THE COLLEGE SHRINK

A Novel By William Haylon

A Terwilliger Press Imprint
Marion

For people struggling with mental health issues, that you may find your smile again.

Applause for *The College Shrink*

"Haylon offers a novel about a troubled college therapist and her clients. Emily Metcalf is employed as a psychologist at an elite institute of higher learning in New Jersey. She loves her job and her daughters and is mostly content with her life. Then her husband, a teacher at a private school, is involved in a scandal that ends their marriage, and Emily finds herself leaning on her clients for emotional support as much as they lean on her, which leads to problematic situations

“Haylon has a distinctive narrative voice—attentive, witty, and all-knowing—and he wields perspective effectively, weaving the reader into the narrative as an active observer. He also compellingly presents characters’ backstories with a storyteller’s flair. His handling of the story’s setting is also strong, as he clearly understands academia and all of its quirks—from the admissions processes to the lack of adequate mental health care to the daunting demands on today’s students. A fine read about dynamic characters coping with trying times, featuring astute narration.”

- *Kirkus Reviews*

“An empathetic college psychologist finds herself in trouble in William Haylon’s intense novel *The College Shrink* … Throughout, the omniscient narrator condenses information from multiple perspectives well … sometimes sardonic, and at other times witty … a text that complements the unease and restlessness of its wide cast.”

- *Foreword Reviews*

“What an utterly charming and engrossing book! … The personalities in this book are most endearing and so well fleshed out, you feel like you know them and they've become your friends by the end of the book. I didn't want the story to end, it was so enjoyable. And I could hardly put the book down, rushing to get back to it whenever I got interrupted in my read … This is a most unusual story and told in a compassionate and endearing voice. I can highly recommend it for a hugely enjoyable experience.

- *LoveReading*

"The narrator knows all, yet is an unattached observer, leaving a trail of insightful breadcrumbs for the reader to follow as the plot progresses …There are moments to gasp and times to shake your head."

- *Readers' Favorite*

"Haylon captures the milieu of the college counselor in many different ways that keep the story engaging and unexpected …*The College Shrink*'s ability to bring to life the college environment and the new adults who face its special challenges makes for an engrossing read. Audiences who enjoy inspections of psychological approaches to life problems and table-turning scenarios in which wisdom comes from unexpected directions will find *The College Shrink* an excellent read."

- *Midwest Book Review*

-

"Author William Haylon's *The College Shrink* is a stunning piece of literary fiction ... It's a true exploration of real-life issues through a beautifully artistic writing style. You will find yourself and others you know in the pages of *The College Shrink*."

"You can see the amount of thought Haylon put into this story strewn across the pages. He carefully chose each word and the sequence in which he told us the events. Everything has a purpose in this story."

- *Literary Titans*

This book is a work of fiction. Any references to historical events, real people, or real places are fictitious. All of the characters, names, places, incidents, organizations, and dialogue in this novel are either the products of the author's imagination or are used fictitiously.

Jacket design by Marile Borden

ISBN: 9798829322342

www.wdhaylon.com

Other Books By William Haylon

I'm Will

The Missing Something Club

Complicated Families

A special thank you to Kate and David.

1

Life

Let's face it, there are good people in this world and not so good people. The special ones who we can count on whenever we might need help, and those we instinctively run away from as fast as we can.

Then there are the lion's share of people we come across who are not quite either. Many because they are too afraid to do what they know is right. Like people who believe that global warming is a major concern but continue to purchase big fossil fuel swilling cars because their neighbors have one. Or people who aren't bigots, but don't say boo when someone makes a xenophobic comment right in front of them. And, of course, those who freely spread falsehoods to hide whatever shameful deeds they or their colleagues may have perpetrated. Like most Republicans in Congress during the Trump administration. Or billionaires paying no taxes.

She had spent her entire life trying to be one of the good ones. Trying to make a difference. As a daughter, student, spouse, mother, friend, citizen. Employee, church goer, PTA member, workout partner, lover. Basically, she was the caretaker for anyone who needed caretaking.

Life is hard. Too hard for many of us to navigate alone. That's why we sometimes need to reach out to someone like her to help us figure it all out. To keep pointing us in the right direction. The problem is that when someone dedicates her whole life to such a noble pursuit, and there is no doubt her pursuit was noble, and ends straying in a way she had never expected she would, it can be catastrophic.

By the end of this story, you likely won't have remembered this forewarning. Because you will have gotten caught up in the people that you meet and their divergent, sometimes amusing lives. All people who needed a caretaker, including the caretaker herself. But you will be better prepared for what's to come if you actually don't forget.

2

The Good Person

In 1975, the year she was born, the year President Ford survived two assassination attempts, the year Jimmy Hoffa disappeared, the year Saturday Night Live premiered, the year the Pet Rock and the Rubik's Cube were introduced, the year Microsoft was founded, the year the Vietnam War officially ended and Patty Hearst was arrested, the year nine new countries gained independence while the Boston Red Sox almost won their first World Series since 1918, the year the disposable razor was originally sold, the year the first woman reached the summit of Mount Everest and Lee Elder became the first black golfer to play in the Masters, the year Moe and Larry of The Three Stooges died, Emily was the 239th most popular female name in the country.

That's how her mind worked, drifting between the notable and the obtuse. Over the past decade, Emily has become the country's eighth most popular girl's name. Right behind Abigail and ahead of Charlotte. Our Emily currently had eleven clients that shared her name. And given the name's popularity and the growing demand for her services, the odds were that she would meet more Emily's this year doing what she does.

Your views of Emily are likely to oscillate during this story. She is attractive in the way that former athletes, which she is, are often attractive. Fit and firm and still with visible muscles, even into her forties and while mostly sitting at a desk ten hours a day. Not to mention having given birth to two children. Her shoulder length blonde hair remains natural in its color, thanks to her family's Scandinavian roots, and her magnetic blue eyes are nothing if not memorable. Though she has added a few pounds in the years since she last competed, she remains strong from taking up rowing on a once dead urban river that has begun to come back to life, unfolding through an old New Jersey manufacturing city near where she lives. A river whose story, in some ways, might be considered to mirror her own. Winding, unpredictable, and recovering. In her little single scull each morning before most of the city is awake, she will first drown herself in perspiration while pounding the river with her oars until her muscles burn past the point of acceptable pain, and then tranquilly rest in the middle of the still sleeping water watching the other rowers, the multihued birds, and the city as it ultimately begins to stir. For three seasons each year, it is part of her incessant quest to both stay trim and to get all her anxieties assembled into some kind of coherent order. Her looks and her morning routine, though, have little to do with the story.

The long hours she works are at a prominent university where she also received her undergraduate, her masters, and her doctoral degrees – not having gone very far since first arriving here when she was eighteen. Her office, home away from home for a person so spectacularly devoted to her work, is in a six story gothic building in the heart of the campus. It was an office of the type that was given to people who weren't deemed to be essential to the university. A tiny room with a window overlooking a parking lot and just enough space to be occupied by a tired wooden desk, three metal cabinets, two threadbare armchairs that were beyond old, and a standing plant that was as exhausted as the armchairs. It was both utilitarian and dispiriting, but as mentioned, it had been her home away from home for as long as she had been working here. As we meet our Emily, she is straightening the file folders that now included her handwritten notes from the day, tapping the ends on her desk so that the papers inside all line up, and safely returning each to the metal cabinets in the corner of her crappy little office. She locks the cabinets, drops the key in her bag, and turns off the desk lamp as she always does, before finally closing and locking the door behind her. All her clients' information private and secure as it was supposed to be.

Her department had been empty of co-workers for two hours, if not longer. She saw eight clients each day, the same as everyone else. Clients who remained young while she gradually grew older. Somehow, she could never get everything done that needed to get done by the accustomed quitting time. She liked to think that it was because she cared more than her colleagues did and spent more time thinking about her clients' many issues. Issues she had assumed a responsibility to help them confront.

She wasn't in this business for the money. That was something she'd grown comfortable with when she first started pursuing all her degrees -- although a little more than the subsistence wages the university was paying her might have been nice. And so she continued to work long days, with no chance of ever being rich, trying to make a difference. But with each year, that mission, as you will witness, seemed to consume more and more of her own life. Something which she would have advised her clients, if they were in her shoes, wasn't particularly healthy.

The world of elite colleges, the only world she had ever worked in, was hardly recognizable from her days as a student. Back when the applications were handwritten or typed. When the school catalog was printed on glossy paper and was mailed to prospective students. When kids wrote their own applications without the help of any paid consultants. Where she once hitchhiked the entire three-hour trip from her home to the campus for an interview as a senior in high school because her family's lone car, an old station wagon with the fake wood paneling on the sides, was being used to take her only brother to a swim meet. Back when hitchhiking was still legal.

In today's world, it is a non-stop competition amongst the best colleges for the most qualified students. The best colleges tear down buildings, including some that had been new when she was an undergraduate, to build newer architectural pinnacles that really have nothing to do with the quality of the education (but they do look good on tours of the grounds). They offer a myriad of orientation options to ease new freshmen to campus (even though none of the options are on campus). Better food (all day breakfast, comfort foods, dairy free, vegetarian, vegan, Asian, Mexican, Mongolian barbecue), options for students to invent their own academic majors (Aesthetics in Television?), and a greater choice of semesters away. Once upon a time, being away from home and on campus was considered a semester away. Classes start later in the morning so the students can get enough sleep. Exams are now in the evening to avoid the all night studying. The students now only pull all-nighters to party, if they are so motivated. And there are more days off to relax, perhaps to rest up from the all-night partying. All to attract the best and the brightest.

Fewer than eight percent who apply are admitted, which no one could have envisioned when the university was founded not long before the Revolutionary War began. Unless their parents donate one of the new buildings, or perhaps try the cheating scandal route of fake student-athletes and bribed coaches, there is no longer the inevitable acceptance for anyone, not even for legacy applicants. The numbers just didn't work given the huge number of alumni, the small number of spaces available, and the school's never satiated desire for diversity. Wealthy alums never comprehend why their uber talented child – Oliver or Caleb or Amelia -- hadn't been selected amongst all the uber talented applicants. You had a better chance if you were a kid applying from some little third world country that would look especially good on the school website. Sandesh or Chantou. All the student's had amazing grades and unimaginable test scores. Not to mention calendars filled with unbelievably impressive extracurricular activities. Some of which were probably even legitimate. Future leaders of our world, no doubt.

And yet here Emily was, the first day the newest of the best and the brightest arrived on campus to launch their academic experience. The beginning of four years of experimenting with who they were. It was the moment their parents had been both hoping for and stressing about since their child entered grade school. And the slots on her own calendar for first-time clients were already almost completely booked for the next six weeks. The best and the brightest were never asked about any mental health issues on their applications, as healthcare privacy rules applied to college applications, too. So the newly accepted students emailed, or more likely their parents called, a month before school started to schedule an appointment with one of the therapists. It had been this way for long time, but it was getting worse as the students' issues grew and the parents' expectations grew.

In earlier years, going home each night, as she was now, was her favorite part of the day. Not because she hated her job. She didn't. But the warmth of entering their tiny little house on a street of tiny little houses was an experience that was hard to replicate. And she got to experience it night after night. The girls, both of them, would be so thrilled when she walked through the front door, ready with big hugs and big stories of their uncomplicated little days. Day care circle time, pre-school sponge painting, and after school play dates in elementary school. The magic of little ones gaining new talents and making friends for the first time. Experiences that were now all such happy memories. There would never be a better feeling in her life than the cuddles from those four pint-sized arms her first few minutes home. Two very different little people, even though they were twins, who were best friends back then and still best friends today. She couldn't imagine ever loving two people as much as she loved them.

He was a teacher, and his days ended much earlier, and he would have dinner well on its way by the time she came through the front door. If nothing else, he was a good cook, which she was not, who liked to cook, which she did not. He seemed, back then, to be happy to see her, too. A little kiss or hug. The subtle electricity of brushing arms as they set the table together. Hands gently swiping after the meal as one of them handed over a cleaned dish to the other to be dried. The little shoulder rub while the girls were getting ready for bed. She had always loved it however he touched her. It made her feel at peace no matter what was going on in her work, or for that matter, any part of her life. Their smiles radiated contentment. Like they were in a good place together, the four of them, building something extraordinary together. She, of course, read all the books about marriage and about parenting, as she didn't want to make any mistakes. Then she would give the books to him, so he could at least feign reading them.

But things change. She did make mistakes. He made mistakes. A few years from now, he will be embarking on his third marriage while she will still be recovering from the first. Not that anyone had ever said it to her directly, but she knew that her closest friends, the ones who had been invited to the small wedding that was all that they could afford, all quietly questioned why she had decided to marry him. She was driven by her work and later, it was clear, would be all about her kids. It was never quite clear what he was driven by. She had her PhD and was called 'Doctor' by her clients. He was mostly a faux intellect with a bachelor's degree in history, who regularly wrote occasionally published letters to the editor of the local newspaper. A slight build – she weighed as much he did – and an always neatly trimmed beard with gold wire framed glasses gave him a sort of nerdish cute look. If that is truly a category of men's looks. He tried to project the image of a college professor, but was only a high school teacher who, after so many years at the same school, was never even a department head. Though he did teach at a well-regarded hundred-year-old prep school where tuition cost over thirty thousand dollars a year for what they call the upper school. And because it was free for the children of faculty, her girls had gone there since kindergarten.

Emily was fairly certain she had loved him when they first married and that her love grew as their relationship matured. And while she occasionally, or perhaps more than occasionally, chided him for not paying attention to what was going on around him, she certainly hadn't been unhappy at any point during their life together. But now it was difficult to figure out what her feelings for him had been. It's what she thought about the most when she sat in her scull in the middle of the river early each morning. It's funny, or maybe not so funny depending upon how one looked at it, that she gave regular advice to her clients about relationships. A topic, it turns out, she really may not have known all that much about.

A few times before him, she assumed she had been in love, or at least in like. In high school, she was president of her little class and captain of three sports. Not to mention the class valedictorian. Very much the big fish in a small Pennsylvania high school that had only eighty kids in a grade. She dated a number of the boys. There was one she liked the most, and she could have seen them having a long relationship. The first one, as a naïve young girl, she ever had an inkling of spending her life with. Mostly cliched dreams that allowed her to fall asleep at night with a smile on her face. But he was Jewish, and his mother was Jewish, and Emily wasn't. They dated and did things when his mother wasn't looking, which wasn't very often. Dating the boy and his mother simultaneously was unfortunately never going to work.

College was different. It was far larger than her little high school. In addition to studying and playing field hockey, she had various campus jobs to help pay her expenses. Still, she found enough freedom to explore and figure out who she was. Initially, she welcomed the greater number of boys than her high school had to offer, and she was happy to flirt with a few of them when the mood struck her. While she wasn't beautiful, in her mind she was attractive enough, as had been described, and so she had choices. But one boy she thought she might like went too far and tried to assault her after a campus party. Something she rarely spoke about but would never forget. Probably she had consumed too much beer and that had made her do stupid things. Still, it was both frightening and wrong. Only she seemed to be the lone person back then who saw it that way.

After college, Emily fell in love with psychology. That was her only other romance before him. She had been determined to build a career, continuing to ignore boys as she had since having been attacked, while she got her masters, wrote her dissertation, which took her forever to get right, and then her PhD. Until he entered the picture by surprise. They were introduced by a friend of a friend, and she found that she really liked being with him. He was four years older than she was and settled into his teaching career, but he appeared to like her as much as she liked him. There seemed to be an even balance in the relationship. He was gentle with her and made her feel comfortable. But that was then. The balance didn't last. His interest waned long before she ever recognized. Hers continues for a still undetermined period, even though he left. She had never considered love to be disposable.

Now she lives alone in the same tiny little house with a mortgage that she really can't afford. The house isn't even in the town where the university is, but rather in a residential section of Trenton, where everything is cheaper for a reason. There are a handful of famous people who were born in Trenton. Supreme Court Justices Antonin Scalia and Samuel Alito, former New York mayor David Dinkins, comedian Ernie Kovacs, the eccentric basketball player Dennis Rodman, and many actors who you might recognize though not really know who they are. But mostly it's a place that when people leave, they don't return.

She'd gotten a second mortgage and bought his half of the house when they split, and, in retrospect, paid him more than she should have. But, at the time, she wanted the girls to have some constancy in their lives. And, at the time, she thought that she would be getting a regular child support check from him. To save money, she kept the heat so low that it made you afraid to get out of bed in the morning when the weather was cool. And she never replaced the furniture he took with him, but rather spread around what remained to make her home look like it was still appropriately furnished. She should sell the house and rent an apartment that she could better afford and fully furnish, but she didn't have the energy to go through that process. Maybe she secretly feared the embarrassment of no one wanting to buy the home where she had worked so hard to create a family. That might well have been too painful a gut punch for her to take right now.

The girls were growing up and now off assembling their own lives, one starting college in Chicago and one in California. Their first time ever apart from one another. She talked to each of them regularly. Usually, they would call when they were walking somewhere – the gym, dinner, the library, to see a friend. Still loving them as much as anyone could ever love two people, and very much missing their presence. Those calls returned to her the little bit of sanity that she needed in her life. And they made her laugh. Even if it was only for a few minutes a night, before they had to go off and do whatever.

So now she would go home to her newly cold, empty house, many of her now solo evenings spent trying to balance the checkbook, without ever having much luck. Which only added to her mounting mental exhaustion. She headed for the parking lot, as she had done literally thousands of times over her almost two decades working here, to her little car that had more miles on it than a car was meant to have. This is what she signed up for when she decided to be a good person. The fulfillment of being the universal caretaker.

Nonetheless, it didn't mean that life didn't suck sometimes.

3

The Other Break Up

There was a whole other story about Jelly before this one. One about her and a boy and a school and about growing up, but in a way that was both heartwarming and frustrating, and certainly less predictable than what would have been expected. But that is for another time and place. You will like her because she is her own person. She is unique in how she talks, dresses, and acts. She is perceptive and smart in a way that we all wish we were perceptive and smart. She is outwardly independent and confident, even though she can be as anxious and unsure of herself as we are. But it is hard to tell. Nobody ever sees that side of her. It is also hard to take our eyes off her because in so many ways we wish we were more like her. She was this way in high school and is even more so in college.

When a person as capricious as Jelly arrives in an entirely unfamiliar environment, you can never be quite sure what is going to happen. It can be like experimenting with mixing different chemical compounds together. You might discover the cure for some uncommon disease. Or you might blow up the building you are working in. She was new to the university, and the university was new to her. But there was no mistaking when she arrived.

"Hello. I'm Doctor Metcalf."

Jelly had streaks of green across her light brown hair, and too many earrings to count. Wearing a blouse and shorts that both appeared a few sizes too big for her, as likely to have been purchased for several dollars from a Salvation Army as anywhere else, and carrying a huge unzipped bag over her shoulder that seemed it might hold everything she owned. Like one could find a baseball mitt or an espresso machine if they looked hard enough. A sort of homeless chic. She was eye-catching in a way that required no expensive cosmetics, which she didn't wear, or designer clothes, which she didn't own.

The university was an amazing collection of students. The natural school government leader who already had a closet full of suits and ties, seemingly someday destined to be elected to Congress. The ripped jock who would single-handedly change the school's athletic fortunes. The nerdy kid with the unending collection of Star Wars t-shirts primed to invent the next famous thing that no one knew needed to be invented. The first college-bound kid in a family that had no money, but who did his or her best to hide that from peers. The absurdly wealthy kid with a widely recognized brand for a surname who would need neither a job nor money at any time in life, but, on occasion, pretended to be scratching nickels together in order to feel better about his or her incredibly good fortune. The students who called home three times each night to see what was for dinner, then to see how the dinner was, and then to say goodnight. The students whose parents had three homes but never called any of them. Black skin, brown skin, blue hair, no hair. Lots of earrings, a few nose rings, a couple of silver balls on tongues. Alcohol, drugs, sex. Mormon, Muslim, Russian, Sri Lankan. Smart and lots of time spent studying the common threads. She seemed nothing like any of them.

"Hi Doc!"

Nobody was ever happy when they first went to see their therapist. Nobody had an exclamation point at the end of their greeting. She bumped fists with Emily and then flopped into one of the tired armchairs, as if she been there a hundred times before.

Almost a quarter of the students at the university now saw a therapist during an academic year. The school had previously limited the number of sessions to seven, enough, they presumed, to help kids figure out whatever they might be wrestling with. In days gone by that had been plenty. In more recent years, more often than not, seven visits weren't even close to being enough. Not even in the ballpark. As a result of the increasing needs, there was no longer any limit to the sessions. The counseling office was not anymore a place to offer simple advice to confused students, but rather had increasingly become a destination to treat kids with serious mental health issues. But it was a growing challenge for therapists to give the students the time that they needed. Particularly when the university doesn't add any new therapists to the department. The one with a collection of small offices with furniture fatigue and lifeless plants. What the university sold and what it delivered were not always the same thing.

"I didn't know that you were bringing a friend with you today, Angela."

He was huge, and he slowly lumbered across her office until coming to rest on the sill of the window that looked out over the parking lot. Maybe 6'6" and well over three hundred pounds, but chiseled, with hands and feet that were of a size that was hard to even describe. Bigger than whatever you are picturing. And he had a bewildered look, Emily could tell, because nobody had yet told him why he was here.

"This is Seth."

"Hello, Seth."

He had a mane of long black hair, three days of a beard, and dressed like someone who didn't spend much time thinking about what to wear. Exhausted jeans, a generic short-sleeved, buttoned down plaid shirt, and work boots that appeared old and worn from heavy use. Again, his whole body was on a different scale.

"Hi," he grumbled.

It was apparent from the outset that she was his Emma Bovary, and he was her Charles. You may have to look that one up, but on fancy college campuses with ungodly tuitions and all the perks mentioned previously, this is the type of thing that is studied. Novels that were written in the 1850's. This is what some professor in another building on campus, with a nicer office with newer chairs and flourishing plants, spends a career lecturing about to his or her students. A university is proud of its professors and welcomes the chance to show them off. On the contrary, they are happy to hide the therapists, not wanting to admit that their students have issues. *A liberal arts education teaches our students how to think*. But *Madame Bovary*? Still somehow most of these students seemed to find jobs upon graduation that quickly paid them more than she would ever make, even though they studied fiction written in the 19th century while she had her PhD in a science.

"So tell me, where are you guys from?"

"I was born in Philadelphia, but I moved to Chicago this summer after my parent's split up. Have always been a city girl. Seth is from a little town in Iowa."

Hence his outfit. Elite universities always want a kid or two from the less populated places like Iowa, so they can boast that they have students from all fifty states, in addition to the countries where Sandesh and Chantou were raised. It wasn't easy competing for the smartest kids in Iowa. North and South Dakota were even more of a challenge.

"I'm sorry to hear about your parents."

"It was brewing for a number of years."

"That can't have been much fun. How are you coping with all that?"

"For another time."

"Okay." Emily paused and made a note on the yellow legal pad that was always in front of her when she worked. "So then, how can I help you, Angela?"

Most of the students who came to Emily's office for the first time fidgeted and looked at their feet or her feet or the diplomas on her wall in the office or the pictures of her daughters on her desk. The young girl looked right at her with incredibly alive eyes. Eyes that made you want to keep looking at them, or even through them, to see what was inside. The eyes of someone who was either going to do something great in her life or flame out in a dramatic way. After getting to know her over the coming year, which is roughly the length of this story, and better than Emily knew any of her other clients, it would still be unclear which would be the girl's destiny.

"Seth and I having been dating for a while. I brought him here because I want to break up."

Seth didn't react, because he didn't know how to react. With either of them. He just continued to sit silently on the window sill, casting a huge shadow that blanketed most of the floor and far wall of the tiny office. Dampening the spirits in the room, much as his demeanor would also soon do.

"You two are freshmen, right?" Emily asked while adding to her notes on the legal pad. Not that she ever needed the help remembering. She had a steel trap. But she liked appearing engaged when she was with clients, so they were convinced she was serious about her work. Which she was.

"Yup." The girl would do all the talking at first.

"And this is your first full day on campus?"

"It is for me. Seth has been here for two weeks for football practice."

"Well, breaking up the first day here is certainly a new twist. I can honestly say that I've never encountered this before. Did Seth know that this is what you were planning to do?" inquired Emily.

"No. Well, not until right now."

"So why am I part of the equation, Angela?" Emily continued.

"By the way, you can call me Jelly. Everyone I know seems to."

"Like the opposite of peanut butter?"

She laughed in a very appealing way. A contagious laugh. It wasn't a surprise that a boy like Seth would want to be with her. Given the way she dressed, there wasn't much left to anybody's imagination.

"I have heard that once before, when someone in high school and I first met," Jelly responded. "Anyway, I thought that Seth might be hurt. Or be angry with me. Or both."

"Does Seth get angry with you?"

"Sometimes. Mostly when I don't see things the way he does. Which is most of the time."

"And you are also afraid he would be hurt?"

"Yes."

"Are you afraid he might hurt himself or hurt you?"

It was a hard thing to fathom, but break ups, at any age, carry with them the risk of violence. Emily was taught this way back in grad school, and it's something you don't readily forget. It's a scary side of the human psyche. One of the many.

"He won't hurt me. He is too gentle for that."

She reached over and patted him on the thigh. Emily guessed that the giant liked being stroked by Jelly. Although the gesture may have added to his confusion given that she was dumping him. Jelly, it turns out, was quite skilled at such misdirection.

Emily had seen this same situation more and more in recent years. As mobile phone use grew, so did the frequency of student couples coming to see therapists to break up. One, they hadn't yet learned how to communicate. Texting photos is not really communicating. Two, it only took a few swipes to find a new romantic interest. And because they'd had sex before they knew each other's middle names, their connection usually had little substance to it. The thing that made them feel good didn't last. These two were only eighteen or nineteen at this point. It was a familiar story, but, unfortunately, not a particularly healthy one.

"Seth, what do you have to say about this?" Emily continued to probe.

"Fuck."

That was what got them here, but Emily wouldn't comment on that just yet.

"How long have the two of you been dating?" she continued.

"About three months," responded Jelly.

Seth, like most new clients, had been looking down at his shoes the entire time.

"Seth, did you ever date anyone before you got here?"

"There were twenty-five girls in my high school class," he responded, still peering at his worn shoes, perhaps hoping for some insight from them into what was actually happening here. "I've dated pretty much all of them."

"How about you Jelly?" Emily asked.

"That's a story for another session, too," she responded to the doctor.

"If you say so. So how did you meet each other, given that this is your first day here together and one of you is from Iowa and one from Illinois?"

"There is a chat site for incoming freshmen," Jelly filled her in. "We met on the site, and then we got together -- the first time in Chicago. After that we began to take the train back and forth."

"So you saw each over the summer?"

"A fair amount actually," Jelly continued. "It's an easy train ride. And his family is hilarious. I milked my first cow while his father and brothers were cheering me on. Foreplay with a cow."

"Sounds like fun. I guess, anyway. Can't say that I've ever done that. And given how you describe it, I now probably never will." Emily watched as Jelly had turned toward Seth to see how he was accepting the conversation. Like she was training a new puppy. An extremely large new puppy. "And yet, Jelly, you want to break up after your time with his family and the cow?"

"It is clear Seth and I aren't a great match. I met somebody else."

"Your first day on campus, Jelly?"

Emily's job was to keep asking questions and then listen until she was able to paint a more complete picture of the problem. The diagnostic was the part of her job that she liked best. It was a little like playing detective. But, as said previously, this couple's problem was not unusual on today's college campuses.

"I work quickly."

"Shit." Seth seemed to prefer the monosyllabic responses.

Jelly wasn't being truthful, and Emily knew it. There are enough activities to keep students occupied on campus the first day such that finding a new boyfriend wasn't going to be one of them. After all, it was just after lunch. Moreover, Jelly had made the appointment well before she arrived at school.

Emily continued with her task.

"What was the connection for the two of you?"

"What do you mean?" Jelly replied.

"What did you do when you were together. Just the two of you. When you were not building your farming skills?"

"Mostly we had sex."

Bingo.

"Did you guys ever spend time talking?"

"Mostly when we were having sex," Jelly continued. "We were both new at it, and we giggled a bunch because we didn't really know what the hell we were doing."

"I see. So Seth, how do you feel about all of this? Do you want to break up?"

"No."

"Why not? And see if you can help me out by using a few more words in your answers."

It took a while to for him to answer.

"Look, I like Jelly. Not to mention that I like having sex, too. With her."

"Can you tell the difference? Between love and sex?"

He didn't respond.

"What, Seth, did you think was going to happen in the long run with your relationship with Jelly? Did you ever think about that?"

Emily needed to get him engaged in the conversation, so she could gauge for herself how likely he was to hurt anybody. Again, in college, this happens more that anyone would hope. And it is rarely a good outcome. This is what she was most worried about with these two. Given his enormity, he could potentially do some genuine physical damage without ever intending it.

"Not really."

"Did you think that we were going to get married?" Jelly jumped in where she shouldn't have.

"I don't think very far ahead, Jelly. Tomorrow is a long way away in my world."

"If there is no long term together, why would breaking up bother you?" The young woman followed up, impatient with her new therapist's plodding questioning.

"I just like you. You're different than everyone I've ever met." He may not have been wrong about that. "And it's something to do besides playing football and studying."

The therapist had heard this before, too. A whole campus of opportunities, but once the students had experienced sex, they couldn't think of anything else to do. Really that was mostly the boys. Boys have a way of confusing love and sex. Actually men in general often did. Maybe even her husband. For the girls it tended to be different. They tended to have sex to keep the boys, until they didn't want them anymore.

Jelly squirmed in the tired chair, likely not sure she was comfortable with the fact that Seth was as attracted to her as much as he was.

"Do you like playing football?" Emily took the lead once more.

"It's okay. It's a whole lot more serious here than it was in high school."

"How so?"

"It takes a bunch more time. Required weightlifting until our shoulders and legs are on fire, visits to the trainers, film sessions that are far too intensive, longer practices, team meals. Way more coaches, and they all scream all the time. We don't laugh and goof around as much."

"I'm sorry to hear that, because I know it's a big investment of your time. Let me ask you this, Seth. How do you feel towards Jelly right now?"

"Not as great as I did ten minutes ago," he replied.

"Do you feel like you might want to hurt her?"

"I wouldn't ever do that."

"Do you feel you would want to hurt yourself?"

Once more, he didn't answer.

She turned to Jelly, as she was, in theory, the client. She had scheduled the appointment.

"Jelly, give me your perspective. Why are you worried about Seth.?"

"Seth is a living irony."

"You'll have to explain to me what that means."

"He wants to have a girlfriend more than anything. He is really intense about it. But when he actually gets the girlfriend he wants – in this case me – he doesn't want to invest the effort in the relationship. It's like he just wants someone to be with him. To help him make sure he is doing all the things he is supposed to be doing. Like Mary Poppins or something. He's actually my first real boyfriend – beyond a prom date that didn't end particularly well – but he has a clear picture of what he wants, which is different from what I want. I don't want to be Mary Poppins. I just want a best friend. Seth has had lots of girlfriends before, and I get the sense that they have all ended badly. Some really badly."

"Is this accurate Seth?"

"She makes it sound worse that it was."

"Did they break up with you or you with them?"

"Some of each."

"How many times did you end up in a therapist's office?"

That caused him to look up for the first time. Surprised by her question.

"Why do you think that?"

"I've been doing this a long time. Sometimes I can just tell." Really, she was just guessing. But that's what you need to do on occasion.

He once again hesitated before responding, likely trying to figure out whether to come clean or not. New clients are not always the most forthcoming.

"More times than I can count."

"Did you ever hurt yourself after a breakup?"

"This really isn't any of your business, but I have had a few moments that I am not proud of."

"I see. Did you ever share any of this with Jelly?"

"Not until now."

This was Emily's job. This is what she signed up for. And she liked it, so long as no one was going to get physically hurt. Which, she had sadly learned through experience, she can't always influence. She would worry about Seth. And worry for Jelly.

4

The Boy Who Came And Never Left

Mana had been here for three years without leaving. He arrived for the first day of his first year, like all the rest, and has never left campus since. Not even for weekends, holidays, mental health days, or summer vacations. He had nowhere to go. The dorm was the nicest place he had ever lived. It had no problem remaining dry during rainy season. He was never hungry, loved studying and learning, and he was appreciative of the professors for their interest in him. He had two friends, and that was enough. They studied together and sometimes went to see the old movies, that were all new to him, shown in the school's science lecture hall on Friday nights for only a couple of dollars.

Mana is the fourth most popular male name in Nepal. He'd been the best student by far in his little village, where there had been only two teachers for a total of eight grades, which is when their education ended. A wealthy American noticed him while trekking across the mountain where the village sat. Mana had been a guide for the man and his group, carrying some of the supplies they needed and helping lead them safely up and down the mountain. He had learned English on his own during trips like these, asking the trekkers to teach him words and quiz him. Many would leave behind their maps and books so he could practice reading at night. The American took a liking to Mana and paid for him to go to a private boarding school in a larger town where he could take advantage of an education that his village didn't have the resources to provide. Every child has dreams, and this had been Mana's for forever and a day. It became an other worldly experience for him. He would never be able to thank the man enough and wrote letters every other week so that the man would be certain of his gratitude.

During those summers, Mana would go home to help tend to the little family farm cobbled out of the rocks on the mountainside and care for their three goats. In the fall, he would again return for a few weekends to help his father and the other village men lead more foreigners on treks up into the mountains. Mountains that had been his backyard when he was a child. The foreigners brought all sorts of expensive hiking clothes and equipment that would sometimes be packed on donkeys who would climb with them. Mana, his father, and the other men often wore only sneakers and sweatshirts. The skin on their feet was as thick as the shingles on the roof of a house in America, and the fall season, which was prime hiking time, was not yet cold for them.

He loved everything about the university, but that didn't erase the guilt he felt about being here. It began a little bit his first year. He had plenty of food, a good place to sleep, and an incredible opportunity. In the world from which he came, if someone got sick, the prospects weren't always great. The closest doctor was over fifty miles away, and the village only had two trucks and fuel was expensive. His parents, because of the hard life they chose on the mountain, were old before their time. They were each only thirty-seven when he came to America but looked older than many of the grandparents who visited students on campus. Skin warped and creased from perpetual sun exposure at high altitudes, made even more damaging by reflections off the omnipresent winter through spring snow. Gnarled brown teeth from sporadic dental care. Hunched shoulders of those who carry supplies on marches up mountains.

As soon as he arrived at the university, he began working twenty hours a week in the dining hall, and, except for what was spent on Friday night movies, he sent every nickel he earned back home. Every single nickel. He ate Thanksgiving dinner in the dining hall with a scattering of others who were like him and passed Christmas vacation alone in his dorm room when the dining hall wasn't even open. He would pilfer enough food when working so that he had something to eat during the weeks the school was closed, and no one knew he was there. Being alone in his dorm with the heat turned down didn't bother him in the least. He had plenty to keep his mind busy, and, as already pointed out, he was accustomed to cold far worse than this. But the guilt of having so much more than his family only became greater with each term he was on campus.

The following year, he got a second job three nights a week working on the graveyard shift at a UPS warehouse in Trenton, sorting packages for morning delivery. He went to classes, took little naps, did his studying, and then he hopped on a bus for work that was filled with many people seemingly at the other end of life from him. Worn out and with diminished hope for their dreams becoming reality. It kept him inspired. On campus, for the most part, he studied in the library, and sat alone while having his meals in the dining hall, reading his schoolbooks to keep up with his work. Sometimes his two friends joined him. One was from Guatemala, and one was from Newark. No other students on campus even knew who he was. Not that they would have cared, as he wasn't one of them. The college had given him a laptop and a hooded sweatshirt with the university's logo, which he wore virtually every day. Even in the cold, again, which didn't bother him at all. But the guilt still did.

This, his senior year, he landed yet another job working security on campus a few hours each weekend evening. First making sure the athletic center was securely closed and later walking students back to their dorms late at night if they were nervous about their safety. After all, the university was next to a city that had its share of problems. And the students on campus drank too much. Usually, it was girls coming home from a late study night at the library or escaping a party with too many inebriated schoolmates. He understood that many of the girls initially never felt particularly safe with him, as he was only 5'4" and barely weighed a hundred and twenty pounds. But he would assure them that his walkie talkie was connected to the campus security command center and worked perfectly well, and he carried it in his hand so that it was always visible, as was the dark blue windbreaker that read SECURITY in big yellow block letters on the back. He had walked snow covered mountains in his sneakers, he would tell them. Real mountains, not the ones they had in this country. He could keep anybody safe. Eventually the girls would get comfortable, as the trekkers had, with Mana as their guide.

Mana clearly wasn't like the other kids on campus. In fact, it would be hard to consider him a kid. Even in the final year of school, the money for all his jobs was still sent back home. With each cashed filled envelope, he included a letter to his family. He always assumed they received all his letters, and he assumed that one of the two overworked teachers in the village would read the letters to them, as his parents were largely illiterate. From time to time, a teacher helped them write a note back, but those were few and far between. He hadn't received one in many months. They could never comprehend how he lived now, and with the passage of time, the little mountain village seemed less and less real to him. He loved his parents, but three years apart is a long time when you have just turned twenty years old. He didn't know if he could ever go back to that world. Which made the guilt increasingly difficult to bear.

So in his rare free time, he made an appointment to see Emily.

"Mana, come in. My apologies for being a few minutes late. I had to use the restroom -- too much coffee."

The young man entered her office like all her new clients, excepting Jelly, initially did. He didn't smile, he didn't look up, and he didn't say anything. Which seemed to be what the best and the brightest were meant to do when you first met them. He was wearing a well-worn hooded sweatshirt with the school's logo. Emily knew that all the kids from humble financial means were given these by the school at the start of their freshmen year. It made the school feel better about itself for bringing them into a world for which many weren't in the least prepared. Typically, from both an academic and social standpoint.

"Have a seat. It's nice to meet you, Mana. I don't get many seniors coming in for their first visit. How can I help you?"

He didn't answer for a while, likely unsure what to say. Even though he had made his appointment to see Emily several weeks ago.

She politely tried again, and this time he responded.

"I can't sleep."

"Okay, that's a start. Every night?"

"Pretty much," he said. "I haven't had a good night's sleep in months. I now survive on dining hall coffee."

"A lot of people struggle to get a good night's rest. Including me. I know the feeling of surviving on coffee. You can trust me on that. What is it you are thinking about when you are trying to sleep?"

He stopped and thought for a minute, looking at his sneakers, which were not Nike or Adidas or UnderArmour like most of the kids wore. Emily didn't even see a logo anywhere on the shoes.

"My family, mostly."

She saw far more young women than men. And it invariably took the young men longer to engage. No different than with Seth.

"Where is home?"

"Nepal."

"Wow. You are a long way from your family. Do you think you might be a bit homesick?"

"No."

Months later, she did some hurried research in the student registry. With Mana, she now had exactly half of the Nepalese students on campus as clients.

"Do you have a special friend at home that you miss?"

"No."

"Is somebody in your family sick?"

"No. At least not that I know of."

"So it seems you're leaving something out here, Mana."

"I haven't seen them or even talked to them in three years."

"You don't ever go home for breaks?"

"We can't afford it."

"Emails?"

"The internet has not yet come to our village."

"Hmm. That's a long time to be separated."

"I feel guilty."

Okay, now they were getting somewhere.

"Why is that?" she asked.

"I have so much here, and my family has nothing."

"You will have to fill me in."

He told her his history, and she took notes. Reaching out to developing countries for students like Mana was a relatively new phenomenon for highly selective colleges. The admissions teams were building recruiting pipelines with modest private schools that had talent. Most of the kids who are in Mana's bucket are from the wealthier families in those countries. Those kids could still afford to go home. But, every once in a while, a student like Mana would be accepted and thrown into the same mix as the rest of the young people. That could be a lot to absorb. A kid who drove the BMW convertible he or she got for high school graduation rooming with someone whose most valuable family asset is a cow or a goat. Most of the time, it just didn't work. It hadn't been thought through. And she and her therapist colleagues got the fallout. She was surprised Mana had made it this far without coming to see a therapist. Most didn't.

"So do you have plans to ever go back to see them?"

"I don't know," he answered.

"But you've thought about it."

"Yes. Of course. As I said, I send them the money I earn. If I were to use some of it to pay for travel back home, it would have to be subtracted from what it is available to them, and they depend upon that money to live. And if I did go, they may not recognize me and the person I have become."

"I think parents always recognize their children, don't you?"

"We are a long distance apart. And we don't have much of a means to communicate. They could be dead, which is not at all improbable as the mortality rate in the mountains where we live is very high. And if they died, I wouldn't know. Who would tell me? The village would split up the goats and the money I send, and that would be it."

"When was the last time you heard from then?"

"Last April. Someone in their village writes a letter for them every so often."

"I see."

It turns out that Mana was a rock. Apparently like the mountain he grew up on. People who go see therapists often cry, even if it sometimes takes a few sessions to get there. Mana, unlike many, was both hardened and quite self-aware. He knew the complexities and contradictions of his situation. But that didn't make it easy. For him, this was a fairy tale, which made his sentiments towards his family, who had little, more challenging. Yet he didn't show any emotion.

She walked around from her desk and sat in the chair next to him. She reached out to hold his hand, and he didn't pull back, as she thought he might. It occurred to Emily that no one had likely held his hand or hugged him since he left his home for New Jersey three years ago. Think about a parent releasing his or her child to a far-off place that they couldn't ever find on a map. They would certainly be proud of their child, but maybe not as much as if he had brought home another five goats. New Jersey meant nothing to them. And they had no idea if he was ever coming back. Hence their quandary and his guilt.

She squeezed his hand. He didn't squeeze back, yet he didn't pull away. After they talked some more, she gave him a homework assignment to create two lists: one, what he liked about home, and two, job options he thought would appeal to him when he graduated, and they made an appointment for him to come back the next week. She was certain he would complete the assignment, but it would undoubtedly cause him to lose even more sleep.

And so it was on to the next appointment of the day.

5

The Event

Our Emily seemed to have been the last to know about her husband's event. She called it an event because it took her a long time to comprehend what it was, and she never believed that affair was the correct term to describe it. Or perhaps that's just what she wanted to believe. Contrary to the advice she gave to others, Emily tended to put her own problems – little money, a house she couldn't afford, a twenty-year career where she had never gotten a promotion, and, of course, the event – into compartments to be dealt with at another time. When that might be was a great mystery. She'd seemed to prefer spending her time contemplating other people's issues.

She came home from work that one evening, the evening where her world unexpectedly unraveled, and there were no hugs from the girls. In fact, there were no girls. Someone had decided that they were going to sleep at a friend's house that night. Moreover, there was no familiar smell of a meal readying on the stove. When she walked into kitchen, it was apparent that not a pan had moved since the dinner dishes had been finished the previous evening. Wednesday was usually pasta night, which was a favorite for all four of them, but there would be no pasta that night. There was only her husband, who was sitting at the kitchen table pecking away on his laptop, with as incensed a look as she had ever seen from him. He was still wearing a well-worn sports jacket that should have been shredded many semesters ago and a tie with which she wasn't familiar. Dark blue with thin mint green diagonal stripes. Usually by the time she arrived home, he had changed into jeans and a t-shirt. He was not, at that moment, the calm, above-the-fray educator he perpetually tried to project. He'd been fired, he told her without even looking up. And, in the first of many instances, he described to her, albeit with much missing logic, how he was a blameless victim. Yet all she could focus on, for whatever reason, was the unfamiliar tie.

The notable and the obtuse.

A few days later, while she was still going on with her life, trying to piece together in her mind what he might have been the blameless victim of, a friend called her at work. He had been her classmate as an undergraduate at the university and was now a successful hedge fund guy and a trustee at the same private school where her husband was a teacher and her girls attended. No doubt giving donations the size of which she couldn't ever imagine. She and the friend had lived on the same hall of their dorm as sophomores. Back when mixed gender college living was still an experiment. He had always been a good student and a good person. They weren't close knit friends who knew the other's most embarrassing stories and were on their respective wedding invite lists, but rather comfortable friends who had randomly seen each other every few years since college and enjoyed when they did see each other. Everyone needs a few friends like this. A big bang for little effort.

Her husband, the friend told her, was fired for initiating a sexual relationship with a female student. The call came on Valentine's Day, which was probably not the most fitting of days for such a call. Not that there would ever be a fitting day for the call she got. A few weeks before, she had put together a Valentine's goodie bag for her husband, which she thought would be fun as she hadn't done this in years. A box of chocolate treats, the miniature peanut butter cups which were his favorite, and those little conversation candy hearts with the corny messages. *Pick Me, Dream Big, Me & You, Be Mine, My Only.* She rediscovered the bag over the summer, untouched on her closet shelf, and devoured the whole thing in a single weekend, with the exception of the *My Only* hearts, each of which she smashed with the heel of her shoe. Not that it made her feel much better.

Her friend suspected that she didn't yet know the truth, and that she should because her daughters, who at the time were seniors at the school, would obviously be impacted in a significant way. Not to mention the impact on Emily herself. That moment, when her friend called, was when the next chapter of her life began.

When you are standing at the altar of your wedding, wearing the most expensive dress you will ever wear, all the closest people in the world to you looking on, this is not what you think about. He was forty-seven at the time of the event – the one with the girl, not the wedding. The girl, and that's what she was, a girl, was seventeen.

Those initial few weeks following the revelation, she really didn't know much of what her own girls were doing, or even thinking, as her mind was somewhere else that wasn't there with them. When your husband has an event, you can become self-absorbed. Emily tried to play the hurt wife, which she was, and understand why he did what he did. She tried to play the thoughtful psychologist, which she also could be, and understand his actions. Finally, it was easier, for a while anyway, to just curse and throw things. He was lucky that he wasn't injured.

Her daughters didn't mention anything at first, for fear of hurting her even more than she was already hurting. But they knew all the details better than she did. After all, sleeping with a middle-aged teacher made the girl somewhat of a celebrity at their school, and the details traveled at lightning speed amongst students perpetually glued to their phones.

They stayed, for the time being, living uncomfortably together in the same tiny house because they couldn't afford anything else, as he was now unemployed. He and she spoke little, and they never again touched each other.

She went back to work in bits and pieces, staying each day until she couldn't focus there any longer. Then she would spend the afternoons simply walking about the campus or her neighborhood in Trenton, too often passing by people she knew but failed to recognize in her melancholy. After which she went home again, where she cooked dinner badly, as he was no longer engaged as a husband or a father, and then ate the bad food with the girls in their bedroom. He would sit for hours at the kitchen table and email back and forth with his attorney, one she never knew he had. All he said to her was to repeat it was a lie from a troubled kid. Always maintaining that he was the victim. Something he seemed to believe the more he said it. She would sleep on the couch, since he had no intention of changing his routine while it was, in his mind, still his home. It was hard to believe that what he had done was true. Which is why for too long a time she did her best to live in a world of denial.

He got lucky, as he should have been in jail. The girl did not press charges as she apparently didn't want the publicity. Or, more than likely, her parents didn't and made the decision for her. After all, it had been college application time, and helicopter parents, whose children are considering the most selective schools, tend to care about little else than those acceptance letters, which were a reflection on them as well. It does make one wonder, though, if we always truly have our children's best interests at heart. If this was, in fact, their thought process, and Emily would have bet all her meager savings that it was, is this what the girl really needed? Emily had spent her career working with college kids and their problems. Elite colleges, she had learned, often weren't the nirvana that the parents thought they were.

When it became common knowledge what her husband did, her friends went silent. They, too, all seemed to know more details than she did. Like they had front row seats, and she was way up in the balcony trying to hear what was going on. When she went to the grocery store, parents from the school would skip over the aisle she was in or pretend that they had forgotten to get something so that they wouldn't have to stand behind her in the checkout line. Though when these same parents were together at the school or at church, and had the conviction of the whole group, all they seemed to talk about was her husband and the girl. Behind Emily's back, they called him a predator, the girl a slut, and her unfortunate. No one thought Emily could hear. But she did. The undoubted reality was that he had taken advantage of a confused young girl who worshipped an older man about whom she likely knew little that was actually true. The other reality, that Emily had a hard timing accepting, was that she married the wrong man.

Eventually, she stopped throwing things, probably because she was tired of then having to later pick up whatever she had flung. And eventually the school wrote a long letter to all the parents, which would place a finality to her denial. Schools tend to write long letters when there is a crisis, and most would agree that this counted as a crisis -- when a forty-seven-year-old teacher is having sex with a seventeen-year-old student. It was a long letter, talking a little bit about what happened and a great deal about the resources available to any students who were struggling with the discovery. What about for the humiliated wife, she wondered while reading the letter for a third or fourth time? At the letter's end, it said he was not the first teacher who had ever done this, and sadly wouldn't be the last. But that didn't make it any easier for her.

Ultimately, she went back to work for good, but work was not much better than the grocery store. In an office full of professional therapists, there suddenly wasn't any advice to give to one of their own. Usually they were full of advice. The correct clinical diagnosis. Which doctor at the pysch hospital was the best equipped to handle a particular client in crisis. What meds should be considered. Why the office layout should be redone. Why they should get paid more and have more time off. The argument for seeing fewer clients per day. Whether Bill Belichick was a brilliant coach or a psycho. But with Emily, they mostly nodded or mumbled or asked her if she wanted a cup of coffee. They had nothing else to offer.

The one exception was a talented psychologist, younger than she was, who was too good for their little department. Too experienced, too bright, too earnest. Too good looking. Beginning in the spring, Monk, as he was called by everyone (his real name was Mark Monkman) began to stop by her office early each afternoon for fifteen minutes or so, when she wasn't doing her walkabouts, to do what the others wouldn't. Talk to her and let her vent about what had happened. He didn't seem to care what specifically she chose to talk about. And not that anything she said made much sense at first. But he listened, and he smiled in a way to try to help her smile again, which didn't prove to be easy. Eventually, she seemed to make sure that she had fifteen minutes available each afternoon. She was surprisingly comfortable with him. And, at some point amidst all the brief visits, he became important to her.

Otherwise, she just saw her clients and lost herself in their problems.

Neither she nor her husband had the energy to try to repair what they had, even if they had wanted to. Once he knew they were done, he hired another lawyer and filed for divorce before she did, so he could steer the process. Which she let him do because she just wanted it to be over. His lawyer would take advantage of her, he would escape Trenton shortly thereafter, and she could start to rebuild.

The whole thing was beyond sad. A few years later, after our Emily had been considered for the assistant director post in her department and instead almost fired, and after her daughters had too many romances of their own to count, the school where her by then ex-husband had taught published another letter that, this time, it sent to all its alumni. The letter detailed the results of what they deemed was an intensive investigation that detailed all the like events they had discovered – Emily called them events for as long as she lived -- that had occurred for as far back as there were living alumni. Her husband, labeled Person #9, apparently had events with two other young students, the youngest of the three girls not yet having been old enough to drive. How do you ever rationalize that? How did she miss that?

But through it all, she particularly thought about the girl. She wasn't mad at the girl's adventure, and she wasn't jealous of her youth. Emily was sad about what happened and worried about what would become of her. Another young person going off to college with malignant problems that likely were not going to go away easily. A college campus with liquor, drugs, and more reckless teachers, where the girl could again hide her real issues from her parents and from herself.

More than anything, she yearned to meet the girl. Not to chastise her, but to help her. And maybe, selfishly, learn the truth.

6

His Family Owned A Cattle Ranch

Until he met Jelly, Seth had never been outside of Iowa, unless you count South Dakota, which from where his family lived was basically going to see your neighbor. Visiting Jelly in Chicago, back when they were dating, if that's what you want to call it, was the farthest he'd been from home. Having her take him by his oversized hand and lead him around the city was one of his best times ever. She was almost as new to the city as he was, yet she was so much more confident, taking him to Wrigley Field, the Lake Michigan waterfront, for deep dish pizza (which he inhaled), and wherever else came to her wired mind at a particular moment. He was nearly a year older, but the reality was that she was far more assured in everything that she did than he would ever be. It didn't seem there was anything she couldn't handle. She seemed to revel in taking charge, while he, on the other hand, was happy to be led.

His family raised cattle. That was his world. He knew how to brand and ear tag the animals, mend fences so the livestock didn't wander off, impregnate the cows, take inventory of the vaccines, and so on. None of which was of any help in his new surroundings. Theirs wasn't a huge ranch, but it provided a living and a lifestyle for his family, and it was all he knew. He learned how to chew tobacco in the sixth grade, right after helping to get one of the herd pregnant for the first time. He was never going to see a cow in his new setting.

For as long as he had been around, his family talked about cattle prices, football, and how much they couldn't stand Democrats. It was the same conversation over and over and over. Then Jelly came to visit, and she was more different than any girl any of them had ever met. She had grown up a million miles away from Iowa, and now she milked their cows. And she asked far too many questions about how cattle prices worked, some where his family didn't know the answers. And she taught them other music besides country. Earth, Wind & Fire, Alicia Keys, Sara Bareilles. None of whom they knew anything about. She gave them articles to read on Democrat politicians they would like. And after they taught her to play poker, she beat them every time and never gave their money back. She said they should all be ashamed to lose to a stupid girl who had never played. When she left for the last time over the summer, his dad was reading a biography of Barack Obama that she had given him. Basically, she was dating the whole family. Seth probably wasn't enough entertainment for her by himself.

Maybe that's why he liked Jelly so much. He knew that even if he ever did find a cow in his new environment, he would never find another girl on campus who would volunteer to go with him to milk the animal.

He was sitting on a bench on a lawn in the middle of campus. They called them fields and quads, but to him they were simply places where grass still grew, which was what he was accustomed to in Iowa. Lots and lots of it. His farm had many acres of unmowed land where the cattle grazed, and, unlike here, no asphalt besides the driveway leading to their house. He never thought he would admit it, but he even missed the days when the local meatpacking plants ran their rendering operations, where they process the blood and other animal waste from the slaughterhouses. In the hot, humid summer, rendering days created a putrid smell that could hold a town hostage. Where the pungency permeated every space. The streets, the playing fields, the school classrooms, the bedroom closets where you kept all your clothes that sometimes had to be re-washed if you had left a window open. He once went to the burial of a neighbor from town that took place on a rendering day, and the smell was so horrible, everyone had to watch the ceremony from their car, the whole time feeling badly for the pastor who stood alone by the gravesite but with no one intending to go stand by his side. Seth may well have been alone in longing for those stink-filled days that reminded him of home. He felt alone in most things now.

Being pretty much the biggest guy on campus wasn't necessarily all it was cracked up to be. Everybody noticed you, which is a little embarrassing when you are limited in what you have to offer. They all assume that you are older and more mature than you are. Seth was eight months shy of his twentieth birthday. He knew he still had a lot of growing up to do and many things to figure out. As much as he liked Jelly, his dating and sleeping with her were probably, in retrospect, not the best things for him at this stage in his life. She was too much for him to handle. He was still happy playing video games and reading detective novels. He had far more friends from Iowa who were serving in Afghanistan and Syria than he had friends so far at the university. And he didn't seem to be making much of an effort to change that. But, mistake or no mistake, he still thought about her all the time. It had been, without a doubt, his best summer ever.

She saw him sitting on the bench by himself. His beard was now full, but you couldn't not recognize a person as big as he was. Jelly sat down next to him on the bench.

"Nice beard."

"Jelly."

"I've been seeing you sitting here after lunch the past few days. How've you been?"

"Fine."

"What have you been up to?"

"Nothing different than when I first got here."

"Have you made any new friends?"

"Not really."

"Have you gotten over our break up?"

"I doubt it."

"You should, Seth. Life is too short. And there are better people out there to date than me."

"How's your new boyfriend?"

"I lied about that. There's no boyfriend. I just figured that it was a better way to let you down."

"You figured wrong."

In her oversized, loose-fitting clothes, he couldn't keep from looking at her, no matter how hard he might try to refrain. Girls from Iowa didn't look like her. He smoldered inside recalling the times they spent fooling around together and the sad thought that he would likely never get to do that again with her.

"So, again, what have you been doing with your free time?" she asked. Looking at him like she still cared more than he would have expected.

"Nothing."

"You must be doing something for fun?"

"I don't have fun here, Jelly! I play football, I take as many naps as I can, and I study as much as I know how so I don't flunk out. There are a lot of really smart people here, you know. Like you. But I'm not one of them."

"The football team stunk in its first game. And I'm not that smart."

"You don't think I know we stunk? It was embarrassing. We would have lost to my high school team. And you understood more about cattle prices than my whole family did. You're smart."

"Are you planning on winning some games this year?"

"We've only played one game. And, yes, we're planning on winning. We weren't prepared for the first game."

"But you played the whole game on offense. And sometimes on defense, too. That's pretty good for a freshman."

"Do you know anything about football?"

"Sure. Boys go out, slam into each other, and put their long-term health at risk, which for some reason makes them feel good about themselves. Only a step or two up from Roman gladiators. The kickers are the smart ones. They don't try to interfere with anyone."

"Interfere?"

"Call it what you want. They keep their uniforms clean and joints all together by running around where nobody else is. Like the clowns at the circus. You, on the other hand, seem to end up on the bottom of a big pile of male hormones at the end of each play."

"You went to the game?"

"It's part of the undergraduate experience."

"Unbelievable."

He wasn't in a good place, and he knew she could tell. Jelly seemed to be able to figure out most things that no one else ever noticed. Which meant that she would feel sorry for him, which is not exactly what you are hoping for when you want to convince somebody to remain your girlfriend.

"You know I'm truly sorry it didn't work out. You are a good person, Seth."

"That remains to be seen. Why are you even here bothering me?"

"It's what I do."

He really did love her smile.

"Kind of strange given that you decided you didn't want anything to do with me."

"I didn't say I didn't want anything to do with you, Seth. I just said that I didn't want to date you. There's a difference. Maybe you should go see Doctor Metcalf again and talk about it."

"I didn't think that the first session was a rousing success."

"Can't hurt to try. I think she is pretty good at what she does."

"You are an expert on shrinks, too, Jelly?"

"Hardly. I just have a good sense about her."

"Too bad you don't have that same good sense about me."

"I worry about you, Seth."

"I worry about me, too. It's nice that I'm not the only one who does."

As Seth stood up, about to head for his room to nap before football practice and ending up under another big pile of male hormones, Emily made an entrance.

"Hi guys. It's such a gorgeous day, I thought I'd eat my lunch outside. Mind if I join you?"

"Hi Doc!" Jelly responded.

Seth didn't say anything, but he did sit back down on the bench, leaving a bit of room for Emily to squeeze in. Looking mostly at his boots, despite the stunning day. People walking by the three of them, jammed together on the bench, still mostly looked at Jelly and her green streaked hair, baggy boys clothes, green high-top sneakers, and electric smile. And she knew it. You don't have green hair if you don't like the attention.

"We're not going to get many more days like this," offered Emily.

"Why do I have the feeling you didn't stop by our bench to chat about the weather?"

"Okay, Seth, you got me. I saw the two of you from out a window in our offices, and it didn't seem like a particularly cheery conversation. I thought it was a good excuse to visit. I do actually need to eat my lunch, you know."

"I was just leaving."

"Oh, stay for a few minutes, Seth," Emily scolded him. "I don't bite. Not that often anyway. How are you doing?"

"I suck."

"Well, that's not good."

"All he does is play football, study, and sleep a lot," Jelly interjected.

"And you know this how, Jelly?"

"He told me five minutes ago."

"Hmm. Do you two ever see each other anymore?"

"First time since we broke up in your office two weeks ago," Seth answered.

"And again, how are you both doing?"

"I already told you I suck."

"I'm fine," Jelly jumped in, "but I'm sad for Seth. We've only been here a couple of weeks. There are a lot of other people to meet, but he doesn't seem to want any part of that."

"Seth?" Emily asked.

"I'm not even sure what I'm doing in this conversation. I never signed up to see the college shrink, but you keep following me around."

"My bad. I'm just trying to help. Interested in making an appointment to come see me, Seth?"

"Why, you think my head is broken because I can't have Jelly?"

"Not at all," Emily replied. "I just know that romances are hard. I know from my own experiences. Sometimes it helps to have someone to talk to."

He looked up at her for the first time in their conversation.

"I'll pass."

This time he did stand up and lumber away. Looking as forlorn as a three-hundred-pound man-child can look. Jelly stayed seated on the bench next to Emily.

"Thanks for coming Doc. I've been watching him around campus for a while. I don't think he's in a great spot."

"I'm glad you gave me the heads up, Jelly. He clearly has too much bottled up inside of him. Not that I'm necessarily supposed to be telling you things about my clients. Although I guess he isn't actually my client, but it feels like he should be."

"It's okay. People find they like to talk to me. It's one of my better qualities." She smiled a contagious Jelly smile. "But for now, you have to make sure that Seth doesn't do anything bad."

"I don't know that I can guarantee that. He certainly hasn't built any kind of healthy connection yet to this place. It sounds like not even with the football team, which is a little unusual for a highly regarded recruit who has been with his teammates now for a month. And the desire to nap all the time is a tell-tale sign of looming depression. I take it that you knew the history of Seth's dating past and that he had sought counseling before."

"One of his brothers mentioned it to me during my last trip out there."

"Ahhh, so there was a purpose to the cow foreplay."

"Of course."

"Did his brother say why Seth sought counseling?"

"He just said that after one break up, Seth had to take a year off from school. He should be a year ahead of me."

"Is that when you began to get cold feet and plan this break up?"

"Roger to that, too."

"What worries you the most?"

"Like I said, Seth being hurt and maybe hurting himself. He may not be showing it, but I know him well enough, and he's not taking this the way he should be. He has no energy and no interest in anything. This summer he was like a little kid and so excited by all the stuff that we did. Have you seen him laugh yet?"

"No."

"Exactly. He laughed all summer."

"I need to get to know him better."

"Good, then we'll work on it together."

"I didn't know that you had your therapist license yet."

"I don't, but that doesn't mean I'm not full of surprises. Plus, I think I can help. So what have you got for lunch, Doc?"

"Why? Do I have to share my lunch with you?"

"I was hoping you would. It must be better than what the dining hall is serving today."

"See if you can persuade Seth to make an appointment in my office. I have a tuna sandwich, an apple, and banana bread."

"I think the banana bread is calling my name."

7

The Physics of Sleeping

The problem with divorce, particularly a sudden one like our Emily's, is that it changes everything. All of life's plans are suddenly no more. The fiftieth birthday trip to the Cotswolds or Italy or the Norway fjords – it hadn't yet been decided. Buying the small unheated cottage in upstate New York with an incredible view, where they could spend their days hiking or snowshoeing, and nights by the big stone fireplace. Because it had no heat, a theme that now seemed to be following her around, it had been potentially affordable when there were two salaries. Visiting the girls in college. She had so hoped, before life had changed, that they would both be admitted to her alma mater to take advantage of the tuition break to which twenty-year employees are entitled. After the event, this was no longer their inclination, which meant taking on huge loans and a whole new meaning to balancing the checkbook.

Inheriting his tightwad Yankee blue blood parents' money when they passed would have allowed them to buy a bigger house in addition to the small cottage in New York. Not that she was hoping they passed. Although ever since giving her a package of six bottles of salad dressing for their first Christmas together, they weren't all that connected. People can so unthinkingly do hurtful things. But the prospects of a windfall had let Emily and her ex dream about the future. Let's face it, most of us are planners. Or, at least, dreamers. But those were no more. Emily would have to figure out the rest of her life all over again.

It's important to understand who our Emily's ex is. Or was. No doubt, it was easier to be judgmental after the event. The best way to describe him was probably as a wannabe. Or a never was. He had a slender Gumby doll body that had few discernable muscles, with a booming voice that didn't fit with the slight frame. With the exception of an occasional hike, very much a non-athlete. But you couldn't tell him that, as he thought otherwise. He was definitely academically smart, and he knew more details that you didn't need to know about than anyone she ever would meet, which was cute at first. Like only a single person out of two billion will live to be a hundred and sixteen years old. Or that in ten minutes, a hurricane will release more energy than all the world's nuclear weapons combined would. Or that a snail can sleep for three years. Or that it's possible to lead a cow up a flight of stairs but not down stairs. He would tell Emily and their daughters stuff like this all the time. But these musings lost their charm after a while to everybody except him. The point was: who cares anymore? No matter how much he seemed to think they should. None were relevant to what was going on in their world, lives that kept getting busier and busier as the girls grew older and her job got more intense. Maybe that was the issue. He was becoming irrelevant, and that wasn't a comfortable place for him.

Since the girls were born, he'd done more than his share of the household chores, including doing the bulk of the grocery shopping, laundry, and yardwork, in addition to the cooking. And he was an attentive father, going to all the girls' games and other school events. He didn't go to church, but it was understood from the beginning that was her thing with them. He seemed to mostly believe in himself. The things he did were helpful, even important, but none of them groundbreaking parenting. While that may be what he pined for, he didn't have it in him.

At times, he could live in his own cloud, where he didn't share his thoughts with those around him, which was unexpected for a man who typically liked everyone to know what he was thinking. He had always been this way. She didn't know how long the young girl had been a part of his cloud. Emily, in retrospect, certainly wasn't any more. She obviously became, over time, the person who simply kissed him goodnight and slept next to him in bed, after which he would go teach his three classes a day, that he knew by heart, and figure out what to make for supper.

He probably spent most of his spare time thinking about when and where he could next diddle the girl. Which wasn't a phrase Emily was proud of using, but it now floated into her mind more frequently than it should have.

Before all of this, he'd had a place in their family. With the four of them, everyone had a spot that made sense. That made all those plans and dreams seem to fit together. It created a feeling that made their family whole and comfortable. Something that had been missing since he left. It was hard to adjust to his being gone after so many years together. For a long time after the event, she couldn't ever really figure out if she might still love him, as he was the only one she had ever thought she had truly loved, or if she should hate him now. This was the type of question that was never easy for her to answer because it pertained to her own life rather than the lives of others. It should have been clear cut, a no brainer, after what he did. But she had always believed in being loyal. And, at times, well after the event and well after he was gone, she would sometimes wonder if she had been as supportive of him as she should have been. If all that happened was, in some part, her fault. It was a thought that would haunt her for longer than it should have. After all, we all do make mistakes.

Anyway, once her husband left, she had a good deal of trouble sleeping. Not unlike Mana, she had too many conflicting thoughts bouncing around in her head. Night after night she would turn out the lamp on her nightstand, pull up her covers, and know she wouldn't fall asleep for hours. She didn't relish that there wasn't another warm body next to her in bed. It was akin to her affinity for touching. Having him there close by to radiate heat on cold nights was as good as any other physical connection. She didn't have to wait for the covers to warm up as he was always in bed before she was – alternating between reading a book and watching a stupid rerun on the television in their room. He also used to repeatedly share the tired jokes from those old sitcoms with anyone who listened to him, which seemed a withering group. *When you look annoyed all the time, people think that you're busy. I'm not superstitious, but I am a little stitious. I happen to dress based upon mood. I'm not so good with advice -- can I interest you in a sarcastic comment? I love sleeping so much sometimes I even dream about it.*

After he was gone, when she got under her now frostbitten covers, after she had washed her face, done everything to her teeth, brushed her hair, put cream on her calloused feet, peed once and then again so she wouldn't have to get up in the middle of the night when her house was freezing, her thoughts were far different. In the past, she would think about her next day's clients and fall asleep quickly doing so. Now, at the same time she was contemplating whether she had been sufficiently supportive of her husband, she would be wondering how to shield her own girls from what their father had done. And protect them from other teachers who might have similar inclinations. How she was going to afford food, the house, and their college. New plans for the future. How she was going to afford the future. Him and his penis. Would she ever see another penis? It would usually be three in the morning before her mind finally turned off, and she found sleep.

Speaking of him and his penis, the thought that took her many years to escape was that they had fooled around in bed only a couple of nights before he was fired. After they were sure the girls were asleep, and when Valentines were in the air. While they didn't do it as often as they used to, as most middle-aged couples don't, they still did it. And on this night, he was the initiator, though she had been happy to oblige. Which she later had a difficult time comprehending given that he already had his nymph. Did he need a change from a hard, youthful young body to a reasonably fit, but noticeably softer middle aged one that now had creases and crevices forming in some unfortunate areas? At her age, hard was now a choice of ice cream. Why did he want to do that?

He fairly quickly got a job teaching history at a community college, a position he was able to keep for the rest of his career, but as an instructor rather than a professor, which she knew pissed him off. But it shouldn't have. He didn't have a single graduate degree, because he would never put forth the effort to get one. No graduate degree, no getting to be a professor. No matter how smart you might think you are. According to the girls, who saw him every other weekend before they went off to college, he quickly hooked up with another woman who was also teaching there. He brought her to their spring softball games and for pizza with them afterward. How does someone do that after spending the last two and a half decades with you flirting, dating, as an engaged couple, newly married, and then comfortably married. How does someone make a break that quickly? Two months after he had moved out. How come, two-thirds of a year later, she wasn't even close to doing that?

She continued to talk regularly, still in short increments, to the same colleague in her office who she knew least but she had grown to trust. The good looking one. When your friends have taken to avoiding you because they have no idea what to say, even though they know more about the event than you do – same for her long-time work colleagues – you need to have someone else to share your thoughts with. Especially when the person you have trusted for so long has removed himself from your life for good and clearly feels no remorse, so quickly launching his next chapter. This colleague was her polar opposite – always late to work, office a shithole, not shy about screaming at his clients for doing stupid things, and always able to leave right at closing time. And still very good at what he did. For those brief periods each day, she seemed to like when he stopped by, and to even look forward to the visits, though she was not quite sure why.

At first, maybe for the first month or two after Monk started coming by, he just listened. That is, in theory, what people in their profession are supposed to be good at. Thank God, he never asked her about her feelings, the way most therapists, including her, would do with their clients. If everyone didn't know that already, they should quit their jobs. Her feelings sucked! He would, as previously noted, instead crack a couple of jokes to try to generate that previously mentioned smile. It was the only time she ever smiled any more. She told him about the trouble she was having sleeping, and, eventually, he suggested that she read before turning out the light at night. Not a mystery or a thriller, but something that was so long and boring that it couldn't help but put her to sleep. Something that she would never in her right mind have considered picking up. Because she wasn't in her right mind, he laughingly said, she would know when she saw it.

So she trolled her daughters' bookcases one night, reliving the fifth grade soccer trophies and seventh grade swimming ribbons which were still there even after they weren't. She didn't know why her kids saved all this crap, but she was happy they did. They were good memories. Even the pictures of proms where she couldn't remember the names of their dates, but where they looked so beautiful – such ridiculously expensive dresses they would wear but the one night and so much make-up that they looked like high-class hookers. But they were her hookers. She looked and looked through the shelves, pulling out their old schoolbooks and thumbing through summaries until she found what she was looking for. He was right. She knew when she saw it. Their physics textbook from senior year. After all, there have been few things ever written less moving than a physics textbook.

Most of us could read a high school physics textbook and have no idea what it is supposed to be explaining. Emily was no different. And so she began to read and immediately fell asleep her first night before finishing the second page. On the second through sixth nights, it was much the same. She slept soundly and didn't awaken during the night, including not having to wake up to pee because she still peed an extra time before getting under the covers, and she welcomed feeling refreshed when she woke up the next morning. And then came night seven. That's when she began to find what she was reading interesting. The notable and the obtuse.

That wasn't the plan – to become interested in what she was reading. She would now read until two or three each morning, her mind, accelerated by learning physics, keeping her very much awake. By the time she had finished her early morning rowing and arrived at the office, where a big cup of Starbuck's latte now became a constant on her desk -- whatever quirky Italian name they gave to the largest size cup – she was even more exhausted than she had previously been.

Her colleague laughed when she told him and half-jokingly suggested that she instead try smoking weed. More than half of her clients used dope on a regular basis. One after the other said that it relieved their anxiety over academics, romance, friendships, body image, parental pressures, sports, and all the other stuff that they had been trying to get in perspective since they became teenagers. Few of them had their lives in perspective. Pot presented an escape, and she was well aware of that.

She had never smoked pot, or done any other type of drug, in her life, mostly because it was illegal, and she was too chicken of getting caught. She had, as you have heard, always largely been a rules follower. But now it wasn't illegal. And she had to get some sleep. So she went to the only cannabis store that she knew of in the area.

There were few people more out of place in a cannabis shop than she was. Unless maybe it was your grandmother or the pastor from your church. It was an eerie feeling for her being in the store, which had opened just a few blocks off campus. Seeing products for sale that she really didn't understand what they were or why they were each different. There were a ridiculous number of unique brands and flavors of weed. Really? Grandaddy Purple? Chunky Diesel? Strawberry Cough? They all look like dried mud balls to her. Had the world come to this? Was she this out of touch? There were students in the store that she recognized and university employees that she knew. If she had been thinking, she would have found someplace several towns away. So she could be invisible. Nobody really expects their therapist to be a stoner. But she was exhausted, so she wasn't thinking. She smiled sheepishly, blushed, paid cash, and got the hell out of there as fast as she could, holding her bag at arm's length as she walked out. Like it carried uranium. Or her divorce papers.

Never did she smoke in the store or in anyone else's company. Because she was embarrassed, because she didn't know what she was doing, because if she got high she would undoubtedly make an ass of herself. Which wasn't a great thing for a therapist on the grounds where her clients dwelled. The first time, she went outside onto the little back deck of her little house, a deck big enough for three chairs, no different than her little office, to teach herself how to inhale, hold, and then release the haze. And cough and spit and giggle and squint her eyes. No one would ever accuse her of being skilled at smoking dope. And no one would be able to claim they got high more quickly.

She had heard that the first time someone attempts to get high, it doesn't always catch on. Not with her. Each inhale from the very first took her mind to an exponentially higher cloud that she really did not want to come down from. Because she was a worrier, and because she was a therapist who saw too many of her clients dependent upon the drug, she became nervous that she would quickly become addicted, that she would burn her tiny house down, that she would too often get the munchies and, therefore, get fat, and whatever else her foggy mind could find to worry about. And that would be after only a couple of deep inhales. She had to be careful afterward not to stumble when she walked from the little back deck to her little bedroom on the second floor, which wasn't far away because the house wasn't all that big. It would be hard to explain to her world if she fell and hit her head while smoking a joint. But the carpet seemed to keep jumping up to grab her feet, and she would too often momentarily lose her balance, and that gave her something else to be anxious about. And then she would lose the argument with herself about whether she needed to change into her pajamas before getting into bed. Typically the big blue ones with the stupid dancing bears that her husband had given for her birthday at some point back when he still liked her.

But boy did she sleep now. It was waking up that became the newest challenge.

8

The Girl

Amidst all the carnage that followed the event, all the changes and pain and time spent struggling to come to grips with her own feelings, contemplating what the future now was, learning how to smooth life for her daughters, afford things, and sleep again, there was one person who was swiftly forgotten. The person without whom there would have been no event, no divorce, no cold little house with not enough furniture. The one who was the most innocent and most guilty. The one who Emily had assumed all along would be the most damaged.

The girl was not the first to ever get involved in what she got involved in. And she will not be the last. But what causes a bright, attractive teenage girl to want to become the solution to a mid-life crisis for a lifelong wannabe? Someone whose shortcomings were clearly so many, yet so invisible to the young girl. Teachers are too often placed on undeserved pedestals. Was it a kid just being stupid? A ruinous home life? A boredom that needed repair? A desire to live on the edge? The fervent belief that this was true love?

Emily had never met the girl, or, for that matter, ever even seen the girl to her knowledge. Not even a picture. She hadn't been familiar with the name her daughters had told her. Via the church gossip circuit, or maybe at the grocery store, she had overheard that the girl had decided to take a gap year to get her life together before going to college. That made Emily both happy and sad. It was probably a good thing for her to have the time to gain a clearer perspective of what was important to her in life. There was no need to rush. But, in her mind, the girl was not responsible for any of this. Which may have been wishful thinking, but that is what Emily's experience told her. In Emily's mind, the girl was missing her first year of college because Emily's husband couldn't keep his fly zipped up. And no other reason than that.

Experience means a great deal in the therapy field. After you face your first anxious client or one who's depressed, anorexic, has a substance addiction, been raped, psychotic, suicidal, or whatever else, you are better prepared to help a second client in a similar situation. But that doesn't mean that you are ever fully prepared. The situations varied too widely across each spectrum. Jelly's break up was familiar but not. The same with Mana's guilt. The girl's romantic fantasy. And so on. Emily had seen them all too many times, but not really. Each was different, and most were demanding.

As it now had become her habit, she went to the Starbuck's one morning to get the big cup of coffee. The leaves on the trees were hinting at changing color. But it was still warm and sunny, and you could continue to pretend that winter didn't exist in this part of the country. On mornings when Indian summer was still teasing them, she would take her coffee and go sit on the same bench on the lawn where she sat with Jelly and Seth, nursing her caffeine and trying to clear her head from her new nightly habit. There was a young girl at the counter who she had never noticed before. The girl should have been attractive, but had dark black circles under her eyes, and she was carrying too little weight, likely wrestling with body image issues which was a condition Emily saw many, many times with her clients. Girls who too often believed what they saw on social media. As her spot in line with all the other caffeine addicts slowly moved ahead, Emily saw the girl's name tag. Elizabeth. She knew right then who she was.

The one we have neglected so far in this story.

When Emily arrived at the front of the line, the girl named Elizabeth politely asked for her order, looking directly at her but without any apparent recognition of who Emily was. Emily paid her, waited for her drink, and left the store, trying the entire time not to stare, but not having much luck at that.

She repeated her routine the next day – the line, ordering her coffee, checking the tag to make sure she wasn't mistaken, trying not to stare. On the third day, she sat at a table in the store rather than on her bench, pretending to read the news on her phone, but not absorbing a single word of what she pretended to read. She thought more about the girl and what made her do what she did. She thought about what the girl and her ex would do when they were together and alone. And then how they would act when they were at school in a group of other students and teachers. The girl never once, to Emily's knowledge, looked over at her.

What do you say to the person you don't know but who has so changed your life? She wanted to meet the girl, talk to the girl. But how do you do that? Hey, thanks for screwing my husband. Talked to him much lately? Want my help in bringing charges against him? Who'd you end up going to the prom with? Not that she would ask any of these. The girl looked like hell already.

But that doesn't mean you can't think about asking them.

9

Mana From Heaven

October begins the dry season in Nepal. That is everyone's favorite time in Mana's home country. In the valleys, the temperature is reasonable, in the low to mid-twenties, and the vegetation is at its thickest following the rainy season. Further up in the mountains it is colder, but nothing like it will be in December and January where it regularly reaches far below zero. The air is clear, and the skies are the brightest blue most days, fostering views of snowy mountain peaks reaching to the heavens that would still make him pause and stare if he were there. And because it is dry season, it is the trekkers favorite time to visit, meaning his family could earn a living, and, once upon a time, he could learn English.

Even though he was exhausted from not sleeping and guilty from his seeming ambivalence toward his family, Mana kept getting done everything he was supposed to be getting done. His papers, his labs, problem sets, reading, dining hall job, UPS shifts, and his turns as a night security guard. And, his conscience, as was mentioned, caused him to send all the money home. Not that it made him feel any less guilty, but he supposed it slowed the progression of his feeling any more guilty. Other students, if he ever talked with any of them besides his two friends, would have thought his to be a miserable college experience. He thought it unparalleled given from where he came. It didn't bother him in the least what they thought. He had no need for drinking, parties, big games, or the accompanying sophomoric activities. It only bothered him what his family thought. And because they couldn't ever really communicate their thoughts, he had no idea what they were thinking. Or even if they still thought of him. Which meant he stayed awake every night considering it.

He came to see the therapist because some girl who he had given a safe escort one night told him he should. It wasn't even a suggestion.

"Mana, I'm glad to see you again."

"I brought my assignment, Doctor Metcalf."

He was not one for small talk about the weather or what was for lunch.

"That's great. How have you been doing since last week?"

One of the things, the many things, Emily would learn about him is that he always answered her questions. She had told him during their initial session that many of her clients typically took shortcuts in their first visits as they tried to figure out if she could be trusted and if she would give them an answer they wanted to hear. Until finally they came to the realization that Emily never really gave them answers. She mostly, she had said, just asked questions.

He told her about dry season and how that had him thinking more about his village and his family because it was his favorite time back home. And even though he had gone away to high school, his school wasn't all that far away, and he could come home to see his family and help out from time to time with the goats and the tiny farm cobbled out of the less than hospitable mountain. It was nothing like the three years and counting sojourn he was currently on.

"So, in other words, you still aren't sleeping," she uttered when he finished his story.

"That is correct."

"How do you manage to function all day?" She watched him as he sat there.

"It's getting harder. I'm finding it difficult to stay focused in my classes or at my jobs."

"Three jobs, right?"

"That's right."

"You are an incredible young man."

"I wished that I agreed with you."

"Really? You accomplish more in a day than most students – or professors, administrators, or therapists, for that matter -- here do in a week."

"I don't think of it that way."

"How do you think of it then, Mana?"

"Until more recently, I have been under the impression that I had much catching up to do, as everyone here has had a big head start on me. I had to improve my English and learn American culture in addition to catching up on my studies, since I didn't have the same academic background as most of the kids here. The school where I'm from in Nepal isn't as strong as the ones where my classmates here went. Now I spend much of my time simply wondering if I am being too selfish and only thinking of myself, rather than of my family. But, as you know, that is why I came to see you."

"Was it hard for you to make the decision to come?"

"Not as hard as I thought. I was walking a girl home from the library really late one night, like almost two in the morning, doing my security job. She started to ask me about where I was from and how I got here. No one ever talks about me when I walk with them. They spend most of their time worrying that I am too small to protect them. Or talking to others on their phones. This girl was different. She wanted to learn about my world. And after I told her, including my concerns about my family and all, she said that I should come see you. So I made an appointment."

Emily smiled.

"Jelly?" she asked.

"You know her?"

"I'm getting to know her better."

"She is a nice person. And her name cracks me up. I liked her very much."

"What do you say we talk about that assignment I gave you?"

He pulled a printed sheet out of his backpack. There were ten neatly spaced bullet points on the page. He didn't do things at the last minute.

"So tell me about the five things you like most about home?"

"Sure.

"Did it take you a long time to come up with the list, by the way?"

"Yeah, like three days. I really had to deliberate over it."

"Why do you think that is, Mana?"

"I thinks it's because I found that I don't remember my home all that well. I was seventeen when I left and was away much of the time in secondary school before that. I haven't spoken to anybody from home since arriving here. I have one brother who was eight at that time and realize that I don't really know anything about him. A few times since last seeing you, I tried to speak the language of my village and found myself trying to remember words that used to come so easily. You fall out of practice quickly."

"And yet your English is perfect."

"I thought about that, too. I have worked very hard to get better at it."

He was talking with her. Openly. He thought that was a good sign as he talked to very few people. Maybe Jelly's recommendation had been right. He couldn't get out of his mind the thought of walking through campus late that night with Jelly asking all about his goats. Jelly was certainly her own person. It was hard to fathom that she was also Doctor Metcalf's client, which she clearly was, as she seemed to really have her act together.

"So what do you got, Mana?" She flipped to a new page on her yellow pad. He wondered what she was writing.

"Okay. The blue sky in the fall. The early sunset in winter. The treks on the mountains with the foreign hikers. Reading *The Great Gatsby* by lamp – it was a book a trekker gave me -- because Gatsby's world was so foreign to me. My experience in higher secondary school."

"Interesting."

"How so?"

"You know, Mana, none of the answers were about the people in your family."

"I have thought about that."

"Did your answers surprise you?"

"A little."

"Did they make you feel guilty?"

"Not really. I was mostly focused on being honest."

"Something I am pleased to hear. Being honest goes a long way in this process."

He felt good about that.

"Now tell me, Mana, what you would want to do after college if you had no family obligations."

"Okay. That took about five minutes. College professor. That way, if I keep up my language skills, I could go back from time to time to teach in Nepal. A chemist developing drugs for a big pharmaceutical company. Actually, it could be a small one, too. Working in a research lab doing similar sorts of work. Writing software code. And being a television soccer announcer."

"You like soccer?"

"I love soccer. I was too small to be any good, but we played all the time in the school yard in secondary school."

"I didn't know that about you."

"Yeah, that would be a blast. I'm a huge fan. My prize possession in my dorm room is a soccer ball that an equipment guy in the athletic center here gave me when I was working security one weekend. He was replacing the older balls with new ones."

"That was nice of him. Do you ever use it?"

"My two friends here and I kick it around sometimes."

"That sounds like a good way to take a break."

"It definitely is. There are other jobs that I think would interest me, too."

"Your lists are fine the way they are. Those are actually two interesting compilations."

He understood the message of how he struggled with the list of his past and so quickly generated his thoughts on the future. That had surprised him. She seemed to know what she was doing.

"Do you think?"

"Yes, I do think. If you had no family, would you consider returning to Nepal?"

"No way," he quickly spouted.

"That didn't take you very long to respond."

"Are you kidding? I love it here. The opportunities are absurd."

It would be hard not to find a better opportunity given from where he came. His family's life was dangerous. Living on a mountain, monsoons, cold weather, few utilities, minimal education, limited health care. It wasn't the formula for a long life.

"Mana, I also think your answers to the questions tell you what you need to know about your future."

"That's what I was afraid of."

"There is nothing to be afraid of. You were honest and straightforward in putting your thoughts together. That makes this process easier, and it typically makes for a better outcome. My one comment for you is to think about just being practical -- you can't please everyone -- and see if that helps ease your guilt. With your education, are you really going to be best suited going back to leading treks from the village? Is that why you having been so steadfastly taking advantage of the opportunities given to you in high school and again in college? There is no reason that you can't send more money home, if that's what you choose to do, because you are likely to be making far more money after you graduate. Why not spend time thinking more about your lists this week and why you put down what you did? I have a feeling you may start sleeping better."

He looked at her.

"You know Mana, one of the goals from our sessions is going to be to get you to smile." She shared a radiant, mother-like smile as she said this.

"I can do that."

"Let's talk more about soccer. Do you ever go to the games here? Or play intramural soccer? Students of all different skill levels play."

“I didn’t know that.”

“If it’s something you enjoy, you should try it. It may help us find that smile. And it’s okay if college life is more than non-stop working.”

“I do go to the movies with my two friends sometimes. It’s fun as all the movies are new to me, no matter when they were made, and it’s another way to learn the ways of this country.”

“Well, that’s a start. I’ll see you next week. We’ll try to find that smile.”

And that began his relationship with Doctor Metcalf.

10

The Statue In Running Shoes

Henry, her newest client, had been an English professor at the university for more than fifty years. He's the one who taught *Madame Bovary* over and over to students who became wealthy capitalists. He was now a Professor Emeritus, having been a tenured faculty member forever and a day. Emeritus was another way of saying that the university recognizes that you are too old to be useful any longer. It's less expensive than a plaque. And even though the little house he owns and lives in is on the campus, he is no longer a part of the campus. More like a statue who people pass by each day but no longer appreciate.

It isn't the norm for an eighty-two-year-old man to schedule time with Emily. Her clients are typically about a quarter that age. In most cultures, the elderly are revered for the knowledge and accomplishments accumulated from all their years on Earth. In this country, the road to old age can too often be littered with people who no longer count. Specialists, including therapists, are engaged by children, spouses, former spouses, girlfriends, business partners, attorneys, courts, and the like to evaluate their capacities. What kind of place the statues like Henry should be living in? Which pills they should be taking? Do they need hired help? How they should be spending their money, why they should no longer be driving, what they should be eating, what they shouldn't be doing with their boatload of free time, and anything else they can dream up. Basically, why they shouldn't enjoy life any longer.

In this story, there are people of all different ages and backgrounds. Still, it wasn't clear at the beginning that Henry would fit into the story. But, somehow, he eventually manages to make himself relevant again. Because even though he was eighty-two, in due course, he came to the decision that he wasn't done yet. Though when he came to the decision, he really didn't know what that meant.

That first day, he stood quietly in her office doorway for several minutes until she looked up from writing notes of her previous client visit on her omnipresent yellow pad. She later told him that she felt as if she had taken enough notes in her years as a therapist to account for a small forest.

"Professor Rosenstein. Please come in. This is an honor."

"You know who I am?"

"Most of us do. You are a legend here. You were teaching when I was an undergraduate."

"I already feel old and out of place from sitting out there in the waiting room with all the students, awaiting the start of our appointment. Please don't make me feel any older."

"My apologies, Professor."

"Call me Henry."

"Henry, it is. It's a nice change of pace for me to see someone in my office who has had a full life experience and hopefully isn't addicted to a cell phone."

"I hate my cell phone. Everyone is too lazy to write in full sentences. And whenever someone texts supposedly catchy abbreviations, which I can't remember from one day to the next, I have to google their meaning. Which means it's not really the shortcut they think it is."

Therapists at the university were responsible for seeing undergraduate students, grad students, and even professors when the need arose. Though, admittedly, the latter was rare. In her two-decade career, she had only seen two other professors. One who had an opioid addiction, and one who had changed his sexual identity. Each of whom required many years of counseling.

"So I'm guessing there is a reason you scheduled an appointment."

"Yes indeed. I have been thinking about this for a while. When you get to be my age, you have a great deal of time to think. I have a good number of things on my mind, and I need someone to talk with. I asked a few of the people I still know around campus and heard that you are good at what you do."

"Well, you will have to be the one to judge that. I'm sure there are some of my clients who, if you asked them, would say that I am a lunatic."

"I like humility."

Henry still had a full head of white, curly hair. And while he had the expected compliments of wrinkles, age spots, and somewhat hunched shoulders that go with being eighty-two, he clearly worked at staying fit. No doubt someone who still exercised, as evidenced by the new black and silver Nike running shoes he wore. With a buttoned down, open collared dress shirt and rolled up sleeves, khaki pants, and the sneakers, he was not an unattractive man, even at eighty-two.

"So what do you want to talk about, Henry?"

"Is this how it works? We just jump right in and talk about me? By the way, you could use a bigger office."

"We could talk about golf if you wanted, but I don't think I'd add much to the conversation. And my life seems to take place only in small places. Small house, small car, small rowing boat. I wouldn't know what to do with a bigger office."

Henry chuckled.

"A rower?"

"It keeps me sane."

"I never had you as a student, did I?"

"No, you didn't. You remember all of your students, Henry?"

"Most of them. Particularly the ones who never said anything in class. They tended to write the most interesting papers. Perhaps because I had no idea what they were thinking."

"I should have taken your class then. You would have liked me."

"Very funny. Am I supposed to be nervous when I come here to spill my guts?"

"It's not a requirement."

"Well, I'm not a golfer. So I guess I might as well jump right to it. Although I will say that I am finding myself to be a little jittery. For whatever reason. I came to see you to talk about getting old. The process of dying. Mortality."

"Huh. I was hoping you might pick something a little easier. I could do fishing? Or even *Madame Bovary*? I read it in high school."

"Emma Bovary brought me many years of joy. There was so much more to her character than people realized. But that's no more. I've taught my last class. My wife of fifty-one years passed away three years ago. It wouldn't surprise me if I have early-stage Alzheimer's. And I can't figure out a reason to get out of bed in the morning."

"I'm sorry to hear about your wife."

"We had some great days together."

"I should probably be asking you for advice then."

"Yes, I read about your husband."

"Ex-husband now."

"I can imagine. From just having met you, my take is that he is a fool."

Emily grinned at his comment.

"Thank you. I can't remember the last time I had a compliment from a client. Or anybody else for that matter."

"I'm glad."

"So let's talk about you. How old were you when you came to the university?"

"We're going back that far?"

"I find it helps me to understand who you are. What makes you tick."

He settled into the chair that seemed about the same age he was.

"I was twenty-eight. I am from the Midwest and moved out here for a job after publishing my dissertation. It was a plum job for a rookie, I was lucky. But I didn't know a soul. My second week out here, I was in my barren little apartment in a building that no longer exists – the lot now houses a Whole Foods -- having just finished going for a run. I've always been a runner. I still run. Not very fast, mind you, but I continue to be able to get from point A to point B. It was a Saturday morning in the fall that I will never forget."

All this fit with her initial impression, which was that he was charming and an interesting person.

Henry continued. "She knocked on my door. Her mother knew a cousin of my mother's, and so she came to welcome me to New Jersey. She'd been here for a year and didn't really know anyone yet. I fell in love with her the moment I looked through the peephole on the door. After inviting her in, I offered her a root beer and piece of toast, which is all I had in my kitchen, and prayed that she wouldn't ever leave. I was so nervous. She laughed in a way that I very much miss, and we sat, talked, and drank root beer for hours at the rickety little kitchen table I'd gotten at some rummage sale. We were married the following summer and honeymooned in a motel down the road in Atlantic City because the university wasn't paying me very much back then."

"That's a pretty good story. Do you have children?"

"Sadly, we were never able to have children. My students became our children. We would often have cocktails and appetizers at our house on Friday nights for anyone who wanted to show up. Jenny, that's my wife, would make big pitchers of Margarita's, and, it turned out, many people showed up. Because our house is on campus, there was no worrying about drinking and driving. We talked about life on the campus, the problems that students faced, and we occasionally talked about literature. I think Jenny did more talking than I did. I loved seeing her interact with my students. I think they came more for her than me. She was entertaining as all get out, and they knew she cared for them. We did these Friday nights with the students for decades. Once you were my student, you were always my student, and always welcome to our little kibitzes. And the kids always came over to watch *It's A Wonderful Life* at holiday time to take a break during exam period. Even though I'm a Jew. Back then, television only had a handful of channels, and the movie was only shown a single time during the season."

"Your students were lucky."

"But then she went and got lung cancer, even though she never smoked a day in her life," he continued. "It was a long struggle, almost nine years of ups and downs, far too many moments of heightened hopes followed by the rug being pulled out from under us, before she succumbed. In many ways, we became even closer during that time. Sharing all the last secret thoughts and dreams that we never had previously talked about. After all, who cared at that point? But, alas, she is no more, and it's just me."

"Were you and she about the same age?"

"Jenny was three years older. I got to watch her suffer through what's probably a precursor to my next chapter."

"We'll get to that soon enough. Do you live in the same place that you lived in together?"

"Yes. It's a small two bedroom house, as it was just us, and, as I said, right on campus. We enjoyed being close to the school's activity. But now I wake up, spend a while convincing myself to get out of bed, put on my sneakers to go for a long, glacial run, and then have nothing else to do and no one I know worth talking to for the rest of the day. Until today when I came to see you."

"Huh."

"I hope you have more to offer than that."

Emily laughed.

"I hope I do, too. That was just a nice narrative, so I was enjoying it."

"With a huh?"

"I'll have to pick my expressions more carefully. Let's tackle one more topic. Tell me more about Jenny's death."

"Really?"

"I'm guessing it's important in understanding who you are and why you are sitting across from me right now."

Henry sat quietly for a bit. Maybe trying to figure out if he wanted to answer her question. His legs were crossed, and his hands folded on his lap. Except for his eyes, the running shoes stood out more than any part of his body. His eyes still had a sparkle to them. Even at eighty-two.

"She was given a diagnosis saying she had a year to live. You can't imagine the perverse impact that has on your mind and your soul. It was like running headlong into a locomotive for both of us, knowing there is no chance that you will best the train. At first, you decide that you want to go do all the stuff that you had never done. The bucket list thing. Then you realize that you just want to be together, the two of you, to reminisce about all your time together. And mostly just hold each other. Until the reality sets in that Jenny felt like crap most days and didn't want to do anything other than sleep.

"But she lived well beyond the original diagnosis. For the first few years," he slowly continued his story, "we continued to sleep in the same bed, and I would scratch her back and rub her feet to provide whatever momentary escape I could from the pain she felt. It was a pain that was always there. For all those years. Eventually we turned my office into a second bedroom to accommodate all the nurses and equipment that now filled the room. We put a second bed in the room, first so I could sleep in there with her, and eventually so a night nurse could get some rest when Jenny slept. We tried every proven and experimental treatment there was. Jenny lived one day shy of nine years after that horrible day when she was diagnosed. She was wonderful, as she was for the whole time I knew her, keeping her spirits up as best she could through the whole nightmare. Truly a saint. But eventually it was just too much. Her last three months were the worst three months of my life, because Jenny, the love of my life, was miserable."

A tear creeped down a crevice in his cheek.

This would be a new one for Emily. One that would end up having many twists and turns along the way that she never could have foreseen. Mortality? The most haunting question for all humankind. And somehow it had ventured into her tiny little office via a charming former professor in new running shoes. Huh.

11

Mark R. Monkman

You are going to both hate and love Monk by the time you finish this story. Don't say you weren't given fair warning. He is as genial and engaging a person as you have ever met. He is smart beyond brilliant. One of the best and the brightest. But. That's probably the best way to describe it. But. Because it's hard to put your finger on it.

Monk was different than the rest of them. As was said, he was off the charts smart and incredibly likeable. In the old days, on weekends in the school pub, his college classmates, though few really knew him, would love the wildly entertaining, oftentimes exaggerated stories he told with great gusto about himself or others. In New York, and later in Boston, his old research bosses, who also didn't really know him, loved to be in his presence because his work was so refreshingly on the spot, which made each of them also look good. His new work colleagues at the university, who knew absolutely nothing about him, nevertheless held him in high regard because he seemed to so readily be able to help untangle client problems into addressable pieces, and because he was so attractive. He was also off the charts out of control. He'd never been married, had no money, and never seemed to meet a cocktail he didn't drink. Which created a problem.

Monk attended the university five years behind Emily. They both majored in psychology, had many of the same professors, and went on, ultimately, to become psychologists. Back then, when he was sober, Monk was shy and kept to himself. Emily wasn't shy, though she typically didn't go seeking out people she didn't know either. It was a surprise, but not a complete surprise, when they ended up together at the last reunion and spoke for the first time. Reunions were held every fifth year, meaning theirs were always on the same early summer weekend. Each of them was attending solo, and they spoke for a long time and got really, really drunk along the way, and, at some point, they kissed. Not like friends kiss, either. He presumed that she remembered, but was not certain, as neither of them had ever again mentioned it. In his mind, at least, he was a funny drunk, not a sloppy drunk, which for some reason she found attractive and caused her to do something that she should never have done. Remember she was married with children and, he learned over time, typically a rules follower. But she also apparently had a history of doing stupid things on campus after too much to drink. That trait seemed to have survived the many years since. They didn't speak a second time until he went to work in her office a few years thereafter. One might say by default.

Too many days now started the same way for Monk. He would be sprawled on the bed in his one room apartment, still wearing the same stained and rumpled dress shirt from work the day before. He would pry open one eye and then the other, his tongue dry as the desert, feeling three sizes too big for his mouth, and his head pounding like kettle drums. The feelings all too recognizable. Slowly, he would turn his head and survey the meager apartment he lived in, the cheapest one he could find. The foot of the bed was no more than ten feet from a barren refrigerator, one that hadn't seen fresh groceries since the day he downsized from his last apartment in Boston. And the one before that in Manhattan. Many days' worth of soiled clothes would be covering most of the available floor space in the small room. Cockroaches that were big enough to ring his doorbell and say hello would periodically scamper out of his sink drain, across the counter, and down into the bowels of his non-working stove.

Everything would seem in slow motion as he tried to raise his tired torso up on his elbows. The scenery in the shithole always confirming the notion that things were getting out of control. But, with his record of continually bouncing to steadily lower paying jobs, it was about all he could afford. So, for the time being, this was home.

He would stare at his plastic department store alarm clock. The blue numerals would stare back at him, showing a time well past when he was supposed to be at work. His colleagues at the office would be disappointed. His boss would be pissed. A new client would be sitting in the waiting room wondering where the therapist, who he or she had waited so long to get an appointment with, was spending his morning when Monk should have, instead, been sitting at his desk. He would flop his way out of bed and peel off his clothes, leaving them where they fell on the middle of the floor with the others, skulk naked into the bathroom, and turn on the shower to let it warm up while he shaved and used drops to mask the redness in his eyes.

It had been happening for too long now.

Monk was built like a swimmer, a man with wide shoulders, a thin waist, and washboard abdominal muscles despite never having played any sport a day in his life. His black shiny hair always seemed to be on the shaggy side, and his sideburns came down to loose points, as his facial whiskers did not grow much beyond half way up his cheeks. He couldn't grow a real beard no matter how long he tried. It seemed that he was most often pale, whether he had been drinking or not.

He had mastered the art of shaving, eye drops, showering, and dressing in no more than ten minutes. He would run for his car, which was just as much of a shithole as his apartment, and speed off to the university, maybe five miles from his apartment as the crow flies. Walking into the office was something to be dreaded. The university counseling department represented a mighty fall from where his career had once taken him. The little department, he too often thought, mostly was there to hold the hands of the spoiled rich kids whose applications had far exceeded their true skills. He had a PhD in clinical psychology, which he completed at age twenty-six, well younger than any of his current colleagues, and had been one of the best young researchers at the largest academic hospital in New York and still possessed a promising career at a prominent psych hospital in Boston before he got fired from each for the same thing. His work was typically stunning, if he said so himself, and he had been published nineteen times before he was thirty-five. He had been on two public healthcare company advisory boards and had been hilarious on the medical conference speaking circuit, where he was at his finest after a couple of cocktails had provided the proper verve for his talks.

Psychology was a family business for him. His grandfather was a well-regarded academic researcher way back when. Both of his parents were still professors at another highly selective college, and they both knew that their lone son was on a different level. He loved psychology. He knew the work, his insights were prescient, and, more often than not, he made a significant difference. Except when it came to himself.

Drinking was and wasn't a problem. In his own mind, he wasn't an alcoholic. Perhaps he was only kidding himself. He didn't ever drink at work – he didn't even think about it -- and he didn't drink when he was home alone. It was the in between that was the problem. Despite possessing a body that carried no more than a hundred seventy pounds, he was able to consume large amounts of alcohol that transformed him from the somber, analytic academic nerd he tended to be by day into a garrulous, charismatic storybook figure after the sun went down. He simply liked the latter person far better. People would remember him, and he very much liked being remembered. His downfall was that he couldn't seem to get to work on time the next morning. He had been tardy way too many times in the past few months and had received more warnings than he deserved already. He was a realist. Heading into the office on this day didn't feel good. He had been here before, and the shame of his attendance performance was creeping back.

It took about twenty minutes to navigate the way to campus. Monk's head pounded the whole way. Lack of food and lack of sleep were killing him, not to mention the poison he had been putting into his body. He jerked his crappy car to a stop in the lot behind the six-story gothic building that housed his department. His parking spot was about as far away as anyone could get because all the others in the building more than likely had arrived to their jobs on time. Once again, he seemed to be last. As he rode the elevator to the fifth floor, perspiration began to slink down his cheeks, both nervous and badly hungover.

The elevator door opened. He wiped away the sweat with the back of his hand and took a couple of deep breaths. His temples were ready to explode, while he was doing his best to maintain some focus. This was going to suck. One more breath, and he blew through the doors that held the department's offices.

To the right, many of the other counselors were already taking a break, standing in a common area to fill their coffee cups for a second time that morning, and gossip about Emily's life behind her back. Something they had gotten amazingly proficient at over the months. Emily was the one good one of all of them. She wasn't a strong person and didn't handle adversity well, but she had something special in her. Neckties had long ago been loosened, shirt sleeves rolled up, pumps slipped off beneath desks, and jackets were nowhere in sight. This was the same group that left work together at five the previous evening. All were friendly, but none were great friends. Coffee breaks together were a way for them to waste time, not become better pals. They worked as individuals, not as a team, and they all thought that they were underpaid and underappreciated. His colleagues continued with their empty conversations, glancing over expressionless at Monk while he walked across the floor to his own small office along the opposite wall from the main door. No one said a word, not even giving a wave or a wink. Silence was never golden in academia; it is a death knell.

As he walked into his office, he now understood. A moving box sat on top of the desk, filled with his few belongings -- his nameplate, a picture of his parents, his personal calendar, a couple of golf plaques from enjoyable outings of springs that had come and gone. Even though he was terrible at golf. On top of the box lay what would be his final paycheck. The contact information -- Mark R. Monkman and the address of his piss ass little apartment -- showing through the envelope window one last time.

This time it was less confrontational. No speeches, no scolding. There were no security guards asked to escort him out. Four jobs in the last seven years. Each job with a continually smaller, less reputable department. His talent was without question. His lack of dependability was his noose. By tomorrow, the office gossip would have turned from Emily to him.

He sat down in his now former chair, in his former tiny little office, and placed his feet upon his former desk. His former colleagues' eyes would not meet his when he walked out. They would all feign being absorbed in a phone call or a conversation with a client. He wouldn't miss the university. He had only been here fourteen months, which in life's sequence was not a long time. It was a less than mediocre job in a place that attracted less than mediocre talent. It was an office full of people aspiring to something else. They were people, with the exception of Emily, who wanted to be working for the big hospitals with the more challenging patients, the better paychecks, and the expensive dinners paid for by the big pharma companies, just as he once had. To have bragging rights at cocktail parties. Though none of them ever would get that far in their careers. He was ashamed that he wasn't even able to keep a job at such at crappy place.

"Hey, Monk."

He looked up from staring at his feet, startled that a friendly voice had dared to be seen with him.

"Emily. I didn't expect any visitors. Usually, my friends have become my ex-friends by the time I get the boot."

Emily sat down in one his former tired armchairs with a kind, warm grin that would be the highlight of his day. She was, indeed, special.

"Well, I should first tell you that I'm sorry Monk. I've been very much focused on myself for a quite some time now, as you well know, and so I didn't see this coming. I should have spent more time trying to help you out."

Monk simply listened.

"You are an incredible talent, Monk," she continued. "You don't belong here. Our therapists, including me, can't hold a cup of water to you, no matter how hard we work. You are too good. I've gone back and read every research study that you have ever published. The research is truly incredible. Even here the work you do is special. It's different. Since I have the next office over, I sometimes sit and listen to you through these paper-thin walls talking with the kids. Most often I'm amazed and wonder why I can't think to say what you do. You get their trust so easily. You hear them.

"And yet, Monk," she went on, "you don't seem sad or mad."

"Embarrassed is a better word," he answered back. "I've gone from being a lead research guy at the best hospital in New York to being tossed by a little college counseling department. Not the career trajectory you dream about."

"Again, I should have more spent time with you. Like you have with me."

"I'm a big boy, Emily. I made my bed."

"How are you feeling?"

"Are you really going to ask me that?"

"Sorry, bad therapist habit."

"Well, the answer is that I'm not really feeling anything. This isn't a surprise. I guess I'm angry at myself for being fired again, but I'm not angry about losing my job here. If that makes any sense. I need some time, I think, to get my thoughts together. Figure out what in life is going to get me motivated again and stop wasting my time. How's that as an answer?"

She bit her lip and bulled ahead. He found Emily quite pretty, particularly when she had a smile on her face, like she did right now. A smile no one else in his former office had seen much of in quite a while.

"Why don't you come over tomorrow night? I'll make us some dinner, and we can talk."

Monk matched her smile, like he was already over the shame of being fired again.

"Is this like a date between two people who are single and not getting any younger?"

Thinking back to their errant kiss.

"No. No expectations. We'll eat – although I warn you that I'm not a good cook – and get to know each other better."

"I've obviously got some baggage."

"You think I don't? My ex-husband traded me for a twelfth grader."

"Men are known to be fools."

"Thank you."

"How about I bring the food and cook? I'm actually a fantastic cook."

Emily neatly wrote her name, address, and phone number on a piece of paper and passed it across the desk to Monk. Then she stood up, looked at him, still with the wonderful smile, and returned to her office to meet with her next client. When he asked her years later, she would say she didn't know what caused her to do what she did. Most likely because she felt sorry for him, as she did for so many people. And they had a history together which had lasted all of about a minute and forty-five seconds or so four years before.

Monk sat and rested for a while. The shame and embarrassment were done, and he had no place to go. He was in no rush. He looked out his window at people walking to their assorted destinations on campus, something he no longer had. He listened to a few of his now former colleagues who were again babbling away outside of his office, trying to pretend that they were busy so that they could minimize their time with yet another of their never-ending river of young clients with mounting woes. People he would never see again. Which didn't bother him in the least. He thought about whether there were any final tasks he should do before departing, but he couldn't think any. This chapter, too, was done.

As he stood and picked up his box of things, ready to make his final unspectacular march across the waiting area and out the office, he saw his next client sitting in a chair. He paused to smile at the person he had seen a couple of times already this year. The young man had a litany of issues and needed intensive therapy. He would never graduate, and his unseeing parents would never forgive the university for this.

"Sorry kid, I got my ass fired. You should try not to do this."

He was somebody else's problem now, as Monk had enough of his own.

12

He Came To College To Block People

Being a therapist is not as easy as it looks in the movies. Except for perhaps those with Monk's gift, it can take a long time to build trust with a client, and without that trust, the therapist will never have a shot at making much headway. Building trust with a person you have never met before is a challenge. Building trust with a person you have never met and who has weighty mental health issues is often beyond that. There are times during the process, progressing from one session to the next and to the one after that, when you surrender to the feeling that you aren't doing your job well. That you aren't really making a difference for the client. Like when the client is a physically gifted but emotionally lost young man who was brought to your university to play football but isn't convinced that is what he wants to do with his life. And even more so when the therapist discovers that her counseling skills don't really extend to the pros and cons of blocking and tackling other young men wearing helmets and shoulder pads. Partly because you're not totally sure who they are supposed to block and who they are supposed to tackle.

Still, Seth came to see her. Whether Jelly instigated it or not, she didn't know. That didn't really matter. He needed someone to talk to.

"Seth, you decided to come for a visit after all. I'm glad."

"It's not easy to get an appointment."

"Sorry about that. There are a lot of your fellow students who want to see a therapist."

"Really? I thought all the people here had the world by the balls."

"You'd be surprised."

"How surprised?"

"I see eight people a day. As do each of the thirteen other people who do the same thing that I do here. And that doesn't include visits to the hospital emergency rooms, which usually happen at night or on weekends. One of us is always on call because students need help in more ways than you might think."

"Mmmm. So I'm not the only screwed up one here?"

"Confused is a better term than screwed up. And the answer is hardly. Have you gotten past Jelly yet?"

"I doubt anyone gets past Jelly. She is different than anyone I have ever met."

"She is, without a doubt, unique."

"I'm trying to move on, Doc. Though I'm not sure I'm succeeding."

It was still hard to get used to the enormity of Seth. His neck muscles seemed to extend from just below his ears to the outer edges of his shoulders, which, in and of themselves, were three or four times the size of hers. His biceps were the magnitude of her thighs and more muscled. His thighs? It had to be hard to find pants that fit over them. And, once more, his hands and feet were too outrageous to try to describe. You really wouldn't want him as your adversary.

"Well, trying is half the battle. So why did you decide to come see me?"

"I need to figure out why I am here."

"In my office?"

"At the university. I know I got in here because I can block. In fact, I'm really good moving people out of the way. I'm big, I'm as strong as you get, and surprisingly quick for my size. I'm also already their best defensive player, and I've never really played defense before. The coaches here have never had a player like me. It's a chance for them to put what has been a sorry ass program on the map. And to put their careers on a map. They need me."

"Why did you come here instead of one of the big football universities? Sounds like you might have had an opportunity."

"I had lots of opportunities to go to the best football programs in the country. They all were interested. They know I'm that good. I just didn't want to be a football robot. Playing football for a living, which is what you do at those big schools, isn't easy. Even here, my body hurts after every game for about three or four days. We play on Saturday, but I'm not feeling like myself until the following Wednesday. My neck, my back, my hips, my knees all ache. I pop Advil like candy. Because I'm so big, other teams typically target me with two or three guys on every down. They try to chop block or facemask me when they don't think the ref is watching. Plus, I can't begin to tell you how many times I get kicked by somebody when I'm on the bottom of the pile. Or they pull my hair. Believe it or not, I usually have a sore head at the end of game from all the hair pulling. I'm thinking of getting a buzz cut."

"And cut off all that beautiful long hair?"

"Okay, maybe I'll re-think that."

"Very funny. Do the other team's players think of these things to do to you on their own, or are they taught by the coaches to do that?"

"No players think of things on their own in college football."

"It doesn't sound like much fun."

"Football is a brutal sport, Doc. I take a beating. I figured I would need to develop some other skills along the way. For when my body gives out. That's why I came here."

The violence of football had been well documented in recent years. The physical toll was only one aspect of it. She was more familiar with the shortcomings of the sport's overly violent culture. The idea of inflicting pain at all costs that the coaches perpetuate. It wasn't healthy when it carried over to the players' everyday lives. Even though she periodically went to games to socialize, she hadn't been a big fan of the sport or its coaches for a long time.

"That's commendable of you. Because you mentioned when we first met that you usually don't think ahead very far."

"You have a good memory, Doc."

For the first time in her company, Seth almost grinned. Clients didn't grin all that much in her office. Baby steps towards that thing called trust.

"I asked you before if you like playing football, Seth. Your answer was ambiguous."

His giant hands fiddled in his lap while he thought about the question again. Clearly, he had some misgivings.

"Hard to say. I've been asking myself that for a while now."

"Since you got to college?"

"More like since I was beginning high school."

"You know, you don't have to play if you don't want to."

"Really? The coaches would kill me, because their careers would go back in the crapper. My parents would kill me. They live for this. My teammates, who are the only people I really know on campus, would ostracize me for giving up on them."

"None of that makes a difference, does it? It's your life, not theirs."

"Do you like sports, Doc?"

"I do. I played three sports in high school, Seth, and I played field hockey here many years ago."

"What else did you play in high school?"

"I played basketball in the winter and softball in the spring. I wasn't nearly as good at either of those, but I always just enjoyed playing. Did you play anything else?"

"We had such a small school that most of the guys who were athletes played all three of the sports the school offered to guys – meaning football, basketball, and baseball."

"Was football your favorite?"

"Nobody has ever asked me that," he answered thoughtfully. "I think they all assumed it was because of my size and because I'm so good at it. And people live for football in Iowa. It's like a religion. But if I was serious with myself, I think I would say that I actually like baseball the best. It is slower paced, you play more games, which means fewer boring practices, and I love tracking all the stats. Plus, I guess, no one pulls your hair. I still cut out the box scores from each game of the Cedar Rapids Kernels. I'm guessing you've never heard of them, but they are a minor league team for the Minnesota Twins. I have so many full scrapbooks of their games, going back to when I was about seven or eight, which I still look at from time to time. Usually when I'm in a funk. Even though I could look it all up online, I keep doing the real cutting and pasting of the printed copy. I must be the only one in the world who still does that."

"What position did you play?"

"Right field. I could hit, and I had a cannon for an arm. They put me out there for four straight seasons. Used to have some great conversations with our centerfielder while we were waiting for somebody to hit the ball in our direction. We became very good friends hanging out there."

"Interesting. Where is he now?"

"On a training mission in Syria."

"I'm sure he's growing up fast there. Do you ever hear from him?"

"No. My mother sees his mother periodically and then passes the updates along to me. It sounds like it's pretty rough, and he's struggling in the world he's now in. I'm not sure I have any reason to complain about my life. What he is doing makes me feel small and insignificant."

"I can understand that. Many of us would probably feel the same way if we ever took the time to consider it, like you have."

"Were you glad you played field hockey here?" Seth asked.

"That's a fair question. I think so, yes. But it wasn't as great as the coaches told me it was going to be when I was being recruited out of my little high school in Pennsylvania, where we only had eighty kids in a class, by the way. Like you said previously, the coaches take it far more seriously here than in high school. Probably because it's their full-time job. They aren't having to teach classes or monitor study halls. I had a hard time, when I first got here, getting all my work done with the heavy sports commitment. That first semester, I also missed much of what else was happening on campus. I can't imagine what it's like at the big athletic schools. But learning to manage your time is a healthy part of the college athletic experience. What I worry about now, as sports have become so intense at all college levels, is whether the coaches are sending the right message to the players about what's genuinely important. I'm not sure they always are. It's become too big a business for everyone involved, and it's not right to place the kind of pressure they do on such young people. Like you, I liked high school sports better. But that's just my view.

"But what about you? What would you do with all the extra time, Seth, if you didn't play football?"

"That's the thing. I don't know, Doc. The rest of my life has been ranching. I don't know if I like that or not either. Just like I don't know if I like football. But it's been hard to figure out what my other options might be."

"Welcome to the club."

"Are you serious?"

"I'm forty-four years old and still wonder what I should be doing with my life. Trust me, you and I aren't alone in this quandary."

"Even with all those diplomas on the wall?"

"Yes, even with all those diplomas on the wall."

"You don't like helping people?"

"I love helping people. It's what I've always wanted to do. Maybe unlike you and football, I still find myself wrestling with whether I'm any good at it."

"Well, I'm hoping you are."

Emily smiled at that line.

"You and me both, Seth. So let me ask you a question. If you could do anything you wanted in life, and money wasn't an issue, what would you do?"

"You mean besides dating Jelly?"

"You really are still struggling with that."

"I dream about her all the time."

"So answer my question."

"My true answer?"

"Who am I going to tell?"

He chewed on his lip for a moment before answering.

"I'd want to act in the theatre. I'm obviously not ready for Broadway, but somewhere with quality actors, where I can see if I can cut it. Right now, I'm only a pretty good actor in my mind."

"You think about acting a good amount?"

"From time to time. When I'm not thinking about Jelly."

He grinned a full grin this time.

"Have you ever acted before?"

"If sixth grade doesn't count, then no."

"Why not?"

"Really big football players don't do theatre?"

"Again, why not?"

"Cause everyone on the team will think I'm a fairy."

"Would that bother you?"

"Yeah. Because I'm straight. And I care about my reputation."

"There is a wonderful theatre program here. Anyone can try out. And not everyone in the cast is a fairy. And fairy is the wrong word. There is nothing wrong with being gay, Seth."

"I have no experience, beyond all the acting I do in my dreams, and I'm probably not any good. And the football team will still think I'm a fairy, excuse me, gay, no matter what I say. And where I come from, and in our church, there is a lot wrong with being gay."

"How do you know that you're not any good at acting? And maybe some on the football team would respect you even more for pursuing your dream."

"You've never played football."

"That's right. But you aren't the first football player who has ever been to see me either. You know, the odds are that there are gay players on your team right now. But let's table the gay discussion for another time. Just remember that one of the great things about college is that the students get to explore. Get to get out of their comfort zones."

"I struggle with that."

"We all struggle with that."

"I don't think Jelly does."

"You may be right, Seth. But she is the rare one."

"So that's my message today?"

"It's not a bad message if that's what you walk away with. How about you make a list of what other things you might want to try during your four years here? There is no rush to get everything done in your first semester, but it's nice to expand your mind and even put a tentative plan together to take full advantage of the opportunity here. It will give you something to think about besides Jelly. And we'll meet again next week, okay?"

"Okay." The big body raised itself from the tired chair. "By the way, Doc. You're in pretty good shape for forty-four."

She smiled at the comment by the nineteen-year-old football wunderkind. He clearly meant it as a compliment and not anything else. Her second compliment from a client in twenty-four hours, no less. And then she wondered why her ex-husband had never said anything so random and so nice while she was still with him.

13

It Wasn't A Date

She would be lying if she said that she didn't think about Monk the entire time between when she passed him the note with her address written on it and when he rang her doorbell the next evening. She kept telling herself that this wasn't a date, that Monk had too much to figure out about himself and how he'd gotten to where he was in his life. Which basically was a cute, engaging, but, nonetheless, flamed out star. And she was trying to figure out how she'd gotten to where she was. Not that she knew what to call it. A jettisoned wife. A no longer necessary mother. A person pretending that she could afford to live the modestly comfortable suburban life she was living. Someone who was afraid to address all her issues, which included not yet having been able to free herself from still feeling connected to the man she married. With a shameful, yet admittedly exhilarating, two-minute exception that she was grateful hadn't gone any farther, Emily hadn't been on a date, nor anything more than that, with anyone besides her ex-husband since she was nineteen. Which she wasn't anymore. But none of this kept her from thinking about each of them.

She knew she wouldn't let herself do anything with Monk. Maybe let's say she assumed she wouldn't let herself do anything with Monk. Remember, the kiss was never something that she would have expected she would do either. Why did she kiss him anyway? That was so not her. Not to mention that it was so against everything she believed in. She still considered her husband to be her sidekick back then. Her lifelong companion. The guy who kept her bed warm. It was a story that she put into a compartment without out ever addressing, along with many of the other things in her life that she should have addressed. But unlike the other things in her many compartments, this one didn't bother

her as much. While it was wrong, it for some reason didn't feel quite as wrong.

It turned out Monk really could cook. He brought linguine, fresh clams, Italian bread, and things for a salad that she wasn't even sure what they all were. And he brought a bottle of red wine. Emily knew he was testing himself. He wanted to demonstrate, to them both, that he could manage his drinking when he wanted. She also knew that people with drinking problems sometimes play this card. Show that they can stay sober to make a good first impression. He would be aware that she knew this. Yet it felt so comfortable from the moment he stepped through the front door of her tiny house. She had feared that her house, and its kitchen with not a modern appliance, the downstairs bathroom that was barely big enough to fit one person, and a living room with so little furniture, would be too unpretentious for a person, who she had learned from their little conversations in the office, grew up in the haughty Connecticut Gold Coast and had been under the bright lights for much of his career. But it didn't turn out that way at all. With the pasta, the wine, and with him, it was nothing short of enchanting.

"How's the sleeping going?"

She sat at her kitchen table, fondling a glass of wine, while he busied himself about the stove, occasionally asking where a needed bowl or a particular utensil might be, but clearly demonstrating that he knew what he was doing. They could talk about whatever they wanted, and she quickly became aware that neither of them spent much of the time that evening not smiling and laughing, even though each of their recent histories would have suggested they do otherwise. But they didn't have to pretend. Which was incredibly welcome. And she could look, without being noticed, at his tight ass while he was getting pots out of the cupboards and tending to the things cooking on the stove. It was fine that the food had to simmer for a while.

"Monk," she sighed, "I think I'm becoming a pothead."

"Not being able to sleep is hard."

"You've had times where you couldn't sleep?"

"Many. Back when I was trying to build my reputation. I'd get anxious whenever I had to give a talk to some group of researchers. Anybody that I didn't really know well. I always seemed to be the youngest one, and I had miserable stage fright and couldn't sleep worth a crap while agonizing about the whole thing."

"Really?"

"I stayed awake for days, or even weeks, beforehand, even though I suspected that they would be impressed by my research."

This was rare for such a seemingly confident person, Emily thought. He wanted to impress them but didn't know if he could. Even if he was likely the smartest person in a room of what were likely all smart people.

"But I don't know if I can hang out here and have dinner with you, since you're becoming a junkie," he joked.

Emily threw her head back and laughed some more. Which felt great.

"Smoking dope is so not me. But it works like a charm. I know I need to stop, but it's hard. It's just so great to be able to wake up each morning relaxed, well rested, and ready to go. It has been a long time since I've been able to do that."

"Since you discovered what your husband did?"

"You got it."

"Well, you need to be careful. You don't want to end up like me."

He was not wrong.

"I have a new client, Monk. He's from Nepal and hasn't seen his family in three years. He is feeling guilty about the life he has now versus the humble little village where they remain. A very impressive kid. He can't sleep either, which is why he came to see me. I can't tell him that smoking dope is a better solution than seeing me as his therapist. Plus, I don't want to run into him in the cannabis store I went to. That would be embarrassing as hell. And I'd suggest your physics books trick, but I suspect he would like reading them even more than I do. So the kid may never sleep again."

"You didn't drive to some other far away town so that you could buy your pot unnoticed?"

The food smelled delicious, but even after he served her, they continued to talk instead of immediately digging in.

"I actually hadn't thought of that before I went," she chuckled. "It's not like I'm familiar with where all the dope stores are, you know. Basically, I know of one. So that's where I went."

"There is something called Google."

"Whatever. I'm an impulsive shopper. Anyway, while you may have whiffed on the initial sleeping advice, you did help a great deal after my husband's little event really devastated me. And for that I am appreciative."

She reached across the table and patted his hand. Which gave her goosebumps.

"That's what you call it? A 'little event'?"

"Okay, maybe not so little. What would you call it?"

"A middle-aged snake having sex with an underage girl."

"Ouch. That stings."

"Sorry Emily, but you must know by now that men aren't always as trustworthy as they'd like you to think."

"Yourself included?" She smirked when asking.

"I hope not." He smiled back. "Anyway, with the exception of my misguided physics recommendation, I have mostly just listened to you talk since first dropping into your office."

They each finally twirled pasta on their forks and began to eat.

"That's why you are good at what you do…holy shit! This food is fabulous. Where did you learn to cook?"

"When you are an only child, you often get more attention than kids who are part of larger families. My father loved to cook. Saturday was always his big night in the kitchen. I would go to the market with him, and he would teach me what all the different fish and meat and vegetables and oils were. Then he would buy some assortment of them, take me home, and I'd learn how to put them all together and cook a meal. I ate well in my youth."

"So, you're smart, handsome, and can cook like a professional chef. How come you have never been married?"

"Ahhh, right to the sixty-four-dollar question."

"One of them, anyway."

"The story about my learning to cook didn't sufficiently entertain you?"

"Of course, it did. But I have a curious mind."

He put his fork down and stopped eating, in order to think for a moment. The first break in their evening's conversation, though not an unhealthy break.

"I guess I've never met the right person. At least that's what I believe. I've actually never even been close. Others might contend that maybe I drink too much to even remember if I've met the right person. But I'm sticking with my story."

"I've been wondering about your drinking, too, as I've never seen you drunk. Or maybe only once. It's a problem, isn't it?"

He stayed silent for a bit more as he figured out how to answer. Their second break. Emily knew he liked her as a person. And he was no doubt physically attracted to her. In her simple mind, he had proved that four years ago when he made out with her for no reason. He'd had too much to drink, and she didn't know if he even remembered. That was the purpose of 'or maybe only once.' But she remembered. Either way, she hoped he wanted to answer her honestly.

"It's funny. I don't drink during the day, and I don't drink every night. I think I told you that before. I try hard to be a good guy. And probably try too hard to be the clever or funny one sometimes. But trying to be all those things can be too much, especially for someone who is naturally shy like I am, and I just have to explode. If that makes any sense. Does that make me a drunk? I don't know that it does. But it doesn't mean I don't have a problem."

"You sound like someone who knows himself."

"It is what I do for a living. Or used to do for a living. I think I know myself. I don't know, however, that I have great confidence in myself."

"So what are you going to do with your life now?"

"Who knows? Maybe I go the next rung down the ladder, which must be high school. I'm running out of rungs. Or maybe I should try something new altogether. Maybe I could open a restaurant?" he said jokingly.

"If you do, I promise to be your first patron. I haven't eaten this well in a long time. But back to the real conversation." Twirling more linguini to shovel into her mouth. Rudely talking while chewing. "Maybe you should try to address why you drink, get a handle on it, and start your career back in the other direction."

"Sounds like you're playing the therapist now."

"It is what I do for a living. Still do as a matter of fact."

He chuckled at her mimicking him.

"Perhaps I can help you," she continued.

"How would you plan to do that?"

Spontaneity was never Emily's forte. She had been considering an idea for the last day and a half. It would be taking a chance, which was not the norm for her, but it didn't feel wrong. Like the kiss. She also could tell he needed help, something she was quite good at recognizing.

"Do you have any money?" she asked.

"Why do you ask?"

"Just answer the question."

"No."

"Do you have any prospects?"

"For what?"

"A job? Adding to your bank account? A place to live that you can afford? A cool position with the FBI? A role in a Broadway show? A romance?" She added the latter nervously. Again, she wasn't really certain why.

"No. No. No. Very funny. Even more funny. And…I don't think so right now. Yet."

"Yet?"

"I'm an optimist by nature."

They sheepishly smiled at each other. Monk had barely touched his wine.

"Come stay with me for a while. I feel comfortable with you for whatever reason. I have space here now. No husband, kids rarely at home. Stay while you figure out your life. It will change your routine."

"Is that it? Roommates?"

"For now, anyway. Neither of us needs anything more than that at this moment, Monk. Our lives are complicated enough as they are." She grinned. "As you know, I have my own demons to conquer. And I suspect that I could use some company. We can help each other out. I'd be happy just to keep laughing every so often again. I've kind of forgotten what that feels like."

He got up to fill the basket with more bread that was warming in the oven. She just watched him. Surprisingly hoping.

"I can live with that. It's the best offer I've had in a long time. I guess I accept."

"Good."

"Thank you. I needed this."

"You're welcome. You can make dinner tomorrow night, too. This food is amazing."

"I told you I can cook."

While she didn't display it outwardly, our Emily was like a teenage girl when Monk came over. Why? Who knows? She was too old and had too much going on in her life for this to be a crush. And he had real problems that if she went too far or too fast would only add to her own. But two other times – once when they were setting the table and once later when she was getting a serving dish out of the closet for him -- their arms brushed. It turns out that still made her insides churn. In a good way. She hadn't been touched by anyone in too long. It was a longed-for feeling. And so she invited him to move in. Knowing they needed to move slowly, but probably hoping that they could touch again. She really missed that.

Their dinner lasted three hours where they talked about their childhoods – her growing up of modest means in rural Pennsylvania and he in academic snobbery in Connecticut. They talked about academics and sports and their first time ever having sex. She in high school with the boy she really liked, in one of those rare moments when they were able to escape the surveillance of the mother who believed only in Jewish girlfriends. And he in Manhattan, a few years after college, when he was mesmerized by a fellow researcher whose intellectual bandwidth, he claimed, exceeded his own. They talked about his time at the top of their profession, and Emily's career treading water for twenty years in the same place she was now. Why he had loved what he used to do (who wouldn't), and why she still loved what she did (most wouldn't). By the end, she'd had three glasses of wine and a spirited buzz because she was both as nervous and as excited as she had been in some time. He had half a glass. Because that's all he seemed to need.

14

The Valedictorian

In the rare moments when you pull back from your job as a college therapist to consider all the students you see, it can be more than a little mind-numbing. Despite all the skills that a good therapist develops around listening, creating trust, being patient, and the rest, no one ever teaches you how to handle the ocean of people who want to see you. And in college, no matter what the students and parents have been told, it is an ocean. So far in this story, you've met four of Emily's clients. Jelly, Seth, Mana, and Henry, the eighty-two-year-old professor. Altogether, she sees forty different clients each and every *week*. And it's taken this long to describe just the four of them. Hard to imagine, isn't it?

If you cared in the way our Emily did, you don't become numb to the work, but you can become mentally exhausted by it. Particularly when the many challenges in your own life are piled on top. The preponderance of her clients are young people with the bulk of their lives still ahead of them. Many of the issues, as stated at the start of the story, are not serious and can be readily handled. But the ones that are more acute can be disturbing, and you need to be at your best to make a difference in those situations. You also need to be able to identify the benign from the malignant. Which can be problematic given the sheer volume of clients seen. There simply isn't much time to catch your breath and think between appointments.

Once in a while a client comes in who you just don't like. There is no other way to put it. And that became the case here for Emily. A student whose issues were so ludicrous that Emily questioned what admissions was even thinking. You won't like the client either and probably will wonder for a long time why she is even in this story. We have the habit of paying more attention to people we instinctively like. It's a shortcoming of who are.

"Hello Doctor Metcalf. I'm Marionette."

"Nice to see you. Come on in." Emily was reviewing the young women's brief file, as she was yet another new client to be seen in the first months on campus. "Excuse my ignorance here, but your student file says that your name is Marianne. Is that a misprint?"

"No, that's understandable. I changed my name."

"To Marionette?"

"Yes."

"Like the puppet?"

"That's right."

"How come, if I may ask?"

"I thought it was a better reflection of who I am."

She was, indeed, stick like, all knees and elbows, with an untamed mop of dark hair. Like the marionettes Emily might have seen as a young kid. Maybe from Mr. Rogers, another elite college best and brightest who only lasted a year before leaving his university. She didn't know why she knew this. Maybe it was that notable and obtuse thing. But she suspected that this girl had an entirely different idea when she came up with the new moniker.

"When did you decide to make this change?"

"Just last week. As such, it's s new to me. But I'm liking the transition so far."

"You waited until the start of school?"

"I'd been toying with the change all summer."

"I see."

"I definitely like it. Do you?"

"I'm hardly an expert on name changes. So tell me, what can I do for you, Marionette?"

"You're the first person who has called me by my new name so far."

"I'm honored."

Marionette neither looked at her feet nor at Emily. She sort of just looked at nothing in particular, but seemed to be enjoying listening to herself talk.

"Well, Doctor Metcalf, I'm unbelievably stressed."

"Amidst this beautiful fall we are having, Marionette? What are you stressed about?"

"Academics."

"Fill me in."

"I don't think I can keep up. There are so many really smart kids here."

Pretty much every student has that feeling when he or she first arrives. Being in a class that is primarily comprised of the most talented kids from the best high schools across the country.

"Well, the university accepted you, and it's a hard place to get into, so I'm guessing that you are no dummy. And the private school you went to in Delaware is very challenging and prepares its grads well for selective colleges like this one. I'm guessing you did well there academically."

"I was valedictorian."

"Good for you."

"It's different here, Doctor Metcalf."

"Similar kids I think, just a year older."

"I'm not doing well."

This young woman was blindly focused on what she wanted to talk about. It was like talking to a robot.

"Tell me, what courses are you taking?"

"English 101, which is required, Chinese History, Sociology, and Political Science."

"That sounds like an interesting set of classes. Fun actually. I always wished that I took Chinese History when I was here. It's such a rich culture. Do you like your courses?"

"Chinese History is for the full year while the others are just for the semester. I picked them because the professors are supposed to be easy graders."

Huh.

"We are still quite early in the semester. Thirteen days to be exact. Have you had a quiz or test yet?"

"Not yet."

"A paper due?"

"No."

"Received an actual grade on anything?"

"No."

"Do you participate in class?"

"All the time."

"Have you been to see your professors during their office hours?"

"I've been to every single one."

Emily had to bite her tongue to keep from laughing. This was beyond ridiculous.

"So how do you know that you aren't keeping up?"

"I can just feel it."

"You can feel it?"

"Yes. I can just feel it."

"Hmm. So you were valedictorian of your class in high school?"

"Is that in my file, by the way?"

"No, it isn't."

"Shouldn't it be?"

"Why?"

"That way everyone will know what I'm capable of."

"Marionette, did you work hard in high school?"

"Morning, noon, and night."

"Is valedictorian what you are striving for in college?"

"It's not a bad aim, is it?"

"Tell me, Marionette, about your family."

"Why?"

"It will help me get to know you."

"It's just me and my father. My mother died when I was two."

"I'm sorry. That had to be hard."

"My dad is a saint."

"What does he do for a living?"

"He is a plumber."

"Are you here on a scholarship?"

"A full scholarship."

"Good for you. I'm sure that made your dad happy. Does he push you to be such a passionate student?"

"Never for a moment. He's been through so much. He idolized my mother, but he never even finished high school. The post-secondary education system is a little foreign to him. Not to sound trite, but he just cares about making sure we have food on the table and that I have a life that will fulfill me."

"What is it that fulfills you, Marionette?"

It didn't take her five seconds to know her answer. Again, she was so singularly focused.

"Doing well on tests. Getting good grades."

"You seem to do that quite well. Have you ever gotten what you would consider a bad grade?"

"You mean besides a 'A'?"

"That's for you to decide what a bad grade would be."

"Then the answer is no. I've never gotten anything less than an 'A' in any class."

"In any class in any year?"

"Correct."

Her father should be happy that he didn't know much about her schooling. She would be hard to live with if he did.

"What would you do if there were no classes?"

"What do mean?"

"At some point, your days of studying will be over. There will be no more tests, no more grades. What then?"

"Are you trying to scare me Doctor Metcalf?"

"Not at all. Let's just say that you are valedictorian again. What then? How does that help you?"

"Well, I'm sure I would get a good job."

"Marionette, people can get good jobs whether or not they are the valedictorian."

"But wouldn't the valedictorian get the best job?"

You must be kidding.

"First of all, there are no best jobs. Different people want to do different things. They are often hired for more than just their grades. Social skills, teamwork, compassion, integrity, and a whole host of other things can come into play. And jobs don't have regularly graded papers and tests."

"That could be a problem."

Emily sighed. She had a feeling that if she asked Marionette what she had for breakfast, the response would somehow include grades, class rank, and how eating was a waste of time that could have been better spent studying.

"Marionette, the world is about more than getting the highest score on a test."

"How were your grades in college, Doctor Metcalf?"

"Better than some, worse than others. The important thing is that I'm doing what I've always wanted to do."

"Really? *This* is what you wanted to do?"

Okay, that really pissed off Emily.

"Marionette, are you trying to make me feel badly about my choice of a life? If people like me didn't choose this path, where would you be sitting right now?"

"I didn't mean to offend you."

"Well, you did."

There was no reply from her tone-deaf client.

"Here's a thought." She would have liked to have thrown this shallow little twit out of her office right then and there. But in her line of work, you couldn't do that. "I want you to think about what you are going to do over Christmas break."

"That's still a ways off."

"Right. But so is graduation, and you're already worried about being the valedictorian. It's different from high school. You will have more than a month off here. No classes, no exams. What will you do with all that free time?"

"I have no idea."

"Exactly. Spend some time thinking about what would be fun for you to do in that period. What would fulfill you. Then come back, and let's talk about it."

"Like tomorrow?"

Unbelievable.

"How about we make an appointment for next week?"

Emily knew from experience that valedictorians weren't always the best hires. Like Marionette, they too often had different ways of looking at the world, not the least of which was that everything was a competition.

15

The Benefit Of Working For Insurance Companies

Moving is typically a significant life event. But for Monk, it was not momentous. He took all the clothes that he hadn't yet ruined via his drinking binges to the cleaners, cleaned out his car, checked out of the pit of an apartment for which he no longer had money to pay the rent, and moved in with Emily. He didn't bring anything except his laptop, his unruined clothes, and what he planned to make for dinner that night. He told Emily that the little else he had, which wasn't much more than his bed and his alarm clock, went to The Salvation Army. The symmetry Emily and Monk experienced during their maiden dinner flowed into their new life as roommates. It was easy for them to be together. He didn't need to show off to her, while having Monk around made Emily more than content. They each now had somebody to look out for and to look out for them, and that felt like a good thing. He took over her daughters' bedroom which kept it all platonic. She didn't tell the girls right away, as they wouldn't be coming home until Christmas, which was still a couple of months away. Meaning she still had plenty of time to screw things up before then.

Being together made it so she could talk about her clients with him. He particularly liked hearing the ongoing story about Mana. Seth was certainly compelling. Even the valedictorian or bust one. It gave them something to share, which they rarely had the time to do when they worked together. Her clients, no doubt, could make for interesting conversation.

Twenty minutes after her last client departed on the initial Friday that Monk was her roommate, and all her colleagues had scattered for the weekend, Jelly was standing in her office doorway. Emily had no idea why. Jelly hadn't made an appointment, nor had she sent any message cautioning that she was coming. But the only thing Emily had on her schedule for that evening was another dinner by Monk, which was quickly becoming her favorite part of each day, but it could wait for a bit.

"Hi Jelly! I haven't seen you in a while."

"Fourteen days, four hours and sixteen minutes to be exact. My hair has changed colors twice in that time. You missed out on all the excitement."

"Hah. Come on in. Have a seat."

Emily found herself a little envious of Jelly. A young woman so willing to do whatever she felt like. So free spirited. Now purple hair, a pair of camouflage cargo shorts, and a gray *Feel The Bern* t-shirt with nothing underneath. With a fit body and incredible eyes. No doubt every straight guy and not so straight girl on campus would watch her saunter by, and there was no doubt in Emily's mind that Jelly knew it.

"How is school going?"

"Pretty cool, Doc. I like it here. I like the freedom. The work is always there, but it's not overwhelming. And it's interesting for the most part. I've even joined the school newspaper and am going to be writing a regular column. You know, 'The World According to Jelly' or something like that," she laughed.

"Well, that's sounds interesting. I guess I'll have to subscribe to the school paper."

"Don't worry. There are about five copies on the table in the waiting room here."

"In that case, my bank account thanks you. So no stress in your life?"

"Not over academics."

"No more complicated break ups?"

"I've stayed away from boyfriends for now. Too much work."

"Hah. That's a new one."

"I try to keep it interesting."

"Getting along with your roommates?"

"I have a single. I do better when I don't have to pretend that I like some snobby rich bitch from Greenwich or La Jolla."

"Okay. If you say so. I'm surprised you stopped by on a Friday evening. Haven't you and your friends usually started your weekend by now?"

She wondered, for the first of many times, who Jelly's friends were. Who she hung out with. Girls or boys? More freshmen or upper class? Studious kids or those who spent too much of their time high? Jocks? Techies? Artists? The newspaper staff? Employees who worked full time in the dining hall? Professors who would flirt with her? Strangers in the bars in Philadelphia? She'd only seen her with Seth, and never anyone else.

"I always see your light on later than everyone else's in here. Figured you could use some company."

"You don't miss much. But you know that you are always welcome to come by. So how's Seth doing?"

"That's why I'm here."

Jelly had flopped down in one of the chairs, the same way she had the first time she showed up. As if she shared the office.

"I figured that you didn't just come to say hello."

"Don't worry, Doc. I'll get around to that at some point, too. Do you know he is thinking about quitting football?"

"I know the thought had occurred to him. Actually, I may have suggested it. But I shouldn't be telling you this as he is now officially a client. Thanks to you, I suspect."

For the second time with Jelly, Emily bent the rules she had always held so dearly. Which is to say, she had always been strident about the privacy of her client information. And then Jelly unexpectedly sprinted into her life.

"Are you kidding me?" Jelly almost screamed.

"What?"

"Do you know how good he is?"

"I have a feeling you are going to tell me."

"You just said he is your client! Haven't you read about him on the pro football scouting websites?"

"Never been my thing, Jelly. Am I supposed to be reading them? I don't even think I know what they are."

"Doc, the experts all say he is already the best football player in New England. If he stays healthy, there is a good chance he is going to get drafted early and make a ton of money, even after going to a two-bit football college like this."

Emily paused. She was trying to figure out if this was really something she should have known. Some relevant research she should have thought to do on her own. She couldn't imagine why Jelly was familiar with pro football scouting reports.

"He said that he might want to try acting."

Third time bending the rules.

"Are you serious? All the plays for the semester have picked their casts by now. The next tryouts aren't until February! Plus, he has no idea how to act. It's a pipedream! The theatre kids here are really good. They've been acting their whole lives. I've been to a few of their practices and seen them. He'll piss away his future and be more unhappy than ever because his teammates will now hate him. And, as a result, he'll just spend more time thinking about me! You know, his fixation with me is not healthy!"

Emily felt the big pit in her stomach that she felt on those occasions she did something stupid. Jelly was causing her to feel that this was one of those occasions. And Jelly went to watch the acting practices? What didn't she do?

"How do you know all this Jelly?"

"Seth and I now have breakfast together every day?"

"What?"

"He came by to see me in my dorm room the other night."

Oh crap.

"What did he want?"

"He was drunk. He told me that he still thinks about me, that he dreams about me, and that he wants me to give him another chance. I told him that there was no chance that we are going out again, but that I would meet him for breakfast at seven o'clock every weekday morning if he wanted to only talk. Not many college kids are up at that time, yet he's been early for each one so far. Which means he can't go out and get drunk the night before. So now I'm playing shrink."

"How drunk was he?"

"Drunk enough. It was like ten o'clock on a weeknight."

"That's not promising."

"No kidding, Doc."

"People too often hurt themselves when they become depressed. Getting drunk when you have never been a drinker is something to be concerned about."

"We need to help him."

"Don't you think that playing shrink, as you call it, is a little dangerous? Maybe above your pay grade?"

"Doc, I'm not sure you have it figured out. I told you we would do this together. That's why I'm eating breakfast with him and filling you in. Otherwise, you wouldn't know what the hell is going on with Seth! I do still care for the guy!"

Emily was quiet for a moment. Trying to figure this all out.

"Do you think this will help Seth, or just make him become more infatuated with you?"

"I also told him that I'm a lesbian."

"Huh."

"You don't look convinced, Doc."

"Are you, Jelly?"

"Who knows. Might be too soon to tell. My parents are lesbians, so that at least makes for a good cover. I told everyone in high school that I was a lesbian so that horny boys didn't derail my studies. I've only really liked one boy in my life, and he never was sure whether to believe I was gay."

"Huh."

"I bare my soul and 'huh' is all I get?"

"You told the boy you liked that you were gay?"

"I wanted to stay in control of our relationship."

"You're not always the easiest person to figure out."

"That may not be a bad thing."

"Impetuous is the word that comes to my mind."

"I'll take that as a compliment. But the term for Seth right now might be 'loose cannon.' He doesn't know where his head is at."

"Do you have any suggestions?"

"No! If I did, I wouldn't have needed to come to see you! Man, you are off your game."

"I won't take that as a compliment. Okay, let's go back to the basics. Is Seth going to hurt himself?"

"I don't think so."

"How confident are you of that?"

"60-40."

"That doesn't give me great faith."

"I can understand that."

"Is he going to hurt you?"

"I hope not. I'm not giving odds on that one."

"Here is my card, Jelly, with all my contact info on it. Keep it with you and call me at any time you become afraid. Okay?"

She reached over the desk to hand Jelly her card. Now you can see the challenge of being a caretaker. She was going home to what would undoubtedly be a great homecooked meal, which should be the beginning of an entertaining weekend with her new roommate. Food, wine, laughter, and that growing warm feeling with Monk. Something for which she seemed to increasingly yearn. Yet now she knew that this conversation with Jelly is all she would think about. Seth and where his head was at and whether he might hurt anybody. She would play it over and over in her mind until she returned to work on Monday. Because weekends could be the scariest time for a college therapist. It must be one of the reasons why so many people instead choose to work for insurance companies.

16

It Had Been Eight Months

Twenty years into Emily's marriage, the switch had somehow been flipped off. Why did this happen to so many couples? How can you know people so intimately one minute and then not know them at all? Once, for better or worse, knowing all that they were going to say before they said it, and now being so completely unsettled before starting a conversation. Do people really change? Is it really that easy to fall out of love? Are most couples truly in love in the first place? Or is it simply the idea of being in love and having a family that attracts them to each other? Procreating and sharing the genes of someone who you later will no longer like or trust or respect?

This was our Emily. Now full of new, unfamiliar feelings and emotions, but having no idea what to do with them. The shock of the event had certainly moved everything to the forefront. If she'd had the time, she could likely study her life for days on end. Maybe figure a few things out. If she wasn't providing counsel to her students or going to see them in the hospital emergency room or smoking dope or worrying that Seth was going to hurt Jelly or being whatever she was being with Monk. What kind of decision was that, by the way? You're cute, I really might like you, so come sleep in my daughters' room? Instead, she stuffed things into her soon to be overflowing compartments and kept the doors closed for as long as she could.

She hadn't seen her ex since he moved out. That was eight months ago. Over their two-decade marriage, the longest they had gone without seeing each other had been five days, when he took the girls one June right after school had ended on a camping trip for some father-daughter bonding. He was off for summer vacation from teaching, while she was still working. When he finally left their little home for good, he took all his clothes, the furniture he deemed was his because he was the one who had picked it out, and his collection of largely ignored hobby equipment – golf clubs, a baseball mitt, his tennis racquet, woodworking tools, and the rest of the crap that he had wasted their money on. All that stuff could now remain ignored in his new closets. The one thing he didn't take was a box of memories from his life with her and the girls. The pictures of their wedding, where he looked good, and she looked fabulous. As tan as she gets and sculpted in a ridiculously expensive dress. The pictures of when Abbey and Jessie were born, and Emily was bloated like a hippo. But a blissful, grinning from ear to ear hippo. Birthday photos with pin-the-tail-on-the-donkey games, no matter whose birthday it was and how old they were. Even after a six-year-old Jessie tried to stick the tail on an open window and almost fell out. It had been their ritual for everyone's birthday, year after year, right up until the event, after which rituals simply stopped. Videos of trips to the zoo, anniversary dinners, visits from both sets of parents, and all that stuff that happy young families do. He apparently had decided that he was leaving behind their past together. Which hurt her and pissed off the girls when they noticed, which didn't take long. How does someone so quickly discard twenty years of memories? She had determined that she would still think fondly about that part of their life together. If nothing else, they created two amazing children out of it. And there were plenty of times where she and he had endlessly giggled ensemble.

Since he left, they had emailed and spoken on the phone, but never seen each other in person. She was not sure why she emailed him about getting together. This was the advice she would have given herself if she were a client. Keep the communication going, because you share children and because it's not healthy to keep that festering feeling inside of you for the remainder of your days. Only now she didn't know him. The whole idea of meeting didn't make any sense given her apparently growing interest in Monk. Maybe deep down she wanted to add to the wall between

Monk and her, make it larger than the one between their current bedrooms. Make it harder for anything to happen between them because she still hadn't figured out how she felt about her ex. She still didn't know. Her mind vacillated more unevenly now than it ever had.

Her ex responded affirmatively to her email with only a few words. *Yes. Where? What time?* They met at a little diner near the campus on a Saturday morning – he made the drive from Philadelphia where he now lived. He looked the same, his brown beard perfectly trimmed, his familiar weekend jeans and sweater, both a little baggier, looking like he had lost a bit of weight that he couldn't afford to lose. His voice remained deep and commanding, for someone who, it turns out, wasn't all that deep and commanding. The voice was probably the first thing that had struck her when they met. A surprising powerful voice for a small man. He spoke not unlike a poor man's James Earl Jones. An actor who Emily adored.

She wondered if her ex noticed anything about her. Whether he remembered something about her looks that had first attracted him to her, or if he thought she looked at all different from when they were still together.

Even years later, Emily wouldn't have been able to tell you why she had decided to ask him to get together. The man who had hurt and embarrassed her so deeply. The man who had so quickly thrown their entire family on the scrap heap. But she did, and he ordered a huge breakfast with eggs, sausage, fried potatoes, and buttered toast, all sorts of grease and cholesterol, and yet he remained a toothpick. She just had coffee and fruit. Throughout their breakfast, she would watch him eat while she picked at her fruit, mostly trying to remember the other things about him, besides the voice, that she had been attracted to, which wasn't difficult, because she quickly discovered that she was still attracted to him. Which was hard to believe after what he did.

"Hi."

"Hello, Em."

The deep voice.

"It's been a long while."

"Yes, it has."

"How've you been?"

"I'm okay. How about you?"

"I'd be lying if I said this has been easy."

"I'm sorry things worked out the way they did, Emily. Nobody deserved this."

"I would agree with that."

"Are you still angry?"

"I have my moments. I had thought we were a team. But it turns out you kept a lot secret from me."

"I have no answer for that. It was hard time in our lives."

"I wish I knew that."

There were many questions that she wanted to ask, most of which she knew would irritate him. But the simple fact is that she wanted to understand why he found a teenage girl so much more interesting than she was, why he left all their history behind, why he pursued sex with her two nights before this whole thing blew up, and if life is really that much better now. The latter which, it turns out, he was not shy about sharing.

"I understand from the girls," she said, "that you are dating again."

"I am."

"Was that hard to do? After you and I having spent so many years together."

"It was time, Emily. We weren't headed in a good direction."

"How come you never told me that?"

"It didn't take Einstein to figure it out. I assumed that you felt about things the way I did."

"Obviously not. You had a fling, and I didn't."

His food came, they paused while being served, and then again while they began to eat their breakfasts. Some of the eggs eventually landed in his beard, but she resisted the urge to wipe them off, which she would have done without hesitation not all that long ago.

"If this is where this conversation is going, I'm out of here. I told you that she was a delusional young girl."

"I don't know that I believe you."

"Okay, that's it. This was a bad idea."

He wiped his mouth, put down his napkin, and began to stand up.

"Wait…we won't talk about that."

She instinctively reached out to grab his arm, like she might have done in a conversation in their kitchen or bedroom back when they knew each other but pulled back before she touched him. It wasn't clear that he noticed, but she likely couldn't have handled the touching again. She would have been afraid of what she might feel.

"Let's talk about the girls," she said.

After an intermission, he decided to stay, which was good, because she didn't want him to go. She still wanted to look at him. Maybe he was just still hungry and wanted to finish his breakfast.

"They seem to be doing well," he opined.

"They are still hurting."

"Why do you think that?"

"You can't go through all of this and not be."

"This is the psychologist in you coming out."

"It never seemed to bother you before."

"I just never said anything."

That hurt her.

"Was that much of our marriage hidden from me? I thought we were in a pretty good place. Was I missing as much as I seem to have been?"

"You were having an affair with your job. I felt increasingly on an island."

"Why didn't you say anything?"

"There was too much to say."

"Too much?"

"Emily, you too often hear only what you want to hear."

That hurt her, too.

So lesson one in why Emily struggled to move on from her past was that she still found her ex attractive. He clearly wasn't going to take any of the responsibility for his actions, yet she found herself checking him out. Lesson two was that he was succeeding in causing her to re-think, yet again, all of the things she could have done better in their relationship. Which didn't make her feel particularly good at that moment. Most spouses who have been so unceremoniously discarded would have been spitting venom. But, for some reason, she was still holding on to something, yet she didn't know what it was.

"If I did, it certainly wasn't on purpose."

"It was what it was, Em."

"What do you think attracted us in the first place? Why do you think we got married?"

He smirked for the first time since they sat down. Not a smile, but a smirk.

"Back to the therapist again?"

"I guess. It's a hard role for me to escape sometimes. It's what I do."

He shoveled some more cholesterol into his mouth and responded while still chewing.

"You were a lot of fun back then. You loved doing things together – hiking, biking, movies, having parties. You were a rabbit in bed. You always asked my thoughts about your work. You were not unceasingly critical of me as you became later. I was never angry with you, as a result."

"I didn't know that I was critical of you."

"Again, too often we don't hear ourselves."

"Don't you think this happens in lots of marriages?"

"That's why so many marriages fail, Emily. But they don't have to. You just seemed to grow tired of me. You seemed to take me for granted."

"Is your new girlfriend a lot younger?"

"No, she's about the same age as you. Not that we need to talk about her. But she is fun to be with. And life is too short not to be fun."

As might be expected, it hurt Emily to hear all of this as well. The one man she had ever thought she had loved, and he had so little trouble writing her off.

"So that's it? I stopped being fun?"

"It was a lot of things, Emily. Don't beat yourself up trying to figure it all out. Splitting up was the right thing for us."

"I wish we could have talked about it."

"Things happened. Unforeseen things."

"How is the girl doing?"

"I have no idea. She ruined my reputation."

"You used to tell our girls that their reputation is the thing that is most important to protect."

"I learned that sometimes it is not in our control."

"Can I change the subject and talk about more practical things?"

"Sure."

"Are you planning to start paying your child support?"

"I'm not rich. I barely make enough for me to live on."

"That's not my issue. The judge said you are required to pay me."

"My bank account is empty."

"We both know that your parents have a boatload of money that will someday be yours. I also heard that you and your new girlfriend were able to go on a trip to London. That doesn't seem fair while I'm scrambling to pay basic bills, including all the girls' expenses."

He didn't say anything.

"And we have college that we have to figure out how to pay for now and maybe even weddings at some point down the road."

She knew she wouldn't call her lawyer to take any action against him because she hated confrontation. She would instead have to keep scraping by. For his part, he had finished his meal, for which she would ultimately pay the bill, and it was clear that he was getting less comfortable with the conversation and ready to move on.

"Can I ask you one more question?"

"Sure, Em."

"Twenty years later, is there anything about me that you still find appealing?"

He was wiping off his mouth and picking the remnants of his breakfast from his beard as she asked the question. He stood up slowly, reflecting on her question, dropped his napkin on the table, and walked away.

That hurt the most of all. It was the question, she recognized, to which she most wanted to hear the answer. But he was onto a new life, that didn't include her in any way, while Emily still found it so difficult to simply dismiss the man who had been her desire and sidekick for all that time. She just wished he had answered her question, even though she knew it wasn't likely going to be one she wanted to hear. She just hated being left in limbo.

They have never talked again face to face. In later years, she went to the funerals of both his parents. At his father's funeral, the current girlfriend was there – she had become his second wife by then. His third wife was with him at his mother's funeral. The second wife must have stopped being fun. Emily and he didn't speak, but she thought it appropriate to go given that his parents had once been a significant part of her life. And they were the girls' grandparents. As such, the three of them went, and she stood in a corner and watched people do funeral things. After he inherited his parents' money – he was their only child – she still never received any financial support.

When her parents got sick and later died, she looked for him at the services, wanting to see how he looked, how wife number three was faring, and if he had ever cared enough about her or her folks to make an appearance. But he never showed his face.

That's when she finally got over him.

17

Henry

He had thought about when and how Jenny would die for a long time before she got sick. Not morning, noon, and night like he thought about death now, but enough to scare him that it might be a painful, tragic, far too soon death, and he would someday be without her. All of which ended up being true. For some reason, perhaps because she was older, he had always assumed that she would die first. And she did.

For the last dozen years, the nine years she was sick plus the three years since, he had been surrounded by the aura of death. These last three years is when he began to think about dying non-stop. It was happening all around him, and he would have no impact. It was not something that a pitcher of Margaritas could solve. And that bothered him. That's why he decided to see a therapist. It was embarrassing and even a sign that he might be losing it, but he needed help.

"I didn't ask when I was here the last time. Do I need to call you Doctor Metcalf, or may I call you Emily?

"Emily is fine."

"It's such a pretty name."

"Thank you, but I had nothing to do with it."

"Of course. But it shows your parents have good taste."

"They would be happy to hear that."

"They are still with us?"

"Yes. Sadly, though, they both struggling with health issues."

"I'm sorry to hear that," he said and then paused. Sitting in the chair in Emily's office that was his peer. "Which perhaps brings me to why I am here. No sense in wasting time, right? What do you think happens to us, Emily, when we die?"

"You've got me."

"Really? You never think about it?"

"I suspect that everyone on this planet has thought about it. Including me. But it's not an easy thing to figure out an answer to. How often do you think about it?"

"Morning, noon, and night."

"Since your wife passed."

"That would be a good excuse to hide behind, but the reality is that I suspect that I have been thinking about it in some way since I was in my early twenties. I just began to think about it far more when she got sick. And now that she is gone, it's all I think about."

"That's a long time to think about one's mortality."

"Yes, it is. I was in college, and our frat was playing a prank late one night, pushing a dean's car up the steps of the administration building to park it in the main foyer. Sophomoric, stupid, and fun. Except that one of my good friends caught his foot on a wheel, fell backwards down the stairs, hit his head, and ended up with a cracked skull. It was a very serious accident. He didn't end up dying, but he was never quite the same person. I have never understood why he lived and others with similarly serious injuries don't. Or why he was the one who got his foot caught."

"This is really what you want to talk about?"

"I read the obituaries each morning like most people read the sports page."

"Well, you couldn't have picked a more abstruse topic to spend so much time thinking about."

"Good word."

"Every once in a while, I have to show off."

They were already surprisingly comfortable with each other. Almost like an old comfortable pair of slippers. Not that he owned any slippers. He always went barefoot in his house.

"Each time I meet someone now," he continued, "I begin to wonder when they are going to die, how they are going to die, and what will happen to the loved ones they leave behind."

"How old were you when you got tenure?"

"Thirty-eight. Why?"

"Bear with me. That's pretty young."

"I was here at the right time. It's a sweet gig."

"How many classes did you teach?"

"Two a semester before I got tenure. Three for the entire academic year after earning tenure. Plus, the option to take a full year sabbatical every six years."

"Did you do a lot of research?"

"I did for a while. Fewer people became interested in publishing books about some long ago forgotten writer. Including me. But the kids seemed to like my classes, so no one gave me a hard time."

"Did Jenny work?"

"She managed a lab for a cancer researcher at one of the big hospitals in town. Right up until she was sixty-five, always loving what she did."

"Do you read a lot of books?"

"Not as many as you might expect from a lifelong English professor."

"How about movies?"

"The last one I went to see was *Schindler's List.*"

"I guess it made a terrific impression," Emily chuckled. "Follow sports?"

"Too boring."

"Gardening?

"Too much work. Why are you asking me all these questions?"

"Again, stay with me. Did you think about your students dying when you were teaching?"

"A few of them."

"And all of your colleagues on campus?"

"Whether I was fond of them or not."

"Have you thought about what is going to happen to me since we met last week?"

"Quite a bit actually."

"I hope I still have a few more years left."

"You see, that's the problem. I never, of course, come up with any answers. I just visualize scenarios. How, when, if. Including how their loved ones would react, even though I typically have no idea who their loved ones are. It's like handicapping horse races. But it's mind numbing to now go through life constantly asking a question, wanting to ask a question, and never having an answer."

"I'll say. Do you have health issues?"

"Everyone who is my age does."

"You mentioned Alzheimer's before."

"Simply pontificating, which I can do sometimes. Have never been tested for it."

"Are you religious?"

"Not particularly."

"Do you believe in God?"

"Yet another question with no answer. It probably depends upon the day of the week."

"Did Jenny know about your growing fixation with death?"

"I thought it was a big secret, but she knew. She was incredible."

"And you think this all began with a frat boy prank in college, where your friend hit his head?"

"Yes."

"I don't buy that."

"What?"

"Henry, who in your life, someone who has been truly important to you, has passed away?"

He put the conversation on hold for a minute. Or two.

"Well, you now know about Jenny."

"Yes."

"My parents died at the ages you might expect them to die. Both were in their late eighties. We had a good relationship, but it was not a surprise when they died."

"Okay."

"My older brother is still living, but we aren't all that close. He lives in Colorado, and we talk by phone once or twice a year."

"But he's still alive. And that's not the question I asked."

"Sorry."

"And?"

"Are you really this good?"

"You will have to be the judge of that."

Henry paused once more before speaking.

"My older sister was nine when she fell out of a window on the third floor of our house. She died immediately. We were very close, even though I was only five at the time. I adored her, and she watched out for me in a neighborhood that wasn't all that safe. Yet one minute she was there, so special to me, and the next she wasn't. In many ways, there was a hole in my life for many years, until Jenny came and filled it."

"I'm sorry to hear that."

"It was a long time ago. Seventy-seven years."

"How did your parents handle it?"

"They didn't. They couldn't. It was never talked about."

"That's never healthy. And so you think about your own mortality as well?"

"Of course. You see, in my previous life, I was far busier and had less time to think."

"Your previous life?"

"Yes, before I got old. When I was getting an education, and then was teaching. I wrote a few books. And, of course, I had Jenny. I had less time to think. Now it's all I have. I think about death far too much now. But I can't help it. Mine, yours, the cop who gave me a ticket the other day, my butcher, and so on."

"I'm guessing that the natural response to all of this would be to ask you if you have a hobby."

"That's really what you want to ask me?"

"No, not so much. But I'm at a loss for words right now, which is unusual for me. I've never had a conversation like this before."

"There's that humility again. I appreciate you not trying to come up with some phony explanation."

"I'm not particularly good at phony. Let me ask you one more question. A very direct question actually."

"Okay."

"Have you ever thought, Henry, about taking your own life?"

"You don't beat around the bush, do you?"

"It's part of my job."

"It's not like that, Emily. I'm never going to hasten my own departure from this world. I am primarily fixated on other people's demises, and I don't want to go nuts thinking about that."

"Huh."

"What do I do, Emily?"

She had been taking notes on her yellow pad as she always did. But now she put her pen down and was silent for too long a time. This, no doubt, wasn't what he was hoping for, but the teaching legend was more complicated than she might have guessed. Yet still so likeable.

"How about we go to Starbuck's and get a cup of coffee?"

For Henry, it was nice to again interact with someone so much younger than he was. Thirty-eight years to be exact. He was born in 1937, and she, he calculated, around 1975. Emily was attractive physically and was obviously bright. When he was a teenager, a long time ago, he and his nerdy friends called that a double treat. He had seen on television recently that a double treat is now what they call a particular brand of dog bone. He watched way too much television these days. Apparently, it provided him company, including now even old reruns of *The Jerry Springer Show* and *Match Game* instead of the news. Man was he crumbling. If he hadn't been so focused on death, he could have convinced himself to ask her to dinner. Just for something different to do. After all, her personal life must have been a train wreck, too.

18

You Can't Save The World By Yourself

The urge was certainly there. Particularly after sitting inches apart on her couch late at night watching some soppy movie, where two ridiculously attractive actors toyed with each other for an hour and a half before finally hopping into bed together. For their part, Emily and Monk went to bed separately each night, just the two of them in her tiny house, and woke up alone. Emily knew that if she pointed to the other side of her bed, he would be as thrilled to jump in as she would be to have him. But she had, in her mind, set out a sort of unwritten syllabus for each of them, and final exams had yet to be taken. Her plan wasn't really a plan. It seemed more that she was hoping to still hang on to some of her past, even though she knew it didn't exist anymore. Which made her afraid of her future.

"I started reading your daughter's physics book last night."

"For entertainment, Monk?"

"I wanted to see if I could get as far as you did."

"And?"

"Didn't make it to the end of the second paragraph."

"Hah. So what does that mean?"

"It means you're a nut."

"And it's taken you this long to figure out?"

"I'm a little slow."

"You may be a bunch of things, Monk, but that's not one of them."

She had been up early, gone rowing, and now was sitting at the kitchen table, having a cup of coffee and reading the Saturday online version of the *Philadelphia Inquirer*.

"So can I ask you something, Monk?"

"You know you can."

Monk didn't shave on weekends, which she found made him look even sexier. He was toasting oatmeal bread for each of them and grinding up an avocado to spread on top. She didn't cook anymore.

"On my way to work each morning, I stop by the Starbuck's to get a coffee."

"You and the rest of New Jersey."

"There is a girl working there who looks like hell. She needs help."

"You can't save the world by yourself, Em."

"I'm pretty sure it's her."

"Who?"

"The girl who was having the event with my ex-husband."

He stopped what he was doing, knowing this was sacred ground.

"And you wanted to talk to her," he confirmed before she even offered her perspective.

"More than that."

"You want to be her therapist?"

"Yes."

"Not a good idea, Emily."

"I know."

"It's wrong in so many, many ways."

"I know. So why can't I get the idea out of my mind?"

"Because you are a natural born caretaker. I know that, and you know that. But, even more, you probably want to learn all the things about her and your ex that you don't know."

She didn't respond.

"Am I right?" he continued.

He wasn't wrong.

"Monk, I can tell she needs help. She's completely emotionless and now even anorexic."

"You don't even know her. She has parents. That's their job. This is a lawsuit and a loss of your license both waiting to happen. Neither of which you would survive. Most importantly, it's probably not a good idea for the girl."

"What would you do if you were me?"

"Change coffee shops. Switch to tea. Try chewing gum. Sometimes you just need to let someone else take on the responsibility. This one is not yours. It can't be, and you need to understand that. And I'm not kidding around. This would be a monumental mistake."

She quietly nodded in agreement.

"So, on another note," he added, "any interest in going for a hike this afternoon? I'm heading to the market this morning. Then the hike. And then I thought I'd cook a nice dinner – I was thinking French onion soup, tamarind glazed chicken, and baby Brussels sprouts."

"*Brussels* sprouts?"

"That's the proper name. They are named after the Belgian capital."

"Okay, smart man, you bribed me. You are also doing a good job of getting me to change the subject."

"I'm serious about changing coffee shops, Emily. You need to get this idea out of your head."

They went and had a wonderful hike up to a beautiful overlook in a town about a half hour north of their home, on an overcast but warm October afternoon, where the rain held off just long enough for them to finish their ramble. Her second workout of the day, alternately talking, laughing, puffing, and trying to beat the rain. Then they came home and enjoyed Monk's gastronomic feast, while Emily had a glass of delectable wine that he had picked out for her, and a local brand of non-alcoholic lemon seltzer for himself. He had pulled together a homemade pie made of fresh raspberries and blackberries for dessert which was equally out of this world. He should have his own restaurant. They ate and talked for a long, long time about her daughters, his parents, and which friends from their pasts they would most like to see again. Eventually playing that game – she forgot the name – where you name three people and decide who to sleep with, who to marry, and who to throw off of a cliff. Sophomoric and dumb, but nobody else was around to pass judgement. Then they hugged a long hug, something new to their routine. But it had been such an incredible day that it seemed fitting, and even though she could feel his interest in doing more when they hugged, they went their separate ways to bed. And then Emily stayed awake for several hours, first thinking about him, then her ex-husband, and then considering the girl. She decided somewhere in the middle of the night to continue going to Starbuck's.

19

A Little Kentucky Bourbon

One of the challenges of being a therapist is that those times when you actually do make a recommendation, the advice that you give doesn't always work out the way you hope. Like when you recommend to the biggest student on campus that he branch out and experience more of what the university has to offer. You're thinking joining a club, attending a couple of talks by famous people, or getting involved in community service. Perhaps visiting with a professor just to chat about something that interests you or trying out for one of the many a cappella groups on campus. Occasions where a person can expand his college experience and meet other people. When he thinks he's following your advice but has a completely different picture of what the university has to offer, it doesn't feel all that good to be the therapist. Usually, you don't know that you've screwed up until after the damage begins.

She had thought she would try to slowly help Seth discover what he really might want to do with his life, but he was the classic one step forward, two steps backward client. With most of his steps backward relating to Jelly. Which wasn't a great trend.

"Doctor Metcalffffff!"

"Seth. You made it for your appointment."

"Yes Maaammmm. And right on time!! With my latest homework assignment!"

"And you're drunk. In the middle of the day."

"Coach called off practice today. Something about a family emergency. Or maybe he had an interview for a new job. Who knows? Anyhow, we decided to have a liquid lunch. Isn't that what I am supposed to be doing in college? Trying new things?"

"I don't believe that getting drunk was part of the package. So is this your new thing?"

"I never drank in my life until about a week ago. My family doesn't drink. I guess I'm catching up. Turns out that I can drink a lot."

As opposed to sitting down in it, he basically fell into one of the tired armchairs, which never had looked so small. Almost, she imagined, like he was sitting on a milking stool back on the farm in Iowa. One of his shirttails was hanging out aimlessly, and his eyes were squinting red. This was, undoubtedly, a Seth that the school had not yet witnessed.

"I'll bet you can. Were you drinking alone?"

"Naaahhh. With some of my teammates. I'm finally getting to know them. They're not bad people. You guys told me this is what I should do."

"You guys?"

"You and Jelly."

"I'm your therapist. She's trying to be your friend."

"You're both doing a terrific job!"

"Are you doing drugs, too?"

"What?! Nope, never. Not on your life."

Besides the untucked shirt, the squinty blood red eyes, and the stumbling into the chair, he had an enormous shit-eating grin. It was called that for a reason.

"So why did you suddenly decide to start drinking? You didn't at home. You didn't your first several weeks here."

"Who knows? Maybe it helps me make friends. Maybe it helps me forget all my worries."

"I thought that's what I was for."

"TBD. Remember, you told me you weren't sure you were any good at your job. But I'll tell you what. If you can get my world right, or get me another date with Jelly, I'll quit drinking. Maybe."

"Maybe?"

"I really do still like Jelly."

"Okay."

"So what are we going to talk about today?"

"I have a feeling that whatever we talk about, you won't remember. Maybe you'd be better off going back to your dorm room and taking a nap."

"Oooh, that does sound good. I love taking naps. Did you know I'm having breakfast with Jelly every morning?"

"Tell me about that."

"Just weekdays. Not weekends."

He wasn't going to remember any of this babble.

"Alright."

"She asked me, so I, of course, said yes. Maybe she'll find me more appealing first thing in the morning."

"Maybe she's trying to be sure you don't do damage to yourself. Like you seem to be doing right now."

"Ahhhh Doc. A little Kentucky Bourbon never hurt anybody."

"You know that's not true. Many people can't handle it. Including most who have it for lunch."

"I'm 320 pounds. I can handle a lot of booze."

"You never drank before. It's foreign to your body. And that shows."

"You don't think I'm a good drunk?"

"No. I think you are out of control, which is never a healthy thing. Why don't you go sleep this off?"

"If you say soooo."

"Will you text me when you get to your dorm room?"

"Okaaayy."

"Straight home, right?"

"Where else would I go?"

"That's what worries me."

20

Another Hiccup

While craving is the word that is so often used to describe a substance dependence, it is more than that. It's a lust that takes over your mind and your decision making in a way that nothing else does. As therapists know, because they see so much of it both in their clients and amongst themselves, it causes more harm than anyone ever suspects.

Monk was no doubt trying. Emily and he were developing a comfortable rhythm. She gave him a cozy home, albeit one where she never turned up the thermostat, and he cleaned, did laundry, shopped, and cooked for her most nights without ever being asked. He didn't have anything else to do, and he was really trying to get his head on straight. He used the time spent doing chores to think. It was clear she liked him. And he liked her. Neither of them, though, tried to push their relationship any farther for obvious reasons, though he certainly thought about it more often than he didn't. It was hard not to when they were living in such close quarters.

Sometimes they went out together for dinner, which was her version of cooking. He didn't seem to feel the need to drink when it was just the two of them, and he told her as much. He didn't feel the need to impress her. He could see a future for them together, a gratifying future, and he could see telling her that once he began working again and had demonstrated to each of them that he could remain sober.

They decided to go together to what once upon a time was called the Homecoming football game, but now was called Family Weekend. College administrators liked to busy themselves changing the names of things. But why not go? They were both alums, and it would be more amusing now that they could go together. Despite all the pageantry and the chance to reconnect with old classmates, he hadn't been to one since he graduated. Probably for reasons that he was afraid to address. She apparently had been a bunch of times and said she always enjoyed seeing random folks from the old days there. And she said she wanted to see Seth play. Jelly, who he had only heard about up to this point, had set the expectations for how good Seth was. And, as often was the case, Emily had an ulterior purpose that was somehow connected to her clients. In this instance, he knew she wanted to make sure that number seventy-seven wasn't intoxicated.

The stadium parking lot that afternoon was festive. They ran into people she knew from college. They saw clients of theirs. Or, at least, clients of hers and former clients of his. It was easy to pick out Seth's family, who had obviously flown in for the weekend. They, too, were bigger than anyone else there and seemed to consume most of the hot dogs at the concession stand. His father wore a classic cowboy hat and a big belt buckle between his expanded belly and his tight jeans. Emily pointed out Jelly, who was seemingly entertaining Seth's entire family. It's possible that they did not yet know that she was now the former girlfriend, but whether they did or did not now know, she had them howling. Making it easy to visualize, Emily told Monk, what Jelly had been like on their farm that summer. There were numerous cars with the tailgates down, grills cooking meat, and coolers chilling beer. As the afternoon went on, Monk seemed to be visiting all of them. He reacquainted himself with a few people from a long time ago, and he made many new friends with people he had never before met.

He was again feeling the feeling, surprised by how much he welcomed it. It had been a while. Becoming gregarious, charming, and so very confident when he had that extra boost. Otherwise, he'd have little to say that anyone would find interesting. By late in the afternoon, when the game was firmly in control for the home team, he was standing up on the hood of a car and leading the parking lot in the school's fight song. And kissing women who had never before laid eyes on him, though not in the passionate way he had kissed Emily. It was all in good fun. Always with a drink in his hand. Always looking for a refill. Everybody's best friend for the afternoon. The one they would all be talking about when they climbed into their SUV's and drove home. More than they talked about the game. Somewhere during the afternoon, he lost Emily. When he last saw her, she was having real conversations with friends and even with a few clients who were not uncomfortable being seen with their therapist in public. His conversations, on the other hand, were insubstantial and amusing.

He remembered once again how much loved this feeling. He did lust for it.

Monk never re-connected with Emily. After the game ended and the post-game celebration eventually waned, and people either went to dinner with their kids or left for home, he couldn't find Emily's car. He wasn't sure he could remember where they had parked. She could have been long gone (likely) or sitting in her car waiting for him (unlikely). She would know that he was drunk. His presence was hard to miss, as he had been all over the parking lot. And she wouldn't be pleased. This is what she was afraid of, why they slept in separate bedrooms, and why she was hesitant to commit. The fear that he couldn't stop screwing up, like he just had again. In his present state, he really wasn't ready to face her. In his present state, he wouldn't be able to come up with any cogent answers to her questions. And he wasn't sure, at this point, that he even wanted to try.

After stumbling around the shadows of the campus for a bit, presenting to anyone who might have noticed what was an embarrassing picture of a drunk, alone, once well-regarded psychologist, who was now almost forty and had little to show for his life, Monk walked into an empty old dorm on the edge of campus that was scheduled to begin renovation in a few months. It wasn't hard to get into the building as he knew where the old delivery entrance was, and he remembered from days gone by that these entrances were rarely locked. He entered the old dorm and kicked in the locked door to one of the first floor rooms, splintering the wooden frame, and creating an enormous bang that echoed down the empty hallway. One where there was no one to hear. This would do just fine for the evening. He had the whole building to himself. No one would know or care that he was here.

Despite recognizing that he'd behaved badly, he still couldn't help but feel spectacular. He'd been the big man on campus. King of the world. Master of his own destiny. Once he got going, he hadn't wanted to miss any part of such a great day, not having realized how ready he would be for such a blowout. Emily and he had been doing their version of being together for more than a month now. She was energetic and smart and sexy. She also had a nurturing side, where, in a weird way, she watched out for him. He didn't want to screw things up, so he had been on his best behavior until now. Coming back to the university, he had just uncorked, putting on yet another performance for people he didn't know. He would feel a huge sense of guilt tomorrow, but for the moment he would enjoy what he was feeling. Again, he felt the lust.

Monk flopped onto the naked mattress of a cheap institutional bed, folded his hands behind his head, and stared at the dorm room ceiling. How many times had he been in this position before in a similar dorm building on this campus? Head spinning, alone with his unpredictable thoughts, drifting off into a deep, peaceful sleep. He had come to the university just after turning seventeen, a rarity in the storied world of the school, and, younger than everyone else in his class. The nickname, Monk, was given to him his first week at school, and he had been called nothing else since. He was smart, but that was hardly different than everyone else here. The extra year that his classmates had on him, or sometimes two for those who had done post-grad to bulk up for athletics or taken a gap year to save the world, seemed like a lifetime. The professors scared him, the girls petrified him, and the boys made him feel inferior. He quietly went to classes, ably did his studying, and found his home at the corner table of the school pub where he gained confidence inside too many bottles of beer and would hold court with clever witticisms after enough booze had kicked in.

At this point, he once again convinced himself that he just had to get some discipline back in his life. But that would have to wait. He would first have to deal with Emily.

Nonetheless, it had been a pretty great day.

21

He's Too Small For This

It's hard to comprehend why violence has to be a part of our world. It occurs in so many places in so many ways. But in an idyllic college setting? Between sunny afternoons sitting on a quad bench, old Friday night movies, Madame Bovary classes, and football game tailgates? Where young people are supposed to be free to explore and figure out who they are and who they want to be. Where the university replaces parental oversight with electronic passkeys to buildings, visible 911 emergency phones, video cameras on dorm entrances and on streetlights, a constant security force presence, and a state-of-the-art emergency text messaging system. Why does violence still exist here?

Sadly, violence can encroach even into utopia. No matter how much utopia costs parents. Some students simply have regrettable violent tendencies. For others it may be a leftover resentment, too often towards their overreaching parents, and that resentment sprouts into anger or more when, for the first time in their lives, they feel the freedom to push back. Often, it's the vicious nature of the more ferocious sports, now being played on a bigger, more competitive canvas with more uncompromising coaches, that transfers over to their daily lives. Sometimes it's a deeply embedded bigotry, usually learned from others, that shows its ugly face when there is no longer anyone to hold it back. Almost always there is alcohol involved.

Being a perpetual caretaker like Emily, the fear of such violence never is far from what she is thinking about, particularly on weekends when bad things are most likely to happen on university campuses. College kids never consider that therapists work during the week and may want their weekend time off for themselves and their families. College kids never consider a lot of things. But good therapists always have certain clients in the back of their minds when the weekend rolls around. The ones who might be trying to deal with more anxiety, stress, or anger than they are prepared to handle. The worry never really goes away for the therapists who still care about what they do. Which is not all of them but is enough of them. And weekends, with their lack of structure for students, generally provide the spark. Again, because that is also when the kids drink.

Emily got a call from the emergency room at a hospital in Trenton. It was the Saturday evening of that same, newly named Family Weekend. It was past midnight, and she had gone for very late drinks and dessert with a few old friends she had run into at a post-game reception at the campus alumni house. She and Monk had gone to the game together, the football team won for the third time in a row, and he fell back into his drinking habits. It was that simple. But it did not completely surprise her. He had been on his best behavior for a while now, though too quickly retreated to a familiar place when he suddenly felt that he was on stage with people he, for some reason, sensed were looking for him to ignite the gathering. Why he always felt the obligation to be the show, she didn't know.

He had told her, more than once, about his insecurity when he perceived he had an audience of people with whom he was unacquainted. Where he didn't know how to act. Where he felt inferior. Even when there was no reason for him to be front and center, and certainly no reason to feel inferior. He could have simply had a couple of hot dogs at the football game, and they could have been on their merry way. When he was with her, he didn't have to show off. They were comfortable together. He was making strides. Or maybe that's what she wanted to believe. When he was back on campus with a group he hardly knew, it was a different story. And given that he was drunk, she had been in no rush to head home to confront him, and had, consequently, stayed on campus far longer than she had planned. But as soon as she hung up her phone, she quickly said her good-byes to hurry over to the hospital emergency room, where they knew her well enough.

She had been there with too many other clients in her twenty years at the university.

For most parents, rape is something that happens to somebody else's child. Until it happens to yours. And it is always Emily's initial thought when she gets a call on a weekend night. One out of six girls on college campuses are sexually harassed in some way during their time on campus. The truth is that the victim is almost always a girl, and the perpetrator is most often a male athlete from one of the more violent sports. It's not that most athletes from these sports are rapists, rather most rapists on campus play one of those sports. Despite the campus enthusiasm for athletics, and the alumni fixation with the memories of their teams so many years later, college campuses would be much safer without football, ice hockey, and lacrosse. The physicality that allows horny young men to dominate their competitors in these sports can translate to their view of women. They sense victory in a surprisingly similar way. And, it cannot be mentioned enough, the liquor just makes it all easier and all less clear.

A few years from now, Emily would learn about an enduring email chain that is shared by a group of the former athletes. Middle aged men who would have been undergraduates at the university around when she had been. Who still tended to use older technology to communicate. The chain apparently continues to grow weed-like with each passing year, adding men from other graduating classes and other sports, and including their stories. The purpose, when it was started by a player from two decades ago, was benign. Reconnect with old friends. Share a happy birthday wish and maybe a funny memory or two. A friend had showed her some of the postings. What was saddening was how too many of these men's emails would easily sink from their original intent to stories about wild, alcohol enabled antics and who they had unceremoniously bedded during their time at the university. All were from men now in their forties and fifties, and they needed to grow up. The Wilt Chamberlain-esque dual hockey and lacrosse athlete who refused to marry until he had slept with a hundred women. A list he maintained to this day to confirm his resolve, while serving as a family court judge and married father of three. He provided the initials of his top ten list to the others on the chain in a show of bravado. She thought she recognized some of them. And the four football players who picked up four women at a bar the night before an away game, had sex with them, eight naked bodies going at it in the same cramped room of a motel the team was staying in. Evidently, they callously tossed the girls out in the middle of the night in order to rest up for the next afternoon's game. All still boasting on the email chain about what they collectively still maintained was one of the greatest nights of their lives. How about their wedding night? Or the birth of a child? One now a district attorney, one an investment banker, one a surgeon, one a high school teacher. All of whom are now available to provide their grown-up services. Another two knuckleheads' goal was to inhale a case of beer while driving the seventy miles back from a party at a women's college in the middle of a blizzard. An example for their children? This is what they learned in college and made them still proud to share twenty-something years later? There were messages about a guy purposely putting his head through a wall at a party, the length of someone's thing, the record for mooning pedestrians in a day, and how many of them had slept with the same woman in college. They should have all been embarrassed. But they weren't.

She was not new to these visits to the ER, and she knew what to expect. Or so she thought. An older nurse, more than filling out her pink scrubs, escorted Emily into a treatment room filled with heart monitors, IV's, respirators, and other equipment, all seemingly on wheels, that she had no idea of their function. A room with too many clinical people coming and going for her to feel good about entering. She was not on call that night for emergencies, meaning someone had specifically asked for her. During the entire ride over in her car, her mind rotated through her roster of female clients, continually coming back to Jelly because of how appealing she was and the way she so freely dressed. What some boy might wrongly interpret as an invitation. She also, no surprise, thought about Seth.

When Emily entered the room, she was stunned. Even though she had been doing this long enough so as not to be stunned by events anymore. But she was. Hanging on a hook in the back corner of the room, covered with blood, was a familiar well-worn hooded university sweatshirt and a windbreaker, with the yellow block letters SECURITY stenciled across the back. In the middle of the room lay Mana, one leg raised in a splint, one eye swollen completely shut, the other swollen but not closed. He had a long, nasty semi-circle gash on the cheek below the closed eye, where the doctor was in the process of sewing stitches to pull the skin together. One hand had an ice pack on it. Emily looked at Mana, and he looked back as well as his single open eye allowed him. The one eye that could still see was so incredibly scared. She wanted to cry right there.

With her previous clients, you weren't always immediately sure what had happened. They were often drunk or high or both from having been at some party, and they were often not speaking all that coherently as a result. Their stories could be hard to follow. Not that being drunk is ever an excuse for what would have happened. It just can make the story more than a little cloudy at the outset. But with Mana, she readily grasped that he was completely sober and hadn't done anything wrong. Which were among the many things that made Mana special.

A campus security officer was already at the hospital. He took Emily aside and explained to her that college security had received a call from three girls asking to be walked home from a campus party. A party, they both knew, where the football team's victory was being celebrated. His sense was that when Mana walked up to fetch the girls, some of the boys had other ideas. They didn't want young, attractive, potential hook ups being escorted away. In their alcohol driven stupor, it got out of hand, and they beat the messenger. The cop said that Mana didn't have anyone else to call, so he asked that Emily be called.

Mana wasn't crying. But he wasn't the stoic young man she had seen in her office. Undoubtedly, he was confused, and, as has been said, scared. He was here to get an education and to earn money to send home. It was that straightforward. This was not part of the plan. He was so small to begin with, and now they had broken her little Mana. What was wrong with these people? They had so much more than he did. He hadn't done anything to hurt them. They didn't even know him. Why couldn't they just leave him alone?

They didn't talk at first. She simply stood by the bed and held his one good hand for the second time since they had met, which he didn't resist, while the doctor finished stitching. Besides issuing requests for bandages, x-rays, shots, and the like to the nurses, the doctor didn't say anything while she was going about her work. Given that it was a Saturday night, she was probably busy. Hopefully not too busy, so she could give Mana the attention he needed. Because he didn't look all that good.

The problem with assaults on college campuses, rape or other, is that no one tends to believe the victim. She, because it usually was a young woman, was drunk. She was asking for it. It was consensual. She didn't put up a fight. Many of the athletes, on the other hand, were big, strong young men and capable of doing substantial damage, particularly when they were intoxicated and didn't realize the extent of what they were doing. Mana, as has been said before, probably weighed a hundred and twenty pounds with all his clothes on. Any football player had more than fifty teammates. He didn't even have a roommate. Their families would have lawyers. He didn't even have a family here. They were taught by their coaches to have each other's back. Nobody had his back. All he had was his therapist.

Mana had been alone on an island his whole time here. He now wouldn't be able to do his jobs for quite some time, which would add to his existing angst. The predators would surely make life hard for him, as they circled the wagons to support their team's perpetrators, finding ways to continue to scare him at every turn. It would be incredibly hard for Mana to concentrate on a shrinking global ice mass lecture in a geology class lecture when the boy in the next seat was whispering what would happen if Mana were to squeal on the boy's teammates. If this is what coaches meant when they preached about having each other's back, they were dead wrong. Another reason to consider banning the sport.

Though she had always played and loved sports throughout her life, Emily thought football brought out more bad than good. Think about how much the coaches are paid at the big schools? The big *non-profit* schools? Where they virtually always are the highest paid public employees in any state by a longshot. Where their damaged players are sent to see people like her. Think about their players who leave school without any skills beyond whatever they do on the football field. Think about the number of athletes accused of sexual assault. The rich coaches are supposed to be their teachers and mentors. Well, it isn't working, is it.

22

The Detectives Came And Somebody Left

Emily spent Saturday night in the hospital with Mana, mostly just being available and holding his hand when the doctors weren't poking, prodding, and doing more stitching on him. She again spent the whole day Sunday there, after they had moved him to a room on one of the general floors, chatting with the nurses and again just being around as he mostly slept. She didn't call or text Monk because, after his feats at the game, she felt he should be reaching out to her. And she was a little miffed that he hadn't. On Monday morning, they did surgery to insert a rod into the tibia of Mana's left leg which had been fractured in two places. When she arrived home that Monday afternoon, having not had a shower or changed her clothes in two days, Monk wasn't there, as she had anticipated he would be. His car wasn't in the driveway, nor was he on the couch still sleeping off a hangover. His closet and dresser had been emptied of all the clothes he had brought with him, which Emily believed was the total sum of everything else he owned. It was quickly evident that he had packed up for a move that was meant to be permanent, only leaving her a cryptic note on the kitchen table that read *'I'm Sorry'* and nothing else. She cried when she read it, all the genuine feelings for Monk that had built up inside of her in this last month quickly fleeing. As if he had known all along that this wasn't to be his ultimate home but hadn't ever told her.

On Tuesday afternoon, she took Mana to the university infirmary, as that's where students go when they are sick or need to recover from being beaten. This wasn't a situation anyone in her world had thought about ever happening. The kid from a little mountainside village in Nepal being assailed by a bunch of drunk football frat boys. Mana had never been to a football game in his life. Nor had he ever been to a frat party.

She helped get Mana set up in the infirmary bed, with his laptop, ear buds, and three pillows that would keep his broken leg raised as the surgeon had mandated, the whole time doing her best to stifle the tears that indicated how emotionally adrift she would soon be. No matter how many times she wiped them away, they just kept coming. Hopefully Mana, who was still sufficiently doped up following his operation, thought she was tearing up for him. She left him to rest and then escaped to a stall in a bathroom in the hallway to have a real cry. One like she hadn't even had when coming to grips with her ex-husband's depravity. She had so looked forward to coming home again each night. To see Monk, to have dinner together, to talk, and to laugh. Even to touch when washing the dishes together. Then they went to the football game, they got separated, he got drunk, and he left her. There were no doubt missing pieces to the story, but none that she could think of that had a particularly positive ending for her. Dumped once again, unceremoniously and painfully. She really liked Monk. There was little doubt of that.

Mana really had been beaten badly. It was hard to understand how college boys would even conjure up something like this. It wasn't life threatening, but recovery would not be fun. Their hope to have sex with unaware college girls was really that potent? It must be if men are still emailing about it more than two decades later. Not all that long after she helped Mana get settled and after she had her cry in the bathroom stall, the campus police came to the infirmary. She had been through this sad process before when her clients had been raped. It's something so distressing that you never want to experience it once, let alone a second or third time. Or beyond, as she had in her years at the university. The detectives needed to learn the details and then figure out who the attackers were. Nobody ever raised a hand and claimed guilt. No matter how guilty they were. Instead, they lied their asses off, and then they got expensive attorneys, when it became necessary, who lied their asses off for them. She superficially knew the two detectives who arrived, having met them during several previous rape investigations, and she had never been impressed. It was not a fun process, and the end result was never satisfying. Mana was likely not prepared for this, nor was she, even with twenty years of doing what she did.

"Do you want to tell us what happened?" one of the detectives asked of Mana.

Her client hadn't moved an inch from where they had first settled him in the infirmary bed. Surrounded by institutional white sheets, blankets, and pillows. The cast on his leg was almost as big as the rest of his body. Wearing a gray t-shirt she had brought him with the logo from her ex's old school, yet another item he had decided to leave behind, and overly baggy pajama bottoms from the hospital, as they would fit over the huge cast.

"I don't know what happened."

Mana's voice was different, muffled by the swelling of now his entire face, and maybe the pain drugs as well. It hurt her to watch the effort he was putting forth simply to answer their questions. At this point, he needed sleep and nothing else. Except maybe her hand to hold, which he was currently doing. But the detectives were going to plow ahead.

"What do you mean?"

One detective was taking the lead, and the other taking notes.

"The people there knew I was coming," Mana replied.

As the two officers stood next to his bed, he started to shake uncontrollably, reliving a trauma that he didn't want to relive. Emily feared that the shaking, as vigorous as it was, would tear some of his recent sutures, and so she found another quilt to spread over him. The experience was terrifying to him, both for what had happened and what he feared was going to happen. He wasn't dumb.

"They threw a blanket or something over my head, and then they tackled me before I even got to the front door. They dragged me around to the back of the house, where no one else could see, and then they started pushing and hitting me while my head was still covered. Some big person was kicking my legs. I couldn't see anything. My eyes were swelling up, and I purposely kept them closed. I fell to the ground and was pretending to be dead, as I thought that it might cause them to stop. Which I don't think it did. One of them cursed and said that my leg had snapped like a twig and was now pointing the wrong way, and they should leave. A few of them were laughing when they threw me in the bushes and left me. I never saw one of them. But it was at least five boys, maybe more."

"You speak English very well."

Emily just glared at the detective.

"How do you know it was at least five boys?" he continued without registering her look.

"I could feel their fists and bodies. For some reason, I was focused on trying to count the number of them. I don't know why. That's the way my mind works. I've always been kind of a math person."

It's hard to describe how he was really struggling to speak. His cadence was slow and deliberate. Far slower than you are reading this story. His voice so foreign. As if a dead man was talking.

"Could you see anything at all?"

"No."

"Their shoes? Their legs? The color of their skin?"

"No."

"Nothing more you can add, Mana?"

"Two of their first punches were to my eyes. You can tell that I can barely see now." He paused to catch his breath, which took several moments. "And the blanket was wrapped around my head and pulled tight around my neck. I couldn't even see down towards the ground. It was choking me so that I had some trouble breathing, which I don't think they realized."

"Do you think you would recognize any of their voices?"

"I don't really know. There was so much laughing. Which freaked me out. There wasn't anything funny about what was happening."

"How long did this attack last?"

Mana was clearly anxious having detectives there asking him questions. Obviously, he had never been through this before. He had to think about this question, still shaking despite the extra quilt.

"I don't know. Maybe five minutes. It seemed like a lot longer though," he mumbled. "I didn't have any idea what was going on. I didn't know why they were attacking me. I only know about three students on the whole campus."

"What did you do after they threw you in the bushes?"

"I lay curled up there for a few minutes. I didn't know if they were finished or not. Still pretending that I was dead. When I figured they were done and gone, I reached around on the ground to find the phone that security gives me for my job – it had fallen out of my hand when they were beating me -- and called the office after I found it. Finding the phone took several minutes as I couldn't see well, as I said, and I was hurting badly. Security came first, and then they called an ambulance."

"Were you conscious the whole time?"

"I'm not sure. They hurt me a great deal."

"I can see that. How are you feeling now, Mana?"

"Not very well."

"We're sorry to hear that, and hopefully you will have a quick recovery."

"Can I try to sleep now? I'm exhausted."

"Of course, you can."

"What happens from here?" Emily interrupted.

"You know the drill, Doc. We start with the people who live in the frat house where the party was, try to figure out everyone who was at the party, and then we talk to them all."

"And?"

"And I think this will be tough. Football players don't have a history of ratting on each other. And the moment they do, the families hire pricey attorneys. I know you have seen this before."

"Can I ask a question, sir?" Mana mumbled.

"Of course, Mana."

"Why did they do this? I wasn't bothering anyone."

The note-taking detective answered matter-of-factly.

"They likely didn't want the girls you were escorting home to leave."

"What?"

"They were hoping to have sex with them."

Mana had a look like this was the last answer he would have ever expected to hear.

"One more question, Mana." Emily had something to which she needed to hear the answer. Then he could go to sleep. "Did it feel like any of the boys who were punching you had particularly big hands? I mean like enormous hands like you have never witnessed before?"

The officers left, and that would be the beginning of a disappointing few weeks where they essentially accomplished nothing. Emily was, of course, frustrated but not surprised. She didn't think that her little client from Nepal expected anything, as nothing in his life to date had been particularly easy. So why should it start now.

During the first few days in the infirmary after the surgery, Mana mostly slept. His leg hurt from the surgery, while the rest of his body hurt from the attack. They gave him painkillers to help. Though his mind was both drained and afraid.

Jelly had somehow heard of the attack on Mana and came to visit him in the infirmary. How Jelly heard of the attack, Emily never knew. Incredibly, Jelly volunteered to help with Mana's care. This was not something many college freshmen would ever consider on their own. They are, most often, too busy thinking about themselves. Maybe even thinking about nabbing an invitation to the next jock frat party, an invitation which for attractive freshman girls like Jelly was easy, and for freshman boys impossible. Think about it.

Emily didn't need help falling asleep anymore. She now would mostly just cry herself to sleep. Because of all the baggage involved with Monk, she had known that any relationship with him would be dicey. That's why she kept it nonsexual. Be prepared for a bad ending, she had told herself. She simply didn't want to listen. The fact that it took merely a month for him to flee only added to her misery. Had she become that easy to dispose of? She thought about calling him but recognized that given he had left so suddenly and without saying goodbye, his feelings weren't going to change.

So the focus, for the moment, became Mana. That would have to keep her sane for now. She didn't really have a choice.

23

Her Name Is Elizabeth

You know what it feels like when someone sneaks up and surprises you from behind? Someone you are never expecting to see? Hopefully in a good way, but not necessarily. Emily didn't spend much time in places where people could sneak up and surprise her. In her tiny little office, where she spent most of her time, you might be able to fit a basketball between her desk chair, when she was sitting in it, and the wall behind her. That's why she was so taken aback when the girl approached her on the same bench on the campus lawn where Emily had met Jelly and Seth. It was a spectacularly sunny and surprisingly warm fall day to enjoy before the familiar New England cold settled in for the long haul, and Emily was having a super-sized café latte while thinking about Mana and Monk, but not necessarily in that order. This, no surprise, occupied much of her bandwidth now. The other thing on her never short worry list was to wonder if Seth, maybe an intoxicated Seth, newly violent from his college football involvement, had been part of the attack that no one professed to know anything about. Something the administration didn't seem to have any appetite to pursue -- they sent Mana a food gift basket and a get well card. College administrations were amazing nimble at avoiding negative attention. It seemed a prerequisite to having a senior title. Sort of like being in Congress.

"I know who you are."

A feeling of sorrow overwhelmed Emily, and it took her a moment to respond. It certainly was not how she expected to start her day, but that was fine by her. It was no secret that she had been hoping for some kind of encounter. The girl didn't look any healthier than the previous times Emily had seen her working the coffee counter. Pale, frighteningly thin, and deep circles beneath heart-wrenchingly limp eyes.

"Elizabeth, right?" Emily finally answered.

"Yes."

"How are you doing?"

The girl hesitated before finally sitting, like the bench might somehow possess a sinister curse that would do even further harm to her. She looked so sad. And she looked so panicked. Not unlike Mana when Emily first saw him in the hospital. The girl was clearly still in so much pain all this time later. Far from the vibrant young woman with a whole life ahead that she should be.

"Is that the question you really want me to answer!" the girl challenged with a surprising whiff of anger in her voice. As if she had been waiting a long time for this conversation. Which she may well have been.

Emily thought for a moment. This was a conversation she so wanted to have, despite Monk's counsel, but she didn't want to say something that might cause the girl to disappear for good. As her ex-husband had. As Monk now had. She didn't seem to be great at holding on to people lately.

"Yes, I think so. I'm guessing that you have been through more than a high school girl should have to go through. You are the same age as my daughters, and I can't imagine their experiencing what you have been through."

"How do you know that I didn't instigate it? That I didn't want it!"

The girl continued to stare at Emily, while Emily, in turn, saw the girl's unkempt hair, lack of any sort of make-up, and simple wrinkled clothes festooned with coffee stains as the sign of a girl who was giving up. But Emily hoped to God she hadn't given up.

"I don't. But I'm guessing that you didn't. My ex-husband, I have learned, is good at being deceitful."

"You can say what you want about him, but I'm the one to blame. I did a really bad thing!"

"It's takes more than one person, Elizabeth. And he was the adult and the teacher."

The girl's head dropped down, and it took Emily a moment to realize that she had begun to cry.

"I'm sorry. So sorry. For ruining your marriage and ruining your family."

Emily instinctively reached over and hugged her. Children are so precious, and, as she knew too well, often too fragile. It can be the most beautiful of days, like this day was. A sky clear and blue and bountiful. People wandering the campus with a little extra bounce in their steps. And yet when there is a child close by who is this distraught, the day becomes dark and miserable for everyone the child touches.

"It's not your fault. My marriage was going to fall apart one way or another. It's not your fault, Elizabeth."

The girl's tears turned to real sobs, while Emily continued, after first pulling a package of Kleenex from her bag and handing it to the girl.

"He wasn't the mentor he should have been. He wasn't the man he should have been, Elizabeth. He took advantage of you. You are the much better person."

"How do you know? You've never met me before!"

"That's right. But I know him better than anyone in the world does."

"I assumed I did, too!"

Young people shouldn't have to hurt like this. It is a feeling that should be reserved for people later in life. People who have taken many decades to screw things up.

"Life can be full of surprises." Emily, having put her coffee on the ground and then forgotten it was even there, spoke again about the man who was responsible for their joint misery. She, of course, was still wrestling with her own share of it. "He is so beguiling, but the reality is that he is also shallow. He fooled me. And he set you up."

"You think so?"

"Yes, I think so. I'm sure that he was quite the flirt. He is especially good at that. I'm sure he knew where he wanted this to go."

"So you don't think I was the instigator?"

"I know you weren't the instigator. That is not something you need to think about."

"How can you be so calm? How can you not want to reach over and strangle me!"

"You made a mistake, Elizabeth."

"A pretty big one, don't you think! My life should be done."

"Your life is just beginning. You still have a great deal to look forward to."

"Every time I saw you in the Starbuck's, it reminded me of what a horrible person I have become. I have realized that I don't know who I am anymore. Or more accurately, don't want to be who I am anymore."

"Do you want to come see me and talk about it?"

"You're a psychologist, right?"

"Come at the end of the day. We can get to know each other."

"I'd like that."

And with that, Emily pointed to where her office was, stood up, and headed off to see her next client of the day.

Even the best laid plans don't always work out. Elizabeth didn't show up at the end of the day. Nor was she there the next morning when Emily arrived at the counter at Starbuck's, as was now Emily's routine. Nor the day after that or the one after that.

Why is it that Emily was so looking forward to seeing her ex-husband's child lover? Let's face it, this isn't normal. The girl hadn't been wrong. She had ruined Emily's family and put it on a track to the great unknown. All those dreams that weren't anymore. And yet she was so disappointed when the girl didn't show up at her office as they had planned. There is little doubt that the girl needed help. This is what Emily did for a living. She thought she could make a difference. Perhaps there was more to it than she thought, and that's why the girl didn't show up. Maybe the girl had been the instigator, as she had said, and her husband was the innocent victim, as he said. Though every bone in her body doubted that.

As she would sit in her office each evening hopelessly wishing that Elizabeth would show, she would feel the guilt creep into her being, like maybe when you were a kid and are waiting to get a report card that wasn't going to be good and knew you would be grounded for the rest of your life by your parents. In her case, it was the other reason why she wanted to talk to Elizabeth that was causing her feelings of guilt. She really wanted to understand, as Monk had surmised, all the things about the girl and her ex that she didn't know."

Was that so wrong?

24

Film Sessions

One of the many things that distinguished Jelly is that she already, at such a young age, understood right from wrong. In her mind, there was no gray area in the middle. She had been to the infirmary every day that first week to see Mana, who was a mess, not understanding why he had been targeted. Why he had been attacked. And it was all so wrong. Hence, she made the decision to make her view on all of this heard. It began on the Sunday after Mana's surgery, when she stormed right into the middle of the football team's weekly film session in a room in the school's athletic complex. She knew the building as it's where she regularly did workout classes after she was done with her academic day. It might have shocked people to learn that she was a fitness nut, given that she had never in her life played on any kind of team. Uniforms were never her thing. She'd been on campus for roughly two months, yet only one of the sixty-seven football players in the film room on Sunday at midday had ever met her. None of the eleven coaches there had. But that all changed in a rather extraordinary fashion.

"What the fuck is the matter with you people!"

Film sessions were something that the team, like most college football teams, did after each game. Coaches used them to dissect what the players had done well in the previous game and what they hadn't, and then parse out grades to each unit with specific instructions on what it needed to fix. Jelly had learned all this via some early googling that morning. She'd been up since six, while most of the campus was still sleeping. Or some, perhaps, just getting in from Saturday evening's activities. The young men were sitting, or mostly slouching, in rows of folding desk chairs, though a few, like Seth, sat on a bench in the back, too big to be comfortable in those seats. Most wore gray team issued sweatpants, a t-shirt, and a hangover.

"He is from Nepal, doesn't know anybody here, is the nicest person on the whole campus – has way more substance than any of you assholes – and still you went and beat the snot out of him last weekend!"

Jelly watched the players sit up a little straighter when she began her tirade. Partly because her accusations caught their attention, and partly, she was aware, because her fit body and loose clothes caught their attention. It didn't take much to excite spoiled little boys.

"Excuse me, young lady," the head coach jumped in.

He was in the front of the room, pointing at various nonsense displayed on a big screen on the wall, and looking like you would think a college football coach would look. Cropped hair, a receding hairline, still with clues of what had likely been oversized arm and neck muscles in his younger days, and zero sex appeal. Most likely, he had never read the front page of a newspaper.

"This is a private team meeting."

"This is no fucking team, Coach! Your guys are criminals. They put a friend of mine in the hospital because they were all drunk and only focused on how to get laid! Did they learn this from you?"

The coach walked over in front of Jelly and put a hand on her shoulder before he spoke again. He wanted to get back to his game films and grades, because that was what he did every Sunday in the fall. It was a part of a detailed, stupid-as-hell teaching program that he probably sold to the administration that hired him and to the students who came to play for him.

"I think, young lady, that you should leave the room."

"Why? So you can fill their heads with more male ego bullshit? Have they told you what they did? Have they made you proud?"

"I don't know what you are talking about, but there are proper channels at the university to go through if you have concerns."

"Concerns? A boy is lying in the hospital with a leg in a cast, a broken nose, more stitches than I can count, and who knows what else. He had surgery on Monday to place screws in his leg. All because your guys jumped him when he was doing his security job. And you want to blow this off? What the hell is the matter with you? Are you the one who taught them how to act like this? You should be in jail, too!"

"Again, you need to leave. You don't belong here."

His voice now showed his growing agitation. He had a schedule to adhere to because good coaches have a schedule they adhere to, and he wanted to get back to his review of the game film. She knew she was pissing him off, and she was just fine with that.

"What do you say we ask your players what they did last Saturday night? I'm sure you will be proud of their responses. They almost killed a student. Again, because they wanted to get laid. Nice priorities, huh?"

None of the coaches saw it because they were staring at her, but a significant number of the players in the room changed course and slumped again into their chairs as far as they could. Athletic yo-yo's. This time not from their hangovers, but likely hoping the coach wouldn't see the guilt on their faces if he turned to survey them. Which he didn't. He wanted to review film.

Three of the assistants ultimately came over, carefully grabbed Jelly by her arms, like she was toxic, and ushered her out of the film room. Anything to please their boss, because they would all want a job like his someday. So they could become assholes, too. Instead of assistant assholes. It was not hard to remove her, as she was not a big person. She looked back over her shoulder while being escorted out and saw Seth on the bench in the back, never a hard one to miss.

"Seth, are you going to sit there and say nothing?" she screamed. "I thought you were better than this!"

He sat there and said nothing, while the assistant assholes locked the door after marching Jelly out.

College infirmaries are nothing like hospitals. They are more like dorms with nurses. It's easy to come and go as you please, and it's easy for visitors to wander in to see you. Mana didn't want any visitors besides Emily and Jelly, but they came anyway.

It was the Monday after the surgery -- a full week had gone by -- and it was the day after Jelly had stormed the film session. It had been six days since the detectives had been for their visit. He had been sleeping on and off. Floating, the nurses called it. It kept him from having to think about anything serious for a while. But that solitude didn't last as he would have hoped.

"Wake up, Monkey!"

Two boys had entered his room, neither of whom he recognized. They were no doubt athletes. There were no nurses to be seen, the two boys having made certain of that. One boy with a buzz cut, sweats, and horrible breath leaned close to Mana and whispered with an obtuse, southern accent.

"How are you feeling?"

Mana didn't answer.

"Cat got your tongue?" said the second boy in a low, deep voice.

Mana just watched through his swollen eyes.

The first boy looked around the room and then leaned over within inches of Mana's face again.

"We're sorry you got hurt, but we are bringing a message from the guys who did this to you. If you rat on anyone, you will be hurt even worse. Got it, Monkey?"

And then they left.

You can't imagine how much more intense his pain was after this. The mind and the body so tightly connected.

25

Hotel Henry

Mana told Emily and Jelly about the threatening visit he received. He was intimidated and rightfully so. It made Emily even more sad, and Jelly even more angry. This wasn't the college experience he deserved. As was always the case, Emily put on her caretaker hat. Mana needed a place to recover. A place he felt safe. And the college infirmary clearly wasn't that place.

She thought about moving Mana into her tiny house. After all, she had the space now, and it would be easy to care for him and to continue their therapy sessions if he were there. But since Mana was a client, she would be breaking all the rules of her counseling department. Her boss, if she knew, would pop a cork, because like so many bosses, liability was her favorite response to pretty much everything. Perhaps except for what kind of coffee do you want or where did you get your shoes, both of which seemed core to her being. Which was not meant to be a compliment. It would also be frowned upon by everyone and every oversight body in her profession. Though that didn't mean she wouldn't further bend the rules at some point as this story progresses.

But she had an idea, and so she called the cell phone he so loved.

"Hello."

"Henry, it's Emily."

"Emily my favorite therapist!"

"Yes. Emily your therapist."

"Favorite therapist."

"I believe I'm the only one you have."

"I'm happy to hear from you."

"Ditto, Henry. How are you doing?"

"Just got better this minute."

"Listen, I'll get right to the point. I've been thinking about your dilemma quite a bit."

"That can't be healthy."

"You're an engaging person. I want to help."

"An old nut like me?"

"Yes, an old nut like you," she chuckled. "I have an idea."

"I'm all ears."

She told Henry the story of Mana, from the goats to his jobs to the Saturday night attack to the threat in the infirmary, none of which was information, she convinced herself, that he couldn't have discovered on his own. Although even she didn't believe her own rationalization of the privacy rules she was supposed to live by. Henry listened carefully, undoubtedly struck by the story. Who wouldn't be?

"He can't stay in the infirmary any longer as it scares him and, who knows, it may not even be as safe as it should be. If I put him up at my house, I'd be breaking every rule that my profession has. So I was wondering if you want a roommate for a while?"

"Me?"

"You know college kids like the back of your hand, and you need a hobby."

"I'm eighty-two, and this is not exactly a hobby."

"Good, you're catching on. You've spent your life helping to mold college students. It appears it's what you do incredibly well. Unless you were fibbing to me. It's your choice. I just thought it might be a good match for two good people I've grown to care about."

"Why did you think of me?"

"Because it occurred to me that you answered your own question when we last talked. As your career moved along, your mind had too much free time. As you said, there was no heavy lifting after being tenured. And then came retirement where there were no hobbies. And now Jenny's passing. Plenty of free time and nothing to keep an obviously bright mind as busy as it once was, and so an experience from your undergrad days has had plenty of room to dance around inside your head and take root.

And with your wife's long illness, the idea of death had the chance to grow like a weed in an underutilized place. Contemplating death became your new scholarly effort. Maybe you need a more positive challenge to fill up your mind."

The phone went silent as he thought about her rationale and all the reasons he shouldn't do this. She let him take his time. He could take as long as he wanted.

"It would be a big change."

"I don't doubt that."

"I don't know if I'm up for the responsibility. Cooking for two, changing bedsheets, tending to his wounds, and all that."

"It's entirely up to you."

"He's a good kid?"

"He's a great kid."

Henry was quiet for a few more minutes.

"What the hell? I expect I can introduce him to Margaritas and *It's A Wonderful Life*."

"Exactly."

"Bring him over."

And, thus, Hotel Henry began. His house was not dissimilar to Emily's. Two bedrooms, a bathroom on each floor. and a deck looking onto a small backyard. Only it was bigger, had more modern appliances, and a more appropriate amount of furniture. Emily delivered Mana to Henry's house the next afternoon and helped set him up, the same way she had set him up in the infirmary, in the second bedroom in the house. Where Jenny had died. The sheets and pillowcases this time were blue flowers and the duvet cover pink flowers, because his wife liked flowers, and Henry had no taste when shopping. Emily had told Mana about Henry, but Mana had no idea the man was ancient. Henry, on the other hand, had not realized from her description how broken Mana really was. After caring for his ill wife for nine years, he worried whether he was up to the challenge once more. After all, he was now more than a decade older than when his wife first became sick.

Sometimes life delivers surprises that you never expect. Jelly rang his doorbell the next day and introduced herself. It was the only time she would ever ring the doorbell. He had no idea who she was or why she was there. She explained that she was a part of the package. Over the coming weeks, she and Henry would split the chores between them – changing Mana's dressings, taking him to doctor's appointments, and working with him on the physical rehab of his leg, which was not, it turned out, a small undertaking. Jelly even took responsibility for helping him bathe as that was an arduous task for an eighty-two-year-old man. And while Mana protested at first at the idea of the one female student he knew from the university helping him shower, she told him to shut up and stop being a baby, and that was that.

In the process, Henry and Jelly began to talk about life on the campus, the problems that students faced, and they occasionally talked about literature. Sound familiar?

26

It Was My Fault

Somewhere in the ten days after approaching Emily on the bench in the quad, Elizabeth made the decision to take her life. The shame she carried in every pore of her body was too much for her to surmount. She assumed there was no person in her existence that she could interact with the way she used to, before she traded it all for the teacher. There was no person, she would think, that she was important to any longer. There was no way in her mind that she could repair the damage that she had caused Emily and her family. So it came to this, and, for the first time since everything went to hell many months ago, she felt at peace.

Ten days later, ten days of our Emily's brain being filled with thoughts of all the bad things that may have happened, of repeatedly scanning the news for unspeakable stories, of having the high school website continually open in a window on her laptop, the girl showed up at her office door after closing time, looking just as sorrowful as she had when Emily last saw her. Elizabeth was no doubt in a chilling place.

Sometimes things happen, and we don't know why. For whatever reason, Emily had made an impression with Elizabeth. For whatever reason, Elizabeth saw a goodness in the woman whose life she had horribly trashed. For whatever reason, she decided that she would go see Emily, to finish their conversation, before ending things. To make sure Emily knew how sorry she was.

"I didn't know if I was going to come to see you again."

She stood frighteningly alone in the doorway.

Emily jumped up from her desk, the rest of her department once again scattered for the night, and basically sprinted over to the girl. She put her arm around her shoulder and escorted her to one of the armchairs. Emily sat in the other, ready to grab her and hold tight if the girl made a move to leave. Really. She'd been waiting for this opportunity since she first learned of the event, and she knew well that she needed to be at her therapeutic best.

There are few things in life more dispiriting than seeing a young person struggle with serious mental illness. It is so challenging for them to start each day trying to understand their purpose in this world. Not knowing who they are. Too often, their time is instead spent thinking about ways that they might hurt themselves. Some wanting to go away quietly and not make a mess, others wanting to create a shattering splash that the people who had caused them pain wouldn't miss.

The increased presence of mental illness in young adults is scary. Her department had hired a company to do a survey of the mental health of their student population a couple of years before. Eleven percent of college students had considered taking their lives at one time or another during their time on campus. The place that was supposed to be their utopia. Remember? That is a number, after learning of it, that she would never forget. Eleven freaking percent. It was triple of what it had been the last time they did a survey, maybe a decade before. The survey results didn't end there. Only one in four of these unsettled young adults go for help. The other three are embarrassed or decide they don't have the time, which is an incredible thing to consider, or think that maybe it's not as serious as they might have thought. Wishing that the dark feeling would just go away on its own like a bad cold.

The university basically had the same number of students it had back then, the same number of therapists, and more funerals for the administration to attend. More letters to write to worried parents and anxious students, advising all of them to reach out to the counselors if they had concerns. That's why Emily and her colleagues were here. The group that was booked out for new clients for the next six weeks. A system that really didn't work.

Now, it may be true that many students are able to plow through and avoid an unnecessary ending. But what Emily had seen more often than she would care to recollect, and remember that once is too often, is students waiting too long to acknowledge how real their problems are. Or maybe it's their parents, so often the real problem, who simply won't offer their children a pause to recalibrate. Parents, especially those with money, are too frequently of the belief that there is only one road to joining the world of the anointed. Which normally means the selective private high school and college that they get their kids into any way they can. Many begin to set expectations when their children are still in elementary school, resulting in the ten-year-old girl who already has a list of colleges she might want to attend. It's just too much pressure that most kids don't need and can't handle. And, hence, the now eleven percent threshold.

As Elizabeth sat next to her, Emily was already imagining the thoughts that the girl had been wrestling with. Likely the girl had pictures in her mind of a bottle of colored pills or bloody wrists or taking a boat far out into the ocean before throwing the oars overboard. After all, the university is less than an hour from the ocean. On the other hand, the university was near several cities that had their share of tall buildings. She shivered just thinking of this, but she suspected she wasn't wrong.

"It was my fault. I started it." The circles beneath her pained eyes were now dark as night.

"How old are you now Elizabeth?"

"Eighteen."

"Do you want to talk to me about it? As a counselor?"

"My parents won't let me see a shrink. I think they keep wondering what I am doing in their family. Like I'm a mistake that they keep forgetting they have. My father works all the time, while my mother plays all the time. They keep telling me I need to be strong. I think so it looks better for them. No cracks in their perfect social armor. What they don't recognize is that I'm not that strong."

"This is what I do for a living," Emily responded in a delicate manner, meant to demonstrate to Elizabeth that she cared. Which she did. "All of my clients are about your age. I've seen a lot. More than a lot. And what you have been through counts as a lot. You're an adult now, hence it's your decision. And, of course, we can do this after hours. There won't be any charge."

They sat silently for several minutes. Emily was looking at Elizabeth the whole time, and Elizabeth was looking at the door.

"I've been wanting to ask you for a long time," Elizabeth finally asked, "how you and your daughters are doing?"

Emily stopped to think. She didn't want to make the girl any more stressed than she already was. Still, she also knew that she needed to be honest in order to build the trust that a therapist needs to build with a client. Particularly one who is on the edge like this one.

"We're okay. I would be lying if I said it wasn't hard. It's been incredibly hard. We've had to adjust how we live and change our plans of the future. But change does happen in life, and we all need to acclimate. There are an awful lot of people out there who have it a good deal harder than Jessie, Abbey, and I do."

"Do Jessie and Abbey still see him?"

"Mostly when he went to their games at school. It's funny that he didn't shy away from that. Not so much over the summer, though, and not since they headed off to college. They are angry, too. But he is their father, so it's a challenge to reconcile what he did with the role he has played for all their lives. Up until now, he had been a good father. Or that's what I have believed, anyway."

"He used to talk to me about them a lot."

Emily hadn't ever considered this. It didn't fit with what he was doing with the girl.

"I'm surprised to hear that. But I've been surprised to hear so many things these past months."

She smiled at Elizabeth with her tender mom smile.

"I started it."

Emily remained silent.

"I was in his class," the girl continued, "and he always flirted with all the girls. Like you had said to me before. I thought that I was the special one, though. He was always patting me on the arm, rubbing my shoulders, pushing my hair behind my ears.

That sort of thing. Always staring into my eyes with a big warm smile on his face."

Emily was familiar with the touching and the smile. It had attracted her for a long time, too.

"I liked it," Elizabeth began to cry, and Emily once again handed her a couple of tissues from her seeming never ending collection. A requirement of the job. "Who wouldn't like the attention? And no one had ever really touched me like that before. Each time he touched me, I so wanted him to do it again. At that point, I wasn't even thinking about the age difference or that he was my teacher and married and had a family. I was just thinking about myself."

The sobbing swelled, and Emily gave her the whole tissue box.

"We were out in the woods in the fall doing a kind outward bound team building day for rising seniors."

"I remember my daughters telling me about that."

"I was on his team, and he was helping me as I was lagging the other kids. Maybe on purpose, I'm not sure. I'm not a particularly good athlete. I took his hand and put it under my shirt and under my bra. He didn't pull back. That's when I knew."

"Why do you think you did that?"

"I've thought about that for a long time." Elizabeth let out a long, pained sigh. "I think I learned it from my mother. She's been fooling around on my father for years. With a bunch of different men. He doesn't know a thing. And she doesn't think I know. But kids are sometimes smarter than our parents expect we are. It seems to make her happy. I just decided to see if it would make me happy."

"And did it?"

"I don't know. I think I liked the attention. Isn't that what high schoolers strive for? I know I liked the touching as I said. I was a virgin before him. And yet when we got discovered, I was relieved in many ways. I would have been happiest with one of my mother's brief flings, I think. He wanted more."

"How so?"

"This is really hard for me to talk about, Doctor Metcalf."

"It's your decision entirely. And please call me Emily."

Not something psychologists are supposed to do. Being called 'Doctor' balances familiarity and respect. Clients aren't meant to be friends.

Emily really wanted to hear the answer, more than she would even admit to herself. The girl took her time. God knows this was so strange, the two of them having this dialogue. But for some reason, the girl seemed to have a sense of comfort with Emily. There was an incredibly long way to go, even if she could help Elizabeth find the strength to give it the time it needed.

"He wanted me to apply to college here so we could continue the relationship."

Which was just sick. And it made Emily physically ill to hear. She threw up in her mouth and had to look away so that Elizabeth wouldn't see her reaction.

"I'm so sorry, Emily."

This was not an easy conversation, and she had to take a moment and drink some water to regain her poise. She may have still been attracted to him, but he was even a bigger shit than she thought.

"Again, Elizabeth, it's not your fault. But let me ask you this. Have you ever told anybody? Your folks? A friend?"

"No. My folks learned about my antics from the school, and then went right into crisis management mode. Everyone else heard via the gossip mill. You're the only one I have ever really spoken to about this. Which is not what I ever expected. Probably the same for you."

"Keeping something as significant as this to yourself, particularly for as long as you have, is only going to add to the hurt. It likely never goes away until you find the strength to talk about it with someone you trust. How are you feeling right now?"

Emily knew that was a stupid question to ask, but she also really wanted to keep hearing the details. Again, what she was doing wasn't being wholly altruistic. Which made her a shit, too. But she couldn't help it.

"Can't you tell by looking at me? I'm a wreck! I am so incredibly mortified for what I did to you! I already knew who you were the first time you came into the store. Kids always know which parents belong to which kids. I got that job on purpose. I'd been stalking you since school started up this fall. You seemed like a nice person, which makes sense cause your daughters are also so nice and seem so balanced. Which has made me ache even more. And since all my friends are off at college, I'm mostly alone. I don't even know if they're still my friends. And I don't care anymore either."

"What do you think about when you are alone?"

"You don't want to know."

"I've been doing this a long time. I expect I already do. We can talk about it if you want."

"Can I ask you a question instead?"

"Yes."

"What do you do to feel better? To hate your husband less. And to hate me less."

"That's a really good question."

Emily shifted positions in her chair before answering. The girl's tears were still flowing. She was engaged in the conversation which was a positive step. Every other therapist Emily knew and respected would have said she was playing with fire. That the chance of something good coming out of her intervention was minimal, and the chance of something bad happening was highly likely.

"And I don't know that I have a great answer, Elizabeth. At first, I was really confused. But I was never angry at you. You were just a mixed-up teenage kid in my mind. I didn't know what you looked like. I didn't even know your name. But he and I had been together a long time, since a few years after I graduated from college. Nobody knew him like I did. I became quite angry. I even used to throw things at him, which he, of course, never picked up." She chuckled at the memory. "And, finally, I've simply been trying to figure out why he did what he did. I don't know that I've figured that out yet."

"Are you still angry at him?"

"I suspect that I will be for a long time."

"Maybe we can be therapists for each other."

Between all her tears, the girl smiled for the first time. This was not going to be easy. She had many layers to uncover and many demons of which to rid herself. But that was enough pain for one day. All of her colleagues probably would have tried to get the girl admitted to a hospital. Emily was betting that she would not hurt herself and come back tomorrow. Which was a risky bet. She also knew that she was doing this to protect her own reputation. Not wanting others to know that she was counseling the girl. The desire for self-preservation shows up at times you don't expect.

"I think I would like that," Emily answered. "See you tomorrow? Same time?"

27

The Definition Of Lingerie

The dangerous side of this utopia is a place of unbridled alcohol, barely in check hormones, dormant rage, and the exuberance of an unfettered group of young people living without adults for the first time. All mixing together without a recipe. For which Mana had paid dearly. His body, with the swelling, bruises, scars, and bandages, looked like hell, but it was ultimately going to heal. It would take a long while, particularly his leg which had been stomped on unceremoniously by a big, unknown schoolmate. But the surgeon sounded confident that it would eventually come around if Mana was diligent with his rehab, which there was no doubt he would be. His psyche was another issue altogether. It was the more challenging rehab. Mana had come so far from his very different life in Nepal. He was smart, disciplined, and hardworking, and he would have many opportunities for a promising future in this country should he decide to remain. A single evening, though, had set him back immensely. Something he didn't ever deserve. Ever.

As for our therapist, she remained pretty down after Monk's sudden exit. She found herself tearing up at times and in places that she didn't expect. Driving to work, sitting in her office between client sessions, bathroom breaks while hiding in a stall, doing the dishes in her kitchen in the evening. And almost always when she went to bed at night now, she had a full rainstorm. It had been a short run, but Monk had allowed her to enjoy life again. Until he dumped her. Something with which she had quickly become too familiar. Ultimately, she was a strong person and would eventually heal. Should eventually heal. Watching out for Mana, as you heard before, gave her something more to focus on. For the moment anyway.

The logistics had changed, but Emily was still Mana's therapist. Each night after work, she would drive to Henry's house to talk, pulling up a chair next to Mana's bed, as he laid there wrestling with his recovery. While he would be up and move about for brief stretches of the day, he continued to spend most of his time hibernating. He had gone into a shell after the attack. Speaking less, smiling less, involved little in the unfamiliar pocket-sized world of Henry's, where he was now living and being cared for. And napping for long stretches. His entire body still hurt when it was required to do much of anything, and he grimaced if you sat on his bed. So she sat in a chair when she went to check on him.

The process of coaxing him out of his shell was, in retrospect, more Jelly's doing. Jelly came most evenings to help with his physical therapy and make sure he ate enough to get his strength back, even if it meant force feeding him when he said he wasn't hungry. She read him stories from the school newspaper. She posted pictures on his Facebook page, so he could stare at himself she said, lying amongst the favorite pink flowered bedroom designs of Henry's choosing, and that made him laugh. Even taking a shower, which had initially been the source of some consternation, was now more like the old *Who's on first?* Abbott & Costello routine. *Who's in the shower?* Mana would tease that he was going to break Jelly's leg so he could give her a shower. Jelly, of course, retorted that it would be greatest day of his life.

Jelly kept a toothbrush and her version of pajamas in Jenny's Room, and she began to sleep in the other bed on those nights when her work with Mana went too late. Or just whenever she felt like it.

But even Jelly couldn't readily erase all the scars.

"Hey Mana."

"Hi Emily. How was work?"

Both he and Jelly had taken to calling her by her first name now that she came by every night, which was fine by her. There were far more acute issues that needed to be addressed than what to call each other.

"Busy. There are too many kids who want to talk."

"They are lucky to have you."

"Sometimes I wonder, Mana. How was your day?"

"I'd be lying if I said it was good."

"Are you hurting?"

"Sure. But a lot of it is not in the way you are thinking."

"Tell me about it."

The doctors had replaced the cast on his broken leg with a smaller one, but it still seemed almost as big as he was.

"I got seventeen emails today."

"I take it they weren't ones you wanted to get."

"Why would someone call me a monkey?"

Shit. Emily knew that most kids weren't born this malicious, with this callousness towards anyone who wasn't like them, but rather learned it from a parent or a coach or some other adult. Still impressionable as young people. The problem is that wherever or whenever they got the religion, it rarely seemed to ever leave them. It just seemed to spread.

"Is that what someone called you?"

"More than one. And a wild yak, a pangolin, a midget, a traitor."

"What's a pangolin?"

"They were looking up on Wikipedia animals indigenous to Nepal."

"Huh."

"They told me to go back home. That if I caused problems for the football team, they would make my life miserable. One said that what I experienced in the first go round would be worse the next time. Another said they'd break me in half. None of them used their personal email addresses."

The best and the brightest, no less. None of this malice, of course, ever showed up on an application. Or later on resumes. But it was there, and it was forbidding. The welcome fake grin from when she first entered the bedroom had disappeared. His eyes were sad once again. She would make sure the detectives received copies of the emails, even though she suspected it wouldn't make any difference.

"This is all hard for me, Emily."

"I know it is."

"I'm scared to go back to my dorm. I'm scared to hobble around the campus. I'm scared to go to classes."

She would be, too, if she were in his shoes. Football was far more important to this sordid group than Mana's dignity.

"Mana, I suspect that I know the answer to this, but tell me anyway. What is most frightening to you?"

"People calling me racist names. People badgering me not to squeal on the football team because they are having their best season ever. Any large athlete I see who I fear is just going to pummel me once more for no reason. I keep having this dream where someone knocks on the door of my dorm room, and I answer it. The whole football team in their uniforms, including helmets and cleats, is there with a blanket, and they proceed to cover my head and beat me. Just like happened for real. Only there are more of them."

"I've seen this before when my clients have been raped," Emily weighed in. "They – and I say they because the rapist's teammates typically support him – try to make life miserable for the victim until she typically leaves the school. Which is what the rapist wants. Their problem disappears. I hope beyond all hope that this isn't what happens with you."

"Again, Emily, what did I do wrong? I just want to do my work and graduate. I don't need to be popular, and I don't need them to be my friends. I just want to get an education."

"Do you recognize any of the players in the dream, Mana?"

He stopped to think about her question. They clearly weren't happy thoughts. He was still petrified of having to again relive the horrible experience.

"I don't know. I seem to wake up when I'm getting beaten up and before I know who they are. But it's different than the real assault where I never moved or made a sound when they attacked me, for some reason thinking that if they thought I was dead they would more quickly stop what they were doing. Which, in retrospect, may not have made any difference. In my dream, I am screaming as loud as I can and thrashing all about, kicking and punching, doing anything I can to try to get them to stop."

Emily had forgotten about his feigning dead, something he had told the detectives.

"Are they coming every night in your dreams?"

"Yeah, pretty much. Remember when I first came to you because I couldn't sleep? Well now I fall right asleep because I'm exhausted by the end of each day. This healing takes so much out of me. But I don't really want to fall asleep now because I know I'm going to wake up some time during the night scared to death again. When I wake up from my dream, my heart is racing like it's going to run right out of my chest. Usually, I'm perspiring like a mad person. I keep seeing that same blanket and basically re-experiencing what I went through."

"I'm so sorry to hear that."

"How long do you think this will last Emily? It's not fun."

"I wish I could give you an answer, Mana. Dreams are hard to predict and can be hard to understand. Although yours are certainly not surprising." Not at all surprising given what he had been through. "But there are some things that I think we can do that might help. I suspect that can start by changing your routine before going to sleep at night."

"I'm willing to try anything."

"Maybe Henry and you can start watching a few *Seinfeld* reruns before turning in."

"I don't know what those are."

Sometimes a therapist needs a therapist. After all, they have lives, too, and the things that life throws at them can be hard, even if they have a doctorate in psychology.

Jelly could tell that Emily, despite all of her inherent goodness, was struggling with her own issues. She had gone to see Emily at her office one evening to talk about plans to get back at the football team for what they did to Mana, because that's what Jelly was determined to do. The campus police were not impressing anyone with their lack of progress, and it wouldn't be fair for the football assholes to get away with what they did. But Emily just wasn't all there. She pretended to be listening, though she wasn't really hearing anything that Jelly said. Jelly snapped at her, but Emily just apologized and continued being spacey. Likely, she was thinking about Monk, who, from what Jelly could learn, was an ex-colleague who had a drinking problem and who Emily had hoped would become more than an ex-colleague. A sober one, no doubt. The fact that there was a bedroom at her house that she had referred to as where Monk slept, and it wasn't the same as Emily's room, indicated that the relationship hadn't gone all that far. But that doesn't mean Emily didn't hope for more.

Jelly went to the market Friday after classes and after working out. She bought some sort of fish and various other things that she presumed would work together to make a meal, and then went to a liquor store for two bottles of wine thanks to her fake ID which indicated that she was twenty-three. She took her bags of goodies to Henry's house, knowing Emily would be there for a therapy session with Mana.

"Rumor has it, it's Friday night," she announced. "None of the four of us have anything to do. What do you say that we open a bottle of wine, make a nice dinner tonight, and celebrate that we had our most demanding rehab session to date, and Mana hasn't yet smacked me when the exercises I put him through were torture?"

Emily was clearly tired from her week of work and worry. If Henry was tired, he didn't mention it. He seemed amused by all of the people and activity. Mana was shyly smiling with the idea of the four of them having a fun evening together, having set aside, for the moment, his morose therapy sessions with Emily. He still had remnants of the black eyes, but the swelling of his face had fully subsided, so he could now see fine, and his voice sounded like his own again. It really was amazing how he had adapted to the language of a new country of unlike linguistics with only the slightest trace of an accent. She really liked and admired the person he was. Fun, though, had been an elusive part of his recovery, and she was determined to change that.

"Henry cooks every night, and we need to give him a break. Can you cook, Emily?" Jelly asked.

"I'm a terrible cook," replied Emily.

"Join the club."

"We could order pizza."

"I think I can cook," offered Mana.

"Mana, you can't even walk," Jelly shot back.

"You don't think I've noticed that? You be my legs, and I will make you a feast. Or try anyway."

"Where did you learn how to cook?"

"Holidays, Emily. I watch the food channels on the TV in the lounge of the dorm after everyone goes home for break. You know, a home cooked meal on the big screen. Figured it is something I should learn how to do." Jelly's baggy shorts were serving a purpose besides her obtuse fashion statement, as they were the only clothes that fit over Mana's big cast. She and he were about the same size. "It looks pretty straightforward."

Henry watched and laughed, before jumping in.

"Did you actually cook the food, Mana?"

"Heck no. Henry, in case you haven't been in a dorm lately, there aren't any refrigerators or stoves in the rooms. But I have a really good memory. I haven't forgotten any of the instructions."

"Have you ever even turned on a stove?" he followed up.

Jelly had already filled four stemmed glasses with red wine and placed them on the kitchen table where their unique foursome sat. The old man with nothing else to do, the boy who had been improperly welcomed to the final year of accomplishing his dream, the woman who had always fretted about all the others she met and was now overwrought with her own reckoning. And Jelly, who was good at keeping secrets. Mana's casted leg rested on an empty stepstool, reminding all what had brought them together.

"Ye of so little faith. And by the way, Jelly, I don't drink."

"That's okay Mana, it's a dangerous habit. If you don't want the wine, I'll drink yours. I'm not planning on leaving here tonight, so I'm not worried about over imbibing. Or drinking and driving. You get to share a bedroom with me again tonight, Mana. I promise to wear my sexiest lingerie."

"Lucky me. And I've seen what you wear to bed," he laughed back at her. "I don't think that's the definition of lingerie."

Everyone recognized when Mana laughed now.

"I'm hurt."

"That's doubtful," he replied.

It was amazing how comfortable together they had become in such a brief time. Only Jelly knew that the reason she came here so often is that it had become her happiest place on campus, too. Way more fun than her dorm life, where non-stop gossiping and sharing showers with shallow girls held little appeal. And it was safer. She wasn't blind, knowing full well that the way she dressed and acted drew attention. She enjoyed the notoriety and wasn't intending to change her ways. But it was certainly a contradiction since many of the boys – too many of the boys – on campus worried her. It made her a target when one or more of them had too much to drink. Or were just pigs in general. She also knew that she probably would never recover from something like that. She could be defiant and vindictive, but she wasn't as strong as Mana. Which is why she never would go to frat parties. Which is why she used Walk Safe. Which is why she spent so much time here at Henry's Hotel. They just were not feelings she shared with anyone else.

"I didn't know that Mana had so much chutzpah in him."

"I don't know what that means Jelly, but I can be full surprises."

"Really?"

"Okay, not so much really. But I've always wanted to say that."

They all hooted, and Mana was the source. That was a good thing.

"So Emily, who did the cooking when it was just you and Monk?" Jelly asked.

Emily blushed. Maybe because Jelly was raising the issue while Henry was present.

"Monk did all the cooking. He is a fabulous cook."

"Every night?"

"Just about. The first night he was there, he cooked linguine with white clam sauce. It was out of the world. Most nights after that, it was a similar feast."

"So where did he run off to?"

"We were just friends helping each other out. It wasn't a romance or anything."

Jelly knew she wasn't being straightforward.

"You didn't answer the question, Emily."

"I wish I knew. How's that for an answer?"

"Evasive at best."

Emily was sitting at the kitchen table, while twirling her glass of wine. She began to tear up, hoping that none of the others would notice. Jelly noticed immediately while she was searching through the bags and pulling out various items to show Mana, who would shake his head either yes or no while he stood on his one good leg, supporting himself on the little kitchen's single counter next to the stove.

"Unfortunately, it's as honest as I can be. He left and never really said goodbye."

"Another woman?"

"Jelly, you don't stop, do you!"

"You're just coming to that conclusion now?"

"I don't know if it was another woman. I certainly have considered that, and, given that we were supposed to spend the whole day at Homecoming together and instead he deserted me, it probably is a fair guess. Or it could be that he just grew tired of me altogether. Or maybe it's something else that I haven't thought of yet."

"There was a romantic interest then?"

Jelly pretended she was loving this, but really she just wanted to help. She had learned that somewhere.

"You like talking about my personal life?" Emily chuckled.

"Of course. But, once again, you didn't answer the question."

"The answer is maybe. But let's talk about something else."

"Suit yourself."

She counted that as a personal victory. Getting her therapist to open the door to her private issues. It's all about building trust. So next she turned to the newly crowned chef.

"Okay Mana, are you going to stay in this country after graduation?"

"I have to make it to graduation first. Without getting beaten up again."

"I think we should go to the administration and rat on Coach Quigley."

"Jelly," Emily jumped in, "we don't know for certain that it was the football team. The campus detectives said that nobody at the party is pointing fingers at them."

"Mana, what the hell are you doing to the food I spent a small fortune on!" Jelly screamed, and Mana giggled.

Mana had pulled out various pots and pans, unwrapping and examining the food Jelly had supplied him with, all while pretending that he knew what he was doing. Emily and Henry didn't care. They were enjoying themselves, with the wine glasses in their hands, the conversation, and the fact that Mana was progressing, which included his opening up to their little world. Jelly found a bag of pretzels that she opened and put in a bowl to occupy them.

Mana was eyeballing his wine glass, as if contemplating asking it out on a date. This meal was going to be interesting. At best. Mana had no idea what he was doing. She couldn't believe that she spent so much money on the ingredients, and he was going to screw it up.

"Emily, you actually believe the administration?"

"That's not the point, Jelly. The university has established a process to follow in these types of circumstances. Universities like to have a set of rules in place for pretty much anything they can think of."

"Actually, that *is* the point Emily. Nobody in the university knows who Mana is. Or has shown much of an interest in finding out. They sent him a food basket for God's sake, and probably feel they have done their job. Although the food basket was actually pretty good."

"Remember," Mana jumped in, "the more noise created, the greater the chance of their coming after me again, which doesn't excite me at all. I'm fine if they just forget me. And no more being a security guard. I'm too afraid now."

"We understand that," Emily responded.

"Yeah, but that's so wrong," Jelly shot back. "To be fearful of the other kids on this campus, when all you want is to live your life the way you want to live it? They never put that on the website."

While she would never admit it to the others, Jelly may have been speaking about herself, too.

"There are a lot of things they don't put on the college website, Jelly." Emily spoke in an empty tone, having been down this path before.

"It is what it is, Jelly," Mana chimed in. "And is there any of the food basket left? Just in case."

They all threw pretzels at him.

"So let's switch subjects again." Jelly was already almost finished with her first of what would be several glasses of wine for the evening. "Is this Monk guy ever coming back?"

"How do you know so much about Monk?"

"It's hard to keep a secret from me," she smiled. "And it's not that hard to figure out when you have a bedroom for Monk in your house, but no Monk."

"It's a long story."

"Dinner won't be ready for probably an hour." Mana was interested, too. "And that can be extended if the story is good."

"I told you I would make a good therapist."

"That you did, Jelly."

"Hey, does anyone know how to turn on the oven?"

"Okay, take the wine away from that guy," chuckled Jelly.

"I've only looked at my glass."

"And yet you're getting drunk?"

"Do you know, Jelly, that you snore when you sleep?"

"Mana! You know that you're not supposed to say stuff like that to a girl? We get self-conscious."

"You get self-conscious?"

"Okay, maybe other girls. But since we mentioned girls, have you ever had a girlfriend?"

"What brought up that?"

"I'm switching subjects again. Answer the question."

"No."

"Been on a date?"

"No."

"How come?"

"I've had a lot going on in my life. Even before all this happened."

"We may have to work on this."

"Let's hope, then, that you find a new diversion."

"I have been known to be a great matchmaker."

They were all having great fun now. In Henry's transformed little house. Which was, indeed, a welcome respite from all that had been going on.

"I'll pass for now. You can work on Emily."

Probably not what Emily wanted to hear. But if she drank enough wine, she'd never remember.

"So Henry," Jelly changed the subject once more, "we've let you off the hook long enough. How do you know Emily?'

"She's my therapist," he replied calmly.

"Wait," yelled Mana above a clanking of pots, "I thought Emily only provides counsel to college students."

"Perhaps she needed a change of pace," Henry chimed in.

"Why did you go see her?" Jelly asked.

"Jelly, some things are meant to be private."

"Not here, Emily."

"It's okay Emily, I'm not afraid to discuss my issues. I'm wrestling with mortality."

"How old are you?"

"Eighty-two. But it's not just mine. It's everyone's. Now including all of you."

It turned out that Mana was a terrible cook. He badly burned whatever it was he was cooking, which became a subject of some discourse. It took him the full hour to destroy the dinner. He did drink his first glass of wine and got funnier, but one was enough for him. They ordered an extra large pizza, and despite the issues hanging out there for all of them, it was the best day that any of Emily's clients had at the university that semester.

While they were waiting for the pizza, the conversation drifted back to Mana and his struggles.

"Let me ask you this, Mana," said Henry. "Is there any place on campus where you think you would feel safe?"

"Meaning not afraid of the slurs, the threats, or the crap getting beat out of me again?"

"Yes."

Mana hesitated and looked at Jelly first. It seemed that they had already discussed the question.

"You wouldn't want to know the answer, Henry."

"Try me," he said.

Mana looked at Jelly once more before responding.

"Here."

The answer shouldn't have surprised Henry, but it did. College kids, in general, liked the autonomy of living on campus. They didn't usually want to go in the other direction. And his house was nothing to get excited about. Mana, though, wasn't a typical college kid to begin with, and now he was a damaged one.

"Why is that?"

Mana hesitated before answering.

"I've been on my own for a long time, Henry. You guys have cared for me like nobody I have ever met. Even though only a few weeks ago, I didn't know any of you."

"Families are important when things are tough," Emily observed, "or, in this case, a substitute family. All of us have been hurt by what you have been through."

"But I can't stay here forever. This is your home, Henry."

Henry smiled, and instinctively reached for his hand.

"Mana, you can stay here as long as you need to. I like having you around, and I'm not going anywhere."

"Really?"

"Absolutely. We'll have to figure out where everyone sleeps should Emily send over more boarders," he winked at Emily. "But one thing at a time."

"You don't know how grateful I am for this Henry. How much better it makes me feel."

Jelly opened the freezer and pulled out a large jug of ice cream. Cow Tracks. Then she pulled out four bowls and began scooping. Ice cream before dinner was her way of sealing Mana's living arrangement. The one she had mapped out with him that afternoon.

"You've been through too much. Time heals. You just must be careful not to rush it."

And that's when they began to call him Saint Henry.

It was nice to be a valuable person again. Being called Saint Henry because he was doing something helpful. All of which was a positive step for Henry, but none of which completely erased his penchant for thinking about dying.

Most nights now, he thought about how Mana was going to die. The vision changed every few nights, but the endings were always too violent, too sudden, and when Mana was still too young. A drive by shooting. Being crushed in a fan stampede after a soccer game somewhere in Europe. A brick falling off a very tall building and hitting him while he traveling along a sidewalk. All when he was still about the age he was now. He admired and cared for Mana far too much now. These were not welcome thoughts.

28

The Next Tomorrow

Elizabeth came back tomorrow. And the next tomorrow and the tomorrow after that. The other woman, or girl more accurately, and the jilted sitting together and talking in Emily's office. Elizabeth knew she still was a mess, but she kept delaying the decision that Emily, at that point, didn't completely know she had made. And that was something. For whatever reason, she was feeling an attachment to the person whose life she had obliterated. And so their unanticipated conversation continued.

"I know that people call me a slut and worse. And I deserve that. What's weird is that I'd never even had a boyfriend before. Or ever been on a date. Even though I was surrounded by them at school, boys were unfamiliar beings to me. Like something from Mars. I never had a brother nor ever even really had a boy for a friend. I've never really understood them."

"Did you think of him as a boyfriend?"

"I guess I did. After a while, I think that's the part I liked the best. More than the physical contact. It made me feel special when he would spend time with just me. We went to an art museum in Philadelphia where he showed me stuff that I didn't know anything about. We walked the beach in Atlantic City. We went to a couple of Trenton Thunder baseball games."

"He had season tickets for a long time, Elizabeth. I had stopped going with him years ago. I got too busy and found baseball boring. Much to his chagrin, our girls didn't like going either. I didn't know that he ever took anyone else."

"I am sorry that it was me." She sat in the same armchair each time, still looking physically as adrift as she did when she approached Emily on the quad. "Doing those things, I think, did make me feel like a girlfriend for the first time in my life."

For the only time in their discussions, she wasn't crying.

"I had this persistent feeling for the first couple of months," she went on, "that I really didn't want to lose him. Like I was in fear of losing him. Sex, I think, is what I did to keep him. I think he liked it way more than I did. One time I went out shopping to buy him a tie for his birthday as I thought he could use some better clothes. I had so much fun picking it out. It seemed that was the kind of thing girlfriends are supposed to do."

"He was wearing that tie the day he got fired. It was the first time I had ever noticed it, and I remember wondering where he got it."

Again, it was hard to believe that they were having this exchange.

"How long was your relationship?" Emily asked.

"About six months. From September of my senior year until February."

"Elizabeth, you don't have to answer this question, but did you have sex a lot?"

It was amazing that Emily could ask her questions like this so calmly. The girl had been screwing her husband, for God's sake. She had stolen Jessie and Abbey's father. How could anyone do this? Anyone.

"It should be harder to talk about than it is. I don't know why. I'm feeling more and more comfortable with you. You must be a very good therapist." She smiled weakly. "After the first couple of months, he wanted to have it way more than I did. Like all the time. It wasn't always that romantic. In his car. On his classroom desk late one night. In cheap motels a couple of afternoons. It wasn't like you see in the movies. Am I hurting you?"

"Of course. Nobody wants to hear this stuff about the person they initially planned to spend the rest of their life with. But it's part of the process. For both of us."

"It already seems like so long ago."

"That's not a bad thing. Why do you think you were attracted to a man who was so much older than you?"

"I wish I knew. Because he is older, and probably because he is a teacher, I think that for some reason I assumed he was wise, and so I trusted him. Like if he thought it was a good thing, then it must be a good thing. I wonder if I was really attracted to him or if I just liked being noticed by someone. Can those be two different things?"

"They very much can, and they often get confused. Let me ask you this. If you saw him again now – in a store or a park or some other random place – how do you think you would react? What would you say?"

Elizabeth had to stop and think about that.

"I have no idea," she finally answered. "Have you seen him since all this happened?"

"Once. I had breakfast with him."

"Was that painful?"

"I spent most of the time trying to figure out why I had been attracted to him. And then I tried to understand how the logistics would work as he is still the father of my two daughters. I even thought about their weddings, if you can believe that, even though neither of them even has a significant other. I'm not sure, though, that I gained clarity on anything. My gut tells me that I probably won't ever talk to him again. So I have to learn how to move forward without the clarity I might have hoped for. But was it painful? Yes, it was. Sound familiar?"

"I don't know if I could handle seeing him."

"You can. I get the sense that you are stronger than you think. I promise you will get by all of this. It's a process."

"What do I do if I see him again, Emily?"

"You will know by then. And then you can tell me what to do."

"You seem so confident, and I'm afraid of who I am."

"Trust me, I'm not as confident as you might think. Elizabeth, I went months without sleeping. A friend suggested I read a physics book to help fall asleep. That worked for about a week until I unbelievably started liking physics. So then I slept even less. The mind is tricky."

"Do you think I will ever know how to have a relationship?"

"A romantic relationship?"

"I'm thinking any kind of relationship right now."

"Yeah, I have no doubt. But there is no need to force it. Just let your relationships happen. You obviously have a great deal to offer. You got overly curious and got into a situation that was too difficult for you to handle at your age. Maybe at any age. It happens to more people than you think. Though they're not all like that. There are still a lot of good people out there in the world – for friendships and romances. We just need to take our time."

"We?"

"I'm wrestling with some of the same issues. I have these same conversations with myself. Time heals."

"You know, Emily, I appreciate what you are doing for me?"

"Ditto."

It had now been four days that Elizabeth had put off killing herself.

29

She Went To All The Games

As was mentioned earlier, unlike so many young people, she had a strong sense for what was right and what was wrong. It may have been the result of a difficult lesson she learned while in high school, but again, that is another story. She wasn't done with the coach. What had happened in the film room was just the beginning. Why? Because that's who she is. She believes in doing the decent thing. And believes in keeping things interesting.

"Hi Coach!"

He was sitting at his desk, his head buried in his laptop, when she sauntered into his office the first time.

"What are you up to?" she asked cheerfully. As if she visited him each day.

"I'm watching films of possible recruits for next year's team."

He had a big cup of coffee in a mug that read World's Greatest Coach, while wearing a polo shirt and a pair of sweatpants both adorned with the school's logo. Which just made him look like a dumb jock. More young players, and their parents, were obviously paying attention to his program because they were winning games. If they only knew his team was Seth, and that the coach was a self-absorbed moron. Give her time.

"How can I help you?" he chirped.

"I just stopped by to congratulate you on having such a good season. It's been a long time for this school."

Jelly naturally was wearing an outfit that couldn't have been more opposite of what the coach was wearing. No logos of any kind. He didn't yet recognize who she was.

"Are you a football fan?"

"I go to all of the games, Coach."

"Well, that's nice to hear."

"The team is playing really well."

He closed his laptop and looked up at her.

"Yes, they are. I'm always glad when somebody notices."

Oh, she noticed.

"I'm sure you are," she answered.

"It's been a fun year so far."

"Really?"

"Without a doubt."

"I've noticed that you haven't punished your players for beating up that student."

There was a quiet moment before he next spoke.

"Now I remember who you are."

"I told you I wouldn't disappear," she said in a way that he shouldn't forget.

"Terrific."

"I saw a video of one of your talks to the alums, Coach. You talked about the importance of your players being held accountable. I was just wondering. Is this just on a case-by-case basis?"

"I think it's time for you to leave, young lady."

"Why? You are a Professor of Athletics. I am a student. The school website talks quite a bit about the easy and welcome accessibility of professors to students. I've printed out the pages if you want to see them, in case you're not familiar with the school's mission."

She wasn't lying. She reached into her bag, pulled out a loose stack of printed pages from the school's website, and stretched across his desk to hand them to the coach. But he didn't take them. Instead, he just looked at her with a growing confusion and irritation.

"What's your purpose in coming here, despite just being a wise ass?"

"I'd heard that you swear a good deal. Never built a broader vocabulary?"

"Fuck you."

"Is that what you want to do? Sexually attack me? I'd be glad to notify your boss about that."

"You are twisting my words."

"It was only a two-word sentence. I'm not sure it even qualifies as a sentence. There's not much there to twist."

"What's your name?"

"My friends call me Jelly. So you can call me Angela."

"What do you want from me, Angela?"

"I want you to kick the football players who beat up Mana off the team and out of the school. That's his name. Mana. He is from Nepal. And he's five feet four, 120 pounds. Don't think your guys really needed to gang up on him, do you? He's about as big as your daughter, Ella."

"How do you know anything about my daughter?"

"I do my homework. That's what newspaper reporters do. By the way, I work for the school newspaper. Five or ten of your guys assaulting her would be ugly, don't you think?"

He was pissed that she had brought his daughter into the conversation. Worked like a charm.

"I don't know anything about the attack you mentioned."

"Well, then I'll be glad to fill you in. Your players were celebrating a victory with a party at their frat house. They were all drinking more than anyone should have. Three of the girls who were invited to the party felt uncomfortable and called security to ask for an escort back to their dorms. In case you didn't know, that's a service that the college offers every night. Mostly to prevent women from getting raped. Mana was working security that night, as he does every Saturday and Sunday night to earn money, which, by the way, he sends home to his family in Nepal because they are dirt poor. Some of the players had other hopes for the girls. When Mana arrived at the front steps of the frat, they jumped him, covering his head with a blanket so he couldn't see them, and then proceeded to beat the living crap out of him. All hundred and twenty pounds. You should go see him now. You'd be so proud of your guys. Broken nose, left leg broken in two places, big ugly scars on his face that will be permanent. I told you all this when we first met, but you weren't listening. I don't think he'll be able to make any more of your games this year. He had successful surgery on his leg, but it will take him the better part of a year to recover. Just in case you wanted to know."

"You're pretty threatening for such a young person."

"I didn't know I was being threatening, but I can be."

"What do you want me to do?"

"I already told you. And then you can quit."

"I'm not quitting."

"Then I'll have to get you fired."

The Coach stood up from his desk, the purple vein in the middle of his forehead, below his receding hairline, now popping out and gesticulating in front of her to confirm that this meeting was over. He was twice Jelly's size, but she had rendered him mute. If he only understood at that point what a pain in the ass she could be when she wanted to be. He evidently wasn't a quick study.

30

Thinking About Other Things Than Dying

When he went to bed at night, Henry still thought about dying. It was too long an addiction, many years now, to be able to quickly surmount. In addition to Mana, he now wondered how, when, and why Emily would die. The same went for Jelly, which bothered him the most. He had a crush on Jelly. Not in the way you are thinking, but a crush, nonetheless. And he had a crush on Emily. In the way you are thinking. Mornings had changed, though, with his new role. In the morning when he woke up, he no longer was thinking about death, and he no longer needed to talk himself into getting out of bed. Instead, he has too many things to do as the innkeeper, which he listed on a never-ending sea of index cards. Shopping for groceries (whatever amount of ice cream he bought, the tenants always told him to get more, and the flavors requested always seemed to change), making Mana lunch (which most often included one of the newly requested ice cream flavors), making a real dinner instead of his previous steady diet of peanut butter sandwiches (dinner was now very much a form of art as no one ever told him who exactly was staying for the meal), cleaning the bathrooms (he had never purchased so many cleaning supplies in his life), changing Mana's sheets (something he had gotten better at when Jenny was sick), taking the young man to his doctor's appointments (always a little dicey as Henry didn't drive as well as he used to -- his eyes were fine, he just too often didn't pay attention as he was thinking when and how all the people he passed on the street were going to die).

Remember, Jenny and he had never had kids of their own.

"So Saint Henry, you are a client of Emily's?"

"I am Jelly. I just started seeing her recently."

She had walked into the kitchen where he was cooking dinner. Either for two, three, or four.

"Because you spend so much time thinking about dying?"

"That's right. Thought she could help me put things in a better perspective. Are you staying for dinner?"

"Dying. Really?"

"Yes."

"I think of that sometimes. And, yes, I'll stay for dinner if that's okay with you."

He stopped what he was doing, which was pouring tomato sauce from a jar on top of some spaghetti he had boiled. He had been a magical teacher, challenging his students to think beyond their comfort zone. Able to get them to take a chance in class, not just give him the answer they thought he wanted to hear. Writing papers that they never, ever thought that they would have the conviction to write. But that skill did not translate to his cooking. He was not a good cook. Probably because he could have cared less about eating. It was simply a way to stay alive.

"You're too young to being thinking of that."

"I have an active mind. I think of a lot of things. So has Emily been able to help you yet?"

"I don't think that I'm a particularly easy client for her. But she is keeping me busy, that's for sure. I'm an innkeeper now."

"So can I ask you a question?"

"You know you can."

"What's it like being old?"

She always kept the conversations interesting, but he didn't seem bothered. As if he had been expecting her question.

"It's different."

"That's not the answer I expected to hear."

"Nor the one I expected to give. I had an incredible career here doing what I loved. Being with the woman that I loved. I couldn't have asked for anything more. Except that I can't shake this thinking about death. Not just mine, but for all of us. Plus people I don't really even know. Which creeps up on me more and more with each passing year. Got any great ideas how to nix that?"

"Give me a few days. I've been known to be full of surprises."

"Why doesn't that shock me?"

"On a more serious note."

"Death isn't serious enough for you?"

"Not yet. You are doing a good thing for Mana, Saint Henry."

"He's a special young man. I'm enjoying having him around."

"Are you just saying that?"

"No. I'm not that polite."

"It's more work that you thought it would be, isn't it?"

"I make my list every night, and then by nine o'clock the next morning I'm anxious about how I'm going to get everything done. I'm supposed to be too old for this. You help a great deal by being here."

"Don't worry, I'm not going any place."

"Why is that? You are a college student. You have your own life."

"College is a step along the way. It's not nirvana."

"I don't think I've ever met a freshman with that attitude. Ever since I arrived on campus, all those years ago, they have mostly been trying to balance getting good grades, getting drunk, and getting laid."

"Being a freshman is a label. I don't like labels."

He thought more about how she would die, fearing it would be too young and tragic. Maybe struck by a car while campaigning to be re-elected to her second term in Congress, as a Democrat from the state of New Jersey. Or Pennsylvania. In her green high-top sneakers, no doubt.

31

Not Everyone Is Good At Relationships

Relationships are hard, and in the world of college students, they can get compressed into short time periods and small spaces. Jelly and Seth had only known each other now for five months, and their relationship was increasingly complicated. In part because they were, too. First, he had liked her romantically. Then there was the sex thing. She afterward had liked him platonically and felt sorry for him. Now she was trying to hate him.

For his part, Seth was as mixed up as he ever had been. His track record with girls was not one that anyone would hold up as a positive example. He hadn't been forthright when Doctor Metcalf had asked him about his previous girlfriends. Every single one had dumped him. Some in a sweet way, some ran as fast as they could and had their brothers or fathers ready with loaded shotguns, if needed. He never did anything physical or violent, but the reality was that some of them feared that he would. Maybe it had to do with his size or maybe it didn't. Either way, it didn't reflect well on him.

The spring of his junior year, he dated the most attractive girl in his high school. She was a cheerleader and the homecoming queen, while he was one of the smarter boys and, no doubt, the best athlete. Seth never wanted to be apart from her. It was unclear why he so often felt this way with the girls he dated, he just did. It's like they made him a more settled, more confident person. He wanted to be one and the same with this girlfriend, more than any girl he had dated up till then. People in rural Iowa tended to marry young, and he assumed from early in the relationship they would get married. She didn't. Both of their families were ardent Methodists, and theirs was an unsullied relationship. He had thought he was being a good person. He had kept his fly zipped, as difficult as that might have been for him, and she had never pulled her dress up over her head. He didn't know if that's why she dumped him or not, which was a part of his confusion after she let go of him for a college guy. And that caused him to crack up in time for final exams.

He dropped out of high school for a year, worked on the family ranch, worked out to become stronger and faster, and escaped by reading as many mysteries or detective books as his could get his hands on. He knew Grisham better than Grisham knew himself. He saw a therapist in a bigger town about thirty miles away every week. While his family was incredibly supportive, the therapist always kept asking him how he was feeling and not much else. It was waste of time. When he returned for his final year, it seemed he had already dated and been dumped by pretty much every girl in their little school. So instead he focused on being an athlete and a student, and seeing where that would take him. Which turned out to be New Jersey. When he met Jelly the summer after graduation, many of the old hopes came back. He was ready to spend his life with her after the first few weeks. The fact that she connected with his family so well only further cemented those feelings.

It wasn't clear to him if she was going to show for their morning breakfasts ever again. She hadn't made an appearance since she disrupted his team's film session. That may not have been strong enough a word. And although the coach never said anything after she was escorted from the team room, the players who had been at the party, which was most of them, were no doubt shaken. Mostly afraid of having their young lives disrupted, wanting to keep their stupidity unnoticed on their road to Wall Street or Palo Alto or wherever else paid obscene salaries.

He continued to arrive early each morning to the dining hall, just in case. One morning, just in case happened. She returned, arriving earlier than he did, and seeming to know that he would be there whether she was or not. It was clear from the outset that this wasn't going to be the warm and fuzzy conversation he would have had hoped if he knew she was coming.

He didn't even bother to get food, as most likely it would end up coming right back up soon after their little summit ended. When he was anxious, his stomach had a mind of its own. She was having a cup of tea when he sat down empty handed at the table with her. There were no pleasantries. No 'Hi, how have you been?' or 'How is your week going?' Jelly jumped right into it, and it was only ten minutes of seven.

"You know who beat up Mana, don't you?"

That's a tough way to begin a discussion with someone you had already thought about spending the rest of your life with. She wore a typical indescribable Jelly outfit, completed by a new pair of purple high-top Converse sneakers. He wore jeans and a XXXL sweatshirt.

"Yes."

"Who was it?"

"I can't tell you that, Jelly."

"Why not?"

"I don't squeal."

"Did you participate?"

"You know I wouldn't do something like that."

"Do I, Seth?"

"Yes."

"And you were hammered like the rest of them?"

"Yes."

"Because that's what you have succumbed to now to be one of the boys?"

"I guess."

"But you know who did it."

"Yes."

"Mana is a friend of mine, Seth."

"I didn't know that."

"Did you even know his name is Mana?"

"No."

"That he is a senior here on a full scholarship?"

"No."

"Did you think to ask?"

"No."

"Mana is a person, you know! He doesn't have anything here besides his scholarship! No parents to go see. No relatives. No nothing. He spends all the holidays on campus. And the money he makes as a security guard he sends home to his parents in Nepal, where they raise goats on a mountainside."

"I didn't know that either."

"And he doesn't know why he was beaten up. He was just doing his job. And now he is scared shitless."

"I'm sorry."

"So then do something about it."

"I can't tell on my teammates."

For the first time, he stopped looking at her, training his eyes instead on the floor. A habit that began with Doctor Metcalf when he wasn't proud of his contributions to a conversation.

"You don't have any friends here, Seth! You're on an island! I'm on as island! Mana is on an island! We're not these spoiled, self-absorbed assholes. Nobody gives a flying fuck about you, except that you are making all of them look good on the football field. It will give them something to brag about for the rest of their lives, even though they didn't have anything to do with it. And they will never look you up again because you won't be able to help them in their new rich boy careers. You don't owe them anything!"

"Jelly, you told me to get involved with the team and focus on football, so that I could have the option of playing professionally if I wanted. You told me that they had to know they could count on me. That if I was a bad teammate, word would get out to the people in the pros who make these decisions."

"That doesn't mean you have to lie like our fucking president to protect yourself!"

"I didn't lie."

"What's the difference? You didn't tell the truth. Mana is hurt. And he's frightened this is going to happen to him again. You can fix that."

"I wish I could."

"Is something going to happen to him again?"

"I don't know."

Jelly's anger was evident. She took a few minutes to glare at him, but Seth never looked up. He didn't want to see those eyes as it would take too long to forget them.

"How could I have ever been interested in you?"

"Please don't say that."

"You're a pig! And I'm not done trying to pin down who did this. I'm certainly smarter than your coach. And I'm smarter than the police. It better not have been you!"

She got up and left. And now he was scared, too. For many reasons.

32

The Thing About Parents

When a person has contemplated leaving this planet by her own means, it's clear she needs help. And it was no secret that's what Elizabeth had been envisioning. It was going to take a long time, but Emily had now signed up for this. Which was stupid. But she had done stupid before. The girl continued to talk to her, and that was a positive.

Still, Emily held her breath as the end of each workday approached, praying that Elizabeth would choose to come to see her rather than the alternative she likely had been considering. There was never an appointment or any kind of previous agreement. It was just sort of understood. And Emily would be uneasy, looking at the clock and peering out the window, until hearing the polite knock on her door sometime after five and until the girl settled into the same tired armchair. Then Emily felt relieved for one more day.

Throughout the whole process, Emily was getting a better sense of why her ex did what he did, and had no remorse about leaving her, the girls, and their history behind. As we know, she needed this for herself. Even if it was selfish, she, too, needed to heal. And this didn't even address the fiasco with Monk, from which she also needed to mend. She was still stuck on the conclusion that her ex didn't like getting older and being forgotten. Being irrelevant. Not that any of us do. Didn't she remember him telling her years ago, one of his quirky anecdotes, about a football player called Mr. Irrelevant who, contrary to his moniker, got all sorts of recognition for being the last one chosen in each year's NFL draft of college players? Her ex's career had plateaued, his life had plateaued, and that's why he needed someone who would idolize him. Maybe the way Emily once did. The young girl, the new girlfriend, and the one after that. She's not sure it mattered who they were or how old they were, so long as he had someone who would make him and his ego relevant again. Akin to the accolades that Mr. Irrelevant got. Emily, Abbey, and Jessie didn't do that for him anymore, so all were jettisoned. Somehow thoughts like this would make her feel better for a day or two. It made the event easier to stomach. Nonetheless, nine months later, and she still thought about him every day, meaning that she wasn't making any more progress escaping his influence than Elizabeth was. The man had, in too many ways, damaged each of them.

"I guess it's that time of the year. It's getting dark out earlier now," Emily started. The lights in the parking lot beyond her window would now turn on shortly after Elizabeth arrived. By the time Emily finished here and walked to her tired little car to head to Hotel Henry, it would be completely dark.

She now sat behind the desk again to create the atmosphere of a more professional session. Even if only for her own peace of mind. To convince herself that she wasn't stretching her role as therapist beyond where it was meant to go. Which she knew she was.

"I kind of like it."

"Why is that, Elizabeth?"

"It's easier to be invisible."

"You like being invisible?"

"I love being invisible."

"So let's talk. Tell me, how are things on the home front?"

As was now her habit, she placed the box of tissues on her desk where Elizabeth could reach them. Thus far the girl's eyes were dry. Thus far.

"Not super. Over the weekend, I decided to sit my parents down and tell my father about my mother's flings. It been long overdue getting this out in the open. They need to begin to understand each other again, and maybe it might also help them to recognize why I did what I did. I told him everything I knew with her sitting right there. Honest and straightforward."

"Wow, Elizabeth. That takes some guts."

"It took something. I'm not exactly sure what. But I felt amazingly calm when I was talking to them. Selfishly, I may have been happy to have the spotlight on someone else in the family for a few minutes. It's the invisible thing."

"So how'd it go?"

"Probably like you might expect. He freaked. She freaked. They basically forgot that I was even there. But I guess it has at least changed the fake dynamic we have been living under. My mother now is pissed at me for telling him. My father is pissed at her and me for not telling him. Our house is a frigid place right now, yet I don't feel bad about opening up the can of worms. My mother never thought about how what she was doing would impact our family. I think she figured she could keep going on having her little affairs with the painters and electricians and lawn guys forever. That's who she fools around with. I told the truth, which makes me feel okay about myself."

"Not to repeat myself, that must have been a very hard thing to do."

"It was, and it wasn't. My mother was wrong to mess with our family. I know that from my own idiocy and what I did to you. There are only three of us. It was time to stop pretending."

"How's your father taking it?"

"He's a mess. You should know better than anyone. He's hurt, and he's mad. He has always been a tough guy, kind of like a military guy, even though he never was one. In his mind, there is a right way to do things, and what my mother has been doing for a long time is so far from that. And he never saw it coming. Until that moment, he may have thought they were in love. Now I suspect he doesn't know what to think. He may need to change his view about therapists and get some help."

She grinned awkwardly.

"That would be an interesting twist. But you are right, that is familiar territory. And it won't be easy for him."

"I think he kind of blames me for this, too, even though he knows deep down it's not my fault. But it's hard to have much of a conversation right now with either of my parents."

The tears finally started to flow down Elizabeth's cheeks, and she grabbed a couple of tissues.

"It also reminded me that I'm forever sorry for what I did to you," the girl continued. "I doubt you can ever forgive me."

"I forgave you a long time ago, Elizabeth. We are past that. You are proving to be a truly good person who I care for very much. So wipe those tears away, and tell me what's the next step with your family?"

"I think it's time for me to move out for a while."

"Not a comfortable place to be, huh?"

"Well, as I said, my father is steamed. He's moving out right away to some little furnished one bedroom apartment in Philly that he could get on short notice. There wouldn't be any space for me there. My mother, on the other hand, has taken to calling me anything but Elizabeth. 'Hey, it's the little slut' or 'How's the tramp today?' She takes none of the blame for her affairs. In her mind, it's somehow all my doing. So when I fire up something like 'right back at ya, Mom' she usually loses it."

"That doesn't sound healthy."

"I have no doubt it isn't."

"So where would you move to?"

"That, of course, is the question. I'm not really on anybody's invite list these days."

It didn't take a rocket scientist to figure out what Emily was already thinking. Henry didn't know he signed up for this.

33

What To Do About The Wins

There is an old adage that Vince Lombardi coined for his players when they scored a touchdown. *When you get into the end zone, act like you've been there before.* Since Lombardi's time coaching in the 1950's and 60's, his line has been borrowed and bastardized for grand slam home runs, great golf shots, a half court hoop to win a basketball game, and many other competitive athletic accomplishments. And, finally, to college football teams that win more games than they were ever expected to win. Most athletes are familiar with the line.

Act like you've been there before.

The following Saturday, the football team won again. Winning was not familiar for this team and this program. The response by the players was to throw an even bigger party in the same frat house with more kegs than the last one. The team was feeling it, and they weren't thinking Lombardi-like thoughts. This was all new to them. Red plastic beer cups were filled and later spilled. People who were not yet old enough to legally drink passed out on random couches. The cannabis store did quite a bit more business than usual that night, much of which found its way to the frat house. Other people, who didn't know each other when the party began, were becoming more familiar than they had planned. Something that could be written about in an email chain in another twenty years.

It's not known if anyone was permanently damaged at this party. A rape, an attack, the beginning of a drinking or drug dependency, unwanted and unwarranted bullying that made someone begin to have body image issues. Much of that would not be discovered for a while.

Seth was a big part of the win again. He was not just good, he was dominant -- both on offense and defense, which was more than unusual in today's specialized football world. He is enormous and agile and has a ferocity that all coaches love. He put the offense on his big back, and they ran behind him. Opening holes in the other team's defense, leaving one body after another writhing in the dirt. When he was playing defense, he was simply couldn't be blocked, with the other side most often assigning three people to try. Even if they could slow him down, it left a couple of his teammates untouched to make the play. The local press that had started to cover his extraordinary performances each week had now expanded to *The New York Times*, which wrote a lead article about Seth and his family. This big, fast, incredibly athletic young man carrying a team not known for football. The big, fast, incredibly athletic young man who, they repeatedly made the point, was getting a privileged education.

He stopped dreaming of the theatre, mostly because he had too many other things on his mind, but he still kept coming to see Emily. His star was growing, but he remained a less than happy star. He felt like a broken person that needed to be recreated, without intending the pun, in a big way.

"I saw the story of you in *The New York Times* on Sunday. That was impressive, Seth. And I loved the picture with your parents. They must have been so excited."

"Yeah. Parents like that shit."

"And you?"

"It doesn't mean anything."

"Really? Most college athletes would be thrilled with that kind of recognition. It likely means you are moving closer to getting drafted to play in the NFL. If that's what you want to do."

"That's a long way off."

"It will be here sooner than you think. You seemed to be limping when you walked in. Did you get hurt in the game?"

"I think I told you before about how I can be the bullseye for other teams. They throw a bunch of people at me on every play. I always come away beat up after a game. Everything pretty much hurts afterwards. Remember how I told you that I keep a big bottle of ibuprofen next to my bed?"

He saw Emily wince.

"Football is a brutal game," she responded.

"Sometimes I feel like I'm selling my soul to the devil. I might get a big contract and get rich, but I also may not be able to walk when I'm fifty. Not to mention the risk of all the brain damage they're finding now."

"You think about this?"

"I try to put it out of my mind before each game. You kind of have to. But then I wake up in so much pain on Sunday morning and sometimes wonder what the hell I'm doing."

"Is that why you started drinking?"

"There are a lot of reasons I started drinking."

"Are you ever going to share those reasons with me?"

"Maybe someday. I have other things on my mind right now."

"Like what if I may ask?"

The newspapers were writing about an image projected by a vicious game, an ambitious coach, and probably even a sports communication director at the university who made a living making things sound better than they really were. The image they created was not him.

"You know what the best part of game day is, Doc?"

"You're going to switch the subject?"

"I think so."

"Okay, so tell me what the best part of game day is."

"It's when the game is over, and everybody has left the stadium. The team is going nuts in the locker room, all the fans are back to their tailgates in the parking lot, and I just sit in the bleachers by myself and watch a few guys who are putting away the equipment that was on the field and cleaning up the crap that people left in the stands. I should go help them, because they are all more than twice my age, but I am too exhausted to move. So I just watch. They all seem perfectly content."

"And you wonder why you can't feel like that?"

"Am I that obvious?"

"I'm getting to know you, Seth."

"Can I change the subject again?"

"You are jumping around today."

"Like I said, I have a lot on my mind."

"Then fire away."

For a college freshman who was having a season about which athletes dream, he was not happy. He was in a funk that began with Jelly, and while that was still a significant issue, there was more that was bothering him.

"Can I ask how Mana is?"

"You can. But why are you interested, Seth? You don't know him."

"But Jelly does, and you do, and he was hurt in a way that he shouldn't have been."

"How do you know that?"

"Word gets around."

"Is that really how you know?"

Seth was silent.

"Were you there at the party, Seth?" Emily asked.

He continued not to say anything.

Emily put her pen down and pushed her omnipresent yellow pad away. Her usually stoic therapist face became even more serious, if that was possible.

"Seth, Mana was hurt badly. He will have physical scars that forever remind him of what happened. Remember, he didn't do anything except his job. He will also likely have permanent psychological scars. For a kid who trekked the Himalayas, who worked two night jobs so he could support his parents while he was here, he is now afraid of the dark. This was the strongest, most courageous student I have ever seen on campus and whoever did this took that all away in ten minutes of recklessness. It was no different that someone being raped.

"I'm guessing," she continued, "that you can make a difference if you decide that you want to."

He looked at her directly. He knew that his eyes were full of something she hadn't seen from him. Some of it was sadness. Some of it was fear. Some of it was empty. Then he rose from his chair and limped out of her office.

The university police were making no progress. A new set of detectives came to see Mana at Hotel Henry. They mostly asked him the same questions that the other detectives had asked. His answers were no different and his entire body, as it did before, was shaking during the questioning. They were going to go back to interview the same people once more, with a more threatening approach, obviously with the hope of scaring a few of them to open up. Seth would be on their list this time. Mana believed in the mantra of letting sleeping dogs lie. He would have been happiest if it all simply went away. He couldn't take another beating.

But no one thought about Mana. The response to the new detectives by all the people who had been at the party – the football players, the other athletes, and even the three girls who Mana was supposed to transport – was to get lawyers. The ones who attacked Mana were afraid of being arrested for what they did. The ones who protected the attackers were afraid of being caught lying to the police. The three girls were worried about getting punished for underage drinking that could get them points on their records or even suspended from the university. They all preferred to hide for a while longer.

34

The Fallout

We haven't heard from Monk in a while. Hopefully you haven't forgotten about him. Emily certainly hasn't. He is still central to this story, although, as mentioned earlier, you are likely to both love him and hate him by the time our story is complete. Which makes for an interesting role.

Monk didn't leave Emily for another woman. Nor did he leave her because he had grown tired of her. It was just the opposite. He left her because he recognized that he couldn't be the person she needed him to be. The person she deserved. That's a hard thing to convince yourself. That you're not good enough for the person you are dating, or trying to date, or however you might have defined their relationship.

The morning after the infamous Family Weekend game, he called his parents to ask to borrow money for rehab, not something that made him proud at thirty-nine years old, with a PhD and a litany of research articles that had been published by scholarly journals. Now back begging his parents for handouts. Then he left Emily's house without saying goodbye. He was a mess and didn't know what to say, after hurting a woman who had been hurt enough. This is not where his life should have been by this point.

Ultimately, Monk had to deal with many issues that he knew existed somewhere within him but had been unwilling to admit to their existence. He had a deep-rooted desire to be admired. An arrogance that was hardly supported by an entire lack of self-confidence, a general fear of seemingly powerful men, an even greater fear of attractive women, an inability to let anyone witness his true feelings, a perpetual use of humor to keep his guilt and his feelings hidden, and too often he used alcohol as a crutch. Even though he was well trained in psychotherapy and would know what to expect, they didn't let him duck anything in rehab. Whenever he started feeling pretty good about coming to grips with any one of his many issues, each painful in and of itself, they raised the next of his shortcomings which served to establish a new low for him. A few times he blew up because he didn't think that they were appreciating him for who he was. A mistake on his part, as he really wasn't anybody anymore. But he no longer had alcohol to fall back on, so temper tantrums were all he had.

The original plan was to stay two weeks, though he ended up extending his stay to twice that, having become petrified of falling back to his old ways. Ways that, it turns out, had been haunting him for a long time. His parents had been more than generous. The clinic was no shit hole. It was a high-class place, and he seemed the only pauper there. He had learned via his own inquiry that the total bill was forty-five thousand dollars, more than fifteen hundred bucks a day. His parents, who were comfortable but, as academics, not overly comfortable, paid the ticket without saying a thing. Maybe it is true that parents never stop being parents.

Even if she had wanted to, about which he had his doubts, Emily wouldn't have been allowed to come see him while he was in rehab. The reality was that even if she could have, neither of them needed the added pressure of their undefined relationship.

One of the things that is so discouraging about rehab is the feeling that you are not doing anything constructive for the world, instead mostly wallowing in self-pity first and then trying to get your act together. Focusing twenty-four-seven on yourself can be exhausting. Even someone who was prone to being on the self-important side of the spectrum like he was. There is nothing new to stimulate your mind. Only old, tired shit that keeps getting regurgitated. He was gaining a newfound sympathy for his clients who couldn't get out of their own way. It wasn't all that easy.

After searching for something to distract his mind in his spare time, time which up to now had primarily focused on thinking about Emily, he remembered that she had not that long ago told him of the guilt from prolonged separation that was encircling a young client of hers. A kid who had restarted his life in this country, leaving behind an entire family in a poor village in Nepal. Monk had been inspired by the story and decided he would try to find a way to connect with the village. It might keep his mind active a couple of hours a day on something besides himself. He could learn about the country, of which he knew less than little, and he thought that he could possibly even do something good for the boy. It might even ease a reconnection with Emily if he could help find a way for Mana – it had taken some effort with his now overly crowded mind to remember the name – to re-engage with his family. So in between sessions with therapists, and suffering through their many assignments, it became his hobby. He began to look forward to these couple of hours each night -- hours that too often he would have previously spent with a drink in his hand – that could be devoted to his little project. Even though he'd never even met the kid.

He spent his time discovering everything online he could about both Nepal and about Mana. Nepal, it turns out, was an amazing country, engulfed by the Himalayas and eight of the world's ten tallest mountains, and stuck between India and Tibet. The flood of new information about something of which he knew little made his mind feel fresh and alive again for those short strokes of time. Learning about Mana's village was a more difficult puzzle. Mana did have a Facebook page that was sparse, but not empty, and included recent comical pictures of a recovery from some sort of bad accident, pictures obviously taken by someone that wasn't him. There were also photos of trekkers from a few years ago, some wearing shirts that carried logos of the companies that had booked the trips for them. Companies that he then reached out to. He learned from Mana's page that he was a member of a club at the university for students from developing countries, which also had a website that he scrolled. A website which shared some details of the members' backgrounds. And Mana had created a LinkedIn site which was surprisingly professional. Eventually, Monk found pictures of Mana as a seemingly content high school student, and so he sent a message to the high school. Each source he perused provided bits of information that added to the young man's story. As he heard back from the trekking companies, he began to get a feel for that world. And while he had done some dumb things in his life, Monk was hardly dumb. Eventually, he located where Mana's family lived. There apparently wasn't much to the village, and it didn't have a website. But he figured out who in the area might speak English, and, for his own amusement, what the going rate for a healthy adult goat was. The answer being, not much.

While there were many false starts, he kept at it because it was a research project that needed a conclusion. It had him feeling like he felt back in those days when he was doing important research and publishing the results. This, though quite different, was possibly important, and he felt a familiar joy each time it got a step closer. It was a feeling that he hadn't forgotten. He was able to reach by email a woman who until a year ago taught in Mana's village and who spoke – or, in this case, wrote – English. She now worked at a larger school in a town a few hours away. Monk explained to her who he was and the concern for Mana. She, in turn, wrote back a surprisingly lengthy missive that she had known Mana's parents and had taught his younger brother at their village school. She relayed to Monk that there was a reason no one had written to Mana in many months. It turns out that his whole family, including his brother, had been killed several months ago, along with much of their village, in a devastating mudslide during the monsoon season. She said it was very tragic and very sad. The village is basically no more, and the survivors have been forced to relocate to lower lands to restart their lives. Not what Monk had expected to find.

No doubt the news would be devastating to Mana. One more hurdle for a kid trying to take advantage of a gift the world has offered him. It was something Monk needed to communicate to Emily, whether she had decided to hate him or not. Kid or adult, everyone deserves to know where his or her family is. And whether they are alive. So he wrote her a note. In truth, he wrote her many notes, all of which, until this one, ended up in the trash.

Hi Em,

I am so incredibly sorry for my actions at the football game and the weeks since. I was embarrassed to have so easily fallen into my old habits that I couldn't bear approaching you. The next day I checked myself into a rehab facility in Connecticut (my parents have more than generously footed the bill) and have been here ever since.

There has been a good deal of time to think while here about who I am and what I have done. Sometimes, though, your mind needs a break from yourself. One of the things I have been thinking about, besides you, is your client, Mana. You told me his inspirational story, which I have not forgotten. I know that he was struggling with his responsibilities to his family, made more difficult because he hadn't heard from them in some time. So I decided to take a crack at it. Again, full disclosure. I really needed something to focus on here that wasn't me. It was good to have a little break. I ultimately was able to find a woman who had taught in Mana's village, including teaching Mana's younger brother. Unfortunately, it's not a great story. Mana's entire family, as well as much of the village, was killed in a mudslide during this past summer's rainstorms. He no longer has a family to go back to. Or even a village.

It is sad information, and I don't know exactly why I decided to work on it. Maybe I felt I needed to do something good for once. Perhaps it was therapeutic. More than likely, I wanted to find a way to be helpful to you.

I couldn't reach out to you until I knew that I was coming to grips with my demons and, ultimately, going to be okay. Which I think I am, but I won't make promises anymore that I am not a hundred percent sure I can keep.

As I hope you know, I have grown incredibly fond of you. And I'm incredibly ashamed for not being a better friend, boyfriend, partner, or whatever you might have hoped I would be. I know I don't want to give up on us, but I certainly would understand if you did.

I do love you.

Monk

The question now was how she would feel upon getting a letter like this from him. Certainly, it filled a hole in the story. She now knew what he did. He also made it clear his feelings for her. That's what saying 'I do love you' in a letter does to a relationship. This was the first time in his life that he'd ever said this to anybody. He'd recognized during rehab that what he had put her through wasn't fair. He knew it wasn't going to be easy for her to figure out whether to take him back or not. Still, he felt that he was ready to face her. Although a drunk can never be certain.

And then he dropped the Mana bomb. On one hand, she may have appreciated all his effort, because she would know it wouldn't have been easy to find Mana's family. On the other hand, she might think he was overstepping his bounds. It would also, no doubt, make her incredibly sad, as it was clear she truly had grown to care for Mana more than she did most of her clients.

Why is it life never seems to get any easier?

35

The Power Of The Press

When people on campus had nothing else to do, when they were waiting in line at the dining hall, or for class to start, or outside a dean's office, they frequently took to reading the school newspaper. Whether on their phone or via the traditional paper copy. At a minimum, there was usually always a spare paper copy in pretty much every campus bathroom stall, the one place where all readers were on equal footing. Administrators, professors, coaches, students, tech support, the cleaning crews all taking care of business and catching up on the school news. The newspaper was hardly *The Washington Post*, but it wasn't bad. It was run by a crew of journalistic hopefuls who made up for their lack of resources and experience with admirable effort and more than their fair share of promising talent. In addition to delivering basic campus news, it was a venue to harangue the administration with alternate views on pretty much everything from campus diversity to socially responsible investing to grade inflation to paying the dining hall staff a livable wage. It also provided a platform for a new columnist who had something to say.

THOUGHTS OF A COLLEGE KID
by Angela Seideman
October 24, 2019

So far this year there have been 17 reported attacks on university students. Many, but not all, have been sexual attacks. After years of rising, the number of assaults has plateaued recently, mostly, it seems, the result of initiatives put in place by the college administration. Three Saturday nights ago, there was a horrific incident outside one of our esteemed jock fraternity houses. A student who was working for security as a Walk Safe guide was attacked. Walk Safe, for those who have never taken advantage of it, is a free service managed by the college's security department that is accessible to any member of the university community between 10PM and 2AM, every night of the week. It makes a walking companion available for those who might be skittish about a late-night jaunt across our enormous campus. I use it. Walk Safe is a great idea. The service is obviously provided to dissuade such attacks as occurred on that Saturday evening.

Security had been called at 11:17PM from a cell phone to request safeguarding for three women who wanted to head back to their dorms from a keg party, and it subsequently dispatched Mana Shrestha to the frat house. Mana is a senior and has been working the weekend Walk Safe shifts since the school year began. At 11:57, campus police received a 911 call from Mana's security phone asking for help, indicating that he had been assaulted and needed aid. Paramedics were ultimately dispatched to treat Mana, who was then taken to a city hospital where he has, if you can believe it, been treated for two swollen black eyes, a broken nose, and several large lacerations that required some intricate suturing. He had surgery on his leg, shattered in two places, two days later.

The university police began an investigation the next afternoon, beginning at the fraternity house, but to date have not been able to find anyone willing to share their knowledge of the attack.

So let's look at what really happened. Mana did nothing to provoke the wrath of the frat boys beyond responding to a call to walk three female students home. Obviously, some people at the frat party had other ideas for the women, and Mana was going to get in the way of that. According to records, the fraternity has 128 members, 49% of whom play football. Only 33 of the members are old enough to drink legally, but five beer kegs had been delivered to the dorm early that evening. The football team had won their first home game of the year. It is no mystery as to what was going on.

Why is it that football wins and out of control beer parties are seemingly synonymous? Have you ever been to a five keg blowout after a golf team victory? How about cross country or track? Tennis? Volleyball? Swimming? There are some amazing athletes on those teams, and they traditionally have far more success than our football team has had in recent decades. Far, far more success.

The football team gets together for film sessions every Sunday at noon after a game. I didn't know that until I began pursuing this story. The five kegs were returned to the liquor store completely empty on Sunday. I know because I went and asked. Five finished kegs means that some of the players were likely badly hungover for that film session. It doesn't take a rocket scientist to figure that out. Are the coaches that stupid not to recognize it? Of course not.

I dropped in on the film session to see Coach Quigley, two days before I officially began as a columnist for this newspaper. He said that he had no idea what I was talking about and had me escorted out by several of his assistant coaches. (I'm not very big and hardly the violent type, so one person could have handled it just fine.) Nine days later, I again went to visit Coach, where this time he was alone in his office. After he cursed at me using what seems to be his favorite unsavory word, he told me to leave.

Coach Quigley is a Professor of Athletics at the school. How would we feel if an English professor – say Professor Lipsack or Professor Delahunty – had a blowout keg party for his or her students and someone was attacked and badly injured. Do you think there would be a campus outcry? Do you think that the campus police would be more diligent in their investigation? Do you think that the university administration would get involved? Do you think pleading ignorance would be permitted? Yeah, me too.

More to come...

She would be a little more familiar to people on campus from now on.

36

The Stress Of Academics

In the entire history of elite colleges, academic stress is the most frequent reason that students visit therapists. Which may not be a great tribute to the best of the best of our higher education system, or to the families who send their kids to these schools teeming with highly competitive kids. And parents. Emily guessed that Marionette would be a regular during her four years on campus, with the caveat that she would sample different therapists during her stay to find the one who most often told her what she wanted to hear. Many of these kids think that they know more than their therapist, which makes you wonder why they go to see one in the first place. It's certainly not because it's a status symbol.

"Marionette, it's nice to see you again. How's the new name working out?"

"I think I like it and am going to keep it. For the foreseeable future anyway."

"Well, that's interesting."

"I think so."

"You've missed your last couple of appointments. Is everything okay?"

"I'm more stressed than ever, Doctor Metcalf. Being valedictorian is going to be almost impossible."

She still reminded Emily of a puppet. Flopping around, easy to talk to, no complicated barriers to climb over, but hard to connect with. Sort of a puppet who was quite comfortable being a puppet and nothing more, so long as she aced all her courses.

"This isn't high school, Marionette. There are two thousand students in your class. The odds aren't in anyone's favor."

"Hey, I came here for help. Not for you to discourage me."

"That's not my intention. I just find it helpful to talk about what's realistic. But what do you say we start by talking about your assignment from your initial visit? Then we'll take it from there. Sound good?"

"Okay."

"So tell me, what will you do with your month off during the long holiday break? Did you have the chance to think about that?"

"That was a good question."

"Sometimes I get lucky."

When she felt clients were wasting her time, Emily could be a wise ass. It didn't happen often, but when it did, she had to strain to keep a straight face. As she was now. Caucusing with Pinocchio.

"It was surprisingly productive to consider. I came up with what I think is a good approach. I figured out that I can use the time to get a head start on second semester classes. You know, establish a schedule where I can do some of the reading and research each day. I checked it out. The second semester course syllabus will be available for each of my classes by the start of break. If I'm efficient, I might even be able to get the whole semester's reading done for my courses before we come back to campus at the end of January. That way I should be ahead of the other kids when classes start up again. Unless somebody else figures this out and does the same thing."

"Huh. I didn't even know what a syllabus was when I got here as a student."

Not even a tiny smirk from Pinocchio.

"I will admit, Marionette," Emily continued, "that isn't what I was thinking. You are an amazingly competitive person. How do you relax?"

"From what?"

"All that stress from studying that you said you had."

"I didn't say that! You are missing the point! The stress isn't from the studying, it's from not getting the grades I need!"

"Take a deep breath, young lady. You haven't gotten any grades yet."

Pinocchio tried her best to hold back, but she wanted to get her retort out before it got away.

"I got my first grade this week."

"And?"

"I got a hundred on a Political Science problem set."

"Well's that's a nice start. So why are you more stressed than ever?"

"Too many other kids in the class got the same grade."

"You compare grades?"

"Of course."

"With people you don't know."

"Have to understand the competition. They want to know as much as I do."

"Huh."

"The bad part is that there isn't any extra credit that I can do."

"There usually isn't in college."

"Well that stinks."

"Marionette, let me tell you a story." She almost called her Pinocchio by mistake. That wouldn't have been good. "The valedictorian in my class was a theatre major. She had a lead role in two plays each year she was here. Those counted as classes for her. She was a very talented actor and never got anything but an 'A.' A perfect report card. She has never, though, worked in the theatre a day in her life since college, as she was never able land a role in any kind of professional show."

"That doesn't sound right. Valedictorians should have the most opportunities."

"You see, that's not the way it works. She had no social skills when she left here. She couldn't carry on a normal conversation about anything. Nobody wanted to work with her."

"Why are you telling me this, Doctor Metcalf?"

"Have you made any friends on campus yet?"

"That will come. I need to get on top of my studies first."

"What if you approached it the other way around? Worked on making a few friends while it's still early in the semester, and then you can focus on the heavy duty studying in a few weeks. I think most of the kids here do that. Grades are soon forgotten. Friends can last for life."

"I couldn't do that."

"Why not? Aren't you interested in having friends?"

"I don't want to be like most of the kids here. I want to be better."

"Have you ever had a best friend?"

"No. To be honest, I've never even thought that much about it. I have my father, and he has me. That's all we have ever needed. I'm more interested in getting perfect grades. I mostly just talk to the teachers. And, of course, to him."

"Would you want a best friend?"

"I'm not sure. I wouldn't know where to find one, and it might take up a lot of time that I don't have to spare."

Okay, Marionette really needed to be pulled back to the real world. How did she get to be so uncompromisingly driven? Not from her father, the plumber. So where does this come from if he is the only person in her life?

"Were there others in your high school class who were as focused on being valedictorian as you were?"

"There were only a hundred and eleven kids in the class. A couple of other kids – one girl who I'd gone to elementary school with and one Chinese boy – were aiming for it. But by the end of junior year, everyone knew that I was going to be the one who earned it."

"And how did that make you feel?"

"Great. It's what I wanted."

"Did you ever go to the school dances? Or to a party?"

"If you are trying to make me feel bad, it's not going to work. As I said, I got what I wanted. I now just have to figure out how I'm going to do the same thing in this environment."

"Have you ever thought about taking a year off and doing something totally different? Something where there are no grades?"

"Like what?"

"I don't know. Teaching English to people who don't speak the language. Tutoring kids who are struggling in school. Traveling across the country. Taking a cooking class."

"Do you think this conversation is really helping me?"

"I was hoping it would. You seem to lead a very narrow life. The university has much to offer that you might enjoy. It can help to round out a person. So they don't end up like the woman I told you about in my class. Let me ask you another question. Have you ever been to a school play?"

"Only when it was required by the course."

"There is a dress rehearsal next Thursday night on campus for one of the fall plays that I was thinking of going to. Want to go with me?"

"On a Thursday night?"

"I know that going with your therapist may not be your favorite thing, but it might help to broaden your horizon."

"You don't get 'A's' for broadening your horizon. You get them for writing great research papers and doing well on exams."

"You know, Marionette, I was valedictorian of my high school class."

It was as if all the air went out of Pinocchio when she heard this.

37

Roommates

Did you ever think at the beginning of this story that Mana and Elizabeth would be roommates? In fact, actually sharing the same bedroom? The room where Henry's wife died? They each needed a place to recover, Henry needed something else in his life, and he only had a two bedroom house. Hence their new status. Jelly, when she stayed over, now slept on the other side of Henry's king-sized bed, what had been his wife's side. Jelly didn't do couches with leftover thin blankets in rooms where you could hear the traffic from the street. Henry found the whole set up increasingly hilarious but was sure to remind everyone that she went to bed after he was already asleep and that he wore a full set of pajamas. And that he slept like a rock.

The two of them, Mana and Elizabeth, would spend many awake hours in the house alone and together. Mana because his body, and his mind, were still recovering, so he was limited in what he could do. His professors, having heard of his misfortune, videoed their lectures for him, which he now streamed on the days he felt up to it. Elizabeth, on the other hand, only worked until noon at Starbuck's and had nothing else to occupy her time. Her former friends were all in college, her parents were fighting bitterly and had forgotten about her for the time being, and so Mana became her sidekick for better or for worse.

"So what's your deal?"

Elizabeth began what would become a daily stream of dialogue on her very first afternoon when it was just Mana and her in Jenny's Room. Because it was clear to anyone who met him that he wasn't going to be the one to initiate conversation with a stranger. Each was sitting atop pink flowered bed covers with their laptops open and buds in their ears, and each looking like hell. It didn't take her too long to realize that being with Mana would be an escape where she could stop thinking about herself. They didn't know boo about each other, but he clearly had a unique approach to his life, so it became a sort of vacation for her darkened mind. Maybe like living inside the Discovery Channel.

"What do you mean?"

"Why are you here, Mana?"

"I got the snot beat out of me by a bunch of drunk football players, and Saint Henry has been kind enough to let me stay here to recover."

"Isn't that what parents are for? Why aren't you living with them? I mean, when you aren't getting the snot beat out of you."

"My family is from Nepal."

"Oh. I don't think I could even find that on a map."

"Don't worry. They couldn't find New Jersey. I live with me."

She was struck by that comment and would remember it for a long time. Actually for the rest of her life. It was who she needed to be. *I live with me.*

"You have no other family?

"No. This is my fourth year of living on campus. I live in the dorms year-round."

"You don't ever take a break? Go on vacation?"

"College is a vacation for me. It beats taking care of the goats in Nepal."

This was a classic layout of a college kid conversation, except perhaps for the twin pink beds. The two of them sitting side-by-side, doing who knows what on their computers and never even looking at each other. It's how relationships begin now.

"You haven't seen your family in all this time?" the girl continued.

"Yeah, that's right."

"Have you called them?"

"They don't have a phone."

"How do you know that they are even still alive?"

"Okay, now you are starting to depress me. The answer is that I don't. It's all very difficult and causes me great guilt. And, if you keep asking me these questions, I might start crying."

He was still staring at his laptop but enjoying having someone to talk to. His new life, focused largely on recovering from his mugging, could be lonely at times. If he was being honest with himself.

"I'm sorry. It's just that I was interested. You have an unusual story."

"No doubt."

"It looks like they beat you up pretty good. How scared were you?"

"I pretended that I was dead, so that they might get frightened and leave."

"Were you just pretending?"

"You mean as opposed to hoping?"

"Yeah."

He thought for a moment.

"I was hurting more than I have ever hurt in my life. I can't even begin to describe it. Even though it probably didn't last all that long, the assault felt like it was going to last forever. One hard punch followed by another. Each brutal kick followed by another brutal kick. These guys were massive compared to me, and their strikes created a pain like I have never felt. One of them got his jollies stomping on my leg. I couldn't believe something like that was happening to me. They called me names that weren't meant for humans. It didn't feel like it was ever going to end. So yeah, there were moments when I was hoping that I could somehow be taken away from all that was happening."

"I'm familiar with that feeling."

"Really?"

"It's nice to know that you have been able to fight your way past it."

"I've been trying, but I will be the first to admit that it's not all that easy. So what about you? What's your deal?"

"I had an affair with Emily's husband."

"I take it you're kidding."

"No, I'm not. He was my teacher in high school, and I was really stupid."

Mana stopped clicking and turned to look at Elizabeth, as much as his sore ribs would let him. She, in turn, stopped clicking, closed her laptop, and turned to look at him. Pausing as if they were waiting for a commercial break in the middle of their conversation. Something like a gecko ad for car insurance.

"And she set it up so you can stay here?"

"Emily is an amazing woman. I didn't have a place where I could live any longer. And Saint Henry, as you call him, has been unbelievably kind."

"Elizabeth, you really had an affair with her husband?"

"Pretty stupid, huh? I am going to her for counseling just like you. My parents split up because of me, so I'm not necessarily their favorite person right now. I'm more like everybody's least favorite train wreck. Emily is helping me recover, too."

"Again, you really had an affair with her husband?"

"Yes."

"How old was he?"

"Forty-seven."

"And how old were you?"

"Seventeen."

"Where is he now?"

"I don't think I want to know."

"Not in prison?"

"It's not something I am proud of."

"And wasn't Emily pissed at both of you?"

"I ruined her life."

"After which she allows you to be another of her VIP clients? Wow, that's amazing."

"I wish it weren't true."

"Well, we all have unforeseen moments in our lives, don't we? I think it's more of a question of what we choose to do next, don't you?"

"That's what I'm trying to figure out."

"I guess we're going to get to know each other pretty well since we're sharing the same room."

"Why does everybody call it Jenny's Room anyway?"

"It's where Henry's wife stayed while she was ill with cancer. For nine years. She passed away in this room. Jelly used to sleep in the bed that you sleep in now. How do you like all the pink, by the way?"

"It suits you perfectly." Elizabeth was surprisingly laughing. "Who's Jelly?"

"She lives here part-time."

"And goes to the university?"

"Uh huh."

"And Jelly is her real name?"

"Real enough. As far as I can tell, that's what everyone calls her."

"So you are okay being bunkies with me, Mana?"

"I'm not really in a position to complain."

"I hear you on that. Will you put the toilet seat down?"

"I'll do my best. Using the toilet is one of my great challenges right now."

"Hah. Let me know if I can help in any way. It would be good therapy for me to do something supportive for someone else for once. So when do I meet this Jelly person?"

"She floats in and out as the mood strikes her. Mostly to help Saint Henry, but sometimes just to have fun at my expense. But trust me, she's worth waiting for."

"If you say so. I'm not planning on going anywhere for a while."

"And not to be rude or anything, but you really slept with Emily's husband?"

38

Yet Another Visit With The Coach

Jelly was never impressed by people who think too highly of themselves. Donald Trump (he was a pig), Rand Paul, Kanye West, Anthony Scaramucci, AOC, Jim Jordan, J-Lo, A-Rod, Lou Dobbs, football quarterbacks including Tom Brady, some of her high school teachers, Lindsey Graham, Harvey Weinstein (he was a pig also), presidents of elite colleges, and private equity guys. She'd never met Emily's ex, but from what she'd heard, she knew she wouldn't like him either – even when forgetting what he did to poor Elizabeth. And she didn't like this coach.

Her disdain for the coach kept her motivated to keep going to see him. His guys had won another game on Saturday, against a bad team, but the win wasn't as convincing as the others have been. Maybe the guilt was creeping in on both he and his players? Maybe the nervousness that there might not be a place for some of them here in the long run? The long-envisioned career paths no more? That's what they deserved for what they did to Mana.

He was in his office anchored to his desk. The door was open, so she naturally walked right in and sat down across from him. His office was way nicer than Emily's.

"Hi Coach!"

She was wearing a classic Jelly outfit. Too large khaki shorts that came below her knees, an unbuttoned, wrinkled-as-hell blue-striped Oxford dress shirt with the sleeves rolled up and worn over a gray Obama t-shirt, plus her green high-top canvas Chuck Taylor All-Star sneakers. Whoever he was. The bottomless bag was hanging over her shoulder. Her journalist uniform, apparently.

"You never answer any of my emails," she continued, "so I thought I would stop in to say hello. I write a column for the school newspaper. Maybe you've seen it."

"I have nothing to say to you."

"The column is actually getting a lot of visibility and plenty of comments."

"That's your business."

"Can I ask you a few questions anyway? Maybe you might decide to respond?"

"Suit yourself."

"Are you now aware of the party that took place several weekends ago at your players' frat house where a student security provider was attacked?"

No answer.

"Do you know which of your players were responsible for attacking Mana Shrestha?"

No answer.

"Have you ever thought about checking in on Mana to see how he is doing?"

No answer.

"Did you know that Mana had three jobs and sent all the money he earned home to help support his parents and brother who live in an impoverished village on the side of a mountain in Nepal? Did you further know that since he was attacked, his injuries have prevented him from earning any money because he is not physically able to do any of the jobs?"

His body language clearly showed he did not know this.

"Did you believe me when I mentioned, when we first met, that I was going to make sure you lost your job?"

He stood up and walked out of his office. He hadn't forgotten. He also probably couldn't believe that an eighteen-year-old non-athlete, who dressed like something he had never seen before, was going to make his life miserable.

39

Saint Henry

He still came to her office each week, if for no other reason than to take a break from being the innkeeper and to have the chance to see her alone. He didn't know yet whether she was a good therapist or not – having the two kids stay at his home was more desperation than a brilliant plan – but he did like being with her. He looked forward to when she came over each night, and he looked forward to their individual sessions, like this one in her office, where just the two of them could interact. He didn't know what that meant, but it meant something. It was kind of like a date for a guy who didn't know anything about dating.

"New shirt?" Emily asked as soon as he walked into her office.

"The kids made me go online with them and shop."

"I like it. The shirt was a group decision?"

"I don't think that I had any say in it."

"Then I love it."

"They keep it interesting, that's for sure."

"So how are you holding up, Henry?"

"Far better than I ever anticipated. The kids bring me energy. I really care about all three of them."

"Is it too much?"

"Good question. It's definitely not too little. The food and housework are fine. Mana and Elizabeth have issues, as you know. Some days turn out to be more of a struggle for them than others. It's just hard to predict when they are going to be down. I try to make sure they know I'm around and available when they are having a tough day. Again, having Jelly there helps a great deal. It's hard for any of us to not be mesmerized by her."

"You were a good person to take this on."

"I've benefitted as much as they have."

"I like that they have taken to calling you Saint Henry. Very fitting."

"Even for a Jewish guy?"

"Absolutely. So, do you still spend too much time thinking about dying?"

"Less than I did, because I am so damn busy now. Thanks to you filling up my house. But still more than you might think. It's been a habit for a lot of years. I'm addicted, I think, like an alcoholic might be. I do find myself, though, also fixated on Mana's recovery and on Elizabeth's recovery. Trying to do whatever I can to help them."

"So that sounds promising."

"I hope it is. Except now I have added Jelly to my worry list."

"Why is that?"

"Have you seen her column in the newspaper?"

"I have."

"She's not going to be making any new friends."

"No, she's not."

"I worry about another violent attack from someone trying to get even. She is making herself a target."

"Do you really think so?"

"I've been around a long time. Far longer than you. I would say that as she keeps pushing the Mana story publicly, the odds will keep growing."

He could talk to her for a long time without being bored.

"So, Emily," he continued, "I think I need a break from my kitchen. Do you want to go out to dinner with me?"

"I'm probably not allowed to do that since you are my client."

"Bend the rules. Or I'll quit being your client. I've followed the rules for too many years. I'm past that. I just want to go have some adult conversation in an enjoyable setting, and I don't have all that many options."

He was hoping that his most sincere smile would be hard for her to ignore. But she left him hanging.

"I do have to tell you about Mana's family, Henry. It's not good news."

Visions of Emily passing were ones that especially weighed on Henry. He never completed these thoughts because they tormented him too much. Her death was never tragic, never preceded by a long illness. Rather her endings seemed to be peaceful, as if she was going to elevate on a dove's wings to heaven, not that he believed in doves or heaven. It was just that the idea of losing this person who had so remarkably galvanized him was, for the first time, beyond anything that his mind was willing to accept.

40

A Story No One Should Have To Tell

So how do you tell someone that his family, who he hasn't seen in more than three years, is dead? That he will never see them again. That there is no village to go back to and rekindle memories. That the first eighty percent of his life has disappeared for good. There isn't any script for this. No one way that works better than another. It wasn't part of her skillset, no matter how much training she had and how many degrees. It's a message that just sucks to have to deliver. And it is still far better to be the one delivering the message than the person on the receiving end.

Emily wondered whether she should even tell Mana the news of his family. It would be adding yet another unfathomable burden on top of his other struggles. Her heart told her to wait, but she knew she would tell him. Except when it came to her own life, her brain usually trumped her heart.

When she did tell Mana, he cried for a long time. Elizabeth was at work, and Jelly at class. Henry purposefully had gone out for a long slow run. Emily had taken the day off to be with Mana. His guilt, the reason he initially came to see her, would reach a new zenith given that he had left his family behind to pursue his own dream, which he had already come to believe was selfish before this happened. Now they were all dead, but he wasn't. Something that it would take him years to overcome. Losing a family member without any warning is beyond hard. Losing a whole family, one who you stopped really knowing, is beyond brutal. Acknowledging that if you had still been there leading treks and tending to the goats, you, too, would have been killed, makes it all just incomprehensible.

He took to sitting on the couch in Henry's living room for long stretches. He would hobble out on his crutches, without his laptop, and just sit. Staring out the window at whatever life passed by. Sometimes he ate the food given to him, sometimes he didn't seem to even know it was there. When anyone talked with him, he might respond in short answers or grunts. Or he might not respond at all because his mind was a world away with his family in Nepal. Elizabeth, when she would return from work, would bring him lunch and then sit with him staring at New Jersey. Sometimes for three or four hours at a time. If she was there, he was more likely to eat his food. And they would speak in slivers. Sometimes she held his hand, too. His sadness enveloped the whole house.

Emily would still attempt to have therapy sessions with Mana most evenings, asking about his family and their life together in Nepal. How big was the village? What was school like there? How his parents met? What kinds of people did he meet on the treks? It didn't get him re-engaged, but she kept trying because her experience taught her that's what she had to do. She had been worried before about the effect of the attack. Now she was even more concerned. She fretted that she had told him too soon, and that, as strong as he was, he might not recover from this.

Per usual, Jelly had a different approach. She wasn't a therapist, but that doesn't mean she didn't think about different approaches. Which she did. Because, she maintained, she was trying to make the world a better place. And everything was her domain.

"Do you ever go to church? Or any place of religion?" she asked Mana one Sunday morning when Elizabeth was sitting with him on the couch gazing out the window, and Henry was making eggs in the kitchen.

"No. Do you?"

"No."

The three of them stayed silent for a surprisingly long time, even though Jelly, as Elizabeth knew by now, was not one who typically could sit quietly for long.

"I wonder if formal religion helps people who are going through what you are going through," she finally said. "To try to make sense of it all."

"Do you really think there is any sense to this?" he responded after a while.

"The only thing that I can figure out is that it lets us keep you. And we like that."

"Whatever."

"I think we should watch a religious service on TV to see what it's all about."

Henry brought scrambled eggs and bagels for each of the four of them while Jelly turned on the television. Elizabeth had grown to adore Jelly like the others did. She believed in her magic. With Henry's exception, as he had already been for whatever kind of run an eighty-two-year-old goes on, they were all still in their sleepwear. Pajamas for Elizabeth, Jelly's cargo shorts and a cast for Mana, and a sleeveless t-shirt and men's boxers for Jelly, with not a bra in the room and no one uncomfortable with that. There were no shameful old men or unchecked horny boys in the group, which felt special. Jelly, in full control of the remote, skipped past the myriad of traditional Sunday Catholic masses until she found what she was looking for. The plates of food sat untouched in their laps while they stared at an unfamiliar Sunday service that Jelly had obviously researched in advance.

"This guy runs a church in Texas," she announced.

"He looks like he has one foot in his grave," Elizabeth quipped.

"He's eighty-four. Sorry Saint Henry."

"Not a problem."

They listened for a while. All four crossed their arms and focused as if it were a lecture required for a class. Or maybe a Trump press conference.

"All he does is ask for money," Mana commented. At least he was talking.

"He has a seventeen million dollar jet, a boatload of expensive cars, and an enormous mansion. He's supposedly worth seven hundred fifty million bucks." Jelly, per usual, had done her homework.

"That doesn't sound right."

"He steals from his people, Mana."

"So why are we watching? We're not going to give him any money."

"Listen to him, Mana."

They listened to him for a while more.

"He keeps telling everyone where they are going when they die," Mana lamented.

"Isn't this what Saint Henry worries about?" Elizabeth questioned. "And, basically, the message is that they had better pay up now to get to a good place in the afterlife."

"Do you believe him, Elizabeth?" queried Jelly.

"Of course not."

"Mana, do you believe that your family has gone to a good place?"

"I believe, Jelly, that they have been returned back to the earth, where we all ultimately belong. Same as dogs, goats, and yaks when they die."

"Do you think that they are in a more appropriate place than what this clown is selling?"

"Yes."

"Me, too. Time to eat." Jelly took a bite of eggs. "Good job, Saint Henry."

"Wait, what's your point?"

"Mana, I don't have a point."

"You don't have a point?"

"Do I have to have one? I just think it's interesting, that's all. Maybe this is what I'll do with my life. I would be a good preacher, don't you think? You know I can make things up like it's nobody's business. And then we could all live in a mansion and each have our own Rolls Royce. Maybe we could hire a few of the brain injured football frat boys to be our butlers."

"Mana and I don't know how to drive."

"Details Elizabeth."

"Can we hire a cook?" Mana asked jokingly.

"Of course."

"I'm hurt, Mana."

"You shouldn't be Saint Henry," he responded. "You're not great, but you are better than the rest of us. Besides, you wouldn't have time to cook. You'll be giving Elizabeth and me driving lessons in your Rolls."

"Now you're getting it," Jelly cajoled.

Mana laughed like he did before he learned his family had all been killed. Yes, he would feel a contriteness for many years. But he understood Jelly's message. They would be together for the long haul. They were now his family.

For the next several weeks, everyone kept Mana engaged. They didn't leave him alone to wallow in grief, even if that's what he preferred to do. And they made him laugh. Watching television evangelists during breakfast on Sunday became part of their routine. Emily never quite grasped their fascination, but she was clearly happy to see Mana making his way back. The silver lining was that he now understood that his future was here with them, which included Elizabeth, too. There was no reason to go back to Nepal.

That Sunday night, after they watched the bogus preacher on television, Henry received a text message from Jelly. He was in his pajamas settling into bed; she was in Jenny's Room doing whatever with Elizabeth and Mana.

If you are going to spend so much time thinking about death, you might as well make a bunch of money doing it like the idiot we watched this morning does. We need to be able to fund our mansion and a fleet of fancy cars.

He laughed to himself the first time he read her message. And the second, and the third. Her message was right. He was being ridiculous.

It turns out that Jelly may have been Emily's equal as a therapist. At least.

41

The Play

From the very first known plays in the Theatre of Dionysus, in the shadow of the Acropolis in Athens, to Shakespeare's London, and, ultimately, to the world's theatre capital in what is now orgasmic Time Square in the center of Manhattan, the stage has been a magical source of entertainment, great joy, and relaxation. A diversion from everyday life. Or, at least, that's what Emily was thinking when she invited Marionette to go to a show.

She met Marionette in the lobby of the campus theatre. Most clients, as mentioned before, don't want to be seen in public with their therapists as it might embarrass them with their friends. That was not the issue for Marionette, as she didn't have any friends. There was a solid crowd waiting for the doors to open -- some staff Emily knew, some professors she recognized, and a boatload of students like her client. Well, maybe not exactly like her client. It had been a long time since Emily had seen someone so uncomfortable with where she was. So out of place. She should have been more concerned about Marionette but had a hard time feeling any compassion given what many of her other clients were struggling through. A shallow young woman, already so self-absorbed by eighteen years old. But Marionette was a client, too. She assumed that calling a time out to enjoy a show on a weeknight would help Marionette to open herself up to the rest of what the college had to offer. And what she clearly needed to begin to experience. Therapists, as highlighted before, don't always get it right.

"Hello, Marionette."

"Hi, Doctor Metcalf."

"I'm glad to see you here. It should be a fun night. Though you don't, I noticed as you walked in, seem all that comfortable."

"I'm not."

"Why is that?"

"I should be studying. I could be using the time to my advantage."

"Marionette, how many hours have you spent studying already today?"

"Two hours and ten minutes in class, forty-five minutes between two professors at their office hours. Eight hours in the library. I get there a six in the morning."

"The library is open at six?"

"The top floor is open twenty-four hours a day."

"You're going to make yourself sick."

"I stretch every morning, eat right, and go for a walk after lunch every day."

"By yourself?"

"Of course. It's my thinking time."

"What do you think about?"

"How I need to be allocating my studying time between courses for the rest of the day. It keeps me organized."

"Have you ever thought about a hobby?"

"No, not really. I have, though, thought about what you said about the theatre girl from your class being valedictorian."

"Yes?"

"That didn't seem fair."

"To whom?"

"Serious students like me."

"What do you mean?"

"She had an easy major. All she had to do was get up on stage and act, and that counted as her grade."

"As it proved out with her career, theatre may be one of the hardest areas of study that the university offers."

"Acting? No way. There aren't any labs. No problem sets. No thirty-page papers. It's taking the easy path."

"So maybe, then, we're in the right place tonight to learn something. You can see the effort these students put into their craft. All the voices and lines and movements they are required to master. It really is extraordinary. I'm looking forward to the performance. I love the theatre."

"Well, remember, you have lower standards than I do."

"You know, that's not a very nice thing to say. I'm doing what I always wanted to do. Trying to help people. You have to remember, getting good grades isn't the same as figuring out how you want to spend your life. You also need to remember that if you talk to other people like you are speaking with me, no one is going to want to hire you. Valedictorian or no valedictorian. Just like the woman in my class."

"I think it's the right start."

"Let's go watch the show. Here's your ticket."

Marionette couldn't sit still during the show. She was already fidgeting before it even started. The show was *The Bridges of Madison County*, which has been both a great movie with Clint Eastwood and Meryl Streep as well as a long-loved play. Emily had seen both multiple times. She adored Clint Eastwood, but she wanted to be Meryl Streep. Even though it was only the dress rehearsal, which is open for free to the whole campus, it was still marvelous, and, as Jelly had said, these kids could really act. Emily was so happy to lose herself in the play and a story of love that might have happened to her but didn't.

At intermission, she and Marionette walked out to the lobby. Marionette went to pee while Emily bought a couple of waters for them. Emily waited long enough to miss the second half of the show, as Marionette never came back. She was off to the library, no doubt. Emily shouldn't have been surprised, but she was. This one was a piece of work.

42

He Kept Showing Up For Breakfast

Seth was sitting alone in the dining hall with a mammoth breakfast on his tray. Oatmeal, eggs, French Toast, yogurt, fruit, and sausage. It required a generous intake to nourish such a large and physically active person. He sat solo. First, because college kids operate on a different clock and, as such, the dining room was mostly empty this early, and second, because he wanted the table to be empty in the unlikely event that Jelly decided to show up. Over the past couple of weeks, she hadn't appeared a single time. Since she had called him a pig. He wasn't ready, though, to give up on the one thing at the university that he cared about, so he came every morning. Just in case.

But Jelly did show up on this morning right at seven, somehow knowing that he would still be there. She came in like a stiff wind off the New Jersey shore which he had not yet seen. In fact, he'd never spent time at the ocean in his life, but that had nothing to do with this story nor his feelings for Jelly. Her bag was slung over her shoulder, and, he quickly noticed, her hair was now it's natural color for the first time since he'd known her. Jelly was always up for change. He was always more comfortable staying in the same rut. Still, the butterflies in his stomach were once again there.

"I've continued coming here every morning, hoping you would show up again."

Which was Seth's way to say hello to Jelly when he no longer knew what to say to her.

"Habits can be hard to break."

"How've you been?" he asked.

"Shitty. How about you?"

"Same."

"Guilt?"

"More than you'd think."

"So what are you going to do, Seth?"

Jelly didn't waste time when she had something on her mind. There wasn't going to be any happy talk.

"I didn't participate in it. And I didn't see it. I was drunk and had fallen asleep in a chair."

"But you knew about it."

"After it happened Jelly. Yes. They got carried away."

"So why haven't you done anything about it?"

"Jelly, because I don't have my shit together!" surprising even himself with his outburst. "I've been here since August. I'm killing myself to be great at something I'm not sure I even like – and in the process sucking up to coaches and teammates to pad my chances. So I seem like a great guy. Which I'm not! My only friend is my therapist. Academics are crushing me. My strategy for the next three and a half years is to find the easiest possible classes I can, just to get through. I'm not exactly what you would call buttoned up, but I do know that I've taken on just about all I can! Oh, and I've learned to drink so I get to take a break from all of my anxieties. And be one of the guys. Which doesn't exactly make me feel good about myself!"

Jelly was silent for one of the rare times since he had known her, while he sat there and stared at his food.

"That's an incredible breakfast."

"I'm not small."

"No, you're not. I went to see your coach again."

"Oh great."

"I told him again that I was going to figure out how to get him fired."

"Super. He knows that I know you because you called me out at the film session you stormed."

"I don't think he was paying attention. He just wanted to get back to continue his affair with his beloved film."

"This is a big time in his career. He's still a young guy. If this team keeps winning, he will get credit for turning the program around and, in his mind anyway, be ready for a job at a school with a bigger program where he becomes more well known, has some of his games on national television, and makes a boatload more money."

"That's what he cares about?"

"That's all these guys care about. Why do you think it doesn't bother them if they treat us like shit? Or if we treat other people like shit?"

Jelly paused again. She could rarely be accused of being the quiet one. She was thinking about something, but he knew that it wasn't spending more time with him, as he would have hoped. He had sufficiently disappointed her. This time she got up and left without saying goodbye.

43

The Columnist

THOUGHTS OF A COLLEGE KID
by Angela Seideman
October 31, 2019

Mana received seventeen emails the other day from other students, and then follow ups each day since then. None of them were from our college email addresses. Let me say that again. None of them were from our college email addresses. Meaning? Meaning that the people who sent them were trying to hide. Chickens. Want to bet that all seventeen were football players? Or maybe even football coaches? You know, the biggest, strongest people on campus. Biggest, strongest, most afraid, most stupid people on campus.

More than one of the seventeen email senders called Mana a monkey. Another told him to take his brown little body back to Nepal. And the rest weren't any better. All leading to threats should he decide to squeal on anyone who had attacked him. Squeal was their word. How about coming clean? Being straightforward? Telling the truth? Accountability. That's their coach's word. Remember Coach Quigley? He has still never reached out to Mana to see how he is. Although just to set the record straight, 41 other faculty members have sent Mana an email or a letter or a care package. Notice that I wrote "other faculty members." If you look at the directory of our faculty, you will see Coach Quigley's name.

This is the year 2019, right? This is one of the most elite universities in the country last time I looked. Check that. In the world.

Why are we giving coaches a free ride for not doing their jobs? Why are we giving football players a free ride for doing bad things? Why do we even have a football team to begin with? I haven't even mentioned the growing incidence of Chronic Traumatic Encephalopathy. Look it up if you don't know what it is.

It's a stupid sport run by stupid people. Remember where the gladiators got the Romans.

More to come...

The first week, Jelly received two emails responding to her column, both basically telling her to mind her own business. One politely, one less so. Both had misspellings, which meant the writers were, in her mind, either drunk or football players.

After the second column, she received thirty-one. More than two-thirds were supportive of her mission. The others were, again, drunk football players. The support felt good. But you couldn't help but be unnerved by the other ones. She was beginning to understand how Mana felt.

44

Green Tea And A Bagel

Forty-five thousand dollars later, there was only a single question to be asked. Did rehab actually work? A month of people challenging how he lived his life. A month of rehashing unfortunate memories. Of questioning so many of his decisions. Of living through the shame. When he walked out the door of a place where he was afraid to leave but where he never wanted to go back, he was no doubt conflicted. How are you ever certain?

Monk sat in Emily's kitchen munching on a toasted bagel and sipping green tea. It was a little past six in the morning. She was spending her early Saturday off rowing on the river, as the available days warm enough to row were waning, while he was enjoying the once demanding experience of waking early enough to see the sun come up. Having been sober for close to two months, he was feeling better about where he was, even to the point where he didn't really feel the need to count the days anymore. But he also knew that there were enough people who had been in the same position and had been wrong. So he kept counting.

Fifty-nine.

Rehab had been brutal. There was no other way to describe it. His hangovers there came from long days of confronting his own behavior, rather than from drinking. Thinking and talking about yourself for the better portion of every day was torture for him. The first few days in rehab, he was numb. After the first few days, he found within himself a familiar emotion. Envy. This time, instead of successful classmates or work colleagues being the foils, it was anybody who didn't have to deal with what he was dealing with. Over the first couple of weeks, he knew that there was no way in hell he wanted to return, and he would be fine being out on his own once again. He'd had enough of rehab. More than enough. And he assumed that he would be thrilled when it came time to leave, but he wasn't. A funny thing happened. Envy was replaced by humility. He found himself surprisingly hesitant to leave. Afraid to venture out again to a world that had not served him well, where he would be without any real safety net. So he stayed for another couple of weeks.

While in rehab, he made the decision that he would start his own therapy practice when he left the facility. After all, he did need to earn a living, and he would have to pay his parents back. It had been Emily's idea after he got bounced from the university. He could ease back into work, coming and going as needed to keep his head on straight. And he could begin to rebuild his reputation, which he needed to do. He rented a little office in the same town as the college, and quickly he got a couple of referrals from his old colleagues. Kids who needed more time than the university could spare. He was happy to be working again, and he was confident that word would spread, and his client base would pick up. He was still good at what he did. Rehab hadn't changed that.

Then there was Emily. For some reason, she still seemed to want to be with him, even if he couldn't figure out why. She was attractive, bright, and engaging, while he represented a walking time bomb. But she seemed to need him almost as much as he needed her. She was still recovering from her unanticipated divorce following a long marriage, and he sensed it was good for her to have a shoulder to lean on. For which he was thrilled.

When he got out of rehab, he went directly to her home, ringing the doorbell rather than letting himself in as he once did. There weren't really many options for him, and he was uneasy waiting for what seemed like forever at the door, having no idea what to expect from her. No surprise, he had thought about little else since he knew he would be leaving rehab. At a bare minimum, he owed her a longer explanation than his two word note.

He didn't know the person who answered, which initially added to the lack of clarity as to whether he was going to be welcome or not. It was an old man with a full head of curly white hair, a pair of somewhat new running shoes with what appeared to be tomato sauce having been spilled on them, and a sparkle in his eyes. Carrying a cup of coffee as he walked. The man let him in, seeming to understand who he was. After a nervous reintroduction, Monk and Emily retired to her back deck, where they could talk in private, wearing sweaters, drinking tea, and remembering what it felt like for that month when they used to converse like this every night. He told her about his getting drunk the afternoon of the football game, breaking into the dorm that night, deciding to go to rehab, not having the courage to share his intuition with her, and the tortuous days he spent in the place coming to grips with his shortcomings. She listened and didn't get mad. Then she brought him up to speed on Mana's attack and shock from the news of his family's being killed, how she didn't follow his advice regarding Elizabeth, launching Saint Henry's hotel, and how she didn't really even know why Jelly was there, but that she was the special sauce. All four of them her clients. She should have been worried about the risk that came with all of that, but, for some reason, she wasn't.

The old man, Saint Henry, waved goodbye through the sliding glass doors that looked onto the deck, recognizing that Emily would appreciate some privacy. Monk and she talked for almost four hours, which had to be a record for him with an attractive woman. But he was happy to talk with her for four hours. It felt good again. By the fourth hour, Emily was managing to grin and chuckle.

In the end, Emily invited him to move back in. Certainly, she couldn't have been completely sure who it was that had arrived, the old familiar Monk or a new improved Monk, but she talked herself into it. Why? Because she had once said he had a cute ass? Because she still cared for him? Because she loved him? Not that she really knew what love was. He really didn't know. But she invited him back, and he said yes again. He once more moved into the girls' room, knowing it was a test and knowing that he was lucky to have another chance.

They were walking on eggshells when he first arrived. But then he met the whirlwind that was Jelly, who came and asked him his intentions while scouring his life's history, with Emily standing right there. His childhood, career, prior romances, favorite foods, how long he took in the bathroom in the morning, and why he was a drunk. Which caused many laughs, and, ultimately, a level of confidence in him as he was being as straightforward and open as he knew how to be.

Monk hadn't been gone all that long, but he hadn't been a part of Emily's life all that long either. While things had changed, the caretaker in her, he suspected, remained. Maybe a piece of it was a defense mechanism for what she had been through. She had seemed to be fearful of being alone after her divorce and after her kids were off to college, having become a caretaker with no one in her personal life to care for. And now, he hoped, that was no longer the case.

45

She Still Had Two Daughters

She'd been doing what she did for a long time. For the most part, her clients respected her for her education, experience, and patience, and most of them picked up on this relatively quickly, believing that she could help them. They almost always showed up on time, addressed her as 'Doctor,' and regularly did the little assignments she gave them. Only a sprinkling of them never came back to see her. She suspected that Marionette would end up in this bucket. When you wear your mom hat, though, it's a wholly different arena. Nobody cares how many degrees or how much experience you have. From your kids' viewpoint, you are never the smartest one in the room. They are. And while they most often love you unconditionally, they also typically believe that you are a lunatic.

As much as she loved and missed them, her daughters hadn't been front and center in Emily's life since they had left for college in August. Which seemed like forever ago. They still talked most nights, and texted all the time, but she had too much else on her mind by the time November had rolled around. In separate schools for the first time, they each appeared to be having a great time, and had come to recognize that their father was still going to be their father, though not someone they could count on for much. And it appeared they could live with that, though she expected that such solace would not be permanent. But since they had departed, the conversations had primarily been about each of them and their new lives, and she kept quiet about her evolving world.

Given all that her girls had been through with their father, she had hoped that going far away to college would be a good thing. She knew better than most, that college was hardly the panacea for a litany of difficult issues, including the front page newspaper fallout of a newly dismantled family. But, like many non-psychologist parents, she put on her blinders and hoped it would be. After all, she would be repaying the loans for their tuition until she was something like a hundred and thirty years old, so it needed to work. Coming clean to them about smoking dope, her emotional state following the break up with their father, the tenants of Hotel Henry, treating the girl who had ruined their family, and whatever her relationship may or may not be with a man who had a drinking problem would be more than a shocker to them. And, certainly, never in their lives were there so many topics to relay all at once. But it was time. So she finally told them the story of her life since they had left, and then she listened like a mother.

While twins, her daughters were not identical, and they didn't really look alike. Abbey looked like her mother. An athlete with an athlete's build and the Scandinavian blonde hair and blue eyes. She was in Chicago and seemed to be loving school and her new classes and new friends. Every time Emily connected with her, she would invariably hear about someone new who could end up becoming Abbey's new best friend when Jessie wasn't around. Like they were auditioning. But no candidate to be new boyfriend was ever mentioned, with was okay with Emily, as there was enough for her to worry about for the moment. Abbey was also the one with the temper. She said she was proud of Emily for taking in Mana, laughed when she heard about Jelly, was cautiously happy about Monk, and absolutely blew her cork when Emily told her the story of Elizabeth. It wouldn't be difficult for you to imagine all that she said to Emily, but clearly Emily was in the lunatic bucket during that part of their conversation. *Helping the bitch who blew up our family!*

Since she never stopped talking, or yelling, it was hard to argue when Abbey lost it with her mother on their calls. So mostly Emily just listened while Abbey raged. Marionette would have hung up quickly so as not to waste precious studying time. Not so with Abbey. She was sure to get her point across and took however long she felt she needed to accomplish that.

Jessie was much smaller than Abbey and was more reserved, which wasn't hard to be. Abbey would become best friends with a tree if she had no one else with whom to socialize. Jessie was drop dead beautiful, looking like neither of her parents. Dark brown hair, dark piercing brown eyes, and a figure that no one in Emily's family could have ever claimed. Whereas Abbey would laugh or scream with each new revelation from Emily, Jessie quietly listened until each piece of the story was done, only interrupting for clarification. Mana actually raised goats? *Yes.* So Jelly doesn't have any problems but she still is living at Hotel Henry? *Part time.* And she is writing newspaper columns to try to get the football team kicked out of school? *Basically.* Including your football star patient? *I'm not completely sure.* And Henry is a professor and a client and taking in your clients? *A Professor Emeritus.* And he might have a crush on you? *Maybe.* Plus we are certain that Elizabeth has stopped seeing Dad? *Yes.* And her parents call her a whore? *Only her mother.* Who is a whore herself? *It would appear that way.* How drunk does Monk get? *I've never actually seen him drunk, but I think the answer is quite.* And you are still smoking weed every night? *No, I don't need to anymore. I sleep fine now.*

Huh.

Jessie was more concerned about her mom being hurt by Monk than she was about Elizabeth. She didn't have a vindictive bone in her body, and she recognized that it was her father who orchestrated the whole Greek tragedy. Trading his family for his peeper. Which only he would have thought was a fair trade. Monk, though, represented another potentially cataclysmic event for her mom, and the first one was only nine months ago, which wasn't long in the scheme of things. It would seem, she told Emily, that she should recover from the first event before opening herself up for the second one. But unlike Abbey, she mostly kept her thoughts to herself. Most of them. She was two hours behind Abbey's time zone, but she would reach out to her sister as soon as she got off the call. Abbey would be waiting, both because that's what truly best friends do and because it was not anybody's typical family dinner table conversation.

The girls weren't coming home for Thanksgiving as the airfare was too expensive, but they would be coming home for Christmas break. Even though they now knew all about it, they would no doubt be in for a surprise with the new set up. Because they would likely be having Christmas with Monk and all the tenants of Hotel Henry. Hopefully, they would see that it made Emily happy.

46

Bedroom Therapy

Ten years ago, Jenny's Room had been Henry's office. When Jenny got really sick, she moved in there as she had so many needs. It was a room that held many memories for Henry, some special and most less so. In addition to being where Mana and Elizabeth slept, did their work, and quietly bonded, it had become Emily's satellite counseling office. She would most often leave work at five now, like the others in her office, and head to what were becoming full evenings at Hotel Henry – Mana's continuing sessions one night, then another with Elizabeth the next, which Emily termed their mutual therapy, and most nights followed by a spectacular, usually lively, and occasionally riotous group dinner courtesy of Monk. Monk had taken it upon himself to help Henry, who he liked very much and respected for what he was doing for the kids. Unless he had a client appointment at his new practice, Monk would go to the market, shop, and then make dinner. They all welcomed his dinners, and he didn't let anyone down. The warmth of those meals the two of them had experienced once before had returned, just in the form of a larger crowd. He was content, and they were again substantiating how much they cared for each other. She loved going to Hotel Henry each night, while her client work on campus stirred her less than it had in twenty years.

"So how did today go, Elizabeth?"

The girl was sitting on the side of the bed, and Emily once again in one of the chairs in the room. The therapist had her legal pad, something she might feel naked without.

"I spent the whole afternoon with Mana and Jelly. It's been a really long time since I laughed like that."

There was a true happiness apparent in her visage that Emily hadn't seen before.

"I'm glad to hear that. What did you guys do that was so entertaining?"

"I made lunch, Emily. They are both dangerous in the kitchen, as you know. And then we sat around the table and talked for a long, long time. Just the three of us. I suspect that Saint Henry left us alone on purpose. He really gets us."

"Anything interesting?"

"All of it was interesting! We talked about Mana's former life, Jelly's crusade to get the players that beat up Mana, and why I became a slut. Then we talked about who our perfect boyfriend or girlfriend would be. Mana couldn't quite figure anything out because he has never been on a date before. But he knew it would be someone from here and not back home. Jelly, of course, described one of each gender. And me, I described someone age appropriate, which was healthy. We also talked about how Saint Henry must be crazy to let us all keep staying here. But in case you haven't seen through us, we love Henry. He's so real."

It is incredible what laughing can do for a person who is hurting. There is no better antidote for someone in crisis. For that moment, she forgets that she is in crisis and can feel a forgotten relief.

"You like living with these guys, don't you?"

"I *love* living with these guys. Nobody takes themselves too seriously. And everybody, especially Henry and you, would do anything for anybody else. It's so different from my house where we do things because they look good. Not because they are good."

"Can I ask you something serious?"

"Whether I'm still thinking about killing myself?"

"You've gotten to know me."

"It's funny, you've never directly asked me about this before."

"It was apparent when I was first wearing my therapist hat. As I mentioned, I've being doing this for quite some time. And while I seem to be breaking all the rules of my profession, I'm okay with it. You are a special person."

"Thank you for that."

"So now you can answer my question."

Elizabeth looked at the bedspread and some of the pictures on the walls of the happier times with Henry and his wife, and played with her hair, before responding. She didn't look like she was going to self-destruct.

"The answer is I'm doing better. Before I came to see you that first time in your office, I had made the decision to kill myself. I was so ashamed of everything that I had done."

"I was worried about that. I checked the newspapers and everything else I could think of each of those days after you missed our appointment."

"Really? You didn't even know me then."

"I was incredibly concerned. It was clear from that first time I met you on the bench that you were a good person. You had a conscience. I can't even begin to describe how happy a feeling it was when you showed up at my office door."

"I'm surprised. I never knew that," the girl responded. "I guess that I still have times where I struggle beyond belief with what I did. The shame and the rest of it. Though it's not all the time anymore. I'd be lying if I said I never think about it, but I've found I can laugh again. And I think that I'm ready to have a life again."

"That's a really positive step."

"I don't know why I can laugh again, but it does feel good."

"You know that if you are ever truly down, you can reach out to me anytime, no matter where I am. Or Henry. Or Monk. Or even Jelly."

"I know. I'm lucky to have you guys. You know what's interesting? Jelly is the same age as I am. In many ways, she seems like she's twenty years wiser."

"She is a unique one."

"She told me that you are her therapist, too."

"Elizabeth, people come to counseling for all kinds of different reasons. One quarter of the undergrad students come every year. Not to mention grad students and professors. There are all sorts of things they want to talk about. Some harmless, some far more serious. It's kept me busy for twenty years."

"Do you ever get tired of it? Or burned out?"

"I have my moments, no different than anyone else in any field. But I still love what I do."

"Why?"

"I like to try to make a difference. I always have. So let me ask you another question. Have you spoken with your parents at all?"

The girl leaned back onto the bed pillows. She was comfortable here.

"I talk to my dad every couple of days. He's a mess, but he really just wants to know how I am. I've told him about the whole set up. He's grateful to you. My mom just leaves me mean, bitter text messages. Which never really helps how I'm feeling."

"Don't let it get you down. Sounds like she has her own issues to wrestle with. Hopefully she'll be wise enough to get help."

"It makes me sad. She is ruining a family, just like I did. At one time, she seemed a much kinder person."

"Let's stay focused on you for now. Keep laughing. And given how crazy this house is currently, I don't think we have any alternative!"

"Can I change the subject?"

"Do I have a choice?"

"Not really."

"You're beginning to sound like Jelly."

"She's a good mentor."

"You could definitely do worse."

"Monk is a good person. We all truly like him. And he really likes you."

"You think?"

"Yeah, I do. So what are you going to do?"

There were getting to be a lot of therapists in the house.

"Take it slow, I suspect. We both have issues we need to come to grips with first. Then we'll see what happens. But you're right, he is a good person. I think we can all enjoy his presence for now."

"For now?"

"I can't predict the future, Elizabeth. But taking things a day at a time seems to be working for all of us for the moment. And that's not a bad thing."

"No, it's not."

The girl said with a smile.

"I've broken all the rules, Monk."

They were sitting at her kitchen table, having returned from what was another raucous dinner at Hotel Henry. The dinner prepared by Monk once again like that of a fine restaurant.

"You certainly have."

"My boss would throw a nutty if she found out all the stuff that I've been doing – sharing private patient information, treating a non-student in my office, regularly having a client over to my house for coffee, having everyone bunk at his home, letting them call me be my first name, drinking with underage clients. Should I be worried about my job?

"Probably."

"Does it hurt to get fired?"

"It's not fun, but you get over it."

"How about a lawsuit? From Elizabeth's parents? Especially her mother."

"It's not out of the question, Emily. You have been taking risks."

"And Jelly's parents? If they find out she has been living in a house full of my clients, unknown to them, rather than in her dorm? They might, at a minimum, vent to the university."

"Possibly."

"I never thought I would veer so far from how I know I should be acting. It's so not like me."

"The question is can you justify it in your own mind? Are you making a difference?"

"Somebody is, I think. I'm just not sure it's me."

"I think that's the $64,000 question to be answered."

"You know I can't afford a lawyer."

47

It's Not All Bluster

At some point in this story, it becomes necessary to address the power of the press once again. It's relevant to where things end up, so now might be as good a time as any. Newspapers, in recent years, have lost circulation and stature to the exploding numbers of cable television news channels and online media options. That's no secret. But they haven't entirely lost being the place where journalists grow up. Hemingway started as a newspaper reporter, as did his third wife who was the only woman at D-Day. As did Tom Brokaw, Bill Moyers, Charles Kuralt, and Andy Rooney. Maureen Dowd, Paul Krugman, Tom Friedman, Mike Lupica, Mike Barnicle, and many other still not quite yet old people continue to have impactful voices from their regular columns. Voices we all still regularly hear.

Over two hundred students at the university work to put out a newspaper five days a week for the entire school year, which is a substantial undertaking by any measure. More cumulative effort than playing football or being a part of the student government. Though unlike the others, with newspapers, we only see the final product. Not the game that gets you there.

At the end of the day, newspapers, for as long as they have been around, remain a platform where voices of opinion, of support, and of dissent can be heard. What the university paper likely didn't realize when it brought on this young freshman with a catchy nickname, was that it was bringing on Hemingway. Another way to say it is that she intended for her words to be remembered, too, which is why she chose the platform. It is a platform, though, which can have consequences when not everyone appreciates what you are saying.

"What are you doing?"

Mana had hopped into Jenny's Room, steadily becoming more agile using his crutches. He had just finished up in the living room doing the morning exercises assigned by his physical therapist, now only needing help when he was doing the more challenging routines, which was once a day before dinner. When Jelly did her best to make him yell – clearly now one of her favorite hobbies. It was the middle of the morning, and his latest tormentor was half sitting, half lying on his pink bed. Or what he now claimed was his pink bed. He sat down in a chair and with the help of both arms raised his casted leg onto the end of the bed where Jelly lay.

"I'm writing my column, Mana."

"Same topic?"

"I'm trying to make you a rock star."

"I don't think it's working. Every time you print a column, I get more threatening emails. On that note, I was called Tonto in an email today. That was a new one that I had to google."

"These guys are all bluster."

"Jesus, Jelly, look at me! It's not all bluster. The cast and all these scars are real!"

She stopped writing, taken aback by an unfamiliar intensity in his reaction, and looked at him seriously. Sadly, he thought. He also thought that she was the only one he had ever seen who could pull off dressing like a hooker without looking like one. As for him, the bandages had been removed, but the scars were still raw, and the ominous train track like black sutures were still in place. It was not the best look.

"You want me to stop this, don't you."

He did because he wanted it all to go away. He wasn't any less untethered being christened Tonto than he was when he was called a wild yak, a pangolin, a midget, a traitor, a cave dweller, a rodent, a scab, and Mongo. But he knew that would be weak of him.

"Jelly, I'm not sure what I want, which isn't unusual for me lately. I know that these people need to be held responsible for what they did to me. Otherwise, they will be no deterrence to other attacks, including probably raping girls. There will be other football victories, after all, and the guys will still get drunk and horny. But, selfishly, I am afraid for me. I can't physically stand up to even one of these guys. I'm no match, and they know it. Particularly after they've had a couple of beers and lost all their humanism."

"And you don't think I can protect you?"

"With your rapier-like words, you mean?"

"Yeah, it would have to be. I'm no bigger than you are."

"That would be a neat trick."

"Here, read the draft of my next column. Let me know what you think." She sent her draft to his laptop. "How's your leg feeling after the stretching?"

"Been better. I think that when my mind hurts, my leg also hurts."

"I know that I joke around too much, but it makes me sad to hear that."

"Yeah, me too."

But it was what it was. There is no roadmap that tells you how to escape from the nightmares, the newfound fear of the dark, and the dread of getting the snot beaten out of you again. He'd no doubt made strides but was still struggling to free himself from all this, as the only thing he had come up with was to hide in Saint Henry's house for as long as he could.

THOUGHTS OF A COLLEGE KID
by Angela Seideman
November 7, 2019

Five days ago, I sent an email to Coach Quigley asking if I could meet with him. As of press time, I hadn't heard back. I sent the same request to the head of the university police department, our athletic director, our esteemed university president as well as her assistant, who I have been told really runs the school. Five emails, zero responses. Just to remind everyone, the university website has a posting which proudly states 'easy and welcome accessibility' of professors by students. Seems like some folks need a refresher on what this means.

But let's talk about the coach. This is his fourth year on campus. In the first three years, his teams won a total of three games, which in a business where coaches jump around like somebody lit their Nikes on fire, his next career stop was more likely to be at a high school, where he would also have to, God forbid, teach classes. Or maybe Pop Warner football, which apparently is football for little kids (I had to learn about it). But this year they are now 6-1. The reason? They have Seth Davis. For those who haven't yet opened their eyes on campus, Seth is the biggest person here. He is also fast, strong, plays both offense and defense, and is easily the best football player this university has ever seen. Coach Quigley brought him all the way from Iowa to play football. The rest of our players are typical of our university. Slow, undersized boys who look good in a uniform and will be working one day for an investment bank or private equity firm where they can sharpen their moral values. Seth makes them all better players on the field.

But for Coach and his staff? This is their chance. If he gets to move up to a big Division 1 football school, it means a multiple year contract worth millions of dollars. He is not going to let Mana's injuries get in his way. Professor Quigley. He incredibly does not know who Mana is. He has never even been to see him. To see the extent of the damage his boys did off the field. My guess is that he hasn't even thought about it. That's because he's busy watching film for next week's game and thinking up another insincere pre-game motivational speech for his boys. That's only a guess. What's yours?

I've started my own process of interviewing players on the football team about what happened at that now infamous party. My one-person crusade. What you'd think the police would have done. And who knows, maybe they did. After all, they are trained to do this. I am not. No one has spoken openly and honestly to me yet, but somebody will crack. In my heart of hearts, I do believe that somebody on the team knows right from wrong and is willing to do something about it. Right guys?

More to come...

"What do you think?"

"I think you are a very good writer, Jelly, as well as a very strong person."

"Thank you. So again, what do you think?"

Mana just stared at her. How does one ever not agree with a person who has such determination? Such charm? He knew he would do whatever she wanted.

"Print it. I'll just be scared for a while more."

"You have an army here to protect you now."

And he did. So long as he never left the little house.

48

A Surprise Visit

Virtually everyone in this story, perhaps with the exception of the one Emily had christened Pinocchio, has struggled with some level of guilt or shame. Two feelings that are not the same, but not entirely separate either. Feelings that they have compromised their moral yardsticks somewhere along the way. They are all learning that the numbness left behind doesn't go away easily, and, in at least one instance thus far, it has teetered on self-harm as the resolution. That never helps in the storytelling.

Our friend Seth had been wrestling with more feelings since he got to campus than he was equipped to handle. His life in Iowa had been, for the most part, relatively simple. Raising cattle, high school sports, and the Cedar Rapids Kernels. The one time when it did get a little complicated, he had to take a year off and get help. Coach Quigley knew some of this but didn't care. He had his player. He never bothered to consider how Seth might endure a new life on a Mid-Atlantic university campus of eight thousand students, and, if the coach had been paying attention, a different set of moral boundaries. The undergraduates, alone, were double the population of the town Seth came from. And his parents, the Trump following, cattle farming football zealots, didn't say anything. Even though they wore big hats and big belt buckles instead of suits, and drove pickups instead of BMW's and Tesla's, they were excited about their kid attending such a well-regarded school, too.

Doctor Metcalf was not as blind as the coach. Seth could tell that she quickly sensed, in that very first visit, that his girlfriends provided his self-worth and self-confidence. Hell, it was no mystery he had already dated his whole town before arriving to campus. When there were no more girlfriends for him in Iowa, he cratered. If he couldn't survive solo in small town Iowa without that kind of support, how was he going to make it here? He had hoped that Jelly was going to be his security blanket, and he wanted to be glued to her. But that didn't happen, and he found his new world an incredible challenge to navigate without her. He instead took to dating his team, because that's what she had told him to do. And he took to drinking too much, because that's what his teammates told him to do.

But with each passing day, he was getting closer and closer to cratering again. He recognized the feeling.

"Seth."

He had pressed the doorbell at Henry's little house, a structure that seemed far too small for a person of Seth's dimensions, and stood quietly waiting on the front stoop in his worn jeans and plaid buttoned down shirt. Until a familiar face answered the door.

"Jelly. What are you doing here?"

It was a Sunday around noon. The football team had won again, three days after Jelly's most recent column bashing them had been published, but Seth hardly cared. Football meant less and less to him as the season went along. Though he never said this to anybody.

"I'm a squatter. Why are you here? Don't you have one of your holy film sessions now? It is Sunday, you know."

"I'm skipping. I realized Coach can't get mad at me even if he knows he should. I'm too important to him. Is Mana around?"

"He never goes anywhere. He has limitations now, remember?"

"Is he here?"

"Yeah, come on in. Mana, you have a visitor," she called out.

Mana, who Seth identified right away, was in the living room with Jelly and an older man, who was introduced as Saint something or other, watching a Sunday television evangelist show, something Seth was fairly accustomed to from growing up in Iowa.

It surprised him, knowing Jelly as he did. But that was not a conversation for this day. Mana got up from the couch with the help of his crutches, and hobbled over to where Seth stood. They were quite a contrast standing next to each other. Mana was about as big as one of Seth's legs. The giant couldn't help but notice the deep gashes on Mana's face, the traces of bruises on his nose, and the size of the cast. He also didn't miss that Mana had cringed when he stood up.

"Hi, Mana."

"You're Seth."

"You know me?"

"Everyone on campus knows you, Seth. You're kind of hard to miss. Sort of the opposite of me."

"How are you doing?"

As big as he was relative to Mana, Seth was nervous when he spoke, realizing that his voice was shaking with each brief line. Mana, conversely, seemed comfortable in the house.

"To be totally honest, I've been better."

"Are you in a lot of pain?"

"In more ways than you might guess."

Another girl, he was introduced to as Elizabeth, had come out of the kitchen, where she was doing the breakfast dishes, to witness the conversation. Unlike most teenagers, they apparently all did chores without ever being asked. The saint, he was told somewhere during the conversation, owned the house. Emily was doing the grocery shopping for the week with a monk, as best as he could decipher. The monk was supposedly the resident chef, who would pick out the food at the store, while Emily simply pushed the cart and, according to Jelly, just looked at his ass when he was reaching for things. A saint and a monk with a nice ass. This seemed a far more interesting place than where he lived on campus.

"I'm really sorry for all that happened to you."

"Me, too."

"It was so wrong."

"I agree with that. Were you one of my attackers?"

They looked at each other while talking, both of Seth's hands shoved deep into his pants pockets, Mana's gripping the crutch handles.

"No."

"Then why are you here?"

"I play football, Mana. I think it was some of my teammates."

"I understand they came after me because they wanted to sleep with the girls that I was supposed to be walking home."

"I don't know that, but it wouldn't surprise me."

"Do you happen to know what happened to the girls? Did they make it home, or did your teammates harass them? Or rape them?"

"I don't know the answer to that either. No one talks about that night."

"You know, those girls didn't do anything wrong. They just wanted to go back to their dorm rooms safely. And I didn't do anything wrong either. I was just doing my job."

"I know."

"Your friends suck."

"They're not my friends."

"Could have fooled me."

Mana was demonstrating a sternness that surprised Seth. He was not shy about standing up for himself. Not that Seth could blame him.

"Is there anything I can do to help you?"

"Like what?"

"I'm not sure."

"Why did you come here, Seth? You can't answer my questions. You offer to help me but have no idea how. Is this visit just to assuage your guilt?"

"I don't know."

"Well, just so you do know, I'm horrified of the prospect of seeing these people again, and I don't even know who they are! I get threatening emails from them all the time!"

"They are afraid of being arrested or kicked out of school."

"They are physically all way more powerful than I am."

"I can protect you."

"How?"

"I am stronger than anyone on the team. By far. I will make sure they know that I will come after them if they touch you."

"As gigantic as you are, I'm guessing that you overstate your powers. One man against the masses is hardly a winnable battle."

"They wouldn't dare mess with me."

"Seth, this isn't a movie. It's real life. If they want to attack me again, to keep me quiet or whatever, they will. Let's face it, they care only about themselves and your precious football team and their careers after they graduate. They'll get drunk, you'll get drunk. No one will be thinking. I'll be the prize again!"

"That wouldn't be good."

"Why don't you just speak up? To the police or whoever?"

"My lawyer told me not to say anything?"

"Your lawyer?"

"My father hired one for me. Same for the parents of all the other players."

"That is so wrong!"

"I know."

"Seth, I can't survive another beating." The sternness was disappearing. He began to cry. And Seth, once again, didn't know what to do.

He had hoped that this meeting would be a positive thing, and, as Mana had inferred, lessen Seth's own shame. It obviously didn't make even a small dent. He really didn't understand people. Moreover, he really didn't understand himself.

49

Skipping Class

Remember the notable and the obtuse? The story seems to have come a long way from that conversation. Have you begun to consider who the real caretaker is in this cast of people that seem to have been connected by something more charmed than fate? Depends upon the day of the week and the time of the day? Sometimes it seems that way. No one? That would be an interesting twist. Especially given the obvious need.

Monk was sitting at the kitchen table at Emily's house, having his usual cup of green tea and working on his laptop. His new practice did not yet occupy him full time, but it did occupy him. He had clients who had their share of issues. Which is the definition of a psychologist's practice.

The doorbell interrupted his thoughts.

"Hey Monk."

"Hi Jelly. What are you doing here? It's Wednesday morning. Don't you have a class like the rest of the students at the university?

"I'm cutting."

"How come? You pay a lot of money to take those classes."

"I don't, my parents do. And they're about to be richer now than they used to be, thanks to me."

"I'm sure that's a good story."

"It's an excellent one, but I'll tell you the details when I have more time to spare. Let's change the subject."

"Why does everyone around here always want to change the subject?"

"It keeps our discussions interesting."

"Half the time, I'm not even sure what you all are talking about."

"That's our magic."

"If you say so. Come on in. I've having tea. Do you want some?"

He led her back to the kitchen table. Monk hadn't been back all that long and was still figuring things out with Emily's posse.

"So how are you and Emily doing?"

"Is this why you're skipping class?"

"I thought it was a pretty good reason, don't you?"

"I'm not sure that I agree with you. But to answer your question, which seems to be a popular one to ask these days, you'd have to ask Emily. She's the more essential one to our relationship."

Jelly sat down at the kitchen table with the cup of tea. Monk closed his laptop, folded his arms across his chest, and looked at Jelly. In all her Salvation Army attire glory.

"Like the outfit?" she asked.

"Splendid."

"She is a special person. It seems like kind of a strange relationship that you two have, don't you think?"

"As opposed to all of the other ones in Henry's house?"

Jelly giggled.

"Yeah, even as opposed to all the other ones. By the way, we're glad to have someone around here who can cook. You really are good. We're happy not to have to go hungry."

"Thanks. But back to your question. She's saving me, too. I have a lot of baggage."

"What's it like to be a drunk?"

"Are you always this direct? Your words are a little sharp for a recovering alcoholic."

"No reason beating around the bush. We all have issues. And I have to make sure to watch out for Emily. So answer the question."

Monk smiled. There was something about Jelly's boldness that was endearing. And there was something about her questions that were frightening. She was so unusual for such a young woman. Though he suspected that she was hiding something. Like he did with his drinking. A bad experience. Something that scared her. No eighteen-year-old kid could be this confident.

"Do you drink?" he asked her.

"Yes."

"Have you ever been drunk? Like really drunk. I don't know what day it is drunk."

"Once. I learned a lesson the hard way. Now I get a little buzz and that suffices. I have never wanted to be out of control again."

"That's a good principle to live by, if you can stick to it. Alcohol is a drug. I start slowly, enjoy a cocktail or two, and then too often proceed to get out of control drunk. Can't remember the name of the person I'm talking with, slur my words, need somebody to help me get home."

"Really?"

"Yes. When you are drunk, you don't have any issues. The whole world is just contentedly floating by. When you sober up, you have ten times the problems that you had before your first drink. Feel like shit, realize that you spent money again that you couldn't afford to spend, not sure what promises you made that will never be kept, not sure who you offended, not sure what you did to embarrass yourself. People who you aren't certain you even know now look at you funny. And your reputation as a credible, upstanding person takes a big hit. After a while, you recognize you can never catch up to the problems that you have created by drinking. Which makes your life miserable. And which too often causes you to drink more. I used to be a star in my field. I worked with the best of the best. I drank it all away. Spent too many years passing out and not being able to get up in time to get to work in the morning. Not something I'm proud of."

"Are you going to hurt Emily?"

"Is that what you really are trying to figure out?"

"We hardly know you. Emily, on the other hand, is our savior. We care for her deeply."

"Does she know that?"

"I hope so. She has been through too much on her own, Monk. She has wounds that were still raw before you came into the picture. And when you came and then bolted, it only added to those wounds."

"Tell me, why are you staying at Henry's house? I know why Mana and Elizabeth are. You, I have no clue."

"Are you playing shrink now?"

"It's a dangerous habit."

"Because despite all the carnage, it is the happiest place I have ever been. Usually I prefer to live alone, but this is better. So I'm the resident trespasser. Every good home needs one, don't you think?"

"Jelly, they may have broken the mold with you."

He was still smiling.

"It's not such a bad mold, is it?"

"No, it isn't."

"Then answer my question."

"I was hoping you'd forget when I diverted the conversation."

"Fat chance."

"I spent a month in rehab beating myself up about hurting Emily. She is beyond special. It was never my intent, and I hope to God that I never, ever hurt her again. I also know that a drunk's promise isn't worth anything. I keep taking it one day at a time, trying to be a better person than I was the day before."

"That was almost eloquent."

"Almost?"

"Yeah, almost. You don't get full credit until you follow through."

"Fair enough."

"Good talk. Okay, now I had better go to class!"

And with that, she was off to pursue her next victim.

50

One Of Them Will Crack

THOUGHTS OF A COLLEGE KID
by Angela Seideman
November 14, 2019

I tried to talk to Scott Harmon, the junior starting quarterback and well-known campus snake. He said nothing. I approached Trent Harrington, a senior tri-captain. He smirked at me and walked away. I had a long conversation with Ray Martin. We talked about everything except what I wanted to talk about, beyond his saying that they were all in the library studying. Matt Gleason, Malcolm Harrison, B.J. Hyde, Alexis Santiago, Obi Tucker, Paul McIntyre, Darren Holmes, Junior Griffin, Fletcher Constable, Michael Conway, Terrence Hendrick, Judson Smith, Hayes Webster-Green.

Nada.

Nobody was at the frat party. Nobody knew anything. Nobody, from my simple perspective, was being honest.

For what? To save their precious football team? To make sure they get their diplomas. To avoid the feeling of having to reconcile with almost killing a person. Remember that these clowns someday may be your lawyer or banker. The guy who delivers your baby or does surgery on your child. Someone's husband and father. Really? Would you trust them if you knew what they knew?

One will crack. Trust me. And when they do, it will be all over.

Oh yeah. I'm getting more and more emails. Many are supportive, for which I am grateful. As for the others, no one is asking how my day is going. Some of these people have some serious mouths on them. Clearly, they are afraid to pick on somebody their own size. I'm about the same size as Mana. My rebuttal to each of you who have written me with unnecessary messages since the last column began is the same.

Chicken shits!

More to come...

Forty-two email responses. Thirty-three positive, eight negative, and one scary as hell.

51

Playing With Fire

Henry took Jelly out for a cup of coffee a few mornings after her most recent column came out. Not the Starbuck's where Elizabeth worked, as Henry preferred the independent places that didn't have CEO's who were paid four hundred times what the servers made. He told her about his history as a professor and the Friday evening get togethers that he and Jenny hosted with his students, including the pitchers of Margaritas. One of the reasons they did this, he told her, was that many of the kids back when he started teaching had issues with him as he was a demanding teacher. Not every student came each Friday night, but all of them came some Friday nights. The conversations with small groups, he realized, allowed them to discuss both frivolous and serious things that built a long-lasting trust that often continued well beyond their graduation. Even if they were pissed at him for a particularly challenging assignment or a grade that disappointed them, he had a platform for discussion that was comfortable for all involved. And he could be direct with them.

Then he told Jelly that she was playing with fire. That unlike small group discussions, the publicly printed word opens her up to the scorn of people that she didn't know. Any random person she walked by on the campus now might have been offended by what she wrote, but she would have no way of knowing, and thus, not be able to protect herself, if needed. It is necessary to be more careful with the messages delivered, he told her. You can't be so ferocious with your words, he said, and not expect repercussions. No matter how supremely talented and captivating she was.

Jelly, in response, told Henry that she loved him for who he was and for all that he was doing for people for whom she had grown to care so much. That he was as good a person as she had ever met in her life. Which made him blush for the first time that he could remember. Then she kissed him on the cheek, which caused him to blush again, told him to mind his own business, and changed the subject.

Which was not the outcome for which he was hoping.

"I've noticed you haven't missed any of our Sunday television evangelist viewings, Saint Henry."

"I will admit to having become obsessed. When I have time, I watch the weekday morning reruns as well."

"It's a different world, isn't it?"

"I take it that the idea of watching these shows was not just meant for Mana, was it?"

"You are a perceptive one."

"I find them irritating and disgusting. Which is unusual for me given that death is my favorite topic. Your point hasn't been missed."

"Who said I had a point?"

"Huh," he responded, and she laughed her mischievous best. "Now I'm answering questions like Emily. But your little scheme has caused me to look at death in a different way."

"So that's a start."

"Yes, it is."

"Speaking of Emily, you really like her, don't you?"

"I think we all do. She is a special person."

"That is not what I asked."

"I know what you asked, and that is my answer. Now let's change subjects again and talk about your columns some more. I wasn't finished, and I'm worried for you, young lady."

He didn't easily give in either.

52

His Best Plaid Shirt

The baseball team, at a university like this, will play more than forty games in a season. Basketball, hockey, and even water polo will all have over thirty matches. If you play football, there are forty games in *your entire four year career.* Despite all the hype, that's it. And if you're not a freshman phenom like Seth, you may have to wait until your junior or senior year and only get to play in half that many. Consequently, each one typically means a great deal to everyone who plays, as there just aren't that many games. Despite all the warped memories of the men on the fantasy email chain of former athletes.

The day before a game always carries with it an inimitable feeling. There is a final Friday afternoon light-hearted practice where no one wears pads and there are no sprints to be run, followed by a team dinner that night which serves the best meal the dining halls have to offer. You play some video games for a couple of hours, and then you go to bed early to get a solid nine or ten hours of sleep. When the alarm goes off the next morning, you are well rested, don't have a hangover, and it's game day. A little jumpiness that morning is a good thing -- all athletes want to be on edge before a game. The nervous energy keeps you sharp. Maybe your stomach has too many butterflies if it's a big game against a good opponent. So sometimes you just don't eat breakfast. But when you put it all together, it is better than Christmas morning. Because on Christmas morning, you don't get to hit anybody.

The last game of the season, which this was, is when you play your rival. Why or how they became your rival can be a bit of a mystery. Something that happened a century or two or three ago and included land and muskets and money and egos. Football hadn't yet even been invented. The home field advantage goes back and forth, and somebody keeps track of the cumulative won-lost records since the beginning of time. Or, at least, since football was conceived. This year was a home game, which meant that if you win, it is the best day of the entire year. The tailgates will start early. The stadium, a holy ground on campus for many alumni, will be packed, and it will be mostly with your fans. Twenty thousand of them, even though it's not big-time college football.

Twenty thousand people is a big deal for a team that until this year won three games in three years. The team actually hadn't won this game in fourteen seasons. The game. *The Game*. Not only did they have a chance for the first time since who knows when, they were favored to win. A season of nine wins would match the school's all-time record, which had been done only once before. The seniors would go out as if they were on a Macy's Thanksgiving Day Parade float. There was excitement and anxiety. Quigley had been over the top all week. He could taste his future. Seth was up early and skipped breakfast because he had butterflies in his stomach.

Jelly was waiting for Seth outside of his dorm. He didn't know she was coming, but he noticed her immediately and walked over. It was still early, but there was already a game day buzz to the campus. She was leaning up against a big tree of some sort. He didn't know anything about tree types. In Iowa they grew corn. It was warm for November and going to be a good day for a game. Players would check the weather forecast every day of the week leading up to the game. And talk to their parents the night before to confirm what they had known for weeks already. When their folks were planning to arrive and, more importantly, what time the reservations for dinner were. Not too early so that they could party with the tailgaters after the game and in the locker room after that. Not too late so they could get to the frat house while the kegs were still full.

"Jelly."

"Long time no see, Seth."

"You're getting to be pretty famous around here."

"I'm trying."

"Your columns are pretty powerful."

"That's what I'm shooting for."

Seth didn't smile anymore. That's what college had done to him. A place where he no longer found contentment in anything he did. He had smiled often before he arrived here. When he was with his family on the ranch, and when he and Jelly were together that summer.

"Does that surprise you?" she asked.

"It probably shouldn't. But you're still only a freshman in your first semester."

"And?"

"And I would have thought it would have taken a little longer."

In a hooded sweatshirt with the university logo on it, oversized gray sweatpants, and her natural color hair, she almost looked like a normal college student. Only the myriad of earrings stood out, because they made her look like a model for a cheap jewelry store. Which may have been what she was shooting for.

"So how are you doing?" she asked.

"How do you think? Thanks to you, no one trusts any of their teammates any longer because they are afraid that you are going to get someone to squeal. Everybody is acting and playing scared because they think they are going to get the boot."

"Including you?"

"I didn't do anything wrong."

"Not telling what you know isn't wrong?"

"You have a way with words."

"Are you still not planning to speak up about what you know?"

She didn't realize until much later that he was wearing his nicest khaki slacks and a new long sleeved plaid buttoned down shirt, one that wasn't worn out like most of the other plaid shirts he owned. And his leather cowboy boots, perfectly shined. In retrospect, it was an outfit she had never before seen. Actually, it was his nicest outfit.

"I'm more conflicted than ever. But the reality is, Jelly, that it's not any of your business."

"You don't owe them anything."

"That's not what we are taught in sports. But I don't owe you anything either."

She had brought Mana into Seth's world with her film session and newspaper column histrionics. Mana had taught him something important, and Seth owed him. More than he owed his coaches and teammates. Or her. It had taken him a long time to figure that out, but now he had. Seeing Mana made all the difference. The scars and the cast and the living in hiding. All because a bunch of his teammates had to get their jollies. He had wondered if others would have changed their minds if they had taken the time to go see Mana. Right now, he didn't care. He wasn't going to the game. He had never missed a game in his life. Not for being sick or for injury, no matter how much physical pain he might have been in, and certainly not because he was conflicted. *The Game.* He was on his way to a meeting with the Dean of Students. Seth was the one who asked the dean for the meeting. Jelly didn't know this, and he wasn't telling her. She would only twist his words and his thoughts.

For the only the second time since they had met, he walked away from her.

He'd never been to a dean's office. This one was in an old building, the room framed with dark wood paneling and shelves filled with too many books for anyone to have ever read. It looked like you would think a dean's office would look. But that didn't mean you would ever want to return for another visit. Even though he hadn't eaten breakfast, he felt sick to his stomach when he entered the office. Seth wasn't exactly sure all of what a dean did, but he assumed that most of it didn't provide a good outcome for the students who had to visit him. Maybe he was wrong, but he didn't really want to find out.

You can guess what was said in the conversation with the dean. Seth was honest. He knew it was the right thing to do. The dean asked many questions and had two other people join in the conversation and add theirs. A woman and two men, who looked like college people tended to look. Smart. They clearly sensed that if the well-documented star of the team was skipping such an important game, it must be serious. None of them seemed to mind being in their offices on a Saturday for this. *How many members of the team were at the party? How many knew about the attack on Mana? Was their underage drinking at the party? Who actually took part in the attack? Had they been drinking? Had they been drunk? Where was he when the attack occurred? Did he see the attack? Did he know the three girls who requested the Walk Safe home? Were they drunk? Were there any drugs at the party? Did Coach Quigley know about the party? The underage drinking of his players? The attack on Mana? Did any of the other coaches know? What was the connection of this Angela girl who wrote all the columns?* Seth didn't know all the answers to the questions, but he knew enough. When he first walked out of the meeting more than three hours later, he didn't know right away if he felt better about himself or not. He had just buried the people he had spent most of his brief college life with. But it didn't take all that long for his feelings to change. He had done the right thing.

He went to a little deli just off campus where he could eat lunch by himself, having handled enough questions for the day. He finally felt like eating and was ready to do so in solitude. On their campus, when the stadium was packed like it would be today, you could hear the roars from pretty much wherever you were. Seth sat in the little deli for the longest time. There were few roars. His team, he could tell, was losing the game badly. He knew they deserved to go down. The biggest games of their lives. None of the coaches or his teammates would ever talk to him again.

Seth's next stop, after the dean and after the deli, was Emily's office. He had asked if they could meet in her office, even though it was a Saturday. She knew something was up, because he had a scheduled game at the same time. She arrived in advance to turn all of the lights on, make a pot of coffee, and prepare for whatever he might say.

"Hi Seth."

"Hey Doc."

"Can I get you a cup of coffee?"

"No, I'm good."

"So how are you doing?"

"You know, this has been my best day here."

"Really?"

"Yeah. I told the truth."

Emily paused and smiled.

"Fill me in."

And he did, going through all the same detail he went through with the dean and his staff. Unusual for Emily, she never wrote a thing on the yellow pad in front of her. She just listened.

When he finished, she smiled some more. Not the soothing motherly smile she had given to Mana and Elizabeth during their first visits, but rather the grizzled therapist smile that showed how proud she was of him. The nice surprise was that he smiled, too.

"I'm proud of you. That's a courageous step."

"Yeah, it was. It was the right step. Mana didn't deserve this."

"No, he didn't."

"After this is all out in the open, he won't need to be scared anymore."

"I think that will feel incredibly good to him."

He paused and looked at her.

"You always knew I was going to do the right thing, didn't you Doc?"

"You think?"

"Yeah, I do."

"I had a suspicion. You are one of the good ones, Seth. Don't ever forget that."

She thought about how long it had taken him to truly trust her.

"I'm leaving here tomorrow."

"For good?"

"Yeah. This isn't the right place for me."

"All colleges oversell what they do. You can't believe all the hype. Are you going to go back to school?"

"Yeah, I figure I'll apply this spring somewhere closer to home. Somewhere I'm more familiar with, and then try not to date anyone for the first couple of years. Enjoy school for what it is."

Emily chuckled at that one. He was over Jelly, which was a hard thing to get over.

"Football?"

"Not sure. But if I do decide to play, I'll find somewhere with a coach who has been around for a while and is comfortable with who he is and where he is. Otherwise, I might give baseball a try." He looked at her with what only could be described as an impish grin. "And someplace where I match up academically a little better."

"I like that plan, Seth."

"I'd like to go see Mana before I leave, if that's okay with you."

"I think that's a good idea."

"Believe it or not, I'm going to miss you."

"I'm going to miss you, too. You are a special person."

"Thanks Doc."

They stood up and hugged, his mass enveloping her until she was almost invisible. It was, indeed, a good day.

53

They Deserved To Lose

THOUGHTS OF A COLLEGE KID
by Angela Seideman
November 21, 2019

I'm smiling as I write this. It's been a good few days as a number of wrongs have been righted.

The football team lost on Saturday. In fact, they got killed. It was their chance to win the league and to tie for the best season record in the university's history. They weren't up to it. They deserved to lose.

More importantly, somebody cracked, just as I said they would. One person. Only one person from the whole team. A person that ultimately snubbed the peer pressure and coaches' empty verbal spasms to tell the truth. To tell what happened. One person. That's all it took.

Four days after the team got rocked, five players were expelled from the school. Not suspended but expelled. Four coaches were also fired – including my buddy, Coach Quigley. It's never fun to see somebody get fired. After all, he has a family and a responsibility to it. But so did Mana. The coach preached accountability. I wonder what he thinks now.

For those of you who care, and I know that there are quite a number of you who do, Mana is coming along. He is working on his leg rehab, and in a couple of months should be losing his crutches and, instead, walking with a cane through the spring. It's a long, hard process, but a step in the right direction. Hopefully his psychological scars will recede as well. He still is uncomfortable going outside in the dark and gets the yips when big, macho, and, too often, bigoted athletes are in his sphere. Since everyone knows who he is now – as far as I know, he is the only 5'4" brown skinned boy with a big leg cast hobbling around campus on crutches – maybe you can go up and say hi. Make him feel welcome as he once did before this all happened.

It's nice when stories have happy endings. I don't know if this is a happy ending, but it seems it must be given how painful the story was. So thanks for listening.

More to come…

54

The Reckoning

She had entered Emily's life the first day of the school year. She was loud, bold, and yet with a sense of purpose. She wasn't the harnessed child of helicopter parents, or if she was, the parents weren't any good at it. She was more her own person than anyone on the campus, and so many would eventually want to be with her or be like her. But she didn't seem to want to let them.

As best as Emily could tell, Jelly didn't have any close friends besides the tenants of Hotel Henry. Nor did she have a romance. And she lived in a single dorm room. When you study college students for a living, as Emily did, you can't help but wonder what it is that drove Jelly. Why is what she does always a surprise and never a surprise. The way she dressed to catch attention. That she stoked fear amongst the coach and his assistants and many of his players, even though she was half their size and knew little about the sport beyond what she had learned online. And, truth be told, she probably did more to help Mana and Elizabeth, and maybe even Henry, get their lives back than Emily did.

"You made an appointment this time."

Emily was sitting at the desk in her office in the middle of the afternoon. She hadn't seen Jelly in a few days and was looking forward to catching up with her in this setting, just the two of them. They didn't really have any one-on-one time at Hotel Henry. No one ever knew exactly when Jelly was going to be there, if she was staying for meals, or if she was spending the night. But they were always happy when she came since it seemed that the energy in the house suddenly multiplied by at least a factor of five.

"I wanted to show that I didn't always have to buck the system."

"Really Jelly? I'm not sure I ever would have believed that."

"I'm kind of a chameleon."

"I don't think I could argue with that. But on a more serious note, you did a good thing."

"Ya think?" replied Jelly, plunking down in the now familiar chair.

"Yes, I do think. An awful lot of people learned from you about what their priorities should be. It was a needed lesson."

"I'm going to miss Coach Quigley." She laughed a classic Jelly laugh.

"Like hell you are."

"What? He and I were soulmates!"

Then they both laughed.

"Emily," Jelly continued on a more serious note, "what do you think happens to a guy like him?"

"That's a good question. I'd like to say that he has learned his lesson. That there is more to life than winning a football game at all costs. He should have, anyway, but I wouldn't bet on it. He's been trained to do things one way his entire life. That's all he knows. My sense is that football is akin to military life for many people, where you never question authority, and you check your conscience with the coat room attendant. If I was a betting person, I'd guess he'd go back to being the same person, doing the same thing somewhere else. He'll never be a big fan of yours, no matter what you accomplish in life. Which I'm sure will be formidable. Somehow, I suspect, he will forever believe he got screwed."

"Like your ex?"

"A lot like my ex."

"That's kind of funny to think about. On another note, I went over to see Seth before he left."

"You still have a way of dropping these little bombs on me. I thought you were forever done with each other."

"Seth has a way of growing on you. Like a vine or a fungus or something."

"Yes, he does."

"He said that he is over me."

"He told me that, too."

"Which, of course, shattered my ego," she joked. "But it's a good thing for him."

"Jelly, I don't think anybody ever truly gets over you, but it would be a good thing for him. I sense he's ready to move on with his life."

"Do you think he will be okay?"

"I do. Even though this wasn't the right place for him, and his experiences at the school were difficult, Seth grew a great deal here. He is a far stronger person than he was when he got here in August. I believe he is going to be fine."

"Heard he had a good therapist."

"Hah."

"Do you think he will continue to play football?"

"I don't think it matters. I believe that whatever he does now will be on his terms."

"That would make me happy. Although I'm sure some other football coach at some other college is going to make it hard for him not to play. That seems to be what they do."

"I suspect you are correct. Hopefully it won't end up as a story you have to write another column about."

"I thought my columns ended up being pretty effective!"

"I think that a lot of people read them. Most importantly, the ones you wanted to read them."

"By the way, I liked your line about checking your conscience with the coat room attendant. Can I use that in a column?"

"Suit yourself. Although I'm not sure everybody knows what a coat room attendant is anymore."

"Let's talk about you then."

"Me? Are you planning to drop another bomb on me?"

"Yup. You have a lot of unresolved issues. But can I go help myself to a cup of coffee first? I need some caffeine. Meetings with therapists put me to sleep."

"Have at it. And I'll assume that last comment was in jest!"

Emily should have known this was coming. Why else would Jelly make an appointment? Just a few months ago, Emily would have thought this dangerous ground for a therapist and ducked the conversation altogether. When you almost live with your clients, as she did now, it seemed that little was not open for discussion. Which she continued to know was wrong. It didn't take long for Jelly to return with her cup filled.

"So I thought that I am the therapist here," Emily began.

"That's the theory anyway. But you have been off your game for too long. Ex issues, including how you are supposed to feel about Elizabeth. Trying to figure out your deal with Monk, I'm sure. Mana's situation, maybe your daughters being gone, maybe finances after the divorce, and whatever else. You have far too much on your plate for a single person."

Emily blushed what she knew was a nice shade of crimson across her fair Scandinavian cheeks.

"How do you keep track of all of this, Jelly?"

"I pay attention. Somebody has to! Hotel Henry is a good thing for the guests, but also an escape for you. You can avoid addressing the things in your life that you really should be addressing."

"Huh. You think you know what you are talking about?"

"I have been watching and learning from the best."

"That's debatable."

"Elizabeth's a good person."

"Yes, she is."

"And your ex-husband, not so much."

"Isn't that supposed to be personal?"

"I read about it in the newspaper. It can't be that personal. He was screwing someone who could have been his child. Hence the not so much."

"Why do you even care?"

"I'm on a mission to make things right in the world. Think I can get some good columns out of this?"

"Nooooo!"

"I was only kidding. I think my next column subject will be about deciding whether to be gay on a college campus."

"You told me when we first met that you weren't sure whether you were gay or not."

"Should make for some good columns, don't you think?"

"I'll say. Anyway, you are right. I haven't recovered from being dumped by my ex. Or from the fact that he preferred a young girl over me. Although Elizabeth is a special person. I've been lucky to get to know her."

"Elizabeth *is* a special person. And living in Hotel Henry has been a good thing for her. It has kept her from killing herself."

"How do you know that?"

"She told me."

Incredible.

"Does everyone just open up and tell their darkest secrets upon meeting you?"

"I told you a while ago that people like to talk to me."

"You are inexplicable."

"And you shouldn't forget that."

Emily would have been a lousy client. While she liked thinking about her life, she never much cared for talking to others about herself. She found it too scary. Always concerned that others would see how little she had her act together. Like Jelly seemed to have.

"So are we done talking about me?" asked Emily.

"You know I can go on forever, but I'm okay being done for now."

"Then let me ask you a question."

"Sure."

"Why do you spend so much time at Hotel Henry?"

"Now you are going to play therapist?"

"It is what I do, in case you've forgotten. And you are sitting in my office. And you are my client."

"Henry needed the help."

"He did. And I will be forever grateful to you for that. Actually, I think we all will be. Everyone is headed in a better direction now. Yet, you are still there. Not spending your time being a freshman in college."

"Monk asked me the same thing. Are you guys trying to get rid of me?"

"No. And I never would. Trust me. But I do want to understand what you are hiding from."

"Meaning?"

"Seth scared you, and you have never come fully clean as to why. You pretend in high school and again in college that you might be gay. You spend most weekends at Hotel Henry, when most kids are out doing who knows what on campus."

When Jelly goes inaudible, it's a moment that you don't miss. It doesn't happen very often. For the first time in their office meetings, she looked at the floor and her feet, like the others did. She didn't look through Emily.

"You wouldn't believe me if I told you."

"Try me."

"I'm afraid."

"Of being raped?"

Jelly looked up, with what only could be termed incredible surprise in her eyes.

"How did you know?"

Emily was calm in her response.

"It seemed the only logical answer."

"You are incredible."

"Hardly."

"I've read all the articles on the incidence of rape at colleges, including this place. It's not a pretty picture. I'm not as strong as Mana is, and we saw what the attack did to him."

"Yes, we did."

"I'm scared to death of a boy raping me. I experimented having sex with Seth this summer because I wanted to see what the excitement was all about. We did it three times, and that was it. He's a great person, but he's fragile. I was worried that he would lose it and rape me when I said no more. So that's why we came to see you. I needed someone who would protect me. And you somehow did."

"And I take it you are worried about others besides Seth?"

"Every testosterone filled jock who walks around campus thinking about getting laid while he's at breakfast, in class, at lunch, while taking an afternoon nap, at practice, at dinner, and while ogling any girl in the library at night who gets up to drink from the water fountain."

"You've thought about this a fair amount."

"I think about it all the time."

"And you never raised the issue with me before."

"I didn't want to lose my allure." Jelly softly smirked.

"There are good, decent boys out there."

"But I have no idea how to find them. Certainly not online, because most of that shit isn't true. Not at campus parties, which aren't the real world. I'm not up for making a wrong decision. And given the way I dress and act, there are far too many curious boys out there who would like to make the wrong decision for me."

"You're not mistaken."

"I was hoping you'd tell me all the reasons why I was."

"Look at me. I have experienced both the very good and the horribly bad side of relationships."

"Have you ever been raped?"

"Someone once tried."

"What?"

Jelly did not expect to hear that, nor did Emily ever expect to admit to it.

"My freshman year here. That's ultimately why I became a therapist. It's not something I talk about."

"The guy didn't succeed?"

"I was an athlete, too. And I'm pretty strong. I was scared out of my mind, so I fought him off with every ounce of strength I had. Gave him a bloody nose and a black eye, which he wore around campus for a couple of weeks."

"So you got over it?"

"You never get over it. I got through it. The police investigated but didn't build a case that supported me. The administration, like most back then, covered everything up. They all made me feel like the one who was at fault because it was at a party, and I had been drinking. I'm sure you've heard many stories like that."

"Sure. Except for giving the guy a black eye. And yet you have stayed here forever, Emily."

"At first, I wasn't going to give anyone the satisfaction of my leaving when I was still an undergraduate. And I had a scholarship to think about. Over time, I began to realize how many kids here need someone to watch out for them. That's why I'm still at this place."

"Thanks for telling me that."

"It seems you needed to know. I recovered, and you are stronger than I am. It's important to be careful. But you don't have to be afraid."

"Can I have a good cry?"

Emily passed her the Kleenex box.

55

Saint Henry's Premonition

Emily's phone rang around six-thirty, while she was pulling her scull up on the boathouse dock after a cool early morning of rowing. The leaves on the trees had largely vanished, many now calmly floating along the river water and collecting on her oars as she pulled them. This early on a weekday morning was an unusual time to receive an unwelcome call -- the head of security was phoning to tell her that another one of her clients was in the emergency room and had asked for her. All she could think of was Mana having been attacked again now that he was experimenting with going to classes again. Before the call was even finished, she started running from the dock, leaving the scull where it was and making a beeline for the hospital, hoping someone else would handle stowing the scull in the boathouse.

The head of security, an older man with a shaved head and an ursine body, met her at the door. She knew of him but had never met him. He had a cup of coffee waiting for her, but she had no interest. It appeared, he said, that one of her client's had been raped. Not another ambush on Mana that she had feared. Her mind once again quickly began to flip through all the young women she counseled, a sensation of unbridled dread creeping inside of her. And then he said it was a young woman named Angela.

Every muscle in Emily's body froze. She couldn't move, and quickly began gasping for air, panic attack like. This is what Henry had warned. And what she had done nothing about. The security boss put a big arm around her and walked her over to a chair in the ER waiting area. One of the football players who had been expelled was all she could think. Was all she could painfully visualize. Bile began walking its way up her throat. The mind and the body so intimately connected. In that recent conversation they had, Jelly had made it clear that she wasn't as strong as Mana, and that she could never survive a rape attack. Now that reality was here.

When she finally unfroze and guardedly entered the curtained room, the same one where they cared for Mana not all that long ago, Jelly was sitting in a hospital bed, wearing a hospital nightgown loosely tied behind her neck, her emotionless eyes staring vacantly. One eye was black and blue, her lower lip was swollen like a tomato, with a nasty cut beneath it, and she had a long scrape across her forehead. Henry was already there in the room, holding her left hand with both of his.

When she heard her therapist enter the room, Jelly turned her head and looked at Emily in a way that the therapist would never, ever forget. An overwhelming pain of what this dazzling young woman had been fearing ever since she arrived on campus. As if Jelly had known all along that this was inevitable. Her peers, supposedly her peers, weren't going to allow her to live her life the way she wanted to live it. They weren't going to let her be Jelly.

"I gave the bastard a black eye," she spoke haltingly in a voice void of her customary ardor. The edges of her mouth curled up into the world's tiniest grin. Emily rushed over and hugged her like she had never hugged anyone before. And she cried with her.

Jelly had been so incredibly special.

The head of security at the university had gotten a visit from his old friend Henry. The former cop was in his last year before retiring; they hadn't seen each other in three years. Not since Jenny's funeral. Not since Henry became a statue. But Saint Henry had new responsibilities now, so he had reached out. He told his friend about Jelly, her free-spirited persona, the way she dressed, and he showed his friend her newspaper columns. And he shared his concern. His friend agreed to put the word out with his officers and asked that they keep an eye on her while the columns about the attack were still running in the school newspaper -- without her knowing as she wandered about campus. Particularly at night when she returned home late from the library or the newspaper offices. They all now had learned who she was, but it didn't help. Nobody had ever anticipated that she went to the library to study before breakfast. While the officers on duty were having a donut at the coffee shop.

A young man had been waiting for her in the shadows of the book stacks of the library's top floor, where she most often studied, as she made her way from the stairwell to her study cube. It had been six o'clock in the morning. Only the most serious and most organized students studied on the top floor this early in the morning. There was a room in the back corner with a large conference table and chairs that could hide what was happening on the carpet on the far side. The door to the room locked from the inside. After grabbing her, he had swiftly put a sock in her mouth, a covering over her head, and then he dragged her into the room. When she exited twenty minutes or so later, she was bloody, bruised, her shirt badly torn, crying, and the only person there to witness this was Marionette, who had been studying with her headphones on. Marionette didn't know what to do at first, but eventually put her jacket and arm around Jelly, and then called security.

The security friend, in turn, called Henry, which is why he was there before Emily. Which threw him into an all too familiar tailspin that he thought he had escaped. It was supposed to be a car accident.

The perpetrator had not succeeded in raping Jelly. The martial arts training, which is what she did at the gym every day after classes, had paid off. Despite her small stature. But that doesn't necessarily make it any easier for the victim. Which is what she now was and forever would think of herself as. They caught him rather quickly. The black eye made it hard for him to hide when he stupidly showed up for work later that morning. He was not an expelled football player, but rather a young man who worked in the library. Jelly never knew it, but she made his day whenever she went there to study. And she went there most mornings. The columns she wrote, and which he read, might have pointed the police in another direction, were it not for the black eye.

The story of the days immediately following the attempted rape is too hard to share, because Jelly wasn't Jelly any more. She was quiet, no longer defiant, not the center of attention as she had always been. At least for the reasons she used to be. She left the school for an indefinite period, uncertain if she would ever return, and went to stay with her other mother in Philadelphia, in a place that was both familiar and comfortable to her because she had grown up there. Struggling to set aside the new nightmares of her first semester of college. After a month or so of hibernating in that apartment, she began to go outside during the day and take solo walks in the cold weather on streets when they were crowded. She was more at peace when she couldn't feel her face or her hands. And she was more at peace when she wasn't walking where there weren't other people. Her divorced mothers put aside their differences and came together again to care for their distinctive daughter, who they both so unwaveringly loved. But nothing of what they did made a difference. And she had no interest in going to see the therapist they thought she should see. She said more than once, when they suggested it, that she already knew a good one for when she was ready.

It is hard to believe that someone could steal what made Jelly special. That thing, whatever it was, that made her magic. The changing hair colors, the green sneakers, her willingness to take on Coach Quigley and the rest of his team, the willingness to spend so much time with Mana. Someone she had only met once before he was assailed. And Elizabeth. And Henry. And, especially, Emily. But the sexual assault stole it from her. And that was so wrong.

One month after the assault, Henry drove the forty-five minutes to Philadelphia to see Jelly, doing his best not to look at people walking along the sidewalks, who were each someday going to die. It proved a difficult thing to do in a sizable city like Philly. He hadn't traveled very far beyond the confines of the university campus since Jenny died. By the time he found the apartment, his head was spinning with morbid thoughts of so many people he would never meet. Back for the moment to where he had been before this whole new chapter in his life began. He pressed the buzzer to be allowed in, and Jelly answered. Even through the metallic pitch of an ancient intercom system, he could tell it was her. She didn't know he was coming.

"Who is it?"

"It's Saint Henry."

There was a pause and then the buzz to let him in.

He surprised himself becoming nervous waiting for the elevator and even more nervous riding it up to the sixth floor, not sure who she would be when he got there. When the elevator doors opened, she was standing at the entrance to her apartment in jeans, a t-shirt, bare feet, and her normal colored hair, looking like she had quickly just run a brush through it. The cuts and bruises that provided a tangible memory of her attack were mostly healed.

"Hi."

"Hello Jelly."

They stood quietly and surveyed each other for a moment. Or maybe two or three.

"You're my first visitor since all this shit went down."

"Really? I'm honored."

"Yeah. Elizabeth texts me once every day. Mana texts me three or four times a day. I've spoken with Emily several times on the phone. But you're the first to come see me."

"I hope you don't mind. I've missed you."

She ran up and hugged him as hard as she knew how, and he thought he might have a stroke if she didn't let up. But she did let up and then grabbed his hand and led him into the kitchen in her apartment. The two of them were far more comfortable sitting at a kitchen table than on an expensive living room sofa.

"How are you holding up?"

"Been better."

"I'll bet."

"You drove here yourself?"

"Yeah. Will admit that I was going a little crazy."

"You know what, Henry? I spent the whole semester being afraid of being raped. I was determined not to change who I was despite that fear. But they got me, didn't they? I didn't think I could handle being assaulted like Mana did. I didn't think I would survive. But you know what, I'm going to make it."

"I'm proud of you."

"And you know what else? You're going to make it, too. I thought I was going to die. First when I was being attacked, and then maybe even pull the rip cord during the few weeks since then. But I decided that I didn't want to be a capstone to one of your nightmares. So, somehow, I'm going to beat this thing. I'm not sure how, because I have some terrifying moments every day. But I'm going to get past this, so you will need to get over your deal as well."

Henry grinned for the first time since Jelly was assaulted.

"You have a deal."

"Promise?"

"Yes, I can promise that."

She stood, walked over to the chair he was sitting on, sat on his lap, and gave him another enormous hug. And they stayed like that for the longest time. It was a good day.

56

His New Family

By the time Mana graduated in the spring, a good deal had changed. Emily and Monk were officially a pair. He moved from the girls' room in Emily's house to the other side of her bed permanently, and they did stuff. Tentatively at first, and then with no inhibitions. That's as much as she was ever going to say about that. They were a great match in every way, keeping life simple, and Emily even cautiously began to plan a future again.

Mana was able to limp up to the graduation podium without a cane, to receive his diploma and an enormous cheer from the graduating students. Thanks to Jelly's newspaper columns, he wasn't invisible any longer. His family – Emily, Henry, Monk, and Elizabeth -- all came to root for him. Jelly came, too, with what was now a smile that sometimes came out of hiding. They had a little party at Emily's house afterwards, and Monk put out a great barbecue spread, because, again, he was the only one who could, and Mana, Elizabeth, Jelly, Henry, and Emily drank wine and took turns dancing on the little deck to music that Mana selected. Which was much like his cooking. With much prodding, Monk even joined in, sans the wine. Everyone noticed that Jelly drank far too much and was mostly incoherent when the evening was still young. They were so thrilled to see her, to have their whole strange group back together again, that they gave her a pass.

Mana had three job offers. None of them were to be a soccer announcer, but that was okay. He was going to go to Indianapolis to research new drugs for a big pharma company. Although Jelly wasn't permitted to participate, because of her affinity for Salvation Army outfits, the rest of them took Mana to shop for new clothes for work, and then Emily and Monk drove with him to Indiana to help get settled in a new apartment. He actually would get paid more than Emily did, but that was okay, too. He would be able to afford to come home for holidays, and they would all be glad to see him. Because Trenton was now his home. The nicest one he had ever had.

Elizabeth had been accepted at the university and was going to attend in the fall. She had made so much progress from the dark place where she had been. Remarkable progress. And she looked beautiful again. Yet she felt she was best off where she could be close to Emily. In fact, they christened the room where Monk had slept as Elizabeth's Room, as it would still be available in the event she ever needed it. And Elizabeth's father visited Emily and Henry to thank his daughter's therapist and new friend. He seemed like a nice man, though nowhere close to having recovered from his wife's disloyalty, and he became a client of Monk's new practice. Her mother apparently was still living in the same house and now calling many people unfortunate names.

Emily's daughters had experienced her new world over the Christmas holiday. They got to know all the cast, and they overcame their concerns about each of them. Saint Henry was, no doubt, their favorite. Most of all, they were happy to see their mother so content again. Their father's second marriage ended not long after it began. But he didn't seem bothered. He quickly found another girlfriend, who no one had any interest in meeting, knowing that it would be short-lived.

Henry quit seeing Emily as a therapist and took up rowing. He knew nothing about it and was in the beginner's class, but he was okay with that. It gave him a chance to see Emily early in the morning to have some adult conversation, and a chance to keep his mind busy on things besides death. Which, when it came down to it, was what he needed to do in order to keep his promise to Jelly, who, by the way, he kept visiting. Most often making the drive he dreaded to Philadelphia, but it was worth it. He didn't have to convince himself to get out of bed in the morning to go see such a special person who needed his help.

Elizabeth and Henry made plans for Friday evening Margaritas once school started, which grew to larger groups of

Elizabeth's friends over her four years at the college. Times which he relished. He knew Jenny would have loved them.

57

The Sequel

Unfortunately, this story isn't over. In real life, most stories don't have perfect endings. It's sort of like when you order something online -- maybe from IKEA or Best Buy -- and are so excited to take it out of the box when it arrives, but it turns out not to be the right size or color or whatever, and you can never get it packaged back into the box the same perfect way it was when it came. It just doesn't seem to fit anymore. So instead of returning the item that you always intended to return, it sits on a shelf in a closet collecting dust until you move again. Story endings can be the same way. They can collect dust for stretches because certain things are never really settled. Perhaps our story ending gets dusty because our Emily is still afraid to address all of the issues in her life.

Or perhaps the problem is simply what was said at the outset. That when you dedicate your whole life to such a noble pursuit, and you end up not being as good at it as you had expected, or even hoped, it can be catastrophic. The thing that was said you were not likely to remember.

It was two weeks after Mana's graduation, and they were back from the trip to Indiana, and both Emily and Monk's graduating classes, again being five years apart, had their college reunions scheduled for the same weekend. It had been five years ago, at the last reunion, when they had errantly kissed. Something they still had never really fully discussed. Emily held Monk's hand as they walked from the parking lot to a big tent that now encapsulated a portion of the familiar great lawn of the university. Emily wore a new sleeveless dress which showed off the muscles cultivated from her morning rowing routine, and Monk thought she looked fabulous. Yet, he knew that she was not excited about being here. To her it felt like they had already done this once before, and that hadn't worked out so well. And this was an even bigger event with more people and more pomp. But she came for Monk. Somehow, the celebration with people he really didn't know, who had never embraced him into their lives, had been the demon of which he had to rid himself. He had so hungered to be one of them. After his painful rehab, Emily and he had experienced eight wonderful months together, where he'd never felt the need to succumb again to his old haunts. He was confident that there would be no regrettable actions this time around. That time in his life had passed.

As she held his hand, she could feel it begin to tremble, and she reached over to grasp it with her free hand as well, as if to warm it from a cold chill. Even though it was a temperate June evening.

"Monk, you know we don't have to do this." She looked at him, but he was looking away, at the stream of people heading in the same direction that they were. "What do you say we go back home? We can cook a nice dinner. Maybe even get naked."

"That's a pretty sweet offer, especially since I'm the one who usually suggests fooling around, but I will be okay, Emily. It's been a long time now since I drank. It won't be a problem."

But she feared that he was only trying to reassure himself.

"You know I love our life together, and it's taken us a long time to find each other and get to where we are." She was surprised to hear herself pleading. There was a looming sequel here that scared her to death. "We don't need anything more than each other."

Monk didn't answer at first. They walked a while in silence, approaching the stone and iron gate that would lead them to the all too familiar lawn. Where she had sat with Jelly and Seth and Elizabeth. The university kept changing, with new buildings being jammed into cramped spaces, but the lawn had been there forever, and probably would continue to be. He stared at the open space, focused on the burgeoning activity, as he spoke to Emily.

"I came here more than twenty years ago, very naïve but filled with great aspirations. The academics were a breeze. I studied hard and smoked the courses. I was summa cum laude, for God's sake. I went to all the talks by the famous people. I spent hours in the library reading the research of many of the professors, even ones who were long since gone. I filled notebooks with observations by classmates during discussions that I thought were brilliant and would sit in my little cube in the library each night and re-read them, marveling at the intellect and energy of those around me.

"And yet, this was the meanest, coldest place I have ever experienced in my life. I was so alone. I would see my professors around campus days after the end of the semester, and they would look at me with absolutely no recognition of who I was. I would go to dinner and sit at a table with classmates, not knowing how to make conversation, and just sit there like a fool, idly listening. No one said hello when I sat down or goodbye if I got up to leave.

"I started to drink to overcome my reticence. To me, at least, I seemed more funny, more audacious. I still think of that shy kid as me, Em. You give me confidence. You let me be who I really am. But I can't forever be dependent upon you. You can't always be my crutch."

"Why not, Monk?" she was pleading again. "It's working, isn't it?"

"It's working great. I've never been happier in my life. But it shouldn't be a burden to you. I need to get over this, so we can move on together. Besides, I'm really proud to show you off to my classmates."

"You are?"

"Yeah, old alum guys love muscles and big knockers."

Emily grinned, but she wished they would turn around and go back to their home. She didn't need any reunions. In fact, even though she had never missed one since graduating, she no longer gave a rat's ass about reunions. The pieces of the puzzle that had been her life all fit together again. And that felt really good.

Move the clock forward nine hours and it's a different story. It's three o'clock in the morning, and Monk is wrestling with the front door lock on Emily's house until finally it opens. He was a campus security officer's last customer of a busy night. He stumbles through the front door and hallway until his eyes meet Emily's after staggering upstairs into their little bedroom. Though the lights are off, the moon shines through the windows, and he can see she is sitting up in bed, her knees pulled up to her chest. Even in the darkness, he can see her pretty face in the moon's light, but there is no happiness to it at this moment. She has been waiting up for him.

For the first time, he becomes painfully aware that he wreaked of booze. He had returned after eight months away, and the demons had won again. They have yet to lose. Even in the darkness, he can make out a tear running down Emily's cheek.

He had made it until midnight or thereabouts stone cold sober and not even considering taking a drink. Seltzer with lime had served him just fine. A little idea germinated somewhere in his busy mind convincing him that if could drink a single beer and then stop, he will have proven to himself once and for all that he had conquered both his missing self-confidence and his drinking habit. Past midnight, the small group of people who made up his comfort zone were gone and in bed. Why he didn't go home to bed, he didn't know. Emily had left a while before, but he decided not to go with her, despite her efforts to again bribe him with sex. It was, all of a sudden, the young kid from Connecticut amongst a whole bunch of familiar faces who didn't remember him. The first beer went down quickly and removed some of the uncomfortable feeling of once again being the outsider in the crowd. The guy who had lost a bunch of jobs, he was engaging with men and women who all worked for investment banks, hedge funds, and corporate law firms. Or, at least, that's what it seemed to him. And they all appeared so implausibly comfortable with each other. They touched one another's arms, put arms around each other, their faces smiling up close. Like they lived next door to each other and swapped spouses whenever the mood struck. They were that recognizable to one another. They were all his classmates, and theirs was a world he didn't know. Monk, once more, remembered that long ago forgotten feeling of being the outsider. The guy who no one spoke to in the dining hall.

The second beer gave him the courage to reacquaint himself with the power elite. The third beer and beyond reminded all of them who he was and demonstrated to all who remembered him that he hadn't changed a bit since his undergraduate days.

58

So What Happens Next?

You Can't Go Home Again. It was the title of a Thomas Wolfe novel that was published in 1940, a couple of years after he died. *You can't go home again.* Isn't that what reunions are? Going back home? To those long ago memories that are sometimes welcoming and warming, and sometimes not so much. For most, though, going back home did not come with the repercussions it did for Monk.

The morning after reunion, he found himself shivering on the little back deck of Emily's house, where just a couple of chapters ago they were barbecuing and dancing, even though it was again a warm, sunny day with a sky as blue as it gets. He had never considered that he would be back in this spot, after being so long without a drink. Without being such a fool. He had a simple but great life with Emily, her inn of students who came and went, and a new solo practice that he surprisingly enjoyed. Cooking great meals, going on hikes, rolling around in bed, and, mostly, sitting together, comfortably cuddling a seltzer, and talking and laughing. Now he had threatened the whole damn thing because he wasn't able to keep his ego in check. It was all too familiar a feeling and one for which he was immediately humiliated. He hadn't forgotten rehab, but he'd unremembered what he learned.

So what do you do if you are Monk? Whatever he decides to say to Emily, it won't be right. It won't be enough. It won't be believed. He was a drunk, and drunks had no standing in these situations.

Emily walked out on the deck wearing her clothes from rowing, with her tousled blonde hair straying in all directions. He slowly turned to her while she folded her arms across her chest.

"What are you thinking?"

His voice was coarse from too much drinking and too little sleep. His eyes pleading for any sign of forgiveness.

Emily had risen hours before he had on this Sunday morning and gone to the river seeking solace. She was obviously jumpy, nervous about what the future held for them. He suspected she was wondering why it was so difficult for her to find a stable relationship. It wasn't wrong for her to wonder.

Monk answered his own question with what he expected would become the most heartfelt apology he ever delivered. Being honest with her was never difficult.

"I'm afraid," he said with a huge sense of remorse. "I'm afraid you're going to show me the door and not ever let me back in. I have a feeling that I blew the best opportunity that I have ever had in my life."

He looked at Emily's eyes. They were not the comfortable, understanding eyes to which he was so accustomed.

"Monk," she slowly responded, holding the stare with his eyes, "I have never been as happy in my life as I have these last months with you. You know that."

She paused to catch her breath, thinking about her next words. Therapists are trained to choose their words thoughtfully, so as to be able to build that trust with a client. So as not to set the client off. Unfortunately for Monk, he wasn't a client.

"But you fucked up. You fucked me up. You couldn't leave well enough alone. You had to go show off to people you, for some reason, want to be your friends. What the hell did they ever really do to you?"

She was genuinely crying now, something she had never before done in front of him. Typically, Emily had always been the stoic. She was tough and strong and sexy. She was the caretaker. Her crying scared him.

"You hurt me, Monk," she continued. "My life is worth something, but you don't seem to think so. I love you as much as I have ever loved any human being in my entire life. But you're a shit. I don't know if I want to be here when you drink yourself into the gutter."

Her words hit him hard. Take your pick of metaphors. He didn't want to live his life without her. He was pretty certain he couldn't survive a life without her. They had grown that close.

"Maybe I should take some time off. See if I can fix things with you."

"Time off from what Monk? Working? Living here? Drinking? Me?"

"Emily, I am not capable of facing life if you're gone."

"Don't give me that guilt trip, Monk. I didn't screw this up."

"I know, Em." His voice trailed off. He was truly ashamed. "Please. Please give me another shot."

"I don't know. I can't do this again." She was sobbing.

He didn't take the two steps required to hug her. To console her. That's how far apart they were at this moment. Two little steps that he should have taken. He knew Emily liked to be touched, and she especially liked to be touched by him. It was a reminder of who they were. In retrospect, it might have made all the difference.

You can't go home again.

Which begs the question, what the hell do you do going forward? What happens next? They had been so happy together. She made him laugh like nobody else ever did. Yet when they were in a gathering with others, he couldn't help but hurt himself and hurt her. They both knew that alcoholism didn't have a switch that you could turn on and off. Too often, it kept coming back. And when it came back, it was messy. It was like trying to put that IKEA item back neatly in the box it came in.

So, again, what happens next?

59

The Bridges Of Madison County

Marionette, the peculiar one who walked out during intermission of *The Bridges of Madison County*, never came back to see Emily. She also apparently changed her name back to Marianne at some point during her freshman year. Neither of which surprised the therapist.

The odds of Marionette, or Marianne, becoming valedictorian were ridiculously small in a school this size and this competitive. Odds too small for this ever to be someone's solitary purpose in life. Emily hadn't gotten that message across to Marionette in their initial visits. And she never reached out to her again, which she did often to clients who hadn't been to see her in some time. Quite possibly, she just didn't like Marionette enough to want to try any harder. In retrospect, she missed the importance of Marionette needing to understand the message and left a time bomb ticking that was destined to go off at some point during college. And, sadly, it didn't take all that long.

Grades purposely come out the third week of summer, giving students enough time to first unwind from the academic stress of the school year. Hopefully providing a less anxiety filled setting than if they were still on campus surrounded by the myriad of other cutthroat students. Marionette got a 'B' in Chinese History, the first imperfect grade she had ever gotten. As with all of her courses, she didn't even know if she liked the subject. But she wasn't going to be valedictorian, that much was clear.

So, she took her life with a razor blade.

This part of the story is tragic enough to just stop it here. Or maybe at the end of the previous chapter might have been better. You had heard before about the eleven percent threshold of students who consider suicide. This no longer counted as considering.

When Emily received the news from her boss, she cried for a long time. A fully blubbering downpour that required a towel rather than tissues. This was so not right for a teenage girl who had her whole life ahead. Who came to see a therapist who may not have been as there for her as she should have been. Emily went to the funeral in Delaware, where there were only fourteen people at the ceremony, including Emily, the minister, and one other representative from the university. A young blonde woman from the dean's office who was, not doubt, attending her first university funeral. Marionette seemed to have touched so few people in her eighteen years.

The moment the casket first was wheeled into the church, a dark wood box covered by a single purple vestment and carrying the lifeless puppet-like body of too young a girl, her father, the plumber who didn't understand higher education, broke down, crumbling to the floor. Two people helped him to his feet, but a few minutes later, he broke down again. He had lost the most important person in his life. Emily watched him from the pew where she sat. Never had she witnessed somebody who had obviously loved so much. To him, she was brilliant beyond what he could have ever imagined. To him, she had all the friends she needed -- she had him, and nobody could ever have a friend who cared more than he did. And he never, ever thought of her as Pinocchio.

Maybe Marionette had, indeed, touched the only person she needed to touch.

The summer was quiet. Emily spent most mornings rowing through the early mist on the old river while she tried to figure things out. The river, on early summer mornings, was less crowded than in the fall or spring as the lucky ones were off to their summer homes, and there were no college or high school teams sharing her space. Hotel Henry was empty. Mana was in Indiana proudly launching his career, Elizabeth was living in a larger apartment with her father before starting college in the fall, and Jelly was still in Philadelphia, quietly spending time with her parents while mending from being battered. Emily's daughters remained on their respective campuses, living in dorm rooms, and getting paid to do research with professors. Both with science professors, in fact.

Marionette's death, of course, haunted Emily. She hadn't focused on Marionette, an actual student at the university, the way she selfishly had absorbed herself with Elizabeth, who was not a student but rather the one who had shattered Emily's own life. She hadn't had a self-serving reason to be as concerned about Marionette. And while she could process in her head what Marionette did, she couldn't forgive herself.

She knew she missed on Jelly, too. Emily spent many nights alone tearing up about that one as well. Henry had warned her of the risks of Jelly's behavior, something that she was all too familiar with from her own first year in college. The reason she became a therapist. But she took no action. Probably because she had been wrapped up in the girl's magic, instead of acting like the therapist she was supposed to be. Letting everything slide until the world came crashing down on such an amazingly vibrant young person. It was hard to escape the guilt of her inaction. She badly missed the old Jelly.

The first day of school the following fall was no different from the previous. Her calendar was already booked for several weeks out. She would know the problems, and yet they would all be different. Some would be beyond challenging. But it would be cathartic for her, and it was time to get back to trying to make a difference with the students. Or so she thought. Henry was on her calendar for that evening, and she would be more than pleased to see him. It had been a while. He didn't need her help anymore, as he had made incredible progress coming to grips with his dying phobia. Though she didn't think that she really had all that much to do with it. They were going to have dinner together, just the two of them. She was looking forward to it, as he was as entertaining as anybody she knew. Moreover, she didn't have anything filling up her social calendar these days. It was evident that, at one point, he'd had a little boy crush on her, and she was okay with that. They both recognized that he was too old for it to go anywhere. It was not like when Monk came over that first time for dinner. There were no goose bumps with Henry. But there was still something extraordinary about him. And he was also the most dependable man in her life. Which counted for something.

So let's talk about Monk. There is a reason that people watch rom-com's over and over again on television. Right? How many times do we re-watch movies with Billy Crystal and Meg Ryan and Tom Hanks? A soupy plot that is capped with a happy ending, where guy gets girl or girl gets guy. Isn't that what you are hoping for here? That Emily and Monk walk off into the sunset together? But remember, this is Emily we are talking about. As attractive and appealing a person as she is, Emily never seems to take the easy route.

She had broken things off with Monk after the reunion flop, and, of course, was immediately not sure if that was the right decision. They had communicated by phone and text a number of times since she jettisoned him. It's possible that she now may have wanted him back more than ever. But, of course, she didn't know how to do that. Does she call him, text him, or do they meet in person? Does she offer him a spot in his old room again or in her bed, or do they just date occasionally? Should she give him an ultimatum about his drinking or a shoulder to cry on? Should she consult with her daughters first? She thought about him all the time, but, per usual, it took her a long time to settle things in her mind. An inordinate amount of time. So, true to form over the course of the summer, their relationship made no progress because she couldn't make a decision.

Monk showed up at the river early one morning in September. He sipped green tea while he waited for her to finish rowing, and he had coffee and a muffin waiting for her. She noticed him while she was still on the water, a fair distance from the boathouse. If she had feelings upon seeing him, which she did, she didn't show them.

"What are you doing here?"

"I've missed you."

"That's it?"

"That's all I've got."

He was sitting on a faded wood bench on the back edge of the dock. She sat down next to him.

"How's your practice going?"

"I'm getting busy."

"I'm happy to hear that. Dating anyone?"

"Not yet."

Emily knew what he meant and that made her grin. She didn't feel the goose bumps this time, but that didn't mean she didn't feel good.

"How's the drinking?"

"My problem is no better and no worse than before. But I haven't had a drink since reunion."

"So how come you came here? You've never seen me row before."

"As I said, I've missed you."

He smiled a big, hopeful smile.

"And that's it?"

"I thought it was a pretty good reason."

Hopefully, you didn't expect Emily to leap into his arms. She never got that script. But she took the coffee, took a bite out of the muffin, letting the crumbs fall where they would on her sweaty shirt, and placed her hand on his thigh. And they began to date again. Slowly. Platonically at first. Because Emily had no more room within her to be hurt again.

So it was not a rom-com, and he would not be without his drinking episodes down the road. At their wedding ten years from now – he had asked her one early morning on that same boathouse bench when she was fifty-four and he was forty-nine -- he passed out in front of the forty or so guests. The first time he'd been drunk since reunion, because he was back in front of a crowd again and still didn't have the confidence to be himself. Yet Emily and he were together for good, so there was a reason to celebrate. And, then again, when he retired once and for all at age seventy-three, after his shaggy black hair had finally turned grey, and they threw a party for him. Once more the center of attention, and once more unable to handle it. But never in between or after.

Deep down he was a good person, and they built a life together.

60

Rules Do Have A Purpose

Rules. Big institutions seem to like a surfeit of rules. They seem to have them for pretty much everything one could imagine. When to be at work and when to leave. What to wear. How to act. A detailed description for how to do your job. Who gets the corner office and the privileged parking spaces. How you can and cannot spend the institution's money. What days you get off. How to arrange your email salutation. Who you can and cannot date.

As we have been told, Emily had always been a strict rules follower. As this story progressed, she became a little less careful with them. A little less compliant. Sharing private information of one client with another, as she had done more times now than she could count, was a no-no. Seeing a non-student in her office. Also taboo. Setting up multiple clients to live in the home of yet another client. There was no formal rule about that, but no one was going to be patting her on the back for putting this in motion. And then drinking there with her underage clients. There were formal rules about that. Oftentimes talking more about her own issues than she did about theirs. Going out to dinner with a former client, who only became a former client so he could see her outside of the office. And then there was Marionette, with whom, in her mind, she broke the most important rule – which was to be irrefutably committed to helping every client.

For a couple of months now, Emily had anticipated that she would be promoted to a newly created assistant director position in the department, as the continued growth of the student's mental health needs was placing a strain on the department's leadership. The competition for the spot was weak, and she could use the commensurate bump in pay. But when her boss happened upon her having what was no doubt an expensive dinner at a restaurant with Henry, it set off an unexpected chain reaction of looking more carefully into her recent track record, which is usually never a good thing. It ended as a meeting in the woman's office, an office which was four times the size of Emily's, with newer furniture and several plants that were all still very much alive. The meeting was surprisingly brief and did not go particularly well. Emily had to grovel to keep the position she'd held for nearly twenty years. Her colleagues, when someone else eventually assumed the new spot, would have new content to discuss during their myriad of coffee breaks.

Emily could have argued that she had done some of the best work of her career during the year of our story, and she could have argued that her clients were all better off because their therapist took a different road. But she didn't, because that wasn't true. She told herself that she would have made the same rule-bending choices all over again. Which was probably also false bravado.

She thought for a long time about changing schools after the embarrassing non-promotion. The university had been a part of her since she was eighteen, when she arrived with a ponytail, two big suitcases, her own pillow, and an uneasy smile. The big fish from the little pond in Pennsylvania. She had grown up at the university. A process that didn't yet seem to be complete. It would be strange not to be there every day. It's not like she had any colleagues that she would miss, because had spent her twenty years in the department tirelessly working rather than building meaningful friendships. But the metal cabinets, the old plant, the empty parking lot, the bench in the middle of the great lawn, the bleachers of the football field, the theatre building, the paycheck with name and address peering through the envelope window. That's what was so familiar to her. That's what was part of her.

It was imaginable that she could go explore some place new. With her experience, she would not have trouble getting a job helping another college deal with the mounting flow of students with mental health issues. New geography, new faces, new experiences. There were many other settings where it could be interesting to live. Vermont, New Hampshire, Seattle, Boulder, Sante Fe, Asheville, Bend, Pocatello. London or Dublin. She guessed there were possibilities.

But since she didn't do change all that well, since she could never really empty all her compartments, there probably really weren't other options. When it came right down to it, for better or for worse, her purpose in life was to still try to be a good person, a true caretaker, in her same little crummy office. Whether she got promoted or not. Whether they paid a living wage or not.

61

It No Longer Felt Impossible

Being assaulted is something that you never forget. Taking the romantic dream of making love to that person who gives you the chills every time you are together, the one who strokes your arm or neck or back in such a way that your immediate hope is to be stroked again, the companion who makes you smile on your worst days, and then turning it into the horror of being physically manhandled by someone dirty, hairy, and disgusting who you won't ever know. Even though he revisits your dreams night after night. Someone who took what should have been a gentle caress and overpowers you until it hurts. Someone who stole an experience which should have made you breathless and, instead, imposes his offensive exhale into your face until you choke on it. Someone whose foul, horrid sweat seeps into your skin so that months later you still want to shower as many times a day as you can. It makes you not want to close your eyes at night because he will be there, and not want to get out of bed in the morning, because he might be there.

For a long time after, Jelly was no longer herself.

Henry – Saint Henry – became the new constant in her life. Not that it was ever scheduled or scripted. It just was. He continued to drive to Philadelphia every day or two to see her, in the process straining to conquer the craziness of seeing people on the sidewalk and envisioning how they would die. Because Jelly's assault had caused his own recovery to shift into reverse. In the December cold, the February snow, the April rain, and the June sun, he kept coming. Because he had made her a promise that he would. And she so needed him to keep his promise. Not that the drive was easy, and not that he didn't nervously perspire through too many undershirts. Not that he should have ever had been permitted to have a license because he concentrated on everything when he drove, except the driving. But because it was for her, he persisted. They might share coffee in the morning or have lunch in the kitchen of her apartment or at a café or go for long walks throughout the city. Most of the time when they did, they held hands. She felt safe with him, even though at eighty-two she wouldn't have been. The two of them would even, at times, when she needed a steady voice, talk on the phone at night before he went to bed, which was many hours earlier than she did. Because he had to wake up quite early each morning to go chase Emily on the river, and because Jelly, as mentioned, was afraid to close her eyes.

In the process, Jelly grew to love Henry like she had never loved anyone. He became her therapist, because he was a better therapist than Emily. More focused, more thoughtful. Less confused by his own issues. Maybe better said, the saint became her savior. He was the most appealing person that she had ever known, and she knew she would miss him terribly when he was gone from this world, and she was still here. He was the reason that she was still here.

They didn't talk what Henry termed happy talk. Conversations with no substance. They talked about life, his and hers. She learned about his growing up in a working-class section of St. Louis, his older sister's death when she was just nine, and the goofy things he did in college. Including pushing the car up the steps of the administration building, a boy getting his leg caught and hitting his head, and what he thinks about when he is contemplating people dying. Even including his vision about Jelly, her campaigning in her sneakers, and the car accident. Jelly learned why he got a doctorate and became a professor, and she learned why he loved Jenny. Which was truly a storybook romance. And how his heart was shattered bit by bit over the nine years she was ill. Always holding out hope and never having any hope.

The funny thing is that he also got to know Jelly better than anyone else ever had. No one had ever been her best friend. No one knew her like a book. But he eventually did, at eighty-two years old. He didn't care if she dressed in clothes that didn't fit. And he didn't care whether she wore a bra or not. Nor that she was opinionated and wore her opinion on her sleeve. This is what they talked about. Just don't publish it in a newspaper, he said, and just don't stop taking martial arts classes. And don't stop being the woman they all fell in love with. Which would be hard for her. But no longer felt impossible.

They had their mutual mission. He wasn't giving up on fixing the dying thing. And she couldn't give up either. He was going to keep driving to Philadelphia, if that's what you called it, and they would have coffee or lunch, and they would go for walks until they were both better.

Again, it no longer felt impossible.

Author Bio

I'm a married father of four living with my wife on the beautiful Southcoast of Massachusetts. A graduate of Williams College and Harvard Business School, I spent a number of years launching start-up businesses before turning my creative efforts to writing novels. Both efforts, it turns out, begin with a blank piece of paper. I've written four novels: *I'm Will (2012), The Missing Something Club (2014), The College Shrink (2022),* and *Complicated Families (2023).*

In addition to raising a family, a big part of my life has been helping to launch (nineteen years and counting) The Nativity School of Worcester, an independent, all scholarship school for underprivileged kids of all ethnicities and faiths. A magical place where students can realize their many capabilities and build a path to a more productive life. Proceeds from my book sales are donated to the school.

Made in United States
Orlando, FL
26 June 2022

19180042R00186